Bride of Fortune

"Delicious, exciting, innovative and colorful!"

—*Affaire de Coeur*

"Shirl Henke weaves a spell as rich with details as the splendid era she portrays. Mysterious, sensual, heart-wrenching, with an ending that will leave you breathless, BRIDE OF FORTUNE has it all!" —*The Literary Times*

"Passionate love scenes, engaging characters and a well-researched, fast-paced plot." —*Publishers Weekly*

Love a Rebel, Love a Rogue

"A fascinating slice of history with equally fascinating characters." —Catherine Coulter

A Fire in the Blood

"Fast-paced, sizzling, adventurous, A FIRE IN THE BLOOD is a true western with a strong-spirited heroine and a provocative, hot-blooded hero who will set you on fire!" —Rosanne Bittner

Paradise and More

"Another of Shirl Henke's wonderfully intricate and extremely well-researched tales, PARADISE AND MORE is a sumptuous novel!" —*Affaire de Coeur*

Return to Paradise

"Strong characters, exotic settings and a wealth of historical detail . . . RETURN TO PARADISE swept me away."

—Virginia Henley

Sundancer

SHIRL HENKE

St. Martin's Paperbacks

ISBN: 0-312-96691-1

Printed in the United States of America

St. Martin's Paperbacks edition / January 1999

St. Martin's Paperbacks are published by St. Martin's Press, 175 Fifth Avenue, New York, NY 10010.

10 9 8 7 6 5 4 3 2 1

In memory of
Aunt Adeline and Aunt Rosemary,
who made room for one more.

Acknowledgments

Singer-songwriter Roy Orbison provided my associate Carol J. Reynard and me with the germ of an idea for this book. "Workin' for the Man" inspired me to envision an outcast from the wrong side of the tracks who plans to woo and wed his boss's daughter so that he can become "the man." That he would fall in love with her was a given in spite of the calculating way he entered into the relationship.

We owe the 1868–69 transcontinental railroad setting to my husband Jim, who suggested the colorful era filled with such fascinating robber barons as Charlie Crocker, Collis Huntington, and Dr. Thomas C. Durant. Our editor, Jennifer Enderlin, also deserves credit for urging us to do another Indian book because she loved *The Endless Sky* so much. When I was stuck for a way to reconcile Cain with his Cheyenne heritage, Jim not only convinced me to do the Medicine Lodge sequence, but researched the ceremony as well.

For all the background research on *Sundancer*, the Public Libraries of St. Louis and St. Louis County were once again an invaluable resource, as was the Missouri Historical Society.

Longtime friend and lifetime railroader with the Missouri Pacific, Robert F. Fallon was so kind as to read the train wreck sequence and share his expert technical advice with us. To research a myriad of historical details, Carol has ventured with grave trepidation onto the Internet. For hours of assistance in "surfing" she expresses her sincere appreciation to Mark Hayford. As always our thanks go to our weapons expert, Dr. Carmine V. DelliQuadri, Jr., D.O., for arming Cain and the whole cast of railroaders and renegades.

Sundancer

Prologue

The "cut hair" rode up the narrow ravine and reined in his chestnut stallion expectantly beside the lone sentinel. Grim-faced and silent, he nodded to the older man. Both knew there was nothing left to say.

"He is waiting," the Cheyenne said, gesturing to the rocky trail behind him.

"Then it will be finished," the younger man replied bleakly.

As he rode past, the old man whispered so softly the "cut hair" barely heard the words, "No, it has only begun."

Not sparing the old Indian another glance, the young half-blood kneed his mount into a slow purposeful walk up the trail. Just before he reached the open clearing beyond the boulder-strewn ravine, he pulled the Patterson revolving rifle from its scabbard and checked the percussion caps on its loads. The Patterson was old, but in the right hands it was still a reliable weapon at seventy yards.

The mounted warrior poised at the opposite side of the flat wide plain was better armed with a new Volcanic carbine stolen in a raid on a wagon train. His hate-filled black eyes studied the rocky ravine, waiting. As soon as he saw his enemy emerge, the Cheyenne gave an earsplitting war cry. He kicked his horse into a gallop, leaning low over its neck, merging as one with the great beast.

The cut hair focused on the horseman, who raised his rifle and fired. The shot went wild. Fragments of sandstone stung his face and hands and sprayed his horse's neck and shoulders as the bullet ricocheted off the rocks. The chestnut danced nervously as the man raised his own rifle and sighted in on his rapidly advancing target.

The Cheyenne fired again. This time his shot found its mark, opening a narrow bloody furrow along the right side of the breed's cheek. He hissed at the white-hot shaft of pain but remained motionless, waiting until the horseman raised himself to fire again. The distance was closing now, seventy yards, sixty, fifty. He steadied the chestnut with his knees and pulled the trigger.

The impact of the slug knocked the Cheyenne from his horse. He landed in the short prairie grass like a broken toy flung down by some angry child. The cut hair rode up slowly, then dismounted. For a moment he stood staring at the widening red stain on the bare painted chest which would never again rise and fall with breath. The rifle lay nearby, gleaming evilly in the bright noonday sun. With a curse he kicked the stock, raising a faint puff of dust on the wind. Though he had dreamed of nothing else, revenge did not seem so satisfying now that it lay sprawled before him. His own blood trickled slowly down the side of his neck. Brushing his fingers through it, he looked at them, then rubbed the gory moisture on his pants leg and turned to his horse.

He had tracked his enemy halfway across Colorado deep into Nebraska. Now it had finally ended. *It has only begun.* The whispered words teased the edge of his mind, but he pushed them aside. Swinging into the saddle, he rode back the way he had come to tell the old man that he had killed his brother.

VICKSBURG, MISSISSIPPI, 1863

"Roxy, darlin'," Captain Nathaniel Darby drawled, undressing her with cool gray eyes. "Give me what I want and I'll let you ride away in the mornin' on a horse pointed north."

Roxanna Fallon stared impassively at the handsome Confederate officer. "You, sir, are a cockroach, the lowest thing God ever placed on His green earth."

Darby chuckled malevolently, but the laughter never reached his eyes. "The way I see it," he replied, picking up a loose tendril of her silver-blond hair, letting it slide through his long elegant fingers, daring her to flinch, "you have two choices." When she remained stone still, the lazy cat-and-mouse game began to tire him. His voice took on a brisker clip in spite of his thick Mississippi accent. "The Confederate States of America can hang you for the spy that you are ... or you can spend one night delivering what you've promised me these past weeks."

"How can you want a woman under such circumstances?" The moment she asked the question, Roxanna regretted it.

Darby smiled again. "To humble your stubborn Federal pride, why else?"

"Not because I made a fool of you and Pemberton and all the rest of old Joe Johnston's Rebs?" Why was she goading him? To destroy the only slim chance to save her life at the cost of her honor?

As if reading her mind, the captain said in a low silky voice, "You'll come off your high horse after a few more hours in that filthy cell with the rats. Think how a rope will feel on your lovely slender neck. You ever see a man hang, Roxy? It isn't a pretty sight, especially when the poor fellow's too light to fall hard enough to break his neck when the hangman springs the trap. Then he slowly chokes to death, face turns blue, eyes pop clean out of his head. ... How much do you weigh, darlin'?"

*   *   *

Dawn broke over the bluffs. Vicksburg spread over the hills like a jeweled tapestry, its whitewashed mansions gleaming brightly in the misty light of early morning. In the stillness, Roxanna Fallon rode away on a horse pointed north.

Chapter 1

His name was Cain and everyone in the Sierras feared him. In Cisco they knew the tall taciturn man with the cold black eyes possessed decidedly quick hands that could shoot or pistol-whip a man before he could get a running start on making trouble. There was an aura of barely leashed violence about Cain that made folks in the rough-and-tumble rail camps shy away from getting too close. Of course he was a breed and that would have set him apart, even if he were not the chief troubleshooter for the Central Pacific Railroad. But Cain's solitary status seemed as much his choice as anyone else's. Except to issue curt orders, he talked to no one but the coolies, with whom he conversed in their mysterious Chinese language. The little foreigners in their lampshade hats and blue pajamas were despised by Americans from San Francisco to the Sierras, but the rare times anyone saw Cain smile, it was when he spoke with them.

He walked with deliberate steps down the muddy plank walk toward the main office of the Central Pacific's construction chief looking neither left nor right, seemingly oblivious of the sweaty laborers and hawk-faced gamblers who stepped aside to let him pass. Cisco was a small ugly gash cut in the splendid heights of the Sierras, its crude log buildings and mud-rutted streets offset by jagged snow-capped peaks, crystalline blue lakes and towering white pine trees.

The feel of snow was in the air. Soon the railroad camps would be buried beneath a dozen feet of it once more. The fierce blizzards meant men would die, frozen in their blankets, buried alive when snow tunnels collapsed, starved when cut off from food or swept away in avalanches. He'd lived through two such hellish winters already. He knew them all too well. That was why he was back at the base camp.

A heavy wooden sign that read CENTRAL PACIFIC RAILROAD, ANDREW POWELL, FIELD DIRECTOR hung over the door of a two-story frame building. He shoved open the door and walked inside. The raw musty smell of wet sawdust combined not altogether unpleasantly with Andrew Powell's expensive cigars. Although the outer room was spartan, the interior where the chief and his high-ranking subordinates held their meetings was far more comfortable, even though Powell spent as little time here as possible, preferring the amenities of San Francisco. He let his associate Charlie Crocker slog around in the mud and snow.

"Where's Powell?" Cain's voice was low, deadly.

The clerk in the chief of staff's office practically overturned the room's lone chair when he saw the look in Cain's eyes. Standing up, he sputtered, "Er, Mr. Powell's in a conference right now, Mr. Cain. I . . ."

Cain strode past him and yanked open the heavy pine door as the clerk behind him wheezed ". . . wouldn't go in there now." He ignored the sputtering little man, shoving the door closed in his face. "We have to talk, Powell."

Andrew Powell leaned back in the mahogany spring armchair and crossed his arms over his chest with a scowl. His long angular face was punctuated with heavy gray eyebrows, a straight patrician nose and a narrow slash of a mouth set against a wide, powerful jawline, an aristocrat's face, hawkish and austere. But his most arresting features were his eyes, dark fierce blue eyes that scorched anyone who crossed him. He tipped his chair forward and stood up with casual grace. "I told Ezra I wasn't to be disturbed, but then you've never possessed civilized manners."

Cain's eyebrows arched derisively. "I stopped trying to impress you with civility. You steamroll over anyone with manners." As he spoke, his gaze shifted to the third man seated opposite Powell. "Morning, Larry."

Lawrence Erskin Powell stood up as well. Unlike Andrew, he was fair-haired and of medium height, several inches shorter than the two tall men flanking him. Lawrence was fine-boned with a round pleasant face that most women would deem handsome. His eyes were blue but a lighter shade than Andrew's, less compelling. At Cain's obvious inference that his father steamrolled over him, the younger Powell blushed beet red as he stammered, "G-good morning, Cain. Father and I were—"

"We were discussing a family matter," Andrew interrupted, emphasizing the word *family* derisively. When Cain stiffened imperceptibly, the older man gave him a chilly smile.

"I'm to be married, Cain," Lawrence interjected, seeming oblivious to the angry tension between Cain and the older Powell.

"Who's the lucky bride? Some San Francisco belle?" Cain asked, his anger sidetracked by the unexpected announcement.

Andrew replied smugly, "Not San Francisco, St. Louis. Alexandra Hunt is Jubal MacKenzie's granddaughter."

Cain's eyes narrowed. "I take it you cut this deal," Cain said to Andrew. It was not a question.

"Of course. When we met in Washington last month, during the congressional hearings. The wily old Scot is hedging his bets. Seems like the Union Pacific isn't laying track as fast as he contracted with them to do. He's tied up half his personal fortune in supplying construction crews."

"A mistake you and Huntington certainly never made on the Central Pacific," Cain interjected dryly.

"Only a fool would, when there's so much government

money laying around. Of course, Collis and I are a good deal better at siphoning it off from our estimable legislators than those fools Ames, MacKenzie and company. That's why the old man wants a marriage alliance. If he loses his shirt with the Union Pacific, he figures he'll get in on our contract to build Central Pacific lines up to Washington Territory and south into Arizona. And in truth, that might be a good deal all around. He has Washington contacts I don't.''

"What do you think of this Alexandra, Larry? You're the one who has to live with her, railroads be damned.''

"I don't exactly know—that is . . . we haven't met yet. Father and I were just discussing the preliminary arrangements with MacKenzie.''

"Of course you agreed to the deal sight unseen.''

Lawrence straightened indignantly. Cain always made him uneasy. "It's my duty as a Powell. After all, men of our class can scarcely marry for love.''

"Men of your class can afford to do as they damn well please, it seems to me, but then I'm hardly in a position to know. I do know only a fool would marry a female he'd never set eyes on. What if she's so ugly she has to sneak up on a mirror, Larry?'' Cain asked, with a smile that did not reach his eyes.

Andrew let out a sharp bark of laughter. "I would never have taken you for a romantic, Cain. It matters nothing what the girl looks like. She's from a good family, gently reared in St. Louis. A man can always find his pleasures outside of marriage.''

Cain countered insolently, "You should know.''

Powell snorted derisively, then stroked his jaw and assessed Cain with those unnerving blue eyes, eyes that had often reduced foes to quivering jelly. "You're hardly qualified to judge my morals. After all, I've never committed fratricide. You killed your redskin brother just to avenge that old fool Sterling, even though you knew he wouldn't have wanted you to do it. I wonder what other abominations you'd be willing to commit if the price was right.''

Lawrence paled, then flushed to the roots of his hair. "Father, please, this isn't amusing."

"Amusing," Andrew mocked. "No, I suppose it would frighten rather than amuse you. Why the hell can't you have the balls this half-breed does, dammit?" he asked savagely.

Lawrence stood stiffly beside the large mahogany desk with his lips compressed in a thin line, his expression one of helpless misery. "What would you have me do, become a gunman?"

"You'd probably shoot your own foot off," the older man replied in disgust.

"I didn't come here for this." Cain looked at Lawrence with genuine pity.

"What did bring you storming in, then?" Andrew countered. "I expected you'd be at the summit tunnel with your precious Chinese."

"That's where I just came from. It's starting to snow again higher up and Strobridge's going to use that goddamned patent blasting oil. Said you'd told him to go ahead."

"I did. We're months behind trying to dig through solid granite. Black powder by the carload won't get the job done. The nitroglycerin oil will."

"With tons of snow massed above the workers, it'll start avalanches. I've already lost seventeen men this month."

"Not men.. Coolies." Andrew shrugged dismissively. "Just because that fool Sterling taught you to jabber their singsong doesn't mean you have to bleed for them. I'm bringing up another thousand from San Francisco next week."

"So they're expendable . . . just like redskins."

"And breeds," the older man dared him, his pulse humming at the leap of fire he saw in Cain's black eyes.

"With a few differences, Powell. I'm not three thousand miles from home, defenseless in a frozen land—I also speak English. Enoch saw to that, too. You've forced them to work like slaves building this railroad, but I'll be damned if I act as Judas goat while any more of them are blown to kingdom come. We can go around the summit tunnel and let it wait till spring for the blasting.''

"No." There was flat finality in the older man's voice. "We get it done now."

Lawrence stepped out of the way, backing quietly into the corner as his father and Cain moved closer together, eyes locked. The tension between them was palpable. He looked from the half-breed's swarthy face to Andrew's, seeing both men in profile, tall, slim and straight, with rugged jaws and burning deep-set eyes, fierce as eagles. He waited to see how Cain would respond to the older man's challenge.

"I quit."

Powell laughed sharply. "You rode all the way from Nebraska to San Francisco, practically begged me for a job—any job—with the Central Pacific."

"Begged? You know better. I've shot men for you as easily as I shot meat for the laborers. This is different. This is where I draw the line."

"You want a raise?" Powell drawled. His eyebrows lifted measuringly.

"You couldn't afford my price," Cain replied, turning away.

As he strode across the carpet, Powell shouted after him, "You've worked all your life to be a white man, but you're still nothing but a dirty breed outside that door. Your price! Who'll hire you for anything more than a surveyor's guide or meat hunter?"

Cain paused with his hand on the heavy brass doorknob. "Jubal MacKenzie will hire me. I'm going to work for your competition and before I'm done, I'll drive you out of business."

HANNIBAL, MISSOURI, 1867

A loud whistle blast from the *Mississippi Belle* echoed across the cobbled stones of the levee as Roxanna Fallon slipped quietly down the back stairs with a raggedy carpetbag clutched in each hand. She was grateful for the noise from the departing riverboat, which covered the faint squeak of Mrs. Priddy's dilapidated steps. Her heart beat so loudly she was certain the old harridan could hear it at the opposite end of the seedy brick boardinghouse.

Lord above, she was glad to be quit of the musty smell of the riverfront, the greasy stale food and hard lumpy mattress inhabited by a whole community of bedbugs. But she hated losing the job with the repertory company. She had received the part of Desdemona in *Othello* and they were contracted for performances between St. Louis and New Orleans on the *Belle*. But the boat had left without her and she had no money to pay the rent.

No use thinking about what can't be changed, she reminded herself grimly for what seemed to be the hundredth time in the past four years. Just as she neared the end of the narrow darkened hallway, a meaty fist seized her arm, spinning her around. Hepsabah Priddy's sallow round face hung over her like a malevolent moon. Acrid garlic breath from last evening's mulligan stew enveloped her as the landlady hissed, "Thought you'd steal off like the sneaky spy you are, didja? I know all about you. No wonder Capt'n Guarrard fired you from his troupe. You're not even good enough to be one of them hussy stage actresses!"

"I'll send you the money when I have it. Since Isobel Darby's seen to it I'll never work in Hannibal again, I've no choice but to leave," Roxanna replied bitterly.

"Mrs. Darby's a respectable Southern lady. You ain't gonna say a word agin' her. Now, either you give me my week's rent or I drag you by that white hair of yourn down to the sheriff's office."

The hold on Roxanna's arm tightened painfully. All she had left to her name were the clothes in her bags and a few pieces of her mother's jewelry that had been in the Fallon family for generations. As it was, she would probably have to sell the scarab bracelet for passage downriver to St. Louis. Perhaps in a city that large she could lose herself so Isobel couldn't find her.

"I have only my clothing, not a dollar to my name, Mrs.

Priddy. Unless I find work you'll never get your money.''

Hepsabah rubbed her free hand across her nose and let out a snort of derision. ''You think I'm stupid? You ain't never goin' ta pay me noways. Least I can do for the Cause is see a Yankee spy like you ends up behind bars where she belongs!''

The landlady was tall and so wide she didn't have any sideways, but she was slow and clumsy. Raising the portmanteau with her theater clothes and last good pair of boots in it, Roxanna swung it hard as she could at the fat woman's head. The blow caught her in the temple and she staggered back, releasing Roxanna, who lunged away and darted down the hallway and out the front door.

The cool damp air felt clammy on the young woman's sweaty face as she ran toward the river. She could hear the old landlady's screeches fading as she put more distance between them. Clutching her two valises tightly, she slipped behind a trellis covered with dense honeysuckle vines. She took gulping breaths and at last her heartbeat returned to normal and the stitch in her side relented.

''Think, Roxy, think,'' she muttered aloud. Was there any other boat departing for downriver today? Hannibal was a sleepy little river town without much traffic. The *Memphis Queen* had pulled in to take on supplies yesterday. Perhaps it might be leaving this morning. But how to get around the sheriff? Surely Mrs. Priddy would have him waiting to search for her felonious boarder. A tight smile touched Roxanna's lips as she knelt down in the shelter of the honeysuckle arbor and began to root through her bags. An hour later, Althea Goodman, an elderly widow, crippled with arthritis, limped up the gangplank of the *Queen*, past the watching sheriff, with a heartrending tale for the boat's captain.

By nightfall Roxanna was on her way to St. Louis. The only river city below Iowa that held Northern sympathies, St. Louis was large and prosperous, a good place to assume a new identity so Isobel Darby could not find her. Of course, it would not be easy. She would have to do far more than simply change her name. The unique color of her hair and eyes presented a problem, as did her options for earning a living. She had become an actress out of necessity, and made an adequate living at it—until her enemy's paid detectives tracked her down each time she started over. Then Mrs. Darby would follow with her tearful lies about the shameless harlot of a Yankee spy who had murdered a Confederate war hero. War hero! Isobel was the one who should have become an actress.

Maybe St. Louis would be different. At least she was familiar with the city, having gone to finishing school there before the war. *Before the war* . . . How different her life had been back then. She had a home, social position, creature comforts—and most of all the love of her family. Mama doted on her elder brother Rexford, but she had been the center of her papa's world, the little urchin who followed him about like a puppy.

That had been how she learned about his work on the Underground Railroad. Late one evening when he had not come home, she'd sneaked out of her bedroom by climbing down the sycamore tree outside the window and went in search of him. She'd found him helping three terrified black men climb into a root cellar beneath their barn. He'd sworn the ten-year-old Roxy to secrecy and from that day onward his causes had become her own. Who would ever suspect a taffy-haired child of hiding runaway slaves in the wagon she took across the ferry into Illinois?

During the years she attended school in St. Louis, she chafed with eagerness for every holiday and summer recess so that she could return to help with her father's work. But those years of camaraderie and adventure had ended one brutal and bloody night in 1861 when a dozen masked bushwhackers had ridden into their front yard with torches blazing. Jerome Fallon had faced them bravely. As long as she lived, Roxanna would never forget her brother holding her back as she screamed and struggled to break free while the night riders tied Papa to a horse and rode away with him.

The next day the sheriff brought his lifeless body back to the family.

Her childhood had ended that night. Mama grieved herself to death and Rexford joined the Union army. To avenge her beloved Papa, Roxanna learned to fight in the only way a woman could. She became a spy.

No sense letting her mind trespass into that abyss. Roxanna forced her thoughts away from the painful memories and considered her old friend Alexa. Alexandra Hunt was from a prominent St. Louis family, a timid, plain young woman, shy and unsure of herself. The brash outgoing Roxanna had pitied her. When they were assigned to be roommates by the headmistress of the finishing school, she had striven to bring the younger girl out of her shell. Although she had little success with that, an unlikely friendship had sprung up, which had endured through the years.

But Roxanna had not heard from Alexa for nearly a year. Perhaps she was married by now or had moved away. Far more likely she had simply lost touch with Roxanna because the theater was such a gypsy life that Alexa's letters could not be forwarded. *Please be at home, Alexa. I need a safe place to stay until I can find work.* The thought that her friend might be afraid to harbor an infamous-spy-turned-actress hovered in the back of Roxanna's mind, but she refused to consider it. No use borrowing trouble. Enough came directly on its own.

Her fears proved groundless. No sooner had the little German maid scurried off to tell her mistress that Miss Roxanna Fallon had come for a visit than Roxanna found herself ushered into the private chambers of Alexa's elegant Lafayette Square house. "Roxanna, it's been ages," Alexa said, beckoning her friend to approach the bed.

Alexa had always been pale and ethereal, but now she looked wraith-thin, her eyes dull and her once pale silvery hair lusterless. Roxanna was shocked at the changes a few years had wrought as she crossed the room and took Alexa's bony hand in hers. It was cold as ice. "You've been ill," she said as a wracking cough seized her friend.

When she recovered her breath, Alexa shook her head. "Just a touch of the influenza, my doctor says. It was you I was worried about when my last letters to St. Paul and Davenport were returned."

Roxanna shrugged. "It's my work. Traveling repertory companies seldom stay more than a few weeks in one place." She did not want to mention Isobel Darby's malevolent pursuit, which had cost her every job and every move. "I should have written you more often."

"That's all past us now. You're here and I am ever so glad," Alexa said, tightening her feeble grip on Roxanna's hand. "How long can you stay—oh, please say it will be over the winter. Ever since Mama died I've been so alone in this big empty house."

"You're more than kind. You know Papa's bank failed after he was murdered and then I lost my brother in the war. . . . Truth to tell, Alexa, until I can find work, I'm quite broke."

"Then it's all settled. You shall stay with me. We shall have such grand times, just as we did in school, as soon as I'm up and about."

But Alexa was not up and about as fall stretched into winter. The terrible cough grew steadily worse and she had an increasingly difficult time holding down food. Roxanna became a combination of nurse and companion, caring for her friend, who the doctor now admitted was dying from consumption.

The winter had been unusually wet. Now, however, outside the bedroom window a pair of robins chirped joyously and the heavenly perfume from the lilacs wafted up on a warm spring breeze. But the beauty of the day was lost on Roxanna as she looked at Alexa's wasted body. Each day she seemed to shrink more, as if the bed were slowly swallowing her.

"You must write your grandfather, Alexa. He's your only living relative. Jubal MacKenzie owes it to you to come to St. Louis," Roxanna insisted.

"I don't want to disturb Grandfather, Roxanna. He's one of the most important men building the transcontinental railroad. The Union Pacific is all the way into Wyoming Territory now. I doubt if a letter could even reach him."

"You still haven't told him you're ill, have you?"

Alexa did not meet Roxanna's level gaze but plucked nervously at the bedclothes. "No, I . . . I have not. I'm afraid of him, Roxanna. All I remember from when I was a little girl is a big tall man with a bristling red beard and a booming voice. He even made Papa quake, and he was ever so much braver than Mama or me. How disappointed he'll be to find out I'm going to die and leave him without an heir."

"Don't talk rubbish! You are not going to die," Roxanna insisted for what must have been the thousandth time.

But Alexa only shook her head sadly. "You know it's true."

Before Roxanna could remonstrate, a soft tap on the door interrupted them and Gretchen entered with an envelope clutched in her hand. "A letter just arrived by special courier for you, Miss Hunt." The maid approached the sickbed fearfully, not wanting to risk contamination. Gingerly she held out the envelope. Roxanna snatched it and dismissed the girl, then opened the heavy vellum envelope and handed its contents to Alexa. The postmark was Denver. *Speak of the devil and up he pops*, she thought sourly. If Alexa wouldn't write Jubal MacKenzie, *she* would. Then, hearing the papers in Alexa's hands rustle, she looked over at her friend. If it was possible, Alexa looked even paler than usual. "What is it—what's wrong?"

The expression on Alexa's face was one of incredulous terror as she handed Roxanna the letter. Her hand trembled violently.

Roxanna quickly scanned the letter, then resisted the urge to crumple it into a ball and toss it out the open window. "This is positively medieval! He can't just announce to you that he's picked a husband for you and expect you to meekly travel to some godforsaken place in the wilderness to marry a total stranger!"

Alexa smiled weakly at Roxanna's vehemence. "The marriage would take place in Denver, hardly a wilderness. Grandfather wants me to join him at his rail camp in Wyoming so we can have some time together. . . ." Her face crumpled. "If only I could go. He has asked me to come west repeatedly—to visit with him, but I was always afraid. I guess I've always been afraid of life and now I wish I'd done so many things—"

"Don't—don't do this to yourself, Alexa," Roxanna replied, putting her arms around Alexa's shoulders. *Like bird bones, so delicate and brittle.* Alexa began to cough again and Roxanna could see the bright crimson stain of blood soaking through the cloth her friend held to her mouth. Life was so damn unfair! Quickly exchanging the soaked cloth for a fresh one, she rang for the maid and summoned the doctor.

Late that night, Roxanna sat in Alexa's room red-eyed from weeping, staring at the empty bed where her friend had spent most of the past months of her life. The young doctor had done all he could, but Alexa's life had literally ebbed away in a slow crimson trickle. "At least her awful suffering is over," Roxanna murmured to herself, but the words rang hollow. The undertaker was preparing her body downstairs. *Papa. Mama. Rexford. Now Alexa. There is no one left for me.*

The wake began the next morning. But since Alexa had led a painfully reclusive life even before she fell ill, there were few callers, all old family friends—except for one. Fortunately, when Gable Hogue arrived, Roxanna was in the kitchen giving instructions to the cook. The instant she saw Isobel Darby's relentless detective, she slipped behind the heavy velvet draperies in the hallway as her heart beat a thudding tattoo. *How did he find me?*

She listened as he discreetly explained to the maid that he was an old teacher of the deceased young lady come to pay his last respects. Dour, sullen Gretchen, thank heaven, did not mention Miss Alexa's old school chum who was currently residing in the house. For once the maid's churlish disposition endeared her to Roxanna. She watched as Hogue approached the bier and studied poor Alexa's lifeless form. Then he turned and strode silently from the house.

Roxanna waited in sheer terror for the next several days as she closed down the house and paid the servants their severance wages. Since she had assumed control of the household finances over the past six months, Roxanna was able to give each employee a bonus with the admonition not to disclose anything about her to Hogue should he return. By week's end she concluded that he must have heard about a reclusive young woman dying who happened to fit Roxanna Fallon's description. Apparently it never occurred to him that the heiress had a friend with the same unusual coloring.

But sooner or later he would find her. He always did. Roxanna was completely out of options at this point. Once Jubal MacKenzie was notified that his granddaughter was dead, the allowance would stop. Where could she go? What could she do to keep from starving to death? The past four years had taught her the utter futility of seeking further employment on the stage. That was the way Hogue always located her for Isobel. But she had no references to become a tutor or governess. Factory supervisors took one look at her pale blond hair and fine-boned aristocratic body and laughed when she applied for honest work. Of course they offered her another sort of work. . . .

"Is that how I'll end up . . . used by hundreds of men, pawed and mauled until there's nothing left of me?" She sat alone in the empty house, listening to the soughing of the cool spring wind as her body was wracked with shudders. To let any man touch her again after Vicksburg was unbearable. To let an endless succession of them use her was enough to fix her eyes on Terrence Hunt's dueling pistols hanging on the study wall. Even death was better than life as a whore.

Roxanna stood up and paced resolutely over to the drapery-shrouded window. "No. I won't sell myself and I won't take my own life." *That was his way out—a coward's way*.

She had a decent sum of money left in Alexa's account—if old Jubal MacKenzie allowed her to keep it once he learned his granddaughter was dead. Someone would have to let him know, since the family attorney here in St. Louis had died suddenly the preceding week.

Thinking of MacKenzie, Roxanna walked over to the desk and picked up the sheaf of papers, his last letter to his granddaughter. An arranged marriage seemed so cold-blooded. No doubt he stood to benefit from some sort of business merger. The prospective groom worked for the California side of the transcontinental, the Central Pacific. Poor timid Alexa, who was frightened to death of men, auctioned off to the highest bidder! Suddenly an idea planted itself with blinding clarity in Roxanna's mind. No! She shook her head, dismissing it as preposterous.

"I couldn't . . ." Her eyes strayed once more to the letter. The old Scotsman had not been to St. Louis to visit his only daughter since her husband died eight years earlier. When Alexa's mother died two years ago, he had been off in the wilds of Canada, negotiating a timber contract for his precious railroad. He had invited his orphaned granddaughter to come to Denver, but Alexa had refused. It seemed MacKenzie was a man who expected everyone to meet him on his own terms or be damned. Already Roxanna did not like the man, and she had never even laid eyes on him!

But he had not laid eyes on his granddaughter since she was thirteen years old either, some relentless voice within Roxanna insisted. He had no idea what she looked like as a grown woman. She and Alexa were both slender, with light eyes and pale blond hair. Gable Hogue had thought Alexa Hunt might be Roxanna Fallon. What if Roxanna Fallon became Alexa Hunt?

Who would be hurt? Alexa was dead and she was alive. She could become Jubal MacKenzie's granddaughter. After all, she was an actress, wasn't she? But she would have to marry a complete stranger. Could she do it? Roxanna sat staring at MacKenzie's letter, trying to read between the lines. "What sort of a man are you, Jubal MacKenzie?" Ruthless, without a doubt. Would the man she was to wed be equally rapacious? Even if he was, he was *one* man. And the marriage would give her some measure of protection from Isobel. As Mrs. Lawrence Powell of San Francisco, even Gable Hogue would never find her. She would be a wife, not a whore.

Alexa had insisted upon giving Roxanna her power of attorney. All she needed to do was withdraw sufficient funds from Alexa's account to travel to Wyoming . . . to meet her bridegroom. Shivering in spite of the warm spring weather, Roxanna stiffened her spine and took a deep breath. "I'll do it!"

Chapter 2

"Nothin' out there but miles 'n miles o' miles n' miles, thet's fer sure," the old driver said as he spit a glob of noisome blackish tobacco into the dust. It landed at Roxanna's feet with a plop. The leathered skin of his face was creased by a thousand tiny wrinkles, looking as sandblasted as the desolate rolling hills that surrounded them. "Time ta mount up 'n skeedaddle if we want to reach the next way station by dark."

Without further ado, Jack Rabbit Sam scrambled up onto the driver's box of the battered old coach Jubal MacKenzie had chartered for "his granddaughter." Roxanna, now Miss Alexa Hunt, was left to fend for herself, which suited her just fine, since Jack Rabbit was dirty enough to sell as real estate. With a sigh, she climbed through the high narrow door. The interior was a bit shopworn and dusty but plush nonetheless, with faded maroon velvet upholstery.

Roxanna sank back into the lumpy cushions and gazed out the window as the coach took off with a lurch. The Nebraska panhandle was as desolate as the rest of the seemingly endless plains following the tortuous course of the Platte River. Gradually the rippling prairie shortgrass had begun to give way to sand hills covered with undulating coyote willow. On the distant western horizon the jagged Rockies brooded, sentinels overseeing the harsh, vast emptiness that was the High Plains. So stark and barren was the land ahead, said one newspaper account, that it could not even rise to the rank of *howling* wilderness. Roxanna, raised in the rich farm country of northern Missouri, agreed.

At least if she went through with the marriage arrangement, her groom would take her to live in San Francisco, a civilized enough city, from all reports. Would she marry this Lawrence Powell? What sort of a man agreed to wed a woman sight unseen, just to further his wealthy family's ambitions? As she mulled that over, Roxanna's mind skittered over the incredible speed with which her life had been swept along since she had written to her "grandfather." Within the week a wire had arrived with detailed instructions for her journey west to join him in Dakota Territory, including the charter of this stage which would take her all the way into the new rail center called Cheyenne, named for a fierce and warlike tribe of savages marauding across the region.

Roxanna shivered, wishing again that the cavalry escort she had been given from Fort Kearny could have continued farther west with them. But the commanding officer had ordered his men to ride down the South Platte, searching for a band of raiders who had attacked a relay station sixty miles east on the trail.

Forcing aside thoughts about scalping savages, she considered the new life she was beginning. Jubal MacKenzie's letter and subsequent wire indicated a certain brusque businesslike efficiency, yet there were hints of warmth, even humor in the missive. The latter qualities were unexpected from a man who would arrange a marriage beneficial for his business interests and then simply inform his granddaughter where and when she was to show up.

One thing was certain. Alexa's grandfather was a very rich, powerful man, used to getting his way. So, most probably, was Lawrence Powell. "Do your worst, gentlemen, I can hold my own," Roxanna murmured grimly as the coach hit another rut in this fiction of a road, slamming her hard against the coach door. Was it her imagination or were they picking up speed? Jack Rabbit always cursed when he lashed the horses, but there seemed an extra edge in his voice now as the whip cracked viciously and the stage bounced and jerked like a child's top spinning out of control.

Then she heard the voices, soft at first, like the soughing of the constant prairie winds. They grew louder. Short swift yips and high, long screeches of bone-chilling ferocity began to fill the air, melded with the pounding of horses' hooves on the hard-packed earth. Roxanna peered cautiously out the window.

She gasped at the sight of a dozen or more Indians galloping across the rolling grasslands. As they gained on the careening stage, she could see their painted faces distorted by feral grimaces. Each rider bent low over his horse's neck, as if he were one with his sweating straining pony. Soon they would catch the stage. Dear God, what would they do to her? Roxanna had faced death on numerous occasions since her ugly confrontation with Nathaniel Darby, but even choking to death at the end of a rope was beginning to look preferable to what awaited her at the hands of these savages.

Just then a rifle cracked. Two more shots followed in rapid succession before Jack Rabbit tumbled silently from the driver's box, vanishing in the thick dust behind the coach. The savages ignored his body as they closed on the stage.

Roxanna cursed herself for ten-thousand-times-a-fool for not carrying the pepperbox pistol in her reticule. A fine lot of good it was doing her packed atop the luggage rack! Two of the savages leaped agilely from their saddleless mounts onto the backs of the lead coach horses, while a third rode alongside the stage itself. It had not completely stopped when he seized the door handle and yanked it open, then reached one bronzed arm inside for Roxanna.

She kicked and struggled fiercely, but would not scream. What little she had overheard en route about Indians indicated that they valued courage above all else. She would not cry or beg, no matter what they did to her. *A vow more easily made than kept,* she thought, as her captor dragged her out of the coach and two of his cohorts quickly pinned her arms behind her, effectively immobilizing her.

She ceased struggling and stared straight ahead while one of the others ran his dark fingers through her long pale blond hair, exclaiming over the color in what she took to be amazement. He pulled the last pins from it—she had long since lost her hat—and held it out like a silken skein for all to admire. Good Lord, would he scalp her here and now? Her eyes darted to the heavy knife at his belt, but he made no move to unsheathe it.

Then it was to be the other first, she thought with a shudder. Well, it wasn't as if she were a virgin who had no idea of what to expect. All men must have the same basic equipment. She would endure. Bracing her spine stiffly, she bit down on her lip and stared into the dark eyes of the ringleader as the warriors moved in closer.

Hell on Wheels. That's what the railroaders dubbed these stops along the Union Pacific line. Cain rode down the wide street of Cheyenne, Wyoming, now silty with pale tan dust that would turn to bog like mud with the next good rain. On the front of a huge canvas tent a banner proclaimed, HAVALAND'S HURDY GURDY. BEAUTIFUL DANCING GIRLS, COLD BEER. In fact, the women were ugly and the beer was warm. A slit-eyed gambler attired nattily in black lounged in the doorframe of a clapboard hotel, rifling a greasy set of pasteboards. The diamond ring on his pinkie finger winked obscenely in the sunlight. Mentally, Cain gave him a week before someone cut his throat in a back alley and relieved him of the gaudy jewelry. The *Cheyenne Leader* ran a daily column entitled "Last Night's Killings." It was easily the largest article in the paper.

"Come ovah heah, darlin'. My, my, ain'tcha a pretty one, longlegs," a black-haired whore with blood-red lips crooned in invitation, eyeing Cain up and down as if he were a big juicy steak and she a starving coyote. As the portable whores of Hell on Wheels went, she was not bad looking, but Cain was not in the mood for sexual diversion.

The sharp pungency of sage and sweetness of prairie clover wafted heady and clean on the ever-present wind as he left Cheyenne behind. Warm sun beat down on man and horse. He watched the great blue bowl of sky, simply content with being, an infrequent occurrence for his restless soul. How often had his Cheyenne uncle tried to teach him the joys of harmony with nature? But letting his mind go blank and his body simply absorb what lay around him was too alien an act for the white part of his soul. And the white part, he had always felt, was dominant.

With his big chestnut's ground-devouring stride, he reached Fort Russell shortly. As the cluster of low adobe buildings appeared on the horizon, he muttered to himself, "MacKenzie's really dumped one on me this time." He reined in at the edge of the parade ground, where a flag flapped smartly in the breeze. A troop of new recruits was being drilled by a sergeant who could outroar a tornado. Swinging down from his mount, the tall half-breed walked up to the headquarters building and shoved open the door, which protested loudly on rusty hinges.

"Cain to see Colonel Dillon," he said to the young corporal.

Before the noncom could respond, the door to the inner office opened and a barrel-chested man with a square, weathered face and thinning brown hair stepped out with a sheaf of papers in one scarred fist. He looked Cain over with eyes that had seen far too much of life. Shoving the papers at the corporal, he said, "Come in, Mr. Cain," then spun on his heel and entered the small cluttered room. Cain followed, closing the door.

Standing in a bright shaft of sunlight pouring in the room's only window, Dillon studied Cain. "So you're the one they call the Scot's Injun."

"I'm Jubal MacKenzie's man," Cain replied tightly.

"You're Jubal MacKenzie's gun," the colonel countered flatly.

Dillon had nerve, he'd give him that. "MacKenzie needs the army's help in town. The thugs and grifters are causing so much absenteeism on our crews, we're falling behind schedule."

"In case you haven't taken note, I have a serious Indian problem out there." One blunt finger jabbed at the window toward the distant mountains. "I was sent out here to pacify hostiles, not baby-sit a pack of drunken Irishmen."

"You were assigned here to see that the railroad is completed with all due speed. Once we have a transcontinental linkup, the army can move troops fast anywhere hostiles pop up."

Dillon snorted. "I doubt it'll be that easy in the near future, railroad or not. Right now I have fewer than one hundred men to cover thousands of square miles. It's damn hard to surround a dozen Cheyenne with two troopers."

"Then I guess I'll have the Vigilance Committee help me handle the problem."

Dillon knew how vigilantes had filled up the cemeteries in North Platte and Julesburg. "That'll be a bloodbath and you know it."

Cain shrugged. "It's your call."

Dillon stiffened and his face mottled red. "Are you threatening me, Cain?"

"Just call it a request. Cheyenne is going to be the biggest railhead between Omaha and Salt Lake, the connecting point for spur lines south to Denver and north into the Montana goldfields. One way or the other, it has to be cleaned up. If you don't do it, I'll have to."

"And you're just itching to unholster that gun of yours and start." Dillon's eyes bored into Cain.

"I don't get paid by the scalp, contrary to what you may have heard." He could feel that damned scar along his jaw twitching.

Dillon suddenly deflated. Placing his palms flat on the edge of his desk, he lowered himself wearily into his chair. "I'll have a detachment in town by nightfall."

*   *   *

By eleven o'clock that night the army completed its work. Cain sat in the Calico Cat Saloon sharing a drink with its proprietor, Kitty O'Banyon, in her private office at the rear of the establishment. The Cat was the most elegant pleasure palace in Cheyenne, boasting two mahogany bars, mirrors on three walls and an oil painting of Venus rising from the sea on the fourth. Even the cuspidors were of polished brass, cleaned nightly.

Cain sat staring into his drink as if the amber liquid held the secrets of the universe. Kitty, a tall voluptuous Irishwoman with fiery tresses and a disposition to match, studied him. "What's eating you, Cain? It's a fine job Colonel Dillon did, if I do say so meself. With the likes of those Chicago shysters riding the rails east, a hardworking female can earn a dacent dishonest living again."

He raised his glass in salute, then downed the whiskey and leaned back in his chair. "I have two new grading crews to drill tomorrow. If only these damn fools knew how to level a grade as well as they know how to level themselves. On the Central Pacific my Chinese died in explosions and avalanches—here, these yahoos catch cholera drinking water out of the ditches, or the pox lying with diseased women, or they die of whiskey poisoning. Getting rid of the syndicate's scum will only slow the rate of attrition, not stop it."

"You take too much on yerself, boyo. Men can be fools. Usually are. Does MacKenzie expect you to be reforming the kit and kaboodle of 'em, then?"

He rubbed the bridge of his nose and smiled self-deprecatingly. "No. *I* expect it of me—at least as far as it concerns our construction schedule. He's paying me a bonus for every man who works his full shift a month without missing a day."

"You don't drink much. You have the divil's own luck with cards, 'n the ladies don't charge you for sportin' fun. Leastways, *I* don't," she added archly. "What is it you're figgerin' on doing with all that money when the railroad's built?"

"Buying an interest in another railroad."

"It's not power yer wantin', Cain, nor money," she said, prompting him.

"Oh, it's the money, all right, and the power."

"It's showing himself, that's what it is. Yer pa, whoever he may be." He looked up, startled, his eyes narrowing dangerously. She raised her hand, chuckling. "Now, before you go getting yer backside all lathered, 'twas yerself who told me—the only time I ever saw you drunk."

He cursed furiously. "The night I came back from the raid on Turkey Leg's village."

"It's powerful upset you were, with a fearful thirst for oblivion. Don't like seeing yer ma's people killed, do you?"

"They were killing our surveyors, attacking the grading crews. I had to track them for the army. At least they rounded up the right Indians that time."

"Even doin' what they did, the Injuns have the right of it to their own way of thinkin'. The Iron Horse will finish them."

"Progress, Kitty. We can't stop it." The words sounded defensive even to his own ears. He changed the subject. "What did I say about my father?"

She shrugged, meeting his gaze head-on. "Only that he left yer ma and you with the Cheyenne 'n went away. Came back 'n packed you off to some boarding school. But you never gave up trying to win his love."

"I never said that, sober or drunk."

Kitty grinned. "You didn't have to, sugar. I been around long enough to read between the lines."

He scoffed dismissively. "Just stick to the lines from now on, huh? I have to go. The A.M. will roll around before I get my blankets half warmed." He scooted the oak-barrel chair back and stood up.

Kitty looked up at him with appraising eyes. "You want yer blankets warmed, you know where to come, Cain. Any-time. . . ."

She watched him turn and walk slowly out the door, then murmured softly, "I hope you find what yer lookin' for one day, and that's the Lord's own truth."

*   *   *

Jubal MacKenzie was a stern Scottish Presbyterian, a self-made millionaire, and an ardent Abolitionist. He had spent the war years as a high-ranking member of Lincoln's Cabinet. Now his passion had turned west to building the iron rails that would link the Atlantic with the Pacific. The future lay in the West, mineral rich, fertile and awe-inspiringly beautiful to a man who had grown up on the filthy streets of Aberdeen hauling buckets of coal for twopence.

Bending over the polished walnut desk in his private Pullman car, Jubal studied the map in front of him with grim concentration, then pushed it aside with an oath and began pacing across the Tabriz carpet. He clenched a fine Cuban cigar between his teeth and stuffed his big gnarled hands in his suit pockets.

That was how Cain found him upon answering the urgent summons which brought him from the camp shooting range. One look at his employer told him that the old Scot was furious. "What's happened, Jubal? More mules dying on short notice at number seven?"

Mac's heavy reddish brows beetled, rearranging the patterns of large freckles that covered his beefy face. The heavy grooves around his mouth deepened as he grimaced, removing the cigar from his sturdy yellow teeth to speak. "A lot more serious than mules or men." His voice rumbled deep, with a heavy burr of Scotland still evident in spite of fifty years spent in his adopted homeland. "You remember me mentioning the marriage between my granddaughter and Powell's son Lawrence?"

"A dynastic alliance that'll cut you in for the Central Pacific's expansion up and down the West Coast."

"Damn, if you aren't a smart young whelp!" MacKenzie studied Cain with shrewd gray eyes, stroking the bristly beard that grew wildly around his face like an explosion of red and gray squirrel tails. "Aye, I want a piece of the Central Pacific. It's a good way to keep an eye on Andrew Powell's greasy soul." He hesitated. "But there was more to it than that . . . my granddaughter. She's been alone back in St. Louis for several years. I needed to provide for her.''

"You sure marrying her into the Powells is the best way?"

"Better that than she choose some fortune hunter like her mother did." Jubal harrumphed in disgust and resumed pacing. For a man of considerable girth, he was agile and quick on his feet, gnarled and tough as a hundred-year-old oak. He waved away the past with one hand, willing it to dissipate with the smoke from his cigar. "This will be a good marriage for her—if she lives to walk down the aisle.''

He tossed Cain a wire from the adjutant at Fort Kearny. Quickly scanning it, he raised his eyes to the old man. "What are you going to do?"

MacKenzie leaned across the desk, his big fists resting on the blotter as he stared at Cain. "What would you do? You know these people. The adjutant says it was Cheyenne who took her. I'm not without influence in Washington. I can wire General Sherman. Have enough troops deployed to cover all Dakota Territory, if they have to reinstate the draft to do it. But I have to act now. When I think of that poor lass in the hands of hostiles—''

"You don't want to use soldiers. If the army blunders onto the camp where she's being held—and that's the only way they'd find her—the Cheyenne would kill her." Cain studied the wire. "This sounds as if they were looking to take a white captive, not just their usual harassment of the stage lines.''

"How could they have known my granddaughter was in that coach?"

Cain shook his head. "They couldn't. They were just looking for someone important enough to trade for.''

"You mean ransom?"

Cain shrugged. "Their version of it, yes.''

"Could you get her out?" The old man's pewter eyes stared intently at the young half-breed.

"If I can't, no one can. Not alive, anyway.''

"I'll pay whatever the bastards want. The money's not—''

"They don't want money, Jubal. With the powder keg we have on the plains right now, there's no way any Cheyenne can come into a trading post to spend cash. They'll want guns, medicine, blankets. Mostly guns, I'd bet."

"Go to the supply train and requisition whatever you need. There'll be a big bonus in this if you bring the lass back safely."

Cain nodded and turned to leave, but MacKenzie caught him with his hand on the ornate brass doorknob. "You do na' think they've . . . hurt her?"

Cain was surprised at the note of uncertainty in the old man's voice. As long as he'd known the old curmudgeon, Jubal MacKenzie had always been loud, profane and decidedly self-assured. "I can't promise you they haven't used her, if that's what you mean. A female captive past puberty is usually given to a warrior as a slave, but since they may want to bargain, there's a chance she's not been touched."

MacKenzie's face blanched the color of whey, making the freckles grotesquely prominent. He shook his head but said nothing as Cain closed the door behind himself.

Chapter 3

For five days Cain rode northeast into the Sand Hill country of Nebraska, cutting trails, stopping at every Cheyenne or Arapaho camp, asking oblique questions, looking covertly for any evidence of a white captive. The law of hospitality among the People was never to be broken. Because of his Cheyenne blood they received him, but that reception varied. He was a "cut hair," one who had turned his back on their way and joined their enemy. Suspicion and thinly veiled hostility hovered around the campfires.

The past five years had been bloody ones on the High Plains. After the Sand Creek Massacre by Colonel Chivington's Colorado Volunteers, the Cheyenne and their allies had raided and pillaged from Julesburg to Plum Creek while General Sherman turned loose the rapacious George Armstrong Custer to reply in kind. To avoid cavalry sweeps, the Indians scattered like leaves in the wind, dividing up into small bands that searched, often in vain, for the vanishing buffalo and other game which the hated Iron Horse was destroying.

After two weeks on the trail he was beginning to fear he was mistaken and MacKenzie's granddaughter had been killed by her captors. Then he ran across a small village of Arapaho, where he learned old Leather Shirt was camped high up on a tributary of the Niobrara. His band had quit the spring hunt below the Arkansas and headed north, a move which puzzled the Arapaho warriors.

"Why does he leave when the buffalo are yet running?" their chief asked.

Could it be? Was Leather Shirt the one who took Alexa Hunt? If not, at least the old man might know of her fate. Two days later, he approached the camp. Riding into it brought memories of childhood rushing back to him. Two small boys, naked in the warm morning sun, tossed a small leather sack back and forth while a cur raced around them, yipping amid their shrieks of glee. A group of giggling young women returned to camp after gathering firewood into bundles which they carried strapped on their backs.

A lone youth stood on a ridge above the village, his body rail straight, staring ahead into the rising sun, oblivious to the commotion below him. Cain knew he would remain perfectly motionless through the day, a test of endurance and discipline to please the Everywhere Spirit.

As a boy he had once dreamed of such rigorous rites of passage . . . until he learned that his white father scoffed at such quixotic savage superstitions. Shrugging away the past, Cain walked his horse toward the orderly semicircle of lodges, pulling the lead pack mule behind him. Each teepee faced east to the sunrise. An old man's chant, greeting the day, echoed across the hillside. The singer reminded him of his uncle. In his earliest years, the old man's morning song had awakened him every day.

As he neared the village, his presence drew attention. Women stirring their morning cookfires looked up curiously. Men repairing their weapons studied him with narrowed dark eyes. One youth clutching a war lance in front of him raised it defiantly as the "cut hair" passed by. A warrior bearing the marks of the Dog Soldier Society stepped in his path. Once Cain had called him friend.

"Greetings, Rides the Wind. I would see Leather Shirt."

"He waits for you, Not Cheyenne." Rides the Wind spun on his heel and led the way, every movement of his body revealing his antagonism.

Sees Much sat in front of his fire impassively. *Did he know I would come?* A ripple of unease prickled up and down Cain's spine as he dismounted. The old man had always had a peculiar ability to divine the future, an ability which no amount of Enoch's teaching could explain away.

Seemingly sightless silvery eyes gazed past him into the flames as the old man stretched out one veiny hand, gesturing for Cain to approach. His body was shriveled with age, like a currant left to desiccate in the sun, yet there was a wiry strength still in it despite the stooped shoulders and gaunt arms and legs. Thinning white hair crowned a small face whose prominent nose and generous mouth seemed too large to fit. He did not smile, but there was an expression of contentment, perhaps satisfaction when he spoke. "My brother has been waiting for you."

"You knew I would come." It was not quite a question.

A voice from inside the lodge replied, "It was our medicine man, Sees Much, who saw the silver-haired woman in a dream." Then Leather Shirt emerged. He stood face-to-face with Cain, as straight and tall as his elder brother was wizened. Leather Shirt had seen sixty winters, yet his long braids were still black, only flecked with gray. His face was harsh and angular, with a large nose and heavy cheekbones. Deep grooves etched like brackets down to a wide mouth that turned down on both sides. Deep-set black eyes studied Cain.

"Then you have the woman I have come for."

Leather Shirt raised his eyes to the heavily laden pack mules Cain had brought with him. "You speak without politeness like a white eyes, Not Cheyenne, so I will answer as crudely. Yes, my young men captured her."

"Because Sees Much had a vision?"

"You doubt, yet you are here," the old shaman chuckled from his spot by the fire.

Leather Shirt's eyes swept over the gleaming chestnut stallion with its silver-trimmed saddle and the .52-caliber Spencer carbine resting in the scabbard. Neither did he miss the .44-caliber Smith and Wesson Model 3 on Cain's hip, nor the expensive hand-tooled leather boots. "You have prospered among your father's people, leaving behind a life that has become hard. Game is scarce and our children cry with empty bellies. Our women gash their arms in mourning for warriors cut down by the white eyes' bullets. We fight your Iron Horse, but we cannot defeat it. We would move north to the Yellowstone country of our brothers the Lakota, far from the belching smoke, away from the Blue Coats. But we must have guns for our warriors to hunt with and protect the women and children."

"And to fight your way past Sherman's army," Cain added. "I have brought guns."

"You have said," Leather Shirt said to Sees Much, "and it is true."

The older man merely nodded, studying Cain with his penetrating sight. Then he spoke. "You must spend time with the People, relearn our ways."

"I am called Not Cheyenne, a cut hair. The People will not welcome me."

"It has been five winters since you killed High-Backed Wolf. Your banishment is ended," Leather Shirt replied. "If your heart did not belong with your father, you could join us." The bleak expression on his face indicated his awareness that Cain would refuse.

"My heart does not belong anywhere."

"It is not a good thing to belong nowhere," Sees Much said softly.

Leather Shirt gave a snort of disgust. "He is just another white man, brother. I told you this was a dangerous thing to undertake."

"Do not be so swift to judge, Leather Shirt," Sees Much rebuked gently.

Leather Shirt nodded and said to Cain, "Lark Song will provide you with a place to eat and rest while Iron Kite sees to your horse and mules. Then we will talk of the woman . . . and other things."

From across the campgrounds, Roxanna watched the exchange between the old men and their visitor. He was dressed like a white man, but he looked as hardened and dangerous as any of her captors. His long lean body was draped with an arsenal. A gunrunner or whiskey trader, perhaps? His straight black hair and bronzed skin suggested that he was a mixed-blood. Yet his features were sculpted, almost classically handsome if one made allowances for the prominent nose and high cheekbones. There was a narrow scar along his cheek that somehow added a raffish allure rather than detracting from his good looks.

Roxanna had observed him ride in, hoping he would be her deliverance, but something had held her back from rushing out to him. Those hard glittering eyes had swept the camp in pitiless assessment. Instinctively she knew they would scorch when fastened on her. She had won a place for herself among these strange, savage people. There was no sense squandering it precipitously on a hardcase like this man. Best to wait.

Looking back over the past three weeks, Roxanna could scarce believe how she had survived the ordeal. After they dragged her from the coach, her captors had done nothing to harm her, only bound her hand and foot and tossed her across the back of one warrior's horse. She was forced to ride like a sack of grain for two days, with only hard chewy strings of meat washed down with muddy creek water to sustain her. Filthy, frightened and exhausted, she was brought before the village chief at last, the old man known as Leather Shirt. His English was adequate, that of his medicine man far better. The chief turned her over to Sees Much, who was surprisingly kind.

Roxanna quickly learned that they planned to ransom her at some point. They were vague about exactly when, but considering the options of torture, rape or death, she decided she wouldn't quibble over details. Several young women were assigned to care for her. Lark Song and Willow Tree could speak some English, supplemented by gestures and hand signs. They communicated well enough.

She learned from Sees Much that she was greatly admired for her bravery. When the warriors captured her she had

The soft rippling hum of cool water invited him to approach a chokecherry thicket. Perhaps a dip would clear his head. He walked soundlessly through the bushes to a fallen log. Tugging his shirt over his head, he tossed it onto the log, then sat on it and pulled off his boots. Just as he stood up and unbuckled his gunbelt, he heard a loud splash, followed by a contented feminine sigh. Cain froze, then peered through a thin spray of willow branches.

The sight which greeted him robbed him of breath. Gleaming long hair, the color of silver and gold melded together, fanned out across the water as Alexa Hunt lazed on her back, kicking just enough to propel herself away from the swifter current. A set of small breasts peeked impudently through the translucent curtain of water, their pale pink nipples beaded with cold. In repose her face looked more mature than he would have expected. It was delicately formed yet surprisingly strong, the nose aquiline and the mouth firm and full. Her high forehead was crowned by arched silvery eyebrows and thick pale lashes fanned down covering wide-set eyes. He wondered irrelevantly what color they were.

Lord, she's a piece! This water nymph certainly did not resemble her grandfather! Cain knew he should not continue to spy, but he could not tear his eyes away as she raised one delicate arm and began to backstroke through the water. Her body was long and slender, elegantly formed. He judged her to be a bit above average height for a white woman. When she reached the shallows and stood up, he could see his guess was accurate . . . and a great deal more. His body leaped to life, setting off the old familiar throb. He'd been far too long without a woman, and this one was certainly forbidden. Jubal MacKenzie would have him flayed alive if he touched Alexa Hunt. Like all the best things in life, she was destined for another.

Deep in thought, Cain did not realize how close she was coming to his meager hiding place until her sharp gasp echoed in the warm afternoon silence. Now she was the one to freeze in shock as clear turquoise eyes peered at him through the sheer curtain of willow leaves. Water glistened on her alabaster skin like small silvery jewels, sliding over the satiny curves of her breasts, hips and calves. He felt an insane urge to run his hands all over that pale skin, to dry it with the heat of his mouth.

Roxanna saw the slight movement of something ahead of her, then realized that it was a man. *Him!* He was half naked, barefoot, no doubt to better sneak up on her. A thick pattern of black hair covered his bare chest, tapering narrowly beneath his tight woolen breeches, now bulging with the unmistakable evidence of his lust. Those black eyes were fathomless as a night sky, piercing her as if he could see through her skin right down to her bones! She should have turned and run, or at least covered herself, but some instinct made her realize that he would expect that. Instead she stared back at him defiantly.

"I can see why Sees Much named you Her Back Is Straight," Cain said as she reached for the buckskin tunic laying on the grass. She held it regally in front of herself, refusing to back down.

Damn his infuriating smile! "Who are you, besides being an ill-mannered lout?" *Not well advised, Roxy,* she thought the moment the words burst from her mouth.

"My name is Cain, Miss Hunt," he replied, the grin of admiration broadening as he tipped his head politely. "Your grandfather hired me to bring you home safely."

"Is this the usual way you earn your money, sneaking around in the brush, spying on your employer's granddaughter while she's bathing? Even the full-blooded Indians have more manners." His face darkened ominously, erasing the cocky grin. Roxanna knew at once that she'd struck a nerve when he stepped toward her in one lithe pantherish stride, blocking her only way out of the thicket.

"I wouldn't advise screaming—unless you want to bring down half of old Leather Shirt's warriors to see all that lily white skin." He did not touch her, but it was costing him dearly. Damn her, but he wanted her—and he hated himself for it. As long as he could remember, from the time he first started to shave, white women found him fascinating and repellent at the same time. The lure of the forbidden, he supposed, a savage in white man's clothing, educated, a curiosity who could eat with a knife and fork, even quote Shakespeare. God above, how he hated his mixed blood! Taking a deep calming breath, he assessed her with insulting slowness, enjoying the rosy flush of embarrassment that tinged her cheeks and spread downward. "That tunic you're holding can only conceal so much. Besides, I've seen all there is to see already."

"You are insufferably crude!" she finally managed to grate out, though her mouth was as dry as dust.

"And you are insufferably arrogant. About what I'd expect of Jubal's get."

He did not grab hold of her. What sort of cat-and-mouse game did he play? Roxanna felt her temper begin to rise again and forcibly tamped it down. "If my grandfather learned that one of his workers had taken liberties with me, he'd have that man's hide." Knowing what Alexa had told her about the old Scot, that seemed a safe assumption!

"So he would . . . but first I have to get you out of Leather Shirt's camp and safely back to your grandfather." He started to turn away, then paused and added, "Oh, I wouldn't wander off on your own like this anymore. I've seen Pawnee sign around here. If they captured you from their enemies, you can bet they'd treat you a hell of a lot worse than anything you've seen yet."

With that ominous warning, he walked past her, heading toward the water. She could see that he was unbuttoning his fly preparatory to shucking his breeches, and for one insane instant she waited, wanting to see the rest of his long-legged hard body. Then his voice interrupted the shocking course of her thoughts.

*Tsk*ing mockingly, he said, "For shame, Miss Hunt. If your grandfather learned you had taken the liberty of inspecting the tools of one of his workers, he might just tan *your* hide."

She scrambled up the path toward the other women,

clutching her clothing in tightened fists. His soft mocking laughter rang in her ears.

When she returned to camp, Roxanna thought the old shaman wore a self-satisfied expression on his face, as if he knew what had transpired between her and the hateful half-breed. Still stinging with fury and embarrassment and some other unnamed emotion, she set to work with Sees Much's granddaughter preparing the evening meal. The simple task of chopping wild onions and tubers for the stew pot soothed her agitation a bit as she listened to the other women's chatter. It took little to deduce that they were excited about Cain's visit.

"This man, Cain, he has visited your people before?" she asked Lark Song.

The pretty Cheyenne giggled and nodded. "Not visit. Him live . . . with mother."

Willow Tree, older and a bit more sophisticated, frowned at her sister's obvious infatuation. "Not Cheyenne is cut hair. Bad heart for People."

"Bad for any people," Roxanna muttered beneath her breath. So these were his mother's people? "Who was his father?" The question seemed to ask itself.

"His Eyes Are Cold, far away," Willow Tree said with a curt gesture, indicating the subject was closed.

Before Roxanna could remonstrate further, Leather Shirt approached with Cain and Sees Much. They were conversing in Cheyenne, apparently discussing the contents of the packs, which the half-breed now began to open. Soon a crowd of warriors gathered, all standing respectfully back from the campfire, watching intently. Cain pulled out a rifle with a shiny brass magazine, which Roxanna had learned on her journey west was a Winchester "Yellow Boy," the weapon most favored by the plains tribes. A murmur of awe went up as Cain spoke, gesturing to the other packs. No wonder they were so heavy. He must have brought a whole arsenal of the coveted longarms!

The discussion continued for a while, then the crowd dispersed and the leaders of the band adjourned inside the lodge, which had its buffalo-hide sides rolled up to admit the cooling breeze. Leather Shirt prepared a pipe and lit it, going through the elaborate ceremonial ritual, which she had watched on numerous occasions since being captured by these alien people.

The women finished preparing the evening meal for the men. Willow Tree ladled a generous portion of the rich turtle stew into a bowl, then said "Take, feed," gesturing to Cain.

A look of consternation flashed across Roxanna's face before she erased it. She had quickly learned that disobeying a command was not tolerated. Lark Song was already bowing before Leather Shirt and Sees Much, placing their food in front of them. Roxanna took the bowl, gritting her teeth at the injustice of having to kneel before that insufferable brigand. If he gave her another of those insinuating grins, she'd dump the scalding bowl over his head, and devil take the consequences.

Cain watched her approach from the corner of his eye, knowing how much an aristocratic white lady would abhor having to perform such a menial task for a white man, much less a breed. The look in those fierce turquoise eyes was murderous, but she schooled her expression to impassivity as she knelt gracefully before him with the bowl. When he took it from her, his fingers brushed hers lightly and she flinched. In spite of hard camp labor, her hands remained surprisingly smooth and pale. Sees Much was going easy on her.

As was their custom, the older men stabbed large chunks of meat and vegetables with their knives, gulped broth from their bowls and wiped their mouths with the back of their hands. Well aware of how a woman like her set store in refined table manners, he knew she must find this appalling. Damning her, he extracted a juicy piece of turtle and chewed it, then drank deeply of the sweet savory broth.

Roxanna felt his eyes on her as he consumed the food. She knelt on her heels as she'd been taught, waiting to bring more food if he wished it. When his long brown fingers had grazed hers, she had almost dropped the bowl. A powerful current of some mysterious sort seemed to leap from him to her and back. She knew he had felt it too.

"Cheyenne women are modest. They lower their eyes in the presence of a warrior," he could not resist jibing when she returned his perusal.

"I'm not a Cheyenne woman, and since I've heard you called Not Cheyenne, you're no warrior either," she snapped back.

He raised the empty bowl in a mocking salute to her. "Touché, Turquoise Eyes. Now bring me some more."

As she snatched the bowl and stormed off, Sees Much said, "You delight in angering Her Back Is Straight. Why, I wonder?" he added in that rhetorical fashion he often employed.

"You had some sort of vision about her; that's why Leather Shirt sent the raiders to capture her. You tell me." He looked from Sees Much to Leather Shirt, waiting.

"I knew you would come with guns to ransom her," Sees Much replied serenely.

"We have need of weapons. The buffalo are scarce, our enemies plentiful—white eyes with the Iron Horse and our ancient foes the Pawnee," Leather Shirt said.

Before Cain could question further, Sees Much interjected, "Our scouts have seen signs of a large raiding party on Lodgepole Creek. It would not be safe for you to leave with the woman now."

"Her grandfather is worried about her. He wants her back as quickly as possible. She's already been missing for over a month." Cain knew rumors about her captivity would leak out if he didn't get her back soon.

Leather Shirt shrugged. "You would be a fool to face the Pawnee alone with a silver-haired woman. Her scalp would make a fine trophy, but you have always done as you wished."

The rebuke in the old man's voice was plain. Cain cursed silently, then said, "I'll wait until the Pawnee leave the Lodgepole."

Leather Shirt remained impassively silent, but Sees Much smiled.

Later that night, Roxanna tossed and turned fitfully on her pallet. Over the past weeks she had grown used to sleeping with only a thin layer of pine boughs and a buffalo robe between her and the hard ground. Tonight, however, she could not seem to settle down. Cain. She knew he was the reason for her malaise. That harsh scarred visage materialized each time she closed her eyes. She shuddered just thinking about spending days alone with him while they traveled farther into the wilderness to meet Jubal MacKenzie.

Perhaps Isobel Darby wasn't so bad after all. She rolled over and closed her eyes, willing herself not to see Cain this time. Finally, sleep claimed her.

Sees Much watched the girl's restless dreaming on her pallet. When she whimpered softly in her sleep, he moved silently to her side and placed his hand gently on her forehead.

"Shhh, daughter, you will wake the others. Come with me."

He rose and quietly lifted the door flap of the lodge and disappeared through the entryway. Roxanna awakened quickly, relieved to be free of the nightmare world. She followed him outside and down to the bank of the stream. The full moon illuminated the way.

Sees Much was waiting for her, seated on a large flat boulder. She seated herself at his feet. Roxanna looked up into the face of the old man who, for over a month now, had been both her captor and her protector. It was a strong face, but a kind one. Sees Much had told her that he had learned the "white man's tongue" from his nephew. From the day of Roxanna's arrival in camp he had assured her that she would be safe and eventually would be returned to her own people with her "honor" intact. Roxanna remembered how she had laughed a secret, bitter laugh at the old man's concern for that honor.

She had grown genuinely fond of Sees Much and learned to trust him. He treated her as a daughter. Indeed, she lived

in his lodge with his two unmarried granddaughters. Willow
Tree and Lark Song had quickly adopted her as a sister. In
fact, the rest of the old shaman's band seemed to consider
her as one of their own. She shared the work with the other
women, but she also shared their simple pleasures and was
free to roam inside and outside the camp at will. She had
felt oddly content—until Cain arrived, which was bizarre,
since he had been sent by Jubal MacKenzie to rescue her.

"What troubles Her Back Is Straight?" asked Sees Much.

"I . . . I had a dream," Roxanna murmured.

The old man nodded and patted her shoulder affectionately. "A very great bad dream to frighten such a one as
you, child."

Roxanna looked again into the gently smiling face and
chuckled softly. But her good humor quickly died. "Yes, it
was a great bad dream, Sees Much."

"Tell me."

"I was standing on a low rise watching a small herd of
buffalo . . . like the one we saw last week. Suddenly, on a
rise directly across from me . . . but far off, I think, I saw a
speck . . . or something like that." Roxanna paused to gather
her thoughts. "Anyway, the speck began moving toward
me. . . . It got bigger and bigger until I could see that it was
another buffalo. The herd was between me and it, but the
herd just parted and my buffalo—"

Sees Much interrupted, "Your buffalo?"

Roxanna nodded and then quickly shook her head.
"Yes . . . well, I don't really mean mine . . ."

The old man again patted her shoulder. "Forgive me, Her
Back Is Straight. It is wrong to halt the telling of a dream.
Go on."

"The herd parted and the buffalo came toward me. He
came right up and stood in front of me. He was beautiful . . . so very beautiful. I wanted to touch him. To run my
hand through his great shaggy black mane. I looked into his
eyes and I knew that he wanted me to touch him."

The girl paused again before continuing. "I forgot to tell
you that in the dream it was dark. Suddenly the sun shone

and I could see there was something wrong. Blood was dripping down along the great shiny horns of the beautiful buffalo and I became afraid. . . . He seemed to be angry . . . maybe hurt. He backed away and began to paw the ground and shake and toss those great bloody horns . . . and you woke me.''

For a long time both the old man and the young woman were silent. Then Sees Much began to talk, almost in a whisper.

''You have dreamed of the Lone Bull. Sometimes he has been driven from the herd by the others. Sometimes his spirit tells him to go his own way. Yet his path will always cross and cross again the path of the herd. He is of the same kind as the herd, yet he is not of the herd.''

The old man was silent. Roxanna waited for him to continue and when he did not she asked, ''It must be important that his horns were bloody. Why were his horns dripping with blood?''

The old man looked at her with an odd expression on his face. ''I am not certain, daughter.''

For the first time since she had known him, Roxanna was sure that Sees Much was not telling her the truth.

Chapter 4

The next day Roxanna learned that Cain had secured her release from Leather Shirt in return for the rifles, but they would not leave the safety of the Cheyenne camp until the Pawnee moved on.

"I understood from reading newspapers—our talking leaves—that the Pawnee were friendly to whites, that the Union Pacific hires them to protect railroad workers," she said to Willow Tree as they gathered wood for the morning cookfires.

"Pawnee old enemy of People. They watch here," she said, pointing to the distant rock escarpment from which a rider could easily look down on the camp by the river. "You go from here, they think you belong to People. Kill."

The way Willow Tree eyed Roxanna's long silvery braid did not reassure the white woman. Shuddering, she applied herself to her task. After all she had survived, a few more days with the Cheyenne would not be so bad, especially when she considered how much she dreaded the journey ahead with Cain.

Troubling thoughts about last night's dream returned. How vivid it had been—and how strangely Sees Much had responded when she described it to him. Secretive . . . and almost pleased! She resolved to confront him again as soon as an opportunity presented itself when they were alone. Just then Lark Song came dashing up, her dusky cheeks flushed with excitement. "Weasel Bear back!"

Weasel Bear was a leader of the Dog Soldier Society, the man whom old Leather Shirt had dispatched to capture her. He was considered to be quite a catch among the young women of the band. But Roxanna thought there was a sullen cruelty about him, especially when he looked at her, as if she were an insect he longed to grind beneath his moccasins.

"He has found buffalo—a day's ride! We are breaking camp to go after them. There will be a great hunt and feasting," Lark Song added in Cheyenne, then translated haltingly for Roxanna's benefit.

The women quickly finished their task and returned to the camp, which was humming with excitement. Roxanna knew the buffalo herds were growing scarcer and more difficult to find due to white encroachment. She had read about the huge beasts moving by the tens of thousands in great undulating waves across the open plains. It would be exciting to see an actual hunt.

All around her the women of the village were busy dismantling lodges. They used the long poles and sewn-together skins from them for travois on which all the parfleches containing cooking and eating utensils and sleeping gear were packed. Young girls watched over the small children, keeping them out of harm's way, while their mothers and elder sisters broke camp. Everyone seemed to work together, as efficiently as a well-oiled machine. Young boys were dispatched by the leaders of the warrior societies to round up the horses, while the older men gathered up all the sacred medicine pipes and other religious paraphernalia. The warriors armed themselves, ready to guard the band's journey to better hunting grounds.

Cain watched Alexa pitch in, helping Sees Much's granddaughters roll up the heavy buffalo hide covering their lodge. She fit in amazingly well, eager to help and uncomplaining as Willow Tree issued orders for more strenuous tasks. Alexa continually surprised him, first with her startling beauty, then her spoiled temper, now her uncomplain-

ing toughness. She was a survivor, no doubt about it, spoiled
St. Louis belle or no.

"Will you join in the hunt, Not Cheyenne, or have you
grown soft as a woman living among our enemies?" Weasel
Bear taunted. His eyes followed Cain's and he added slyly,
"Your white blood calls to the pale one, but she will not
have a mixed-blood even if he is a cut hair."

Cain's scar seemed to writhe as the muscles of his jaw
clenched. He had hated Weasel Bear since they were small
boys. The Dog Soldier had joined Cain's Cheyenne brother
in tormenting a young half-blood. "The woman is nothing
more to me than I to her. I will be paid very well to return
her to her family. Do not think to interfere. I have already
spilled Cheyenne blood. I would not shrink from doing it
again." He saw the blaze of fury in Weasel Bear's eyes and
smiled chillingly.

"You will not hunt, then." Weasel Bear spit on the
ground in contempt.

"Oh, I will hunt. Sees Much and Leather Shirt are old
and have need of the meat." Cain watched Weasel Bear's
face darken with rage at the rebuke. As the nearest kinsman
who was a fit young warrior, Weasel Bear had the responsibility to provide for the two old men.

"I will see they do not go hungry, unlike you who cannot
wait to return to the white eyes." He turned his back on
Cain and stormed away.

"You have made a dangerous enemy," Leather Shirt
said, coming up to stand beside Cain.

"There is nothing new in that," Cain replied, weary of
confrontation. "He is only one among many."

"Is your father, His Eyes Are Cold, among those many?
You belonged to him, and he deserted you."

Cain looked into the old man's fierce black eyes, so like
his own. They were unreadable . . . like his own. "I do not
belong to anyone," Cain said flatly.

"Will you spill more Cheyenne blood, as you have
boasted?"

"I do not boast. I warned him to stay away from the white woman, that is all."

Roxanna finished packing the travois, which groaned under its heavy load. One of Forked Ear's little boys sat crying nearby while his harried mother and sister strapped a heavy cook pot onto their load. Roxanna approached the toddler and sat down, offering the consolation of her lap. Eagerly he climbed onto it and cuddled, sucking his thumb contentedly.

As she stroked his shiny black hair, she gazed across the crowded camp, her eyes straying until they rested upon Cain. He looked even less civilized this morning, having changed into the buckskin breeches and shirt so often favored by frontiersmen. The soft worn leather clung indecently to his slim long-legged body, the decorative fringe fluttered in the breeze, seeming to beckon seductively with every move he made. His shirtfront was open, revealing that black hairy chest, and his feet were ensconced in high laced moccasin boots with soft soles. If he could walk so silently with hard-soled riding boots, how much more soundless would he move now! Just thinking about the humiliating scene in the water yesterday brought stinging heat to her cheeks. How would she endure their forthcoming trip together?

Suddenly, feeling someone watching him, Cain turned and his dark eyes collided with Alexa Hunt's disturbing pale ones. "White eyes," he murmured, tipping his hat in mock politeness. She raised her chin and looked away, every inch the haughty heiress even if she sat cross-legged on the prairie grass clutching a naked Cheyenne baby on her lap.

The day was long, hot and dusty as the column of people wended their way west toward the headwaters of the Niobrara. Small children rode on the heavily laden travois while the women and old people walked patiently beside them. Youths were responsible for keeping the large herd of horses under control. All the warriors were mounted, some riding point while others formed a strong line of defense from the head to the rear of the snaking train. Everyone remained watchful for the Pawnee, but when they neared the outer perimeter of the vast buffalo herd and camped on the banks of a wide creek, there was no sign of the ancient foe.

The sound of the crier echoed across the arc of teepees as the sun inched its way above the horizon, sending rays of rosy golden light filtering inside the open door flaps of each home. Although she could not understand the crier's words, Roxanna knew he must be proclaiming the Elk Warriors' instructions for the hunt, for their society was in charge. The women boiled a porridge made of roots and served it to the hunters, who ate, then quickly prepared themselves for the day's activities.

"Come. We will watch," Sees Much said to Roxanna as she observed the warriors riding out of camp. Cain, bare-chested, rode his big chestnut with a stripped-down saddle. Although his hair was shorter and his horse saddled, his skin was bronzed and his cheekbones and nose hewn in the same strong mold as the other warriors. Still, the aquiline cast of his features set him apart, as did the dark shadow of a beard across his jaw and the hair on his chest.

He's an Indian yet not an Indian, she thought as she nodded, following the old shaman. *An Indian yet not . . .* The thought seemed to echo something Sees Much had once told her, but she quickly dismissed the idea as they crossed the shallows of the creek and walked up a steep rocky rise. When Roxanna looked down on the flat bowl of the plain, her breath caught in her throat.

Spread below them lay a vast herd of bison, just as the eastern newspapers described it, a milling bawling sea of dark brown, undulating endlessly to the distant skyline.

"Once all the lands from the great Staked Plains below the Red River to the land of the Mother Queen to the north were filled like this," Sees Much said.

"There must be thousands . . . too many for the mind to take in," she replied in an awe-filled voice. A small calf, newly dropped, gamboled beside his mother. Roxanna smiled. "Why, he's a different color than the rest."

"All newborns are yellow. Their fur darkens with age—all except the white buffalo, which is sacred to the People."

As they spoke, other women, children, and the men too old to hunt, assembled quietly along the rim of the escarpment. The buffalo, with their poor sight and hearing, did not notice, since the people were careful to approach downwind. Then the mounted warriors appeared below them, walking their horses slowly forward in a wide arc, forming a semicircle amid the northernmost tier of the vast herd. Unconsciously, Roxanna searched for Cain's distinctive figure. Sees Much followed the course of her gaze and smiled, saying nothing.

For several moments the great beasts continued to graze obliviously. Then the wind shifted to the south and a muffled snorting echoed across the plain as the bison sensed danger. In an abrupt shift of mood, the placid herd erupted into a frenzy, their sharp hooves pounding across the hard-packed soil like thunder. Thick clouds of dust enveloped them and the yipping Cheyenne stretched out on their horses in swift pursuit. Shots rang out erratically, mingled with cries of triumph as several of the buffalo went down.

"The new rifles work well," Sees Much said to Her Back Is Straight. "It is good that the Lone Bull brought them."

Straining to see Cain through clearings in the dust, Roxanna's attention caught on the words "Lone Bull." Her head jerked around and she looked at Sees Much, startled. "You called him the Lone Bull?"

"That was the name his mother Blue Corn Woman gave him. Always as a boy he was an outsider, proud and stubborn in the face of the other children's cruelties to one who was half white."

Roxanna blanched, remembering her dream. "Last night you said you didn't know why I dreamed about a lone bull with bloody horns."

"The Powers have not told me what the blood means yet," Sees Much replied with a troubled sigh.

"But you knew who the buffalo symbolized," she persisted.

Sees Much nodded. "I saw a silver-haired woman in a dream two moons ago."

"Me?"

He smiled. "Yes, child, you—and it was clear that you would be the means to bring the Lone Bull back to his people . . . if only for a little while. There is a healing which must take place . . ." His words faded away as if he meant to speak further.

Roxanna started to question him, but just then Cain's chestnut, galloping hard, approached the side of a big bull. Weasel Bear cut in hard on the opposite side. Both men seemed intent on bringing down the same prey. Cain reached it first, leaning over with his Spencer aimed at a spot just behind the beast's shoulder. Roxanna watched the quarry go down when he fired. Then Weasel Bear caught up. Shouting an infuriated oath, he swerved his piebald into the chestnut's side, raising his rifle butt and clubbing Cain hard in his back.

A loud gasp tore from her throat as Cain was knocked from his saddle, vanishing into the thick dust and sharp hooves of the stampeding herd. "He'll be killed!"

Sees Much closed his eyes, seeming to pray as the dust swirled. They stood by helplessly. Roxanna stared, trying to find the chestnut in the melee. Then she saw Cain. His left foot must have been caught in the stirrup, but rather than being dragged to his death, he had clawed his way back, hand over hand up his own leg, seizing the *sudadero,* then gaining purchase on the edge of the cantle, finally seizing the pommel until he could throw his right leg up and remount.

Cain hunched over the chestnut's neck, grabbing his reins, then guided the horse clear of the stampede. Roxanna and Sees Much raced down the rocky hillside toward him. By the time they reached him he was slumped over his lathered mount.

"Take care. Help me lower him to the earth," Sees Much

said when Cain began to slip from the saddle, unconscious. The herd had all passed them now, although the vibrations still jarred the earth as the old man grabbed one of his arms and Roxanna the other, half dragging him free. When they stretched him out, he came to with a ragged oath.

"My ribs," he gasped.

Then Roxanna saw the widening red stain. "He's bleeding!"

Sees Much calmly examined the wound. "He has been gored by one of the buffalo when he was knocked from the saddle."

"Saddle . . . saved my life," Cain grunted through the pain.

Sees Much smiled as he slipped off his shirt and used it to apply pressure to the wound. "You must always be a white man. This time it was good that it is so."

"I'll fetch help," Roxanna said, dashing off toward the women whom she prayed would have medicines and bandages.

"What happened?" Cain asked, fighting the surging waves of blackness.

Sees Much's face was bleak. "Your cousin, Weasel Bear, struck you with his rifle butt. You had both chosen the same animal and you took it first."

"He . . . always hated me," Cain said, as he watched Alexa run fleetly across the ground, gesturing wildly to Willow Tree and several older women.

The old man pushed the bruised and bloodied area on Cain's side while he held the makeshift compress against the ugly gash. "Even now your eyes cannot tear themselves from her. She is your fate, I think."

"She is trouble . . ." Cain gasped as merciful oblivion finally enveloped him.

Outside the lodge where Cain had been taken, Roxanna sputtered, "But I'm not a nurse. I faint at the sight of blood!"

Sees Much only stared impassively, totally unmoved.

"Look into your heart, daughter. Blood is not what you fear. You did not faint when you helped me take him from his horse. I do not think you will now. I must have a woman to assist me."

"Why can't Willow Tree or Lark Song do it?"

"They are gutting the buffalo which the Lone Bull killed. Now, that might make you faint," he said with amusement, recalling her reaction the first time she had been instructed how to kill and clean a pair of snared rabbits. Clutching his medicine sacks, he ducked and entered the open door flap, expecting her to follow.

Reluctantly she did. Cain lay on his back, breathing shallowly. When he heard them enter, his lashes fluttered. Turning his head, he looked at Roxanna through pain-glazed eyes, then blacked out again. Sees Much knelt beside the pallet and opened the leather pouches, removing various herbs and powders, along with several long strips of thin softly tanned doeskin. Then he reached up and began to unfasten Cain's breeches and pull them down his hips.

"What are you doing?" she blurted out, although it was perfectly apparent.

"I must see if his ribs are broken and cleanse the wound. He cannot remain covered with the tight white man's clothing," Sees Much replied reasonably. "Come help me. Pull on the pants legs."

Ugly memories from Vicksburg shuddered through her mind, but realizing that Sees Much waited patiently for her assistance, she forced them aside. A man was injured and in pain, she reminded herself. But this was not just any man. What was it about Cain that disturbed her so? Surely she did not believe Sees Much's oblique references to the dreams which led to her capture.

She knelt at Cain's feet, from which the moccasins had been removed, and began to tug on the pants legs while the shaman shoved them below his narrow hips. When his sex was revealed, she caught a glimpse of it lying limply in a dense thatch of black hair, then quickly averted her eyes. The male member would always be ugly to Roxanna.

Sees Much covered Cain's hips with a light blanket, then removed the packing he had placed over the wound. Congealed black blood crusted to his side and had pooled on the skins beneath him. Gently, Sees Much probed the ribs around the gored area, then instructed Roxanna, "Hold the compress against the wound while I turn him."

She moved closer and did as he instructed, but when the shaman rolled Cain on his side, she cried, "The bleeding's begun again."

He nodded as he deftly examined Cain's back, where a large ugly black bruise was forming. "Weasel Bear has much to answer for. Always he had an uncertain temper. It is good he has run away to hide his shame for this dishonorable act." Satisfied no bones in Cain's back were broken, he turned him once more and reached out to take the compress from Roxanna.

Her hands were red with gore. "Can he survive losing so much blood?" she asked.

"It seems more than it is. The danger in such a wound as this, deep and narrow, is that the blood remains inside and poisons. That is why we must draw out the bad blood." He pointed to a small mortar and pestle, then reached for a bag filled with dried red dock roots. "I will grind these while you fetch clean water from upstream and set it to boil on the fire."

When she had done as he asked, she watched as he poured the steamy water over the pulverized roots until he had made a sticky poultice. While it cooked, he cleaned Cain's wound of the dried blood. Satisfied with the cleansing, the old man began to apply the medicine, then opened another pack and removed a fistful of dried cattails, which acted as a soft absorbent bandage.

"Now we must bind his ribs. At least one has been cracked where the buffalo's horn struck him."

To assist him in swaddling Cain's body in the long strips of soft doeskin, Roxanna had to kneel by the half-breed's side and lean over him. She could feel his heat, touching his flesh so intimately, knowing he wore nothing beneath the blanket. As they finished the task, a stray lock of night-black hair fell across his forehead and she reached up, gently stroking it back without realizing what she was doing.

Sees Much beamed to himself as he gathered up his medicines and implements. "I will sit with him through the day. Go and eat, then rest, for you will take the night turn when I grow weary."

Cain fought his way up through what seemed a deep well of blackness and pain. Blinking his eyes, he tried to focus on the blurry figure leaning over him. All he could make out was a silvery halo glowing around her head. *Alexa.* Had he said it aloud? Before he could decide, the ache in his side roared to life and he sank back into the dark well.

Roxanna sponged his face with a cool cloth, then rinsed it out and applied it again. When he first rode into camp, she had thought his features harsh and dangerous, but lying unconscious, she could see the incredible male beauty in them, the best of two worlds, red and white. She touched his beard-stubbled cheeks with their high Cheyenne bones, then ran her fingers over the ridge of his straight nose and elegantly sculpted mouth, recalling the whiteness of his smile in that bronzed face.

How would those lips feel pressed to yours? Where had *that* appalling thought come from? She removed her hand with a startled jerk and sat back, looking away from Cain's face, so young and guileless in repose. The bucket filled with soaking feverweed caught her attention. No help for it, Sees Much had shown her what she must do repeatedly through the night. Cain was burning up.

Roxanna squeezed the excess moisture from a fistful of the herb. She began to rub his hot dry skin with it, unconsciously comparing the lean hard muscles of his long body to the Confederate officers she had encountered during the war. The men who ranked high enough to merit her attention were older, with thickening midsections and flabby muscles. Using her feminine charms to wheedle information from lascivious men with hot sour breath and rough grasping hands had been an unpleasant task. Tending this beautiful man was not.

Roxanna finished rubbing his arms and chest, then moved on to his legs. When she reached the nexus of his body, she hesitated.

"What are you waiting for?" Cain's raspy voice whispered. He almost laughed at the horrified widening of her eyes when she jerked her hand away and looked in his face.

"You were unconscious, feverish. I was told—"

"I overheard what you were told. Do it," he commanded, wondering if she possessed the nerve . . . wondering if he did.

"If you're awake and clear-headed enough to issue orders, you don't need me to bathe down your fever," she said in a breathless, angry voice, throwing the clump of herbs back into the bucket with a loud plop.

"You're right, I don't. But I bet you're better at raising temperatures than lowering them. Aren't you?"

Roxanna paled. Those dark glowing eyes seemed to be peering into her very soul—as if he knew! She rose and dashed out of the lodge.

Cain stared into the flickering light of the fire, listening to the lonesome wail of a coyote, or perhaps a Pawnee scout. He wanted to be quit of this dangerous place and all its painful memories, quit of the troublesome silver-haired woman who was destined for Powell's heir. Was nothing ever to belong to him? Or he to any place or anyone?

With a snarled oath of pain, he turned his face from the fire and drifted into a troubled sleep.

Over the following days as Cain mended, Sees Much insisted that Her Back Is Straight tend to him in spite of her protests. Gently but firmly, he brushed aside every excuse she made or reason why Willow Tree would be better suited. Finally, in exasperation, she worked up her courage and approached old Leather Shirt. The forbidding chief always made her feel uncomfortable, as if he had judged her and found her lacking.

"I do not want to care for the Lone Bull. Cannot one of the women of your people do it?" she asked, meeting his unnerving dark gaze head-on.

He studied her silently, as if measuring his reply. "He is no longer the Lone Bull. His name is Not Cheyenne. He is white. You are white," he said as if it were an accusation. "And he has paid many rifles to have you."

"He does not have me," she blurted out, then reddened in mortification. "I don't belong to anyone."

"Your thoughts betray you," the old man said. "Return to Not Cheyenne's fire." He raised his arm and pointed, a gesture that allowed no argument. As Leather Shirt watched the young woman trudge back to the lodge, he pondered her declaration. *I don't belong to anyone.* "Sees Much, my brother, you are right." The old chief's smile was almost sympathetic.

Your thoughts betray you. That evening as she made her way back to the lodge where Cain was waiting for supper, Leather Shirt's words rang in her ears.

Willow Tree and Lark Song had roasted a large piece of buffalo hump, along with chunks of dried lung. The latter delicacy she abstained from trying. Dishing up the meat, along with a honey-sweetened bowl of chokecherries, she carried the food inside.

Cain was sitting up, leaning against a pair of the heavy parfleches, using them as a backrest. He looked up at her, noting the rosy flush of her cheeks. She had been tense as a treed cat around him ever since that night he awakened while she was bathing him. What had set her off now? He said nothing, just watched as she knelt, placing the food before him. She was graceful as a society belle in spite of being dressed in doeskin clothing and sitting on the bare dirt floor of a smoke-filled lodge. When she arranged the meat on the board with a knife, she started to rise and leave.

Suddenly he wanted her to stay. "Don't go—join me. You must be hungry."

Roxanna was startled. The invitation seemed impulsive and earnest, two qualities she never suspected Cain possessed. One silvery eyebrow lifted. "Surely a mere woman cannot eat with a warrior."

"I'm Not Cheyenne, remember? I can do whatever I choose, and I choose to share my food with you . . . if you would consent to join me."

Something made her sit back down, perhaps the watery weakening in her knees. She reached for some of the choke-cherries as he carved the charred dry slab of bison meat into palatable slices, offering her one.

"It's not beef, but it's not bad," he said as he helped himself to a piece, ignoring the desiccated lung.

"You're right, you aren't Indian, are you? I mean . . . you don't seem to like being here even though you were born here," she said, curiosity winning out over wariness at last. Many things that Sees Much and Leather Shirt had said over the past days since Cain's arrival intrigued her. The Lone Bull intrigued her, she admitted grudgingly.

A guarded look came over his face as he asked, "What have you been told about me?"

She shrugged. "Not much. That you were named Lone Bull by your mother, Blue Corn Woman. That your father was a white trader they call His Eyes Are Cold . . . and you chose to leave. Now they call you Not Cheyenne." A sudden thought occurred to her. "Jubal—my grandfather—he isn't your father?" Surely there was no resemblance to the old daguerreotype on Alexa's mantel.

Cain breathed easier, a difficult feat with his ribs still bound. Then a bitter half-smile touched his lips. "No, Jubal's my employer, no kin."

That confirmation brought a bizarre rush of relief to Roxanna that she chose not to examine. "Why did you leave these people?"

"I didn't leave. I was banished," he replied flatly.

"Why?" Her dream of the young buffalo with the bloodied horns returned. Sees Much had understood its significance but had refused to share it with her. Suddenly she felt a sense of foreboding as she studied the injured man's harsh expression and moody black eyes.

Cain had never told any white person his story, but suddenly he felt the need to share it with Alexa Hunt, spoiled, arrogant eastern heiress. The look of genuine concern—and confusion—in her eyes made his breath catch. This attraction was madness. Best to end it by telling her the truth . . . or at least part of the truth.

"I killed my brother." A cold feral smile spread across his lips, then vanished, leaving his face desolate. "Cain. I chose the name to remind me of the blood on my hands."

There was a well of self-loathing in those words. Horrified as she felt at the admission, Roxanna sensed his pain. "You would not have done it without a good reason," she said softly.

"I thought it was a good one then . . . when I was young, in pain, alone. . . . I was my mother's second son," he began and the years rolled back.' "Her Cheyenne husband was killed by whites when my brother, High-Backed Wolf, was three years old. Then my father came to one of the meets. He was a trapper and trader. He married Blue Corn Woman according to her people's ways and I was born. Maybe it would have been different if he'd gone Indian, the way many of the mountain men did, and lived with us. But he went away often and I was left for High-Backed Wolf and his friends to torment whenever my mother wasn't looking. Sees Much was good to me, but it wasn't the same as having a father to teach me to become a warrior. I lived for the times my father would return, but as I grew older those times were further and further apart. You see, he had a city wife, a white woman and another son, a white heir who counted. I was nothing to him."

The bitterness in those words made her wince in empathy. For all her loneliness since the war, Roxanna had spent a happy childhood surrounded with parents and a brother who doted upon her. She waited and he resumed his story, staring into the fire as the twilight thickened.

"Finally when I was ten years old my father returned. He had been gone for years. Some vestige of conscience, maybe, but I think it was because he couldn't let the savages have something that belonged to him . . . even if he didn't want it himself. He took me to be educated at a mission over on Big Sandy Creek in Colorado Territory. It was run by a man named Enoch Sterling . . . the kindest, gentlest soul who ever lived. He'd been a Methodist missionary in Canton, China, for many years. Then something drew him to minister to the Indians. The Cheyenne called him Good Heart, a fitting name.''

''And you found a father to replace the one who deserted you.''

Her flash of intuition took Cain by surprise. He nodded. ''He never converted me, but he did give me the benefit of his considerable classical education. I can read Latin, even speak Cantonese, the former not very practical out West but the latter quite useful. I stayed with Enoch at his mission for nine years. All the while I kept writing to my father and Enoch saw to it that he answered back now and then, but he never returned to visit me.''

''What brought you back to the Cheyenne, then?''

''My mother fell ill the winter I turned twenty. As she lay dying, she sent word that she wanted to see me . . . I hadn't been much better about visiting her than my father was about me. I came to Leather Shirt's camp while my brother and his friends were off raiding.

''There had been trouble building between the whites and the Cheyenne during the late fifties. Increasing numbers of whites started pouring across the immigrant trail, settlers bound for Oregon, miners for Montana and California. A detachment of soldiers from Fort Lyon rode down on a camp of Cheyenne where some of our kinsmen lived and massacred them. High-Backed Wolf whipped up a bunch of hotheads in the Dog Soldier Society to take revenge. Weasel Bear was one of them.

''My mother died the day after I arrived. I felt good that I had come back to see her one last time . . . until I returned to the mission and found the smoldering ruins. Enoch . . .'' He struggled to say the words, the images still choking him with horror even after nearly eight years.

"Enoch wasn't dead. They'd tortured him and left him for me to find. . . . My brother's war lance was driven up inside his belly. With his dying breath he pleaded for me not to kill High-Backed Wolf." His voice broke, but he was so lost in the telling now that he did not realize how it affected the white woman. "I swore revenge on his grave.

"High-Backed Wolf knew I'd come after him, but he made me work to find him, rampaging across the plains, burning and killing from the Bozeman Trail down to the Staked Plains in Texas. I caught up with him—or he let me finally find him, I was never sure which—when he had returned to visit Leather Shirt's band.

"Sees Much tried to reason with me. Leather Shirt threatened to kill me, but they both knew neither of us would rest until one was dead." At length he looked up from the fire and met her eyes. "After I'd killed him, the tribal elders decreed banishment, which didn't matter much to me by then. There was nothing left for me here."

Roxanna had never heard another human being sound so utterly alone as Cain. What could she say to assuage such pain? The silence stretched on for moments, but oddly neither seemed to mind, for there was a strange new sense of communion between them. Some impulse made her reach across to him and place her hand over his.

Cain looked down at her small pale fingers as they lightly brushed the back of his large bronzed fist. Then he raised his eyes to hers.

Chapter 5

Roxanna returned his gaze and her breath caught at the look of naked longing in his obsidian eyes. He opened his palm and encircled her wrist with long tapered fingers, pulling her toward him. Hypnotized, she came willingly into his arms as he guided her hand, placing it against the hard furry wall of his chest. She could feel his heart thudding swiftly and knew her own must echo its wild cadence.

His eyes never left hers, reading assent in their turquoise depths. Slowly, ever so slowly, he lowered his mouth to hers, waiting, testing to see if she would pull away at the last moment. He almost wished she would. This was madness. She was MacKenzie's granddaughter. The old man would have his head on a platter, not to mention his cock and balls! But she didn't pull away. Instead she leaned toward him ever so slightly with a little catch in her breathing. Her lips parted . . . warm . . . soft . . . irresistible.

He was going to kiss her and she was inviting him to do it. During her years as a spy and actress, many men had made advances. Their pawing and slobbering had been loathsome. But this . . . this . . . would be different.

Cain held back the furious rush of lust that made him long to crush her mouth to his and plunder it. Instead he tasted the firm tenderness of pale pink, exalted at the slight quiver in her lower lip as he brushed it, then nipped it softly,

tugging it between his teeth until she gasped and dug her
nails into the bunched muscles of his shoulders. When her
lips parted he rimmed the small round O of her mouth with
his tongue and quickly dipped it inside, touching hers, then
retreating. She responded tentatively, flicking the rosy tip of
her tongue to his lips. Losing control, he covered her mouth
with a groan of animal pleasure.

His lips molded to hers, enticing her to open her mouth
fully. This time his tongue did not taste and dart. Rather, it
swept against her teeth, twined with her tongue, dancing
along the sensitive sides, plunging in and out. She clung to
him with a whimper that was not quite fear, not quite pleasure, yet something that she could not deny.

Roxanna felt his hand cradle her head and his fingers
weave their way into her hair, pulling it loose from its plait
even as he tugged on it, bending her body backward for
better access to her mouth. His free arm pressed her tightly
against his chest. She could feel his heat, so unlike the feverish weakness of that night when he lay unconscious. Now
it was potent, male, hungry. She should have been frightened, shocked, repelled. Instead the answering heat spreading through her burned away everything but the consuming
need to feel his body, his mouth, his hands on her.

Cain grazed the lush softness of her breast with his fingertips, feeling her flesh tighten, the nipple hardening to a
pebbly point. She was a vision of pink and silver and white.
The image of her standing naked in the stream would be
engraved on his mind's eye for the rest of his life. But she
was as unattainable for him as snow in the Sahara—except
for right now. *Now I could have her*

And he would. Her hands slid up around his neck, pulling
him down as he lowered her onto the soft furs of his pallet.
She whimpered when his mouth left hers, but arched up
when its heat trailed soft wet kisses down her throat and
across her collarbone, nuzzling the edge of her tunic where
her breasts swelled.

Roxanna felt his hands unfastening the ties of her tunic,
felt the tautening of her nipples as her breasts ached, reso-

nating with the throbbing low inside her belly. She must stop this! It was wicked, utterly insane! Would she throw away her whole future for a stranger, a half-breed gunman who was probably an outlaw? Then the scalding heat of his lips suckled her breast and the world spun away from her. She dug her fingers into his night-black hair, urging him on as he moved to the other breast, murmuring indistinct love words in that soft gravelly voice.

Cain ignored the throbbing of his wounded side and bruised back for the more urgent ache of his groin as he lay her back and covered her. He could feel her long slender legs part, ready to receive him when he plunged deep inside her. Just as he began to unfasten the fly imprisoning his swollen sex, a low sharp cough broke through their blended pants and moans. The traditional Cheyenne greeting outside the lodge was like a dousing of ice-cold river water. Cain recognized Leather Shirt's voice as the old chief cleared his throat and coughed impatiently a second time.

One instant Roxanna was buried beneath his hard hungry body, desperate to have him take her to a place she had never been before. The next, she was alone, shivering in shock as he rolled away from her with a guttural oath and began refastening his breeches. She lay sprawled like the whore she now felt herself to be, legs spread, tunic rucked up, breasts bared in the cool evening air. The smell of greasy cold meat and sweet fruit blended with wood smoke and the unmistakable musk of sex. Her stomach churned sourly as she sat up and refastened the shoulder ties of her tunic with trembling fingers. Cain watched her with hooded eyes, further adding to her mortification.

Then he called out something in Cheyenne. When she had finished repairing herself, he spoke again. Leather Shirt opened the door flap and stepped inside. He did not deign to look at her but exchanged several harsh sentences with Cain, then turned and departed as abruptly as he had arrived. Humiliated as she was in front of the chief, Roxanna was grateful for his interruption. *What would I have done if he hadn't come?*

"Regrets, Silver Hair?" Cain taunted, hiding his anger for the loss of something that had stretched between them far transcending momentary lust. *No. It was only lust, nothing more. Better that I didn't take her,* he thought savagely. He knew he lied, but he refused to examine why.

"What did Leather Shirt want?" she finally asked, no longer able to bear the uncomfortable silence.

"You mean besides breaking up our little—"

The ring of her palm connecting with his cheek wiped the smirking look from his face. Shame churned deep in her gut. She was merely a plaything to him, just as she had been that ugly night in Vicksburg. She expected a blaze of anger and was surprised when he merely sat back, his face expressionless.

"I suppose I deserved that." At her suddenly wary startled look, he tried to explain the unexplainable. They had to do something if they were going to travel together all the way to MacKenzie's rail camp. "Look, neither of us set out to make this happen, Alexa . . . it just did. Hell—" he combed his fingers through his hair—"you helped Sees Much save my life. I owe you better than . . . Aw hell."

She stared down at her tightly clasped hands. "And I owe you for finding me and bargaining for my freedom. So I guess we're even, Cain." She stood up quickly, wanting desperately to get away from him, to bring her tumbling emotions under control and sort everything out calmly, the way she normally did.

Before she could flee out the door, he said, "Leather Shirt told me the Pawnee have ridden south. It's safe for us to leave in the morning."

She did not turn around, only looked back over her shoulder to ask, "Are you well enough to travel?"

He rubbed his side gingerly. "It's sore, but I've had worse. Yeah, I can ride."

"Then I'll be ready." With that she vanished through the lodge door.

*   *   *

"How strange that I could think of nothing but escaping when I first was brought here. Now I'm sorry to leave your people. You have been kind," Roxanna said to Sees Much.

The old man took a puff from his pipe and set it aside. They were alone in the lodge, as both his granddaughters were at the dance being held to celebrate the departure of the Pawnee enemy from Cheyenne hunting grounds. He looked at the lovely young woman whose courage and goodness had touched him. "My heart is glad to hear these words. You were brought here for a purpose. I was merely an instrument."

She smiled. "To bring fine rifles so the People could hunt?"

"No, that was only a small blessing for us. There are greater things than these which will unfold in your world and ours before we meet again . . ."

She looked at him curiously. "You've mentioned before this dream you had about capturing me—and the Lone Bull. . . . Where does he fit into it? You never did explain my dream about the buffalo with the bloody horns."

"He has told you the reason for his banishment." It was not a question.

She nodded. "That explains why the Lone Bull had blood on his horns, I suppose, but what about me?"

"The death of High-Backed Wolf was long ago. That cycle comes to a close now, I think. Perhaps you are his healing, for he has great need of healing, do you not agree?"

"Yes. I've never met a man so . . . alone." She groped for a better way to explain her feelings about Cain but found none. "But I cannot absolve him for the death of his brother."

"You can love him. That will be enough."

Her head raised abruptly and she felt her cheeks flush in the firelight as her eyes met his. "Love him?" she echoed, her voice scratchy, startled. Had he learned from Leather Shirt about what transpired earlier in Cain's lodge? This old shaman's good opinion of her mattered as much as her own father's had when he was alive.

"Love him. The rest will be revealed to us all in time."

*   *   *

You can love him. Sees Much's words echoed in her mind
as she bade farewell to the friends she had made during her
sojourn with the Cheyenne. Old Leather Shirt stood sternly
apart, an unreadable look on his face. Did he condemn her
as a loose-moraled white woman after hearing her and Cain
last night? She had learned, contrary to what whites believed, that the Cheyenne had exceedingly strict rules regarding chastity. Then he nodded to her in his cool
measuring way, as if saying, *Go in peace, Her Back Is
Straight.* She did not smile but gravely returned his gesture.

"We miss you," Willow Tree said, pounding her heart
with one strong brown fist. Lark Song echoed the sentiment
as they embraced her while Sees Much stood by.

Cain watched their leave-taking, amazed at the affection
Alexa Hunt had for these people. Any other white woman
in her position would have shucked the dust from her boots
as swiftly as she could and ridden away. Leather Shirt remained impassive as he stared at Not Cheyenne. *That's all
I'll ever be to him, Not Cheyenne,* he thought bitterly as a
long-ago scene replayed itself in his mind.

He had come to the chief when he returned from Enoch's
destroyed mission, asking for justice and finding none.

"What if it had been Sees Much who High-Backed Wolf
had killed? Would you think it wrong that he die for his
crime then?" he had cried.

"Only your white blood would allow you to kill one of
the People. High-Backed Wolf would never do such a thing.
His heart was bad to kill the white medicine man, but he
will not die for it, nor suffer banishment, for he has not
killed one of us. That is our law. I have said."

"Then I want no part of your law, for it has never applied
to me or my kind! You make it clear that I never belonged."

"You chose in your own heart long ago. You want only
to belong to your father's people."

"Then no one will mourn me when I am banished. They
can mourn High-Backed Wolf, who will pay for his sins. I
have said!"

Sees Much watched the Lone Bull and knew he was re-living the hurt and anger of his last parting from the People. Would there be a time when he could come among them with joy? If only the Everywhere Spirit would grant an old man this prayer. The arrival of Her Back Is Straight was a good sign. Perhaps it would be so. The shaman was certain she could help the Lone Bull . . . if only the proud outsider would let her.

As they rode away from the Cheyenne encampment, Roxanna observed that Cain never once waved or looked back. "Banishment must have been painful for you. Don't you have any relatives left alive in the band?" she asked.

"Sees Much is my great-uncle. Leather Shirt is my grand-father," he said bleakly, then lapsed into silence, not inviting any further comment or questions.

She digested his statement, not really surprised by it after she thought it over. There was a certain physical resemblance between the two tall lean men. What Indian features Cain possessed he had inherited from his grandfather. She was equally curious about his white ancestry but knew better than to broach the painful subject. The father who had spurned Cain's love was an even more jealously guarded secret than his Cheyenne family.

Roxanna mulled over the reckless passion that had almost overwhelmed them last night. He was right in saying neither of them intended for it to happen. Lord knew he had tried to hold her at arm's length with cool taunts, even insults. But something kept drawing her to him. The dream? Or his loneliness and vulnerability? Those were certainly traits they had in common, that and a surfeit of pride worn like armor to protect them from any more of life's cruelties.

Fate in the guise of his grandfather had intervened to save them from hopelessly compromising themselves. Cain was an employee of Jubal MacKenzie. What would have happened if they had slept together and then she had to face him once she was married to Lawrence Powell? In conscience could she even have gone through with the marriage?

Somehow the arrangement had never seemed real to her. She had tried to convince herself that an arranged marriage to a stranger was better than the awful fate to which Isobel Darby would consign her. Back in St. Louis the scheme had seemed workable, but with every mile she rode closer to it, her confidence waned.

All because of Cain.

No, that was not true, she assured herself. It was the idea of binding herself for life to any man. During the war she had discovered men were lying, deceitful and brutal. The idea of letting another one touch her made her skin crawl. *But you were desperate for more when he touched you.* Roxanna stared at Cain's dark forbidding profile. He had not shaved for the past two days and the beard stubble made his face even more piratical. All he needed was a big gold ear loop to complete the picture.

"We'll camp here for tonight," Cain said, breaking into her preoccupation. He swung down from his horse, then walked over to the dun mare he'd secured for Alexa. She was struggling to dismount without letting the narrow skirt of her tunic ride up and reveal even more of her long legs. With a sardonic smile he extended his arms and encircled her waist, lifting her from the saddle as if she weighed nothing.

Roxanna was slender but tall for a woman, unused to feeling dwarfed by men, but the Cheyenne were an unusually tall race and Cain a big man even among them. His fingers seemed to burn into her skin through the buckskins as he lifted her from the saddle, then placed her gently on the ground. She clasped his shoulders, feeling the fluid power of his muscles, and swallowed hard. *Big mistake, Roxy,* she thought as soon as those black eyes met hers. Before she could gather her wits to thank him for his assistance, he broke eye contact and released her abruptly, turning away.

"I'll rub the horses down. You start a fire. Don't make

it a big one. We should be in the clear, but I don't want to attract any visitors,'' he said as he began to uncinch his chestnut's saddle, tossing the fancy silver-trimmed rig onto the grass, then proceeded to work on the dun.

His physical recovery amazed Roxanna as she watched him perform such strenuous tasks with little regard for what had been a life-threatening injury a scant week ago. Outside of an occasional wince or grunt of discomfort, he betrayed no weakness from the goring.

When he noticed her standing still, he turned, raising one black eyebrow sardonically. ''I assume you were taught how to build a fire after spending over a month with the Cheyenne?''

Roxanna could feel her skin heat with embarrassment.

''I can build a fire,'' she murmured, turning to survey the campsite. A small water hole a dozen yards away was thicketed with pine and red cedar. She walked over and began to gather some dry wood.

Cain looked at the western sky, which was streaked with fiery red and gold as the sun dropped quickly behind the distant lavender ridges on the horizon. The beauty of the scene always moved him, but the dark purplish and steel gray clouds billowing down from the north were cause for concern as they rapidly obscured the sunset. The wind began to gust ever so slightly, carrying a chilling bite in it. Any time of year on the High Plains was chancy, but late spring was the least reliable. There had been unseasonable warmth for several weeks, but after growing up out here, he knew a foot of snow by morning would not be unusual. It would be dangerous for two people alone with little for miles around to offer shelter.

Nearby there was a shallow arroyo carved out of the soft sandstone by centuries of spring floodwater. On the north side of it, a stone embankment overhung the ravine, offering some meager protection if the elements turned ugly. He had passed by it while tracking Leather Shirt's band. That was why he'd stopped here before dusk. Once he finished rubbing the horses down, he quickly resaddled them before feeding them.

Roxanna observed his actions, puzzled. Why did he resaddle the horses and watch the northern horizon? He had not spoken a word to her since issuing those preemptory orders about the fire. This was going to be a horribly long trip if after only one day the two of them were reduced to this uncomfortable silence. Finally, when she could stand the tension no longer, she asked, "Are you afraid the Pawnees are out there?"

Cain sat by the small fire, carefully checking the action of his Spencer. "I've seen no sign of Pawnee," he replied, never looking up as he lay down the carbine and picked up the Smith and Wesson revolver.

Roxanna was stung by the cool dismissal and turned back to basting the pair of jackrabbits roasting on the fire. *I'll marry Lawrence Powell—I don't care if he has two heads and both faces are uglier than the back end of bad luck!* She stabbed a knife into the meat viciously to test for doneness, making believe it was Cain's thick hide. A spray of fragrant juice trickled onto the fire, causing it to flare. "Dinner is served," she said in a level voice, damned if she'd let him goad her into a childish tantrum.

He set aside his weapons and eyed the northern sky uneasily, then stood up. A sharp wind raced along his buckskin shirtsleeves with a wicked snap, biting icy cold on his skin. "Hurry up and eat. This may be the last hot food we get for a while," he said, breaking off a hunk of the rabbit and devouring it.

"Why?" she asked, puzzled by yet another unexplained shift in his mood. Nonetheless, she took a generous bite of rabbit.

Raising his arm, he pointed to the iron-gray clouds billowing down on them. "Storm's coming."

"A little rain never hurt anyone. May in St. Louis—"

"This isn't St. Louis. We're nearly a mile high on these plains with nothing between here and the Arctic to stop the wind roaring straight down on us. Out here they call it a blue norther and it squats down on its hind legs and howls like a thousand timber wolves once it gets going. This warm spell we just had only makes it worse—rain can turn to hail.''

''Hail.'' Roxanna nervously scanned the open trackless plains to the far distant shelter of the mountains. The scrubby pines and cedars by the pool looked pitiful indeed in the face of a possible hailstorm.

As if to punctuate her thoughts, the wind, already brisk, gusted up a stinging cloud of dust, nearly dousing the campfire.

''I think we'd better head for shelter,'' Cain yelled above the keening wind.

''Where?''

He kicked out the last of the fire and grabbed the horses' reins. ''Take the food packs, leave the cooking gear,'' he said as she began gathering the tin plates and cups.

By now the clouds were scudding low, the wind flattening the high grass to the ground. As the strength of the gale made her stumble backward, he took the food pack from her and tossed it over the chestnut's saddle. Wrapping his arm around her waist, he started to run toward the ravine, pulling the skittish horses behind them.

Like the living thing he had named it, the wind grew stronger, snarling and enraged, driving into them as they struggled against it. Roxanna clung to Cain as he bent into the wind, his long legs eating up the ground. Abruptly a narrow crevice opened up in front of them and they scrambled downward.

Just as they reached the flat rocky bottom of the gully, the wind died down as quickly as it had blown up. ''Is it over?'' Roxanna asked.

Cain looked up at the clouds hovering malevolently above them, smothering the sky. ''It's only begun,'' he replied grimly. All at once an earsplitting clatter began. Balls of hail the size of small crabapples pounded down on them like angry white fists.

Not even attempting to speak over the din, Cain sheltered

Roxanna in the lee of his shoulder as he dragged the terrified horses behind him until he reached a small overhang of rock. At once he pushed her as far back under it as he could, then pulled the horses in front of them, giving them what meager protection the niche could provide. He tied the reins securely around the tough roots of a chokecherry growing out the side of the overhang. The terrified animals huddled together, nickering and stamping their hooves as the hailstorm whitened the earth around them.

Roxanna felt the sting of the wind driving along the floor of the narrow ravine. God, they could be buried alive down here! She held her hands over her ears and huddled against cold hard stone. Then Cain knelt beside her and took her in his arms, covering her with his body to protect her from the wind and absorb the shock of stinging hailstones which blew past the horses' legs into their inadequate shelter.

Cain had pulled a bedroll from the saddle and now unfurled the heavy wool, cocooning them inside it. He felt her shivering uncontrollably and stroked her silky hair with his hand, cradling her head so it did not touch the rock beneath her. Gradually her trembling stopped, but she clutched his arm tightly, pressing her body to his until he could feel the soft mounds of her breasts and the long contours of her legs entwined against him. The scent of her was in his nostrils, subtle yet heady, not the perfume she'd employ in civilization but far more compelling. He could feel the small hot puffs of her breath against his throat and groaned aloud. The sound was absorbed in the cacophony of the storm.

Roxanna pressed her face against the crisp dark hair of his chest and felt the steady thrum of his heartbeat in spite of the deafening downpour. His body sheltered hers, absorbing the punishment doled out by the elements. Wind and hail pummeled his back, which was already badly bruised, yet he held her securely beneath him. She inched her arms around him and spread her hands over the painful injury to his side and shoulder blade, trying to protect him in some small way. His fingers tangled in her hair, gently cupping her head just as he had last night in the lodge when he kissed her. Roxanna felt safe, cherished, utterly at peace in the midst of violence. In Cain's arms it was as if she had come home after a long, long absence.

Gradually the hail slowed, then stopped, but the wind continued to howl ferociously, stinging them with sand. Cain could feel her burrow deeper beneath him. Every tiny movement of her body rubbing against his was agony. He felt himself growing hard and knew the bulge in his trousers pressed into her belly. He wondered if she understood what that meant. Sometimes silly white virgins did not, or so he'd been told. The women he consorted with were never innocents.

Cain was not at all certain about Alexa Hunt. She certainly should have been untouched, from what he knew of the way she had been brought up, the only child of a wealthy St. Louis socialite. She was around twenty years old. Cheyenne women—and lots of frontier white women too—had their first baby at sixteen or younger. The way she had responded when he kissed her confused him. There was a wellspring of passion in her combined with an odd sort of reticence that seemed more wariness than inexperience.

If he acted on the overwhelmingly foolish desire to bed her, they would best be served if she were not a virgin. Whether she was or not, he would be jeopardizing everything he had worked for if he made love to her. Jubal had plans for her that would never include a half-breed gunman. No matter how much the old Scot had come to like him or rely on his judgment, Cain knew MacKenzie would see him dead for it. When Alexa raised her head and nestled her face against his throat, he tried to remind himself of that fact.

Roxanna could feel him shifting his weight uncomfortably, trying not to crush her. The wind continued to howl. Over his shoulder she could dimly see the dull grayish white of the mounded hailstones. They could die out here all alone on the trackless plains. No one would find their bodies until their bones were bleached by the elements.

Cain's heat and strength were life and she was drawn to that. She was drawn to him. When her lips accidentally

brushed the pulse at the base of his throat, he jerked abruptly
and tightened his hold on her. Her breasts ached with a
strange new fullness she had only felt for the first time last
night when he had uncovered them and touched them with
his mouth. Just thinking of that caused her to arch involuntarily against his chest.

He cursed beneath his breath as the aching in his groin
intensified. Did she know what she was doing to him? He
nudged his leg over her hip, increasing the pressure of his
erection against her belly to see if she would respond.

She had felt the subtle bulge in his trousers grow, unaware at first of what it meant. She had been attacked head-
on with sex, never lain snugly and willingly in a man's arms
while his ardor grew. When Cain shifted his position, he
was making clear his need. After her unwilling and brutal
initiation to sex, she should have been frightened, repelled,
angry. But Roxanna was surprised to realize she was not.
Rather she felt a low, warm current of excitement eddying
in widening circles, deep in her belly, tingling in her aching
breasts, speeding up her breathing until she was dizzy and
clutching at his shoulders. Her hands climbed up to his neck
of their own volition and bracketed his face. She dug her
fingers into the shaggy black hair of his head while her
thumbs rubbed slowly against the harshness of his bearded
cheeks.

His eyes glowed in the dim light as he looked down at
her, suddenly aware that the wind had stopped. The storm
had passed, swift and deadly as a racing mountain cat
pouncing on its prey. He could see the pale light in her eyes
as she met his harsh gaze. "Are you sure you want this?"
his voice rasped, raw from sand and wind, and he waited
for her reply.

Chapter 6

"I thought we were going to die," she whispered, pressing her lips to the strong brown column of his neck, willing him to say something more before she committed herself. When he too held back, she murmured, "We're crazy to do this. I'm supposed to marry Lawrence Powell . . ." Roxanna felt Cain stiffen the moment she spoke Powell's name.

"You know about the arrangement," she said, unable to keep the accusation from her voice.

"Yeah, I know about it," he said, rolling abruptly away from her. Angrily he stood up and stepped from beneath the shelter of the overhang, needing desperately to put distance between himself and the woman. *What the hell does she want from me?*

Roxanna felt suddenly bereft of the warmth and comfort his body had given her. She lay stunned, watching as he untied the horses' reins. The thick white hail littering the ground made sharp crunching noises beneath their hooves, bringing her out of the numb trance. She sat up, brushing the faint remnants of sand and dust off her buckskins.

She drew in a shaky breath and tried to tell herself it was for the best that he had refused to interfere with Jubal MacKenzie's plans. The bitter aching lump in her throat made her realize just how dearly she had wanted him to . . . what? Tell her that he loved her? That he wanted to marry her himself? *Well, Roxy, I guess you have your answer. Even an outcast like Cain doesn't want you.*

Love and happy endings were the stuff of fairy tales. Being worthy enough to belong to someone was a girlish dream, shattered that morning she'd ridden away from Vicksburg. Even if Cain had wanted her as Alexa, he would not want Roxanna. He did not know her, but he did know he would lose his job if he lay with her. One brief encounter to satisfy his lust was certainly not worth it. *It wouldn't have been worth it for me either*, she stubbornly assured herself.

As he led the horses out of the ravine, Cain mulled over his brush with disaster. He suspected that she had been waiting for him to spout some nonsense about love and promise her a wedding ring. Alexa was an easterner, completely unaware of what it meant to be a breed out West. She probably thought her grandpa's money could buy anything. Hell, if he was fool enough to marry her, she'd learn quick enough what civilized white folks thought of one of their own who stooped to consort with a man like him. She'd be disinherited and widowed inside a week.

Alexa Hunt was young and naive, but he should know better. *No excuse in hell for letting my cock override my brain*, he chastised himself. A dangerous mistake he had never made before in his life. Oh, he'd taken chances, risked death on more than a few occasions, but never over a woman. No, in the past he only laid his life on the line for cold hard cash and the chance to better his position in a world where the deck was stacked against a nameless half-caste bastard. Damn lucky she'd reminded which way the wind was blowing before they both regretted it.

Roxanna climbed up from the ravine, clutching the bed-roll they had wrapped around them during the fury of the storm. His scent still clung to it faintly. She wanted to throw it down, almost did, but then something inside her made her hold it fast instead. Tears stung her eyes and she blinked them back furiously, damned if she'd give him the opportunity to see how his turning away had hurt. At least he had been decent enough not to press his advantage. He did not deceive her with promises of love which he never intended to keep.

Be grateful he's an honest man. Faint amusement at that irony was tinged with sadness for all the deceptions she had practiced in twenty-three short years of life. A small burble of hysterical laughter welled up, but she quashed it, asking instead, "Why aren't we making camp in the shelter of that gully?"

Cain did not trust himself yet to look back at her. "Too dangerous if rain comes later on in the night. That arroyo could turn into a torrential river in minutes and trap us," he explained as he checked the gear on his chestnut. That's when he noticed the bedroll was missing and remembered why.

"Here," she offered woodenly as he turned, shoving the blanket at him, quickly withdrawing her hand when his fingers brushed hers as he took it.

He felt her flinch and her hurt and anger cut through him more keenly than a slap. Sighing, he said, "Look, Alexa, I apologize for what happened back there—"

She cut him off, saying, "Nothing happened, Cain, nothing at all." At his look of patent disbelief she added in her best boarding school voice, "At least nothing we should dwell on any further."

He nodded. "We can make camp over by those trees. The hail's not so thick underneath. Use some of those broken-off branches to sweep the earth around it clear for our bedrolls while I get a fire going."

She did as he ordered without speaking. Soon they had made camp once more, with two pallets laid out beside a cheerily crackling fire. The cool night air hung heavy, freezing their breath in front of them. Roxanna thought the weather perfectly suited the mood. She lay for hours that night staring at the dark vault of heaven stretching above her, unable to sleep, longing for the sweet comfort of his embrace. He had made her feel so safe, sheltered from the storm, but the storm was over now. Time to get on with her life, she reminded herself grimly, and rolled over, turning her back on the man who had rejected her.

Across the other side of the small fire, Cain too lay awake, acutely aware of the woman he had held in his arms. His body still throbbed with desire for her. He cursed himself for seven kinds of a fool, knowing he would wait out the night sleepless. By the time they reached MacKenzie's work camp, he'd have to prop his eyes open with matchsticks just to see where he was going!

Jubal MacKenzie read the telegram and let out a sigh of blissful relief. Thank God Alexandra was safe. Cain estimated they'd reach Cheyenne in two more days. Propitious timing, since the Powells were scheduled to arrive on the twenty-third in Denver. He had held Andrew Powell off with excuses and evasions ever since his granddaughter was abducted. Finally the Central Pacific chief had wired him last week that he must either produce the girl and sign the agreement or their whole deal was off. MacKenzie suggested Denver as the logical place for such an announcement, saying the prosperous mining center was far more civilized than the wild Hell on Wheels railroad towns on the Union Pacific's trail.

The trip south into Colorado provided more time for Cain to return with Alexa. Now he would make it without a day to spare. Cain's wire was deliberately terse, simply stating that he would arrive with his "package none the worse for the journey." Jubal took that to mean the savages had not harmed her in any way, or at least he prayed that was what Cain meant.

Horror stories of Indian atrocities against settlers abounded on the frontier. Conventional wisdom stated that any white female taken captive was better off dead by her own hand than alive after the red devils finished with her, but being a Scot who made his first fortune back East, MacKenzie rejected the idea out of hand. However, he knew the power of ugly gossip and how it could destroy a young woman's reputation east or west, hence the carefully worded telegram and sizable bribes to ensure the silence of the stage station manager and telegrapher who had originally notified him of his granddaughter's abduction.

Cain knew how to follow instructions as well as he knew savages. They had met the day the deadly half-breed had coolly walked into a crowd of half-drunken track workers and faced them down, saving MacKenzie's life in the process. He had offered Cain a job immediately and never regretted it once in the past year. No one else could have located Alexa so quickly and quietly. Much as Cain hated his Indian blood, it had certainly proven valuable this time. Jubal sat back in the heavy leather chair behind his desk and steepled his fingers, idly trying to imagine the two of them together, Cain forbidding and taciturn as always, and Alexa—what about Alexa?

MacKenzie could not even picture what she might look like at age twenty-one. All he had was one blurred photograph taken on her fifteenth birthday. He had not seen her since she was twelve—or was it thirteen? Guiltily he realized he did not remember. Well, he would make it up to her now, or young Powell would. The boy had seemed quiet and affable when they had met in San Francisco last fall, attractive enough to the ladies, he supposed. Let the old warhorses like him and Andrew keep their noses to the grindstone while their children enjoyed the fruits of their labors. Thoughts of the interest in Central Pacific spur lines he would gain from the alliance made him rub his hands in anticipation.

He opened a desk drawer and took out a bottle of ten-year-old bourbon. Pouring himself a small shot, he savored the smoothly potent aroma, then raised it with his usual salute: "To America, the land of opportunity—and damn good whiskey!"

The tall black-haired woman stood on the porch of the way station looking as out of place as a lead crystal goblet beside a dented tin plate. Picking up the skirts of her plum silk traveling suit, she stepped off the rotting boards, which creaked in protest. Dusty, vile, smelly cesspool that the stop-over on the overland stage route in western Nebraska was, she did not care. Misery and inconvenience were a small price to pay for what she had just learned. She allowed herself to smile, thin red lips turning faintly upward as one of the odious shotgun guards assisted her in climbing up into the stage, which was bound for Cheyenne. Once there, she would assess her next move.

Luck had finally come her way, she mused as the coach started off with a lurch. She ignored the obscene curses of the driver lashing his team and thought back over the past year. How terrible—frightening, really—to have lost all trace of Roxanna Fallon. For a while it had seemed as if the earth had simply swallowed the damnable creature. But any-one as distinctive-looking as the Fallon bitch always re-ceived notice.

That was how her agents located Roxanna in St. Louis at the time of Alexandra Hunt's death. By then the tricky ac-tress had assumed her dead friend's identity and escaped west—right into the hands of a pack of ravening savages. She closed her dark brown eyes and imagined what they might do to a white woman, especially one with all that pale silvery hair. She only hoped they had not simply scalped the strumpet without first using some of their fiendish torture on her . . . or far better yet, done what was whispered about out in the barren wilderness—made her a squaw, the "fate worse than death." Any decent woman would kill herself first.

Of course, Roxanna Fallon was not a decent woman and she did possess an unnerving knack for survival. That was the reason for enduring this last leg of the journey to the infamous Hell on Wheels, Cheyenne, in what was soon to be the new territory of Wyoming. If Roxanna Fallon had somehow escaped the savages and was masquerading as Al-exa Hunt, the pleasure of exposing her as a fraud despoiled by bestial red heathens would be the finest revenge imagi-nable.

Isobel Darby rested her head on the upholstered seat back

and dreamed of fashioning one last final humiliation for the woman who had destroyed her husband's brilliant career.

The city of Cheyenne in the spring of 1868 had six first-rate hotels, over a dozen fine restaurants, a school, three churches . . . and seventy saloons. Its population was roughly ten thousand. Next to the saloons, the cemetery was the busiest spot in town.

"Once the rails reach Laramie, half the transients—whiskey peddlers, card sharks, whores—will pack up their gear, whole saloons and bordellos, and ride to the next stop on the road. Last fall there was a gold strike up at South Pass on the Sweetwater. The city filled up with miners over the winter. Now that the weather's breaking in the mountains, they're already gone. Still, since your grandfather plans to build a roundhouse and repair shop here, the place should prosper well enough," Cain said.

At the mention of Jubal MacKenzie, Roxanna quickly forgot about the excitement of the raucous city. Soon she would meet the man who was supposedly her grandfather. Could she pull this off?

Cain sensed her nervousness, different from the tension that had simmered between them since the night of the storm. "How long since you've seen Jubal?"

Roxanna moistened her lips, unconsciously fussing with the heavy skirt of her riding habit. "Eight years. I was only a skinny girl then."

A dark light gleamed sardonically in his eyes as he looked her over. "I think he'll be pleased enough with the way you've grown up. So will your bridegroom," he added grimly, kneeing the chestnut into a swifter pace. He had stopped at a well-stocked trading post on the North Platte to purchase a few suitable articles of female clothing for Alexa. She could hardly ride up to Jubal's private Pullman car dressed like a Cheyenne squaw. The cheap ready-made twill riding skirt and white cotton blouse were hardly elegant, but her curves filled them out admirably. He had guessed right about the sizes. *Don't think about it*, he admonished himself, remembering her slender long limbs entwined with his.

Roxanna followed him as they approached the outskirts of the city, feeling the scorn radiating from him. Twice her body had betrayed her with this . . . savage . . . and now he dared to look down on her for going through with the marriage to Lawrence Powell. A wave of desolation washed over her, leaving her to wonder about what might have been, but one lesson Roxanna Fallon had learned well in life was to forget what might have been and focus instead on what was.

They rode down Eddy Street, as wide open and raw as any boomtown described in the dime novels that were becoming so popular back East. The Whitehead Block was an imposing two-story frame structure a city block square, housing all manner of business and professional offices, but just down the street sat one of the loudest and most gaudy pleasure palaces in the West, "Professor" James McDaniel's Eddy Street Saloon. A huge stuffed grizzly peered malevolently from one window while a pair of rare white monkeys played inside a cage at the door. An immense pipe organ blared out a lively tune, deafening passersby on the street.

Brawny Irish track workers and rough hard-rock miners rubbed elbows with nattily dressed gamblers, while hard-eyed *"nymphs de le grade"* leaned over second-story porch rails, waving feather boas and other more personal items at potential customers. Nothing up and down the length of the Mississippi had prepared Roxanna for this spectacle. An advertisement for a production of *Titus Andronicus* would otherwise have caught her eyes, but as soon as Roxanna saw the long gleaming private rail car sitting on the side track, all she could think about was Jubal MacKenzie.

What sort of a man missed his only daughter's funeral and ignored his only granddaughter? Building railroads must indeed be his obsession. Of course, she was forced to admit he had repeatedly offered Alexa the chance to join him out West and been refused. Somehow Roxanna could never envision her timid friend having enough nerve to go through with a marriage to a complete stranger. But "Alexa" would do it now—if Roxanna could fool the shrewd old Scot into believing she was his granddaughter.

They dismounted and Cain handed the reins of their horses to a youth, instructing him to see that the animals were rubbed down and properly stabled. She stared at the inlaid mahogany and rosewood door as Cain assisted her aboard the platform at the rear of the car. "I didn't know Mr. Pullman's sleeping palaces were operating on the Union Pacific."

"They're not. This one's private. Old Doc Durant bought it from the government after it was used to carry President Lincoln's body back to Illinois. When Jubal came west to manage the work crews on the line, he appropriated it." He knocked and a gruff voice called out for him to enter.

Roxanna stepped into the opulent maroon and gold splendor of an immense parlor filled with overstuffed blue brocade sofas and chairs, marble-topped tables and white lace Austrian shades. A huge polished walnut desk dominated the far corner of the room. Behind it stood a powerfully built giant of a man with a barrel chest and a thick middle. His ginger-colored hair and untrimmed beard were liberally streaked with gray. Weather-blasted and sun-darkened, his face was spotted by large freckles. Shrewd gray eyes peered at her from beneath brushy eyebrows, now raised appraisingly.

Nervously Roxanna stepped forward, feeling almost as intimidated as the real Alexa would have. "Hello, Grandfather."

His thick lips split in a wide smile as he spoke with a slight Scots burr. "Welcome, lassie. I'm relieved to see yer safe at last." He walked around the desk and extended his arms as she approached, clasping big gnarled hands over her arms as he inspected her. "Ye do na' have the look of the MacKenzies aboot ya," he said at length, quirking one beetled brow as he stared at her.

Roxanna's heart skipped a beat before he slapped one

meaty palm against his leg and added, "And it's right good · you take after yer Lindstrom grandmother. I'd scarce want a granddaughter to look plug ugly as me!"

Roxanna wracked her memory and recalled the Norwegian woman Jubal had wed back in Pennsylvania. "Grandma Abbie gave me my hair, Mama always said, although I never knew her."

"I miss her yet and she's been gone over thirty years, God rest her soul. Perhaps that's why . . ." He shook his head as if pushing away deeply buried thoughts and looked over to Cain. "I owe you for this piece of work."

Cain nodded. *More than you can imagine, Jubal.* "She wasn't hard to find once I reached the Sand Hill country. My hunch was right. They wanted to trade for guns." He said nothing about the band being his mother's people and hoped Alexa would not either. "I'll leave the two of you to get reacquainted. I have to check the progress the gun squads have made while I was gone."

Roxanna could read nothing in his level gaze. His face was as expressionless as any of the full-blooded Cheyenne she had met. He touched the brim of his hat to her in what passed for a polite gesture. "In case I neglected to thank you for rescuing me, you have my undying gratitude, Mr. Cain," she said in her best finishing school voice.

Jubal observed the exchange between the two young people and knew immediately that something was wrong. As soon as Cain closed the door, he turned to her. "Cain's a hard man. I do na' expect he was much easier on you than the Indians. Were you hurt, lassie?" he asked gruffly, taking her arm and ushering her to a camel-backed sofa.

"No. Frightened at first, but it was soon apparent they meant me no harm. Their old medicine man had a vision about me. . . ." This sounded ridiculous, as if she believed the superstitions of the Cheyenne. Sees Much's wishful dreams about her and Cain were certainly nothing she should ever confess to Jubal MacKenzie. She would never mention her own dream! "He thought I was important, that someone would bargain for my freedom."

Jubal pursed his lips. "A curiously astute guess."

"When your Mr. Cain arrived, they easily struck an agreement."

Jubal poured a glass of sweet sherry for her, a stronger libation for himself. When he handed it to her she accepted it, trying to ignore the sickly smell of the loathsome stuff, but when she raised it to her mouth he seemed to sense her repugnance. "The sherry's not to yer liking?"

"Mama didn't approve of spirits," she equivocated. Both Mrs. Hunt and Alexa were temperance, but he would not know about his granddaughter's sentiments, since she was too young to voice an opinion when last he saw her.

"And you?"

The studied gleam in his eye made her wonder if this was a test of some sort. *Take the plunge, Roxy.* "I prefer a small touch of real liquor if I'm going to drink at all." She eyed the amber liquid in his glass. "Is that Scotch whiskey?"

He shuddered. "Never acquired a taste for the peat-flavored stuff. This is a fine American invention, ten-year-old sour mash Bourbon."

She smiled. "St. Louis's own. Madam Chouteau was quite fond of Bourbon, so the old story goes."

He poured an inch in a glass and exchanged it for the sherry, then raised his own drink. "Just a wee dram. To America, the land of opportunity—and damn good whiskey!"

She touched her glass to his and sipped the smooth corn whiskey, then smiled. "Here's to both."

"You just might have grown into a girl after my own heart, lassie."

Roxanna sighed inwardly, relieved. The first test passed. She could like this sly old curmudgeon. How sad that the real Alexa would have disappointed him.

Jubal tossed down his drink and poured himself another, then dug his fingers in his woolly beard, studying her. "So you spent—what must have it been—a month, living with the Indians. Yer tougher than you look, lass."

Roxanna had learned to size up men during the war. This

one was nobody's fool. "After losing both parents so young, I had to learn to fend for myself. I had no family there to look out for me."

"I sent for you, but you refused to come west. You wrote it was full of snakes and Indians and you were afraid." His voice was defensive, guilty in spite of his gruffness.

"I was only eighteen when Mama died. I had to grow up."

"A bit late, but better than never," he said grudgingly, tossing off the last of his whiskey.

"Being alone, I've learned to rely on myself."

"Is that why you agreed to marry the Powell boy—because yer more afraid of being an old maid than you are of coming west?"

Roxanna followed his example and tossed down the rest of her whiskey in one gulp. "I'm not afraid of being an old maid and I don't need a husband."

"Then why did you come here to marry Powell?" he asked, leaning forward in his chair, ready for checkmate.

"You would have cut my allowance if I refused," she said baldly. Men made up all the rules and forced women to follow them, damn them!

Jubal surprised her then. A deep slow laugh began rumbling out. "You are a saucy wench! Yes, I damn well would. But somehow I do na' think I can make you wed against yer will if you do na' like young Powell."

"If he's as rude as Mr. Cain, be certain I'll refuse, Grandfather." She could not resist saying it, but refusing the legal protection of marriage would be risky.

"Cain certainly put a burr beneath yer blanket. Is it his Indian blood?"

"No. I liked the Cheyenne well enough. They're proud of who they are. I don't think Cain likes who he is at all."

"Yer a shrewd one for being so young. He's not at peace with himself. An outsider, always keeps people at a distance. But he's a good man for this work."

"You like him."

"Aye, I do," he admitted.

"Perhaps because you're a little like him," she suggested, smiling.

"You may just be too clever by half," he said sourly. Her clear turquoise eyes studied him. Wanting to change the subject, he picked up the decanter. "Another hair of the dog before I see yer ensconced in Cheyenne's finest hotel?"

She held up her glass and winked. "Just a wee dram, Grandfather."

Jubal MacKenzie chuckled and poured.

Roxanna sank down into the big copper tub with a sigh of pure bliss. The hotel was not as fine as some on the Mississippi, but better by far than most in which she'd stayed. Jubal had reserved the best room in the house—a suite, really—composed of a small sitting room and a spacious bedroom with a large dressing closet and this heavenly tub. After days of dusty travel, washing in muddy creeks, this was decadent. She lathered up and let the soft glistening soap bubbles soothe away her tensions.

Things had gone well with Jubal MacKenzie. They had taken a quick liking to one another. She could understand him in ways Alexa, sheltered child of privilege, never could have. He was gruff, loud and profane. He drank. But he was also hardworking and willing to accept people for their abilities rather than their pedigrees. Born to solid middle-class comfort in Scotland, Jubal had lost everything as a small boy when his father died bankrupt, leaving him to fend for himself on the streets of Aberdeen. He had come to America, survived by his wits and prospered.

She certainly knew enough about surviving by her wits, although she had yet to prosper much—until now. If only she could charm Lawrence Powell and his formidable father half so well as she had Jubal. But what if she detested her prospective bridegroom? Despite Jubal's assurances that he was pleasant-natured and good-looking, she could not trust the wily old man's opinion when he had so much to gain from the alliance. Still, she had made her bed and now she would have to lie in it . . . with Lawrence Powell.

Leaning her head back on the rim of the tub, Roxanna closed her eyes and Cain's scowling dark face flashed before her. He was the reason she was having second thoughts about Powell, damn him. She should be grateful that she had not succumbed to his rough seduction . . . if it could justly be called seduction. Certainly it had been a near thing. She remembered his mouth on her breasts, his hard long body pressed against hers, the rasp of his whiskers on her fingertips as she touched those bold hawkish features . . . A warmth began to steal over her owing nothing to the tepid water in the tub. Her mind turned to the scene in the ravine when she had been . . .

She sat up angrily, breaking the spell. He had made clear his feelings for her and they did not include love or permanence, certainly not a decent offer of marriage or the security and wealth the Powell name would give her. Cain was just as Jubal said, an outsider, a bitter loner who fit in nowhere and cared for no one.

"Soon Alexa Hunt is going to meet her future husband. Forget about the half-breed gunman and get on with your life!" With that admonition, she dunked her head and began to shampoo her hair.

Gable Hogue had worked for the Widow Darby for nearly four years and he did not like her. She was impatient and always putting on airs as if she were better than the man who worked for her. Since he had been fired from the Remington Investigation Agency in Chicago, jobs had been scarce. She did pay decently—when she received the information she wanted. He'd tracked Roxanna Fallon up and down the Mississippi, locating her each time she joined a new theatrical company. She'd almost given him the slip for good in St. Louis. It had been a lucky fluke that he caught her trail after Alexa Hunt's funeral. Smiling in anticipation of the hard currency Isobel Darby would pay him, he headed down Sixth Street to their prearranged meeting place.

Yes sir, her silver-haired quarry was here in Cheyenne

right enough. He'd seen her himself, no mistaking that looker. Registered as Alexa Hunt, she was set up at the best hotel in Cheyenne. Not a bad switch, he thought with admiration, trading in her grease paints for a rich granddaddy. Not to mention surviving captivity with some red savages. Once that Darby bitch found out, poor Roxy Fallon would be better off with the Indians. Too bad. He was gaining a sneaking respect for her resourcefulness in spite of the merry chase she'd led him on. But Gable Hogue always went for the money first.

Once apprised of her hated enemy's amazing resurrection, Isobel planned her strategy. As a genteel lady from a fine old Mississippi family, she would be welcomed to a crude frontier city such as Denver, where rough miners and illiterate stockmen still outnumbered gentlemen two to one and soiled doves were a dozen times more numerous than women of refinement.

When she arrived, it would be so easy to let slip the juicy gossip about poor Alexa's captivity by the Indians. How shocking that she survived it, she would *tsk*, the clear implication being that a nobler woman would not have. She would not even have to expose the hateful harlot as a fraud to ruin her. Then when that ruthless old railroad baron saw her usefulness to him end, Isobel would play her trump card and inform him just exactly who the viper was he had taken to his bosom.

She sat down at the writing desk in her room and began to compose a note to Nathan Baker, the editor of the *Cheyenne Leader*. That should get things moving along nicely before she left for Denver.

Chapter 7

"How the hell did this get out? I'll hog-tie that damned editor and sell him to the Cheyenne," Jubal ranted, throwing down a copy of the scurrilous *Cheyenne Leader*. He cursed some more and stormed across the office. Word of Alexa's shocking abduction and rescue by his unsavory half-breed "Injun" was spreading like wildfire up and down the rail camps. It was inevitable that Andrew Powell would hear the ugly rumors by the time they reached Denver.

Cain listened to Jubal, then said, "I brought Miss Alexandra in after dark. I even had her put all that hair up under her hat so no one would remember her. Maybe you didn't pay those men at the relay station enough to keep them quiet, or a man from Fort Kearny hit town and started talking when he heard your granddaughter was here with you. I can check around, find out," he said. Kitty would know the source of the gossip. Nothing on "the line" got by her.

MacKenzie sighed. "I do na' believe that would serve anything now. The cat's out of the bag, lad. All I can do is take Alexa to Denver for the betrothal as planned. Brazen it through and dare old Powell to back down." Jubal clamped down on his cigar so fiercely he bit through the tip, muttered an oath and threw the expensive smoke into the cuspidor.

Cain knew Andrew Powell would never agree to the marriage once he learned about Alexa's time with the Cheyenne. That she'd spent time alone with him would only enrage the old bastard all the more.

Better not to borrow trouble for MacKenzie—or his granddaughter. Maybe the rail camp gossip wouldn't reach as far south as Denver. *But you want it to, don't you?* an inner voice nagged. Did he? Did he want Alexa left standing at the altar, deprived of her blue-blooded bridegroom? Absurd. It was hardly as if he wanted to marry her himself. Or did he? The idea, far-fetched and fleeting, whispered to him once again, curling enticingly around his mind. He brushed it away. Jubal would never agree to it. Neither would Alexa, after the way they'd parted. But then she had agreed to marry Larry boy sight unseen just to please the old man.

Cain left Jubal fuming and rode down to Kitty's place. He was long overdue for some sexual recreation . . . and a little conversation with the shrewd madam as well. One way or the other, it would be wise if he went to Denver with MacKenzie and his granddaughter. At least he would know firsthand how the situation resolved itself. Besides, he wanted to see the look on Alexa's arrogant little face when he walked into the ballroom, even if he was there as a paid employee instead of a guest. How the hell had the woman gotten so deep under his skin that he cared what the hell she thought? Or what happened to her?

He pushed open the swinging door of the Calico Cat and walked inside. After a bottle and a few hours of Kitty's charms he might just completely forget about that little silver witch. To hell with the harebrained idea. It would never work out anyway.

Roxanna stood at the head of the receiving line with Jubal towering over her, exuberant in his greetings to all the movers and shakers in Denver society. Everyone who was anyone in the gold capital of America had turned out to meet MacKenzie's granddaughter, including a goodly number of merchants, bankers, mining magnates and railroad barons escorting their ladies who were all decked out in silks and jewels.

The glittering assembly of notables was there to observe the final burying of the hatchet between the building-site chiefs of the Union and Central Pacific. It would be quite a show, to see the canny old Scot and the ruthless San Franciscan, archrivals since the race for the rails began back in '64, actually shake hands instead of drawing pistols! The vehicle for this was ostensibly the engagement between MacKenzie's granddaughter and Powell's son. Although not official, rumor had it that the announcement might actually be made that very night.

"Alexa, this is my old friend Nathaniel Hill, chemist and world traveler," Jubal said as a portly gentleman with a walrus mustache shook her hand effusively. "Nate's cornered the market in Denver real estate—along with Hank Brown and Davie Moffat."

As Roxanna smiled, Hill nodded politely while he and Jubal exchanged small talk about Union Pacific politics and the directors back East. "Did you see that fancy new portrait of Tom Durant?"

"The one they hung in the Omaha depot last fall? Aye. Dinna' look a thing like him."

Hill looked bemused. "Oh, why not?"

"The good doctor had his hands in his own pockets—instead of somebody else's," MacKenzie replied sourly. Nate Hill burst into raucous laughter and Jubal joined him.

As the men talked, Roxanna extended her hand to Mrs. Hill, who smiled shyly, a fragile swallow of a woman overshadowed by her robust spouse. As the receiving line wended its way past them, Roxanna continued smiling and making the appropriate responses, while nervously scanning the vast ballroom in the Imperial Hotel for her first glimpse of Lawrence Powell.

There was an air of hushed expectancy about the crowded room and some undercurrent which she could sense yet did not understand. Some of the men had eyed her as if she were still an actress, not quite leering but not truly respectful either. Others looked her over with avid curiosity, as if she were some sort of circus freak. Many of the women seemed stiff and formal, almost to the point of being rude, as if dragged by their husbands to meet her.

Jubal did not appear concerned with the peculiar behavior of so many of his associates. He was loud and jovial with many men like Hill, going out of his way to laugh and make jokes. Was he covering up something? Her first thought was that somehow her real identity had been exposed by Isobel Darby, but that was absurd. A man like Jubal MacKenzie would not tolerate such a deception, much less attempt to soothe her feelings after she had made a fool of him.

The only other possibility was almost as dire—they knew she had been an Indian captive and that Cain had ridden in alone to buy her freedom. That would explain Jubal's hovering protectiveness, the forced joviality. It would be just like him to think he could suppress a scandal by sheer force of will. But she knew a man as ruthless as Andrew Powell was reputed to be would never be forced into anything. Would he and his son even attend her gala tonight or simply break off the agreement with no further ado?

As if to answer her question, a tall man with a face as harsh as a bird of prey strode imperiously across the room toward them, followed by a younger man who was considerably shorter with none of the hard-edged features of the elder. Although they did not bear any discernible physical resemblance, Roxanna knew they were father and son, Andrew and Lawrence Powell.

As the older man approached Jubal, the guests parted before the newcomers like the Red Sea for Moses. The two old enemies were of a height, freezing blue eyes meeting steel gray levelly, but there the resemblance ended, for while Jubal was barrel-chested and heavyset like a bulldog, Powell had the lean look of a greyhound.

"MacKenzie," he said stiffly, offering one elegantly manicured hand, the hand of a powerful man who used his brains, never his fists, to succeed in the world.

Roxanna watched Jubal extend his gnarled beefy paw, its

freckles and weather-blasted roughness testimony to long hours spent out in the elements. "Yer late, Powell, but I believe that's prophetic. The Union Pacific will be through Salt Lake before you even get out of the Sierras." Mac-Kenzie smiled, but the forced humor never reached the cool gray depths of his eyes.

"We've just completed the summit tunnel and it's all downhill from now on for the Central Pacific. You'll be up against your first real test soon—the Rockies."

Roxanna was so absorbed in the electric exchange between the two old pirates that she completely forgot about the tan-haired young man standing beside Andrew Powell until he stepped forward and smiled disarmingly.

"I'm Lawrence Powell, and you must be Miss Alexandra Hunt," he said, taking her hand in both of his and squeezing it ever so slightly.

Roxanna recovered herself quickly, returning his smile as she gazed into a lightly tanned face that was round and even-featured. His chin was a bit weak and his eyes were a lighter shade of blue with none of the predatory fierceness of Andrew's. "I am pleased to make your acquaintance at long last, Mr. Powell," she replied, waiting for some feeling, some spark of attraction to leap between them. But none did. Nothing.

"Please don't be so formal. Under the circumstances, don't you think it permissible to call me Larry?" he asked, still not relinquishing her hand.

Roxanna nodded. "If you will call me Alexa." Jubal had been right about Lawrence. He was attractive in a mild sort of way that drew none of the magnetized stares focused on his father. All for the better, since Andrew looked as ruthless and deadly as a hawk.

"Please allow me to welcome you to the West, Miss Hunt," Andrew Powell said, fixing her with an icy gaze but not offering his hand. "I understand you're from St. Louis. I do hope you found your journey out here . . . pleasant thus far?"

Until now, she wanted to say. His look was anything but

welcoming and the remark about her journey west made clear that he knew about her abduction. She looked to Jubal for guidance, wishing he had not tried to protect her from the inevitable.

Moving forward to take Powell's arm, MacKenzie said, "It would seem the young people have struck it off, Andrew. I think it would be best if you and I repaired to the bar and let them enjoy the party."

The elder Powell bowed stiffly to her, then gave his son a meaningful glance before turning away. Roxanna could sense every eye in the room riveted on the two of them as Jubal and Andrew walked away.

Lawrence's expression narrowed for an instant when he made eye contact with his father, but then the warmth returned when he looked back to her. "The orchestra is playing the first dance. I believe it's customary for the guest of honor to lead off. Would you do me the honor, Alexa?"

From the mezzanine across the room, Cain watched Lawrence Powell sweep Alexa into his arms and whirl across the floor to the strains of a Strauss waltz. She would have stood out in any glittering assembly even if she were not the guest of honor. Her hair was caught up in an elaborate mass of loops and twists piled atop her head and intertwined with pearls. Her pale aquamarine silk gown glittered softly in the flickering gaslights, hugging every seductive curve of waist and breasts, revealing the creamy whiteness of a good deal of skin, which had been lightly sun-kissed when he brought her back from the Cheyenne. She must have soaked in milk baths for this requisite pallor, he thought grimly, his mind at once conjuring up images of her silky naked flesh glistening in the bubbles.

Just then she threw back her head, laughing at some sally of Larry's. He was holding her with just the right degree of propriety for a prospective suitor. Trust him to do everything by the book. But if his old man didn't break the engagement, there would be no rules for Larry to worry about. He would have Alexa to do with as he pleased, bury his fists in the mane of silver-gilt hair, suckle those pink-tipped breasts and bury himself deep inside the beckoning heat of her lithe slender body. Cain squeezed his eyes shut tightly for a moment to clear his head of the disquieting thoughts, then looked down and realized that he had clenched his hands so tightly on the marble balustrade that his bronzed knuckles shone white as the stone.

He stepped back, releasing the railing, but not before his eyes met Alexa's as she suddenly looked up when the music stopped.

Roxanna had sensed someone was staring at her for several minutes, but dismissed it given the circumstances. She was the guest of honor and ugly rumors about her were no doubt being whispered around the room. But this feeling was different somehow than the sly darting glances of people talking behind their hands. Then the orchestra finished its piece and Lawrence released her. As she stepped back, her gaze raised to the balcony across the floor and her eyes locked with Cain's.

At least she thought it was Cain. He looked so different, it was hard to believe he was the same unshaven disreputable half-breed who had ridden into Leather Shirt's camp, armed to the teeth. He still looked dangerous but in a totally different manner. His piercing black eyes skewered her intently, emphasizing the harsh planes of his bronzed face and straight unsmiling mouth. The somber elegance of his black evening clothes complemented his gleaming ebony hair, now freshly barbered. That long lean body was made to wear such clothes, she realized with shock as he turned away from the balustrade and walked off like a sleek black panther stalking his prey. Yes, still dangerous, very dangerous, but sophisticated in an urbane way she would never have imagined.

Lawrence's eyes followed hers and he realized who held her mesmerized for that brief moment. "I see he works the floor for MacKenzie now just like he did for us."

"I beg your pardon?" Roxanna said, embarrassed. How utterly reckless and schoolgirl-silly to have been caught staring at Cain! "You know Mr. Cain?"

"He worked four years for my father, rather in the same capacity as he does for your grandfather—he's a gunman hired to deal with trouble—brawling trackmen, tinhorns, any sort of toughs on the line."

Cain was scarcely dressed to subdue drunken railroad workers tonight, but Roxanna did not want to discuss him with her prospective husband. "I didn't realize Mr. Cain was employed by the Central Pacific. He spoke very little after securing my release from the Cheyenne. You do know I was abducted and held for ransom, don't you, Larry?" she asked, deciding the direct approach was best.

As they strolled past a palm-lined corridor heading toward the terrace, he replied, "You're very brave to speak about it." His expression was grave, leaving the rest unsaid.

"There's not much to speak of. The Indians wanted guns for hunting and knew somehow that my grandfather would be willing to trade them for my safety. They did not harm me." She looked directly at him as she spoke, trying to gauge whether or not he believed her.

He squeezed her hand reassuringly. "That's a great relief. We heard the most scurrilous rumors—that is—Father was afraid—no, I mean . . . I'm making a terrible botch of this, aren't I?" His smile was embarrassed and boyish and utterly irresistible.

Roxanna felt herself warming to him even if there was none of the sizzling summer lightning she felt with Cain. *Damn Cain!* She returned Lawrence's smile. "It's all right. I think my grandfather was worried about the gossip, but I expect now that everyone can see I'm unharmed, it will die down."

"I certainly hope—that is, I'm sure that it will. Would you care for some refreshment?"

They chatted about superficial things, her life in St. Louis, his in San Francisco, the race between the Union Pacific and Central Pacific. He was young and earnest, occasionally inept, but so sweet about it that she did not mind. Roxanna quickly realized from his frequent references to his father that it was Andrew who made all the decisions in the Powell family. The thought of living in the same house with that hawk-faced man made her shudder. She hoped if she and Lawrence married that they could move into a place of their own, but it was too soon to consider that.

After several more dances, Jubal approached them with an older couple whom he introduced as Jonah and Sarah Grady, a wealthy mine owner and his wife who were interested in investing in railroad spurs. The men excused themselves and headed to the bar, leaving Roxanna in Sarah's company. She was a slightly plump woman with graying brown curls and merry hazel eyes that protruded from their sockets.

"Those men will talk railroads until they've laid tracks twice around the equator," she said warmly, taking Roxanna's arm. "Why don't we repair to the ladies' sitting room? While the gentlemen smoke on the terrace you can relax for a few moments."

Roxanna felt relieved and pleased at the prospect. "To be honest, Mrs. Grady, my facial muscles are about locked from smiling at so many people. I would dearly love to rest a bit."

They found one of the small parlors on the mezzanine set aside for the ladies and took a seat on a delicate damask upholstered settee near the back of the room, secluded by several large potted ferns. Roxanna sighed in contentment and arched her back to relieve the terrible tension of being "on stage" in her role as Alexa Hunt. Just as she was about to reply to Sarah's question about her hairdresser, a woman's high whiny voice interrupted them.

"I tell you, Emmaline, it's absolutely shocking. That Hunt hussy sashaying around with decent God-fearing white women after letting a pack of greasy bucks have their way with her. Why, any woman with an ounce of self-respect would've killed herself before she'd submit to that fate."

"Now, Berta, maybe the savages didn't harm her. She doesn't look as if anything dreadful happened," Emmaline suggested.

"Humph! They say that the Scot's Injun, Cain—why,

he's little more than a savage himself—brought her back. She spent days alone with him on the plains. If the redskins didn't touch her, you can be certain *he* did!'' Berta responded.

''I do suppose you're right. Imagine spending weeks with those savages and then—''

Roxanna rose from the settee and stepped around the potted fern. ''And then falling for Mr. Cain's charms?'' she interrupted curtly.

Emmaline, a small wisp of a woman, crimsoned with embarrassment and fanned herself, but the big horse-faced Berta stepped forward belligerently. ''You have no shame.''

''With good reason. I have nothing to be ashamed of, unlike some catty backsniping gossips I've encountered,'' Roxanna replied with a cool disdain she was far from feeling.

''Why, I've never,'' Emmaline gasped.

''This city has enough of your kind already, but they normally keep their place down on Cherry Creek,'' Berta hissed.

''You seem acquainted with the locale. So tell me, Berta, what is it like down on Cherry Creek?'' Roxanna inquired dulcetly.

For a moment she thought the big woman was going to strike her as a dull red flush blotched her beefy sallow face, but then she turned and swept from the room, sending one of the palm plants wobbling when her outdated wide hoops struck the pot. Emmaline scurried after her, leaving Roxanna and Sarah alone.

Roxanna seemed to wilt, all the cool bravado of moments earlier evaporating when Sarah placed one arm around her young companion's shoulders and said, ''My dear child, you must pay no mind to women like those.''

Roxanna rubbed her temples with her fingertips, then raised her head and faced the kindly woman. ''This is all over the city, isn't it?''

Reluctantly Sarah nodded. ''Give them time, my dear,

and people in Denver will find something else to gossip about.''

''I'm not so certain that I'll ever be accepted in polite society, regardless.'' Just then several young women entered the retiring room, all chatting at once. ''If you'll excuse me, I think I need to be alone for a few moments.''

With a worried look, Sarah Grady nodded, watching Alexa Hunt walk proudly from the room. What a pity for such a splendid young woman to have survived so much and then fall victim to the petty viciousness of Berta Wolcott.

Roxanna made her way down the long dimly lit corridor, unaware of her surroundings as thoughts tumbled chaotically in her mind. What would happen now? Would Lawrence Powell break the engagement because of the scandal? What would Jubal do? She realized her speculations about his loquaciousness were correct. Roxanna considered what to do if Jubal's hoped-for merger failed. Remaining with him, posing as his granddaughter, was always a risk. If her well-kept secret about the Indian captivity was out, how much more difficult would it be for someone to uncover her real identity? The corridor dead-ended, but one door to her left stood ajar. Hearing voices down the hallway, she stepped inside, blinking to accustom her eyes to the gloom.

Where can I go? Who can I turn to? She stood alone, shivering in the darkness, her arms wrapped around herself. Then she aimlessly turned and walked across the floor, refusing to give in to the tears that stung behind her eyelids.

Suddenly a steely arm clamped around her waist, pulling backward until she slammed into the hard wall of a man's chest, a very tall man's chest. All her breath was crushed from her as she tried to turn and push away her assailant, but he was too strong.

''The party's downstairs. You're a long way from your fiancé. Have a lover's quarrel already?''

Cain's silky low voice made her freeze. What else could go wrong tonight? ''Let me go,'' she demanded.

''Mmm, I don't know. Feels pretty good holding you

close the way Powell did,'' he replied, smelling the delicate essence of lilacs from her silvery hair.

"Larry was a gentleman. He didn't take liberties the way you do.''

"That's what you call it, now—taking liberties? I reckon you took a few yourself back in that storm . . . only I didn't object—but then you're right, I'm no gentleman.''

"At least we agree on one thing,'' she gritted out, turning toward him when he released her. He crossed the floor in two long strides and raised the wick on the gaslight, then stood facing her with his arms crossed over his chest. The expensively cut black wool suit molded to his long legs. The stark white shirtfront contrasted sharply with his bronzed face, now scowling at her. Earlier, from a distance, Roxanna had not seen that he was still armed. Now with his jacket hanging open, she saw the butt of a small pistol protruding from a shoulder holster.

"Don't you go anywhere without carrying a weapon?''

Cain shrugged and the sapphire studs on his shirtfront and cuffs winked at her mockingly. He responded matter-of-factly, "Not when I'm working.''

"Working? At a ball?'' She dimly remembered some comment of Larry's about Cain working the floor, whatever that meant.

"Whenever you put a hotel full of rich men together with a bar full of whiskey, there's bound to be trouble. If not from them, then from business rivals who weren't invited, sneak thieves—''

"And you thought I was a thief?'' she asked incredulously.

"I heard someone enter Jubal's conference room in the dark while I was checking next door.''

"If this is so almighty private, then don't leave the door standing open next time.'' She started to walk by him, desperate to escape for the tears she had banked earlier suddenly seemed ready to deluge her.

"Whoa, princess, not so fast,'' he murmured, snaking out a long arm to intercept her.

"What are you going to do—arrest me?" She stiffened in his arms, fighting the urge to weep with every ounce of her willpower. But then Cain always seemed able to break that willpower without even trying.

He could sense her trembling and drew her nearer. "You're strung tight as a high-wire in a circus act." He placed his hand on her shoulder, feeling the silky bare skin, massaging it gently with his fingertips.

"Don't—please, don't." Her throat was raw. She hated herself for pleading.

"You've heard the gossip, then?" He cursed when she refused to reply, standing rigidly in his arms, refusing to look at him. "Did Larry boy tell you the engagement is off?"

"No," she replied too quickly.

"It will be. But he won't have the nerve to face you. Old man Powell will inform Jubal—if he hasn't already."

"Will that make you happy? Why should you care whether or not someone else wants me? You don't want me!"

"Like hell I don't!" Cain dug his fingers deep into her pearl-strewn hair, forcing her head back as his mouth ground down on hers in a ravaging kiss. He pressed her silk-clad body against his, tilting his hips intimately into hers, feeling the soft pressure of her breasts against his chest.

This kiss was no gentle exploration or swift teasing foray into her mouth. He slanted his lips across hers and plunged his tongue deep inside with swift wicked strokes, leaving her breathless . . . and hungry for more. She could feel the hard rigid pressure of his erection riding low against her belly and his fist tangling in her hair, pulling it loose from its pins as his fingers massaged her tender scalp. He tasted hot and dark, a potent blend of tobacco and despair that sent an answering need singing along her veins, just as it had every time they touched. She could feel those sapphire shirt studs digging into her bare flesh above the low-cut gown. Her breasts grew taut and ached for his mouth on them once again. Without her realizing it, her hands curved around his shoulders, pulling him closer, closer.

Cain released her lips, then moved along the curve of her jawline, down her exposed throat, to the wildly fluttering pulse that beat there. He buried his face in the lilac-scented cloud of her hair, inhaling her essence, then swept his hand down to cup her breast and raise it to his mouth like an offering. The pale creamy swell seemed ready to pop from its silk cocoon as he nuzzled it, feeling her fingernails digging into his back through his jacket. When she arched against him, his knees nearly buckled. He wanted to pull her beneath him on the carpet and take her, rucking up the billowing ball gown, feeling silk-clad legs wrap tightly around his hips.

Just as he was about to give in to the temptation, the sound of footsteps and men's voices echoed from down the hall—coming this way! "Quick, into the other room," he whispered, shoving her through the open door. Taking a seat on the corner of the heavy cherrywood conference table, he straightened his clothes and smoothed back his hair, draping one arm casually across his thigh to conceal the telltale bulge in his trousers.

Cain was able to get rid of the two half-drunken mercantile owners with a minimum of fuss once he pointed out to them that the mayor's suite, to which they'd been invited for drinks, was at the opposite end of the hallway. As soon as they ambled out the door, he quickly closed it, then pulled open the other door, where Alexa was hiding.

She was gone. The French windows leading onto the outside balcony were open, the lace curtains blowing softly in the night breeze. One swift glance up and down the long porch indicated that she had made good her escape from him. It was no doubt for the best. If they'd made love there on the floor she would have hated him afterward. Already he knew the arrogant stubborn little chit well enough to be certain of that.

"I should be grateful," he muttered to himself, combing his fingers through his hair in frustration. "She'd probably have run crying to Jubal.'' The minute he said the words aloud, he knew they weren't true. Alexa was too proud to admit that she'd succumbed to passion, least of all with a man like him—and too honest to lie about her own complicity in the act.

''Princess Alexa, what will happen to you now?'' he wondered as he closed the French windows and retraced his steps back into the conference room. Powell was certainly going to break off the deal with MacKenzie. After the firestorm of tittering gossip that swept the ballroom tonight, the Indian-hating Central Pacific chief would see no other option. Perhaps not least of all because Alexa's name had been linked to Cain's own. That for sure would disgust the aristocratic Andrew Powell. And weak-livered little Larry would go along with whatever his father said.

Would Jubal send her packing back to St. Louis? Cain doubted it. The old man was too stubborn to bow to gossip. But then he might be moved to protect his granddaughter from further hurt by sending her away, perhaps even to the East Coast or Europe. It was that protectiveness that had backfired tonight. The old man should have warned the girl what she would be up against this evening—Christ, as if she could be oblivious to the backbiting! Anyway, it was no concern of his.

Then why did it eat at him so fiercely? He could still see the tears she tried to hide glistening in her aquamarine eyes, feel her trembling in his arms. He'd found her alone in the dark but not the way he'd described to her. He knew she was no intruder because he'd seen her wandering down the hallway like a lost soul and followed her. When she stepped inside the dark, deserted room he knew she wanted to be alone—but was powerless to grant her wish.

From the moment he saw her gliding across the floor in Larry's arms, a vision in silk and pearls, he had ached to hold her again. ''Forget her, Cain. She's nothing but trouble for a man like you,'' he chastised himself as he walked down the long deserted corridor leading back to the mezzanine. There was a lot of work to do before the night ended.

But the idea nagging in the back of his mind would not let him alone. The day MacKenzie had commissioned him to search for his granddaughter, he had first thought of it, then dismissed it as crazy, a pie-in-the-sky dream. When he saw her emerging from the stream at Leather Shirt's camp, it recurred with sudden impact, for she was a beauty, not the homely spinster he'd imagined. He knew the chances of keeping secret what had happened to her were slim and he also knew what Andrew Powell would do when he learned the truth.

This is your golden opportunity to take something away from the bastard—something he's too stupid to value.

But it was not so simple as that. Jubal might fire him for his temerity. Even if the old man agreed, Alexa might spit in his face. *Alexa.* She was dangerous, very dangerous. He desired her too much. That gave her power to wound him in ways that he had never even let himself imagine before. But she was the key to it all—to destroying Powell and achieving everything he had dreamed of since he had been a boy in Enoch's classroom.

Cain walked down the wide marble stairs and began another discreet sweep of the ballroom, looking for potential trouble. As the night grew late, guests often drank too much, resulting in fisticuffs. Occasionally an uninvited visitor tried to steal some man's money clip or woman's jewelry. This was as much a part of his job as controlling brawling track workers or negotiating with hostile Indians along the trail.

He was tired of living by his fists and his gun, tired of risking his life, tired of working for wages—albeit in recent years the wages had been damn good. He wanted what the men at the top had—the powerful, independent rich white men who built railroads and empires. But those men were risk-takers. None—not Powell, not MacKenzie—got where they were without risk.

If he didn't take the risk, he would never be given another chance like this. Would the price of his dream be too high?

"There's only one way to find out."

Chapter 8

"But Father, she's beautiful and innocent—I can sense—"

"You couldn't sense a polecat if it sprayed a whole damn prayer meeting!" Andrew Powell spat out contemptuously. "You're thinking with what's between your legs, not what's between your ears."

Lawrence reddened at the crudity. "That's not true."

Andrew's lethal blue stare skewered his son, who instantly backed off.

"What I mean is . . . Alexa was quite forthcoming about the whole ghastly experience. She assured me that the savages didn't abuse her—they only wanted to trade her for guns."

"Which *Cain* so handily supplied. In the most unlikely event those bucks didn't use her, do you suppose *he* would pass up the opportunity?"

Lawrence shifted uneasily from one foot to the other. The tight collar of his silk shirt was constricting his breathing and the superfine jacket he wore was growing warmer by the minute. A damp sheen of perspiration dotted his flushed face. Unclenching his hands from their white-knuckled grip on the bar in his father's office, he took a calming breath. "Do you think he really hates me that much?"

Andrew snorted dismissively as he poured himself a late-night libation. "You scarcely matter to him. But he damn

well hates *me* that much.'' He jerked loose the black silk
tie at his throat and took a deep swallow of the fine, aged
cognac.

"This is all going to be horribly embarrassing after the
ball tonight. Everyone there expected that we'd announce
our engagement. Alexa will be—''

"The hell with Alexa!'' Powell slammed down his glass
furiously. "When my agents first reported that the girl had
been taken by Indians, then brought to MacKenzie by Cain,
I hoped it was all a mistake. Damn, I wanted that entrée to
MacKenzie's camp. Inside information about the Union Pacific would have been useful, quite useful. . . .'' He took
another swallow of cognac and stared into the amber liquid
pensively. "The gossip tonight spread across that ballroom
like wildfire. Even that silly chit of a girl must've heard
something. She looked pale as a ghost by the end of the
night. She's ruined in our circles. I will not have the Powell
name linked to a woman soiled by savages. For all we know
she could be carrying Cain's bastard in her belly.''

Lawrence paled, sucking in his breath.

"Never even thought of that, did you? A redskin bastard
for your firstborn heir.''

Lawrence's shoulders slumped dejectedly. "Well, I suppose there's nothing else to do. I'll have to—''

"You will do nothing. I will inform MacKenzie the marriage is off. That wily old fox thought he could bluff his
way through this mess with me none the wiser.''

"His mistake,'' Lawrence said softly.

"Yes, his mistake, indeed,'' his father echoed, savoring
his last swallow from the cut-crystal glass. "No help for it,
we shall just have to rely on other expedients to see that the
Central Pacific wins the race across Utah.''

After receiving Powell's tersely worded message that morning, Jubal had fumed and stormed, cursing Andrew Powell
and his spineless son, the Central Pacific Railroad, the Cheyenne Indians and the gossiping old biddies of Denver. He
had been awkwardly solicitous in explaining the broken en-

gagement to Roxanna, assuring her that everything would turn out all right in the end. But Roxanna knew better. The whispers, the pointed stares, the men who leered knowingly and the women who held their skirts away from contamination when they passed her on the street, none of that would ever go away.

A hysterical burble of laughter choked her. Here she was, Alexa Hunt, Indian captive, faced with the same social stigma she had endured as Roxanna Fallon, spy. The irony of the situation did not escape her. She had expected Jubal to make prompt arrangements to send her packing, but the old Scot surprised her. He did not suggest that she should run and hide. Rather the opposite. He was fighting mad and ready to take a stand. If she had the courage to stay with him and hold her head up proudly, the two of them would face down the gossips.

She had done that for five years. At least now she would not be alone. Jubal's wealth and power were a considerable deterrent to the sort of persecution she had suffered before. She refused to dwell on what would happen if he learned she was an impostor. What would happen if he knew she would have let Cain take her on the floor last night like some harlot? If they had not been interrupted . . . She shook off the thought, terrified of where it would lead. Her first reaction to the news of the broken engagement had been a heady sense of relief. In spite of liking Larry Powell—or perhaps because she did—Roxanna had not wanted to marry him. But if that relief stemmed from her attraction to Cain, she was three times a fool.

He wanted only one thing—her body, and even that only in passing. He had made clear that he did not love her. In fact, he bitterly resented the hold their mutual attraction had on him. A man like him was the very last sort she could rely upon, the last she should ever care for.

I don't care for him. I'll never love any man, she repeated her vow to herself stubbornly. Still her wayward thoughts turned to Cain irresistibly. He would soon hear that she was free, if he did not already know. Might he . . . ? "I'll be damned if I sit around like a whipped puppy waiting on the high and mighty Mr. Cain to come riding up to save me," she gritted out. As if he would.

Denver, nouveau riche and newly respectable, waited outside her window. She would not hide indoors on a beautiful day. Let the fine folks of the city gossip about her to their hearts' content. Miss Alexa Hunt was going for a ride!

Cain walked into MacKenzie's suite, his usual cool, self-confident manner in place. He had been taught as a boy living with his mother's people to conceal his fear, learned the lesson doubly well after moving into the white world. Now he would see how good a bluff he could run. He was about to take the risk of his life. Sweat trickling down between his shoulder blades reminded him of that. The next few moments would make him or break him.

Jubal looked up from the mountain of papers on the table serving as his desk, waving Cain to have a seat. "How are the gun crews working out? You never did give me that report before we left Cheyenne."

Cain eased into the chair and stretched out his long legs, shrugging. "Kennedy at least has his squad hitting the target half the time. Davie's men can be ready to fight off an Indian attack in two minutes flat, but Wiley couldn't organize a pissing contest in a brewery. He's hopeless. I told him I was giving O'Mara charge of their group. He's a galvanized Yankee who knows how to lead men."

Jubal harrumphed. "I find it difficult to trust a man who'd trade sides in a war, but I'll defer to yer judgment."

That's a good start, Cain thought, pleased as he leaned forward in his chair. "I didn't come here to talk about gun crews, Jubal."

MacKenzie put down the timber contract he was about to hand Cain and studied him. "What's put a bur under yer blanket, then?"

"I know Powell's backed out of your deal and the wedding is off."

"So will everyone between the Rocky Mountains and the

Pacific Ocean by this afternoon,'' the old man said sourly, waiting to see where this would lead. He was suddenly very interested. *Let him play out his hand. . . .*

"The scandal has ruined Alexa. Are you sending her back East?" He knew MacKenzie never ran from a fight.

"No."

"No white man who knows she's been a captive will touch her, Jubal," Cain said baldly. "You've lived out here long enough to know that's true."

"Aye. Even if it isna' a thing against the purr lass."

"Hating someone for something they can't control isn't fair, but when it comes to Indians, it's the code of the West," Cain said with a bitter half smile.

MacKenzie steepled his big blunt fingers and leaned back in his chair, studying the younger man. *Like yerself.* "Go on," he prodded.

He knows where this is leading. Damn, he should have known the wily old Scot would be one jump ahead of him— MacKenzie was two jumps ahead of everyone else. "I'll marry Alexa."

Jubal bit the end off one of his cigars, lit it and inhaled deeply before he replied. "Are you in love with the lass?"

Cain met his level gaze head-on. "I've never lied to you, Jubal. No, I'm not in love with her, but I'd treat her kindly. She's a beautiful woman—and I happen to be the only man in a position to know she's never been touched."

"Would it bother you if she had been?"

A strange look passed over Cain's usually inscrutable face for an instant, then vanished behind the mask. "I don't honestly know. Being part Indian, I shouldn't look at it the way a white man would."

"But yer white in yer thinking, not Cheyenne." MacKenzie was pleased when Cain's bronze face flushed.

"I don't suppose I'd like it any better if a white man had used her rather than a red one, but that's beside the point. She's still a virgin and there's not a man alive outside this room who believes it."

"And yer willing to marry a ruined woman who's the

brunt of everyone's gossip. Christian charity, lad? Or do you want something in return?''

A dark smile etched itself across Cain's swarthy face. "You finally cut to the chase, I see.''

"Aboot time somebody did,'' Jubal retorted.

"You fired Brent Masterson two months ago and never replaced him. I know you figured young Powell would take over. Now that's out. I want to be the operations chief.'' The words hung on the air like cigarette smoke in a crowded saloon.

Jubal took a long slow draw on his cigar, then exhaled. "So you want to be 'the man.' '' He grinned wryly. "You certainly have a prize set of ballocks on you, lad.''

"You know I can do it. Hell, I've been doing half of Masterson's work for the past year already.''

Jubal knew that was true. Cain possessed keen intelligence, a surprisingly good education and fierce ambition. His Indian blood was the only impediment to his success in the railroad business—or any other business, for that matter. "Alexa is my only heir. The man who marries her will inherit my estate when I die.''

"You're not apt to curl up your toes anytime soon that I can see. I want the chance to prove to you what I can do, not the opportunity to squander your damned millions.''

"To prove it to me . . . or someone else, I wonder?'' MacKenzie murmured almost to himself.

Cain did not respond to that, only asked, "Will you consider it?''

"Aye, I'll consider it, Cain.''

After Cain had left, the old man stared at his desktop, lost in thought. Eventually, a smile spread slowly across his face. Slowly, the smile gave way to a chuckle. Jubal MacKenzie, builder, had a very interesting idea.

Roxanna could feel the stares as she rode down the street. Some fresh clean mountain air would be welcome after the reception she had received in Denver. How long until they returned to Cheyenne? Perhaps she could convince Jubal to take her with him to the Union Pacific work camp farther up the line. Even if she was the center of gossip, she would enjoy the excitement of seeing history made on the transcontinental.

Lawrence Powell watched Alexa ride out of the city, headed toward the mountains. The grizzled old stableman accompanying her for protection looked mean enough to bite off a buzzard's nose. Not much of a chaperon, but then her days of worrying about such social niceties were certainly over. He cursed his rotten luck and wondered if what his father had intimated was possible.

She was a real beauty, with all that silver gilt hair, milky skin and wide turquoise eyes, the kind of woman any man would be proud to have on his arm. Her body was exquisite as her face, slender and fine-boned yet nicely curved. The elegant rose pink riding habit she wore accented her tiny waist and the soft swell of her bosom.

Yes, she was stunning. A pity, but he knew what he must do. Kneeing his horse into a canter, he rode out to intercept her, glad for her choice of such an isolated route. If his father learned that he had approached her, Lawrence knew the old man would be livid.

Roxanna recognized her former fiancé almost immediately. *Fiancé.* For all of a few hours! She wondered if he had been the one to spurn her. Somehow she suspected not after seeing the way the elder Powell controlled his son. She felt a bizarre stab of pity for Larry Powell, then laughed at the incongruity of that—she the fallen woman feeling sorry for the millionaire's fair-haired son.

"Good afternoon, Miss Alexa. I'd say I ran into you quite by accident, but I'm afraid I'm a terrible liar."

Roxanna watched his fair complexion pinken. *He's embarrassed.* She smiled coolly. "Good afternoon, Mr. Powell. I take it you intended to speak with me discreetly?"

"It would have been awkward going to your hotel after all that's happened." He gestured vaguely with one hand, then lapsed into silence, eyeing the old man who had reined in his mount a distance behind them.

"Yes, most awkward indeed," she agreed. For one awful moment Roxanna imagined that he had come to ask her to be his mistress now that she was too tarnished to be his wife. This would scarcely be the first time in her life that she'd been offered such a tawdry proposition.

But then he dispelled the thought as he stammered, "Alexa, I apologize for what's happened. You're a lady who deserves better. If it weren't for my father . . . well, I would never have broken the engagement. I suppose you think me a cad for going along with his decision."

"Considering everything, no," she replied evenly, relieved at this turn in the conversation. *I could never have married him.*

"I tried to reason with Father, to explain that nothing happened to you, but he never listens to me."

She detected a sullen note of bitterness in his voice. Being Andrew Powell's only son and heir must not be an easy life, not an easy life at all.

"All he thinks of is what society deems proper. They're a bunch of backbiting gossips who no one of consequence should regard."

"But they do. We all must live by their rules, Larry," she said softly, once again reverting to the familiar address as he had.

"I just wanted to tell you how much I regret breaking the engagement—and to assure you it was not my idea."

He looked into her eyes, his face so round and smooth and boyish, almost like a puppy who expected to be cuffed. Andrew Powell had much to answer for, she decided. "I appreciate you taking the trouble to seek me out and say that."

"What will you do . . . now? Go back East?"

She shrugged. "I don't know. Grandfather isn't one to slink away when he's been insulted."

"But that's a man's reaction. A lady like you shouldn't have to endure such indignity because of his pride."

She smiled at his own indignation in her defense. *If only*

you knew how much worse I've already endured. "I shall survive, Larry."

"I know I don't appear very reliable at present, but, Alexa . . . if you ever need a friend . . . I want you to know that you can count on me."

"Thank you, Larry. I appreciate that, especially considering how unsettled my future is right now."

He extracted an embossed card from his coat pocket and handed it to her. "My address in San Francisco and a place where you can wire me in an emergency."

He really was serious, she realized as she placed the card in her skirt pocket, then smiled at him.

"If ever I'm in trouble and my grandfather can't help me, I shall call upon you."

"I've decided to accept yer deal," Jubal MacKenzie said without preamble when Cain walked into his office on the Pullman railcar.

Over a week had passed since the debacle in Denver. Cain had returned to the construction camp outside Laramie the following day, but Jubal had other business to conduct in the larger city. He and Alexa had remained behind for another day, then made the dusty journey via private coach.

Cain had answered the old man's summons early this morning with considerable curiosity—and more than a bit of trepidation. Would he be summarily fired for his brass—or would he get Alexa and the position which he had wished for so long? He had his answer. He nodded to Jubal. "I wasn't certain you'd agree to mixing MacKenzie blood with a mongrel strain like mine. I'll treat her well, Jubal."

"There's one condition," the old man said, raising a gnarled hand in caveat. "Alexa has to agree to the marriage."

The tension in Cain drained away, but a subtle simmer of anger replaced it. "You were willing to give her to Powell without asking her opinion."

"Do na' get yer back up. If she'd told me she couldna' abide the Powell boy I wouldna' have forced her either."

A ghost of a smile touched his lips. "Besides, yer the one who brought up yer mongrel blood, not me. I frankly do na' give a damn what color yer ma was as long as you do the job for me, but women . . ." he shrugged helplessly. "They set store by different standards and Alexa's been raised in a sheltered environment."

Cain banked the anger, realizing the blunt old man was merely stating facts. MacKenzie had been, all in all, far fairer to him than most men in his position would ever have been. "Alexa will have me, don't worry," Cain said with a confidence he was far from feeling.

"Will she, now?" Jubal gave Cain a measured look.

"Don't say anything about our arrangement. Just let me talk to her."

The old man dug his fingers in his beard, which had been considerably shorn by a Denver barber, and asked, "You seem awfully sure of yerself. Just exactly what passed between you and my granddaughter while you were alone together in Nebraska?"

"Nothing," Cain replied flatly. "If I'd touched her, you'd have had me flayed alive and we both know it." The fact that he had almost touched her in spite of that he judiciously did not mention.

"Aye, I would have. I suppose it's lucky for you things turned out the way they have now," he added enigmatically.

Roxanna had found the week on the road with the rail crews almost fascinating enough to take her mind off the mess in Denver. If Cain still invaded her dreams at night, the days were filled with new sights and sounds to distract her. Each morning at dawn the loud jangle of the cook bell awakened the Union Pacific town on wheels. The first day she had roused herself from a restless sleep to watch another mile and a half of track being laid in the relentless push to the Pacific.

The construction camp of track layers, which followed the grading crews, was itself mobile and ingeniously designed to Jubal's exact specifications and included over twenty work cars. Besides Jubal's own elegant Pullman in which the two of them had private quarters, there were bunkhouses for the men, kitchens, dining rooms, storerooms, tool houses and an arsenal built on wheels, even a blacksmith shop for the horses and mules which pulled the endlessly arriving wagon loads of rails, spikes, fishplates and bolts, shipped all the way from foundries across the Mississippi River.

The polyglot of brawling workers ate in shifts in the long dining cars where they were crammed in like sardines. In the interest of efficiency, their tin dinner plates were nailed to the narrow plank tables and washed between servings by a boy none too carefully wielding a mop. The men staggered into the mess hall on wheels in the predawn light, grumbling and wiping sleep from their eyes, eager for a cup of bitter black coffee to revive them for the backbreaking day's labor.

And backbreaking it was, as Roxanna observed the amazing efficiency of the tracklaying crews from a discreet distance. Like the few other respectable women, all wives of higher-ranking employees, Roxanna was not allowed near the crude and blasphemous workmen. But even from a distance she could hear the oaths of teamsters rise above the crack of their whips as they urged their teams onward, heavily laden with thousand-pound iron rails and the fittings with which to join them into a metal ribbon stretching to the horizon.

She took to rising early and riding before breakfast. The jovial banter of the crewmen blended with the smell of boiled oats, horse manure and dust. As they neared the highest point on the transcontinental route, over eight thousand feet in elevation, the wind carried a brisk thin bite in spite of the clear blaze of the sun. Roxanna loved the clean smell of sagebrush and mountain yellow rose and even grew accustomed to the less fragrant odors indicative of progress.

Of course she was not allowed to wander far from camp, for raiding Indians were always a threat. This morning she had overslept and hurried to throw on her riding habit, eager, for some unnamable reason, to escape the luxurious confines of Jubal's mobile palace. Without bothering the old man, whom she knew was already poring over surveyor's reports, supply orders and payroll accounts, she slipped out the back and headed for the livery car, where a fleet roan mare was kept, assigned for her personal use.

Already anticipating the wind in her hair and the freedom to gallop up to the ridge and look down on the beehive of activity below, she walked briskly down the tracks, passing bewhiskered old teamsters and burly young workmen, all leathered dark by years in the sun and wind. All of them tipped their hats respectfully. Some were bashful around the boss's granddaughter, while others returned her nod with sly appraising looks. She ignored these.

The big smithy, Shamus Manion, smiled when she approached the car. "Top o' the mornin' ta ya, Miz Alexa. You'll be wantin' that pretty little roan," he said, putting down his anvil. He directed a gangly youth to fetch the mare from the rope corral and saddle her. Then he turned back to Roxanna. "You be careful out there today. We had a wee bit o' trouble last night. One o' the men, right full of liquor he was, came sashayin' into camp after midnight and picked a fight. A right royal row he started too. Half a dozen men were involved before Cain put a stop to it."

At the mention of Cain's name, she paled. "Was anyone hurt?"

"A few bruised knuckles and split lips for the ones left standin'. Cadwallader Cooke didn't fare so well. Himself it was who started the fracas. Cain used his pistol on that thick Welsh head, not that it'll teach that one much. You can be sure he has a fine headache this mornin', though. Cain fired him then and there. Sent him packin', but the blockhead made some pretty ugly threats on his way out o' camp."

"That must've been what I heard when I awakened last night. You don't think he'd return and cause more trouble, do you?"

"Niver know with the likes o' that one. Cain packed him on a handcar and sent him back to Cheyenne, but I'd keep a sharp eye out. Stay close,'' he admonished as he took the reins of the roan from the stockboy and assisted her to mount.

''I'll be careful,'' she said, scanning the ridge which was mostly open grassland with a few clumps of aspen and spruce scattered randomly about. ''Not much place to hide up this high.''

Since Shamus always fretted about her safety, she saw no particular reason for concern about Cadwallader Cooke. He was miles from here by now, probably nursing his aching head in a Cheyenne saloon. She urged her fleet little mare up the gently sloping ground until she reached a copse of spruce, then turned to watch the activity in camp. Out of the welter of color, movement and noise, her eyes quickly found Cain riding his chestnut stallion between the lines of sweating, straining men who lifted the steel rails from a wagon bed and carried them to the end of the track.

Why did he always have to stand out in any group, no matter where it was? She remembered how he had looked in elegant evening clothes that night in Denver, dark and dangerous as an expensive eastern gambler. ''I imagine the ladies secretly swoon over him, even when they're pretending to be shocked by his Indian blood,'' she murmured irritably to herself, tearing her eyes away as he dismounted at the horse corral.

Well, they were both pariahs now, she mused bitterly, feeling a flicker of reluctant kinship for the half-breed. Jubal was constantly assuring her that life would be better once the Union Pacific was completed and they could return east. No one there would have heard the scurrilous rumors about her. After the years and miles she had already spent trying unsuccessfully to live down her past, Roxanna doubted it.

She still harbored a lurking dread that Isobel Darby would pop up to unmask her, leaving her bereft even of Jubal MacKenzie's support. Odd, in the brief weeks she had spent with the old man, she had come to respect his canny intelligence and enjoy his gruff company. The thought of seeing betrayal and hurt in his eyes disturbed her deeply. She had never meant to hurt anyone, but already her desperate gambit posing as Alexa Hunt was turning into a disaster almost as bad as her past life as Roxanna Fallon.

Deep in thought, Roxanna did not see the figure slip from behind the spruce tree as she dismounted and walked her horse to a nearby outcrop of rocks. While the mare stood patiently, she took a seat on sun-warmed shale, which was sheltered from the wind by a stand of spruce. Then his voice interrupted her solitary musing.

"Well, sunbeam, hain't ye a pretty one."

Roxanna gasped, jumping from her perch to face a tall cadaverously thin man with a small head that was sporting an ugly reddish black bruise between strings of greasy tan hair hanging on his forehead. Cadwallader Cooke! Malicious green eyes, set close together in a mean narrow face, stared speculatively at the curve of her breasts. She tugged on her mare's reins as the horse shied nervously, reacting to the ripe odor of sour sweat and sourer hatred.

"I'm not your sunbeam," she said coldly, patting the shying mare's neck to calm her. "Why don't you leave now and I won't report you for your rudeness?"

"Report me rudeness!" he sneered. "The Scot's Injun cain't fire me twice. Ye be the old man's granddaughter. A proud un, hain't ye?" he whispered as he moved nearer, stepping between her and the mare.

"Cain will come if I scream. This time he'll do a lot worse than crack your thick skull," she threatened. The nauseating smell of his body swamped her with ugly memories of the prison in Vicksburg. Roxanna felt her knees tremble and fought to keep from gasping for breath as her heartbeat accelerated. She stared him down, knowing there was nothing else she could do, praying this time it would be enough.

He laughed. "Hain't nobody down there going to hear ye, least of all that bloody bastard Cain. High 'n mighty ye be for a female who spread her legs fer redskins. Probably fer Cain too. Well, now ye'll give ole Caddy a turn," he said as one long bony arm snaked out and wrapped around her waist.

As Roxanna screamed and struggled, the mare whinnied in fright, then bolted away. Cooke ignored the horse, concentrating on the woman, whom he pulled to the ground in spite of her flailing legs and sharp nails. He held her down, straddling her body, while he attempted to pin her arms and stop her clawing at him.

Roxanna could feel his weight bearing down on her, imprisoning her arms and legs. Panic began to engulf her as the old feeling of utter helplessness hovered. *Don't give in, don't give in*, she repeated to herself as his fetid breath fanned her face. She turned her head away and screamed again, bucking to dislodge him.

"Ye be a strong one fer being so skinny," he grunted as he lost his balance and rolled to one side.

Roxanna could feel his long bony fingers digging into her shoulders to stop her thrashing. Then her temple struck a jutting piece of shale and everything faded into merciful oblivion.

Chapter 9

As if it were not bad enough to learn Cooke had over-powered the handcar operator delivering the troublemaker to the Cheyenne jail, Cain had just learned Alexa was riding about unescorted. Then he heard her screams coming from the copse of trees surrounding the rocky outcrop ahead and spurred his horse forward, cursing. Before he reached the cover of the trees her cries ceased abruptly. Then he saw her lying limply as the filthy bastard straddled her body, tearing at her clothes.

Cain pulled the chestnut to a skidding halt and leaped from the saddle. "Cooke!" he yelled, to keep the man's hands from baring her breasts. Before Cadwallader Cooke could do more than swivel his head around, Cain was on him, knocking him across the hard rocky ground with a fist planted squarely in the center of his face. Blood spurted from Cooke's nose as Cain felt the satisfying crunch of cartilage snapping.

Cooke bleated in surprised pain as he fell backward, then rolled up, clawing at the pistol stuffed in the back of his belt. He was still raising it, his thumb on the uncocked hammer, when Cain's bullet tore into his body. Cadwallader Cooke flew backward against a large sandstone boulder, then slid slowly down and crumpled into a ragged heap in the dust.

Giving the corpse only a brief glare, Cain turned, holstered his Smith and Wesson and hurried to Alexa's side. He could see she was breathing and began to check for injuries. The son of a bitch had torn the buttons off her blouse. He did what he could to pull it together, covering the soft delicate mounds, remembering how sweetly they had responded beneath his hands, his mouth. She expelled a little breathy sigh as he picked her up and carried her into the shade of a spruce.

Roxanna awakened in Cain's arms. At first she was disoriented, her fluttering lashes rising so that his harsh dark visage filled her field of vision. "Cain, what . . . where am I?" For an instant she thought they were still in the Cheyenne camp, but then Cadwallader Cooke's assault jarred her back into the present and she stiffened with fright.

"Shhh," he soothed, stroking strands of gleaming hair away from her face with gentle hands.

"That awful man—Cooke?" She winced when she raised her head.

He felt her shiver and the rage that had seized him when he saw that pig violating her washed over him once again. "Cooke's dead."

The flatness of his tone matched the shuttered expression on his face. "You killed him." It was not quite a question.

He ignored it, asking instead, "Where are you hurt?"

She raised her hand and gingerly touched the side of her head where a small lump was forming. "I struck my head on a rock, struggling—trying to get away from him." Cain examined the area with surprising gentleness. She felt the urge to let him soothe her with those marvelous bronzed hands, remembering other times when his fingers had touched her . . . and his lips. His angry voice quickly broke the spell.

"If you ever ride out of a rail camp alone and unarmed again, I'll paddle that lovely little ass of yours and lock you in the stock car for a hundred miles. What kind of a place do you think this is—some goddam Missouri plantation?"

Roxanna sat bolt upright in spite of the throbbing in her head. "I've been educated sufficiently to know geography. I've even been taught rudimentary politeness. Something sadly deficient in your education, you oaf!" His fierce scowl shifted into a mocking smile, which only added to her anger.

"My humble apologies, princess, but you do bring out the worst in me."

"I suspect that's because it's always lurking right under your skin," she replied tartly.

Cain chuckled. "Oh, you get under my skin, all right."

"I don't want anything to do with your skin—or any other part of you. You're insufferably rude—"

"And you're a reckless spoiled brat. Any female who steps outside her door without a man to protect her is fair game on the Union Pacific. I can't believe Jubal let you ride around like this. It's a miracle you weren't attacked by half the men in that camp."

"I suppose they all think I deserve it after the gossip that's been circulating about me," she said despondently, lowering her head into her hands to massage her aching temples. That was when she noticed her blouse gaping open, the buttons torn off, revealing a good deal more of her anatomy than was respectable.

When she tried to scramble away from him, clutching the cloth together, he held her in his arms. "Not so fast. You'll hurt yourself more if you fall, little fool."

"Let me go," Roxanna whispered, suddenly feeling all the violation and dirtiness of Cooke's bestial attack along with the humiliation in Denver and so many others long ago. She craved a bath.

Cain held her effortlessly as she struggled to escape his embrace. "Alexa, I'm sorry. I was . . . frightened because you placed yourself in danger. If I hadn't come up here looking for you . . . Cooke would have done worse than the Cheyenne ever thought of doing. I should've killed him a long time ago."

There was a hardness in his voice when he spoke of Cooke that did not quite register because she was focused on what he said before that. *If I hadn't come up here looking for you.* "Why were you looking for me? To paddle me for riding unescorted, or were you simply going to lock me in the stock car without the benefit of a trial?"

She looked so small and vulnerable, sitting on his lap with her hands clutching the remnants of her blouse protectively over her breasts. His smile now was genuine, gentle. "I never thought of locking you up when I rode out here, but maybe that's not a half bad idea."

She looked at him warily. "Why?" she asked. As he released her, she edged off his lap to sit on the ground across from him. Roxanna had hoped for a certain security in placing even a few feet of distance between them, but his dark piercing eyes would not grant it. They skewered her intently.

"You know why old man Powell broke the engagement?" he asked bluntly.

Roxanna's cheeks heated, but she continued to meet his eyes. *Why is he asking me this?* "You know that gossip is all vicious lies."

"Yeah, I know, but that doesn't stop it," he replied enigmatically.

"The vaunted Powell name can't have a breath of scandal attached to it," she said bitterly.

"I didn't bring up the broken engagement to hurt you, Alexa."

"Then why, Cain?" She sensed a coiled tension in his body, like a great sleek panther, poised to spring yet holding its powerful body under the tightest control.

"Because I want to marry you."

The words dropped between them like stones. He said nothing more, only waited for her to respond. "You're a bit late with your proposal, aren't you?" The anger began to churn in her then, oddly mixed with hurt. "Why didn't you ask me that night in Leather Shirt's village—or even the night of the ball when we . . ."

"Almost made love?" he supplied. "I couldn't, not while you had a chance to marry into society. If I'd taken advantage of you—forced you into marrying me as the only honorable course after you gave me your virginity—you'd have come to hate me."

He combed his fingers through his hair and looked away, at the far western horizon with its jagged pale lavender ridge of mountains. She studied his profile, bronzed and harshly beautiful as the wild landscape at which he stared. Then he swallowed, painfully, and Roxanna realized what he was saying. She placed one hand on his arm, tentatively. "I could never hate you, Cain, even when you make me angry enough to kill you."

He turned to her with that old mocking smile back in place. "We do strike sparks off each other, that's damn certain. It wouldn't be easy, Alexa. I'm a breed, no matter how white I live. I've always been outside the pale of respectable society. Most men like me marry Indian women— if they marry at all. I never thought to marry . . . until the day I saw you standing mother-naked in that river."

She remembered the scorching hunger in his eyes when he had boldly interrupted her bath. The same glittering light blazed in them now and she knew he saw an answering hunger in her eyes. "I'm hardly respectable marriage material myself." Thoughts of that long-ago night in Vicksburg flashed through her mind and she flinched, then suppressed the never-buried feelings of horror and shame, rushing on to say, "Grandfather thinks if we went east it would all be forgotten."

"Could well be. Is that what you want to do?" he asked guardedly, volunteering nothing more, sitting very still.

She shook her head. "No, it isn't. I don't want to run away from my past." *Not anymore.*

He let out the breath he had been holding. "I just don't want you to regret your lost chance to marry a man like Powell."

"I never wanted a man like Larry Powell." *I wanted you.*

"Then I guess you'll marry me," he said with a crooked smile, reaching out to pull her back into his arms.

"Yes, I guess I will," Roxanna replied just as his mouth came down on hers, hard and hot, his lips working their

magic. His tongue danced across her teeth, then plunged
deep inside her mouth until she arched against him, wrapping her arms around his neck and burying her fingers in
his thick night-dark hair. She felt his heart pounding as her
bared breasts pressed against his chest. One powerful arm
held her tightly while the other hand stroked her satiny silver
gilt hair.

She cried out when his mouth moved from hers, traveling
lower down her jaw to her throat. Then he buried his face
in the fragrant cloud of her hair as she brushed small frantic
kisses over his face, pausing to trace the narrow white scar
on his cheek with the tip of her tongue.

He groaned, breaking away from her and holding her by
her shoulders. His breath came in great panting gulps as if
he'd just run a great distance. She reached out, cupping his
face in her hands, eager for more kisses and caresses that
he wanted so dearly to give. But he held her at arm's length,
shaking his head until he could speak. "No, Alexa. Not
here, not like this. I'm not some savage and I won't take
you like one. We'll be married first and make love in a soft
bed with candles and wine . . . and privacy. Besides," he
added with grim humor, "there's a dead man over there."

She looked down, feeling the heat in her cheeks. "I've
never behaved like this with any man . . . but you."

Cain smiled and tipped her face up by touching her chin
with his finger. His smile was pure male predatory posses-
siveness. "I know . . . and I like it that way. You belong
only to me, Alexa."

You belong only to me. Cain's words haunted her that night
as she lay in her big soft bed in Jubal's railcar. The old man
had taken the news of her decision to wed Cain with surprising equanimity. She had half expected him to rail about
her marrying beneath the MacKenzie name or even fire Cain
summarily for having the audacity to touch a white woman.
Instead he had nodded to Cain, saying only that they would
talk later.

Jubal had lectured her sternly about her folly in riding so

far from camp, repeating the same warnings Cain had given her, albeit in a gentler fashion. Roxanna had acted duly chastened this time, still half expecting some question about her acceptance of Cain's proposal. The only thing he asked her was whether she was certain about her decision. Upon receiving her assurance that she was, he awkwardly embraced her and told her Cain was a good man. No one spoke of love. But considering that love had not entered into the arrangement with Larry Powell, she supposed it was reasonable that Jubal would expect this marriage to be no different.

Shouldn't a grandfather want his only granddaughter to marry for love? The question nagged at her. But then neither Jubal nor Cain knew she was not Alexa. Nor was she the innocent they both assumed. Nathaniel Darby, God rot him, had arranged that. She swung her legs over the side of the bed and stood up, reaching for her robe. Belting it, Roxanna hugged herself in silent misery. There would be no sleep now. Whenever she let down her guard and allowed thoughts of Vicksburg to surface, the nightmares haunted her, ugly visions of herself soiled with blood and semen, clinging to the back of a horse.

I need a bath. The thought came as it always did—as it had that night in the wilderness when she rode north in shame and despair. As she had made the ghastly trek to Federal lines, she kept telling herself what had happened was not her fault, that she was a victim, not a fallen woman. But all she had been able to think of was purging herself with lye soap and hot water. Once she reached safety, her strong young body was cleansed and healed in that dreamed-of bathwater. But deep inside of her soul, Roxanna Fallon still felt as defiled and filthy as she had the hour she rode away from Vicksburg.

Through the years since, many a fellow thespian had remarked on Roxanna's zealous penchant for cleanliness, often making it the joke of the company. One leading man in Memphis had dubbed her "Lady Macbeth," little knowing how close to the mark his barb had struck. Roxanna paced, trying desperately to hold her demons at bay.

But even if she succeeded, what would it profit her? Cain's harshly chiseled face and burning black eyes accused her. What would he think on their wedding night?

Would he be able to tell she had already lost her virginity? There was no way she could fake the awful pain of Darby's first thrust or the subsequent blood. His assault had been meant to punish. Surely if Cain had been the one to take her maidenhead it would not have hurt so much. That thought brought even greater pain. She pressed her knuckles to her lips in anguish. He should have been the one, and he had been cheated of his rightful due—in more ways than her virginity. "Liar and impostor," she murmured in the stillness, calling a spade a spade. Somehow deceiving a stranger she did not know so that she could marry him for his money had not seemed half so dishonest as deceiving a man she had come to love in spite of the fact he had no money.

"What can I do? Tell him the truth and risk losing him— or bind him to me through marriage and risk his distrust if he realizes I'm not a virgin?" She stared out the window into the darkness. The night gave her no answers.

The infamous half-breed gunman, the Scot's Injun, and Miss Alexandra Hunt of St. Louis, were married two days later in Cheyenne. The wedding was scarcely the gala event that had been anticipated when she was to marry Lawrence Powell in the Episcopal cathedral in San Francisco. The small private ceremony was held in a storefront church on Hill Street and conducted by the city's only Presbyterian minister. Cain and Roxanna exchanged their vows with due solemnity. Jubal MacKenzie and Reverend Fulmer's wife were their witnesses. After the reverend had pronounced them man and wife, Mrs. Fulmer brought forth the reverend's book for the bride and groom to sign.

"You must put down your full Christian name, Mr. Cain," the reverend prompted carefully.

"My name is Cain. I earned it," he replied in that cold

deliberate tone Roxanna had come to know so well. When he approached Mrs. Fulmer, who stood by the register, she backed away as if he held a scalping knife in his hand instead of a pen. He signed the single name with a bold flourish, then he handed the writing instrument to his wife.

With trembling hands she forged "Alexandra Hunt Cain" under the old harridan's thin-lipped disapproving stare. She could not help but wonder if the document was legal. But they had pledged themselves to each other before God and tonight those vows would be consummated.

After leaving the hostile presence of Mrs. Fulmer, Jubal took the newlyweds to the Pilgrim House Hotel for a wedding supper. The lobby off the dining room was crowded with the usual assortment of frontier types who frequented an upper-class hotel—traveling businessmen in expensive dark suits, leather-faced cattle barons in hand-tooled boots and occasionally their wives, well decked out in what they supposed were the latest eastern fashions.

Still feeling tense and awkward in their new roles as husband and wife, Cain and Roxanna said little, letting Jubal ramble on about his problems building a bridge over Dale Creek Canyon outside Laramie. As they wended their way toward the dining room, a few people who had heard about the shocking marriage between MacKenzie's heir and his half-breed subordinate stared and murmured among themselves. Jubal ignored them.

"I think we'll have to go at least one hundred thirty feet high because the wash is nearly seven hundred feet long. Timber's only a stopgap. We need iron supports but Durant and Company say the Union Pacific can't afford it." He snorted in disgust.

From the corner of her eye, Roxanna suddenly caught sight of a tall dark-haired woman dressed in dove-gray silk gliding down the hotel stairs. Something about the tilt of her patrician head, the hauteur of her carriage made Roxanna turn for a better look. Hate-filled brown eyes glared at her. A slow, malicious smile of triumph spread over Isobel Darby's thin elegant lips, then vanished.

"What is it, Alexa?" Cain asked when her hand stiffened on his arm and her step faltered abruptly.

Roxanna tore her gaze from her old nemesis, trembling violently. *Why now?* her mind railed in silent misery.

"Yer white as a wee ghostie, lass. What's wrong?" Jubal demanded.

Isobel Darby swept past them without a murmur, vanishing out the front door. Whatever game she played, she did not intend to unmask Roxanna before her marriage was consummated, although from the look she had given Cain, it was quite apparent that she knew precisely what was going on. "I . . . just felt a trifle light-headed, that's all," she temporized, glad of the steady strength of Cain's arm supporting her. *My husband.*

"We just need to get a bit of food in you. Bridal nerves," Jubal said to Cain with an indulgent smile for his granddaughter.

Cain studied his wife's pallor and wondered. They entered the crowded dining room, which exuded a certain rustic charm, its walls lined with racks of elk and deer antlers and a snarling grizzly's head mounted over a large fireplace. The heavy-hewn pine tables were each set with a bouquet of spring wildflowers. Jubal signaled a waitress who deferentially showed them to the table he had reserved in an alcove away from the noise of clattering crockery and whispered conversations.

Most of the diners were talking about them, Cain was certain. He had spent a lifetime becoming inured to sly glances and sotto voce murmurs behind his back, but he knew Alexa had not. Was she already regretting their marriage? The way she held tightly to him as if drawing support from him did not indicate regret. Perhaps she was feeling as confused and ambivalent about their arrangement as he was.

Cain did not intend to love his wife. Ever. He had been hurt too painfully in the past. Everyone he had loved had either died like Blue Corn Woman and Enoch or had betrayed him like his father and High-Backed Wolf. He would never be caught in that terrible trap again. Cain had assured himself that this woman was purely the means to an end. He had not lied to Jubal when he promised to treat her well, but he had not said he would love her either. Then why should it bother him so much if she was upset at the way people were reacting to their marriage? He'd warned her how it would be, he thought with an angry, silent oath.

Roxanna could sense a subtle change in Cain's demeanor as they took their seats at the table. He had been guarded and distant ever since they had met for the ceremony, but he had almost always been that way. Only for those brief moments in the Cheyenne camp had he let her inside the wall he so carefully erected around his heart. He desired her but acted as if he resented it. If so, why had he asked her to marry him in the first place?

Pity? She shuddered. No, her husband did not pity a woman he considered to be a spoiled headstrong child born to privilege. He simply wanted her as he said, and the only way he could have a woman like Alexa Hunt was through marriage. Of course, he had never spoken of love, but she had cherished the dream of teaching him to love her . . . to heal her. Would she have the chance—or would Isobel poison their relationship before it even began?

The first course of the bridal feast Jubal had ordered was set before her and sparkling pale gold champagne was poured. The men raised their glasses in a toast to her. Roxanna smiled and sipped. The expensive wine tasted like vinegar on her tongue. *Don't let Isobel Darby ruin this marriage. She's destroyed everything else in my life,* she pleaded silently, wholly uncertain if her prayer would be heeded.

As they ate dinner, Cain watched Alexa push small pieces of the roasted squab around on her plate, eating scarcely a bite of the hearty feast. By the time the traditional wedding cake was sliced and served, it was apparent that she could eat nothing more. "I think this has been a long day for Alexa. If you'll excuse us, Jubal?" he asked the old man as he pushed back his chair.

MacKenzie's florid face reddened in embarrassment as he nodded to Cain. "I have those architect's blueprints for the bridge to review yet," he harrumphed, all too aware of the bride's nervousness. "I'll see you in the morning—not too early," he hurriedly added, then flushed again as she kissed his cheek.

"Good night, Grandfather," Roxanna said with a grave smile. If only he knew the real reasons she was so terrified! Cain's arm felt strong and reassuring as he guided her through the hotel lobby, stopping only to pick up the key for their suite at the desk. The clerk, an elderly man with a harelip and close-set eyes the color of rusty nails, handed it to him disdainfully as if he were a British butler forced to serve a chimney sweep.

With every step nearer their quarters, Roxanna's tension grew until she was wound tightly as a wire on a reel. Cain unlocked the door and let it swing in on well-oiled hinges, then suddenly reached down and scooped her up in his arms. As her arms encircled his neck she gasped in surprise. He said gruffly, "It's traditional," then walked over the threshold into the sitting room with her holding on to him for dear life. She always felt so safe in his arms. *Never let me go, Cain.*

But as soon as he stood in the center of the room he deposited her on the carpet and stepped back, letting his eyes sweep over her, from the small pale pink feathered hat perched atop her carefully pinned-up curls to her matching pink dress of silk pongee, cut in the latest fashion with a bustled train trimmed with delicate Austrian lace. The soft color deepened her turquoise eyes and highlighted the gilded splendor of her hair. Although cut demurely high, the bodice of the dress clung seductively to the swell of her breasts and the skirt hinted at the curves of her hips. "You're beautiful," he said hoarsely.

Roxanna met his eyes and saw the banked fires in their ebony depths. He was beautiful too, severe yet sensual in black, with only the sheer snowy lawn of his shirt for accent. He wore those same sapphire cuff links and studs that she had noted the night of the ball and she imagined pulling them out, revealing that bronzed chest with its springy black hair. Her mouth went dry as she studied the harsh lines of his face. Unable to speak, she stepped hesitantly closer to him and reached up, letting one fingertip lightly graze the scar on his cheek.

His hand, large and dark, enveloped hers as he pressed it to his mouth, inhaling the faint scent of lilacs that clung to her skin. Her pulse thrummed frantically through the delicate blue veins of her wrist. Taking a deep breath, he placed both his hands around hers and held it between them like a pledge.

"I know you're frightened, Alexa. I've never taken a virgin before, but I'll go slow and try to make it good for you."

She placed her other hand on his. "Yes," she said simply, studying the contrast between his long dark fingers entertwined with her small white ones. Soon their naked bodies would be similarly intertwined. A spark of the heat and urgency in him seemed to leap to her. As he drew her toward the adjoining bedroom, she tried to banish from her mind Isobel Darby and the threat she presented. If all else was snatched away from her, she would have this night with Cain, her husband.

The bedroom was commodious with a large oval cheval looking glass standing in one corner and a chest-on-chest of carved oak against the far wall. A royal blue carpet covered the new pine floor planks. A large four-poster bed dominated the room. The coverlet of deep gold satin had been turned back, revealing pristine white sheets. Roxanna stared nervously at the sensuous invitation of the bed until Cain broke the spell by brushing the side of her neck with his lips.

"Take off that hat and I'll be your lady's maid," he whispered.

She stepped over to the mirror and dug into the fluffy pink feathers, extracting the ten-inch hatpin which held the concoction in place. When she placed it on a table with trembling hands, Cain came up behind her and began to remove the pins from her hair until it spilled like molten mercury down her back. As she stared at their image in the glass, he took a fistful of curls and held them to his cheek, rubbing the fragrant softness against his skin.

The subtlety of the caress warmed her. His hands, amazingly adept with tiny hooks and button loops, unfastened her gown and lifted it in a fluffy cloud over her head. He untied the tapes of her petticoats and let them fall to the floor. Then he began unlacing her corset cover while his lips nuzzled her bare shoulder. His dark head bending over her pale flesh reflected starkly in the mirror as the last dying rays of sunset came trickling through the lace window curtain across the room.

Roxanna reached up with one hand and buried her fingers in his hair, pulling him closer until she could feel a faint tremor pass through him. He desired her with a fierce savage passion yet held himself in check. She realized with a bittersweet pang that he did not want to frighten her.

"Why do women wear these infernal contraptions?" he murmured as he tossed her corset onto the carpet. "You don't need it." As if to illustrate his point, his hands encircled her waist, massaging the sensitive flesh of her sides and belly through her chemise. Frissons of heat spiraled in her stomach at the touch of his fingers and her breath caught raggedly.

Cain smiled against the silk of her hair. She was left standing clad only in her sheer batiste chemise and pantalets. He turned her to him to study the perfection of her body directly. Even the mirror could not do her justice.

"Just as I remembered at the water's edge—your legs, the curve of your hips, the sweet turn of ankle so delicate it shouldn't hold up a butterfly," he said hoarsely.

"I'm not that fragile, Cain," she replied, resting her hands on his chest. He was still fully dressed and she stood practically naked in her high heels!

As if reading her thoughts, he picked her up and carried her to the big bed, laying her carefully on the plumped-up pillows. He sat down beside her and took the calf of her leg in his hand, sliding off her silk slipper, then peeling down the filmy stocking. He repeated the process with her other leg. When he turned to pull his own boots off, she quickly seized the edge of the bedsheet and pulled it over herself. Her previous experience with being undressed before a man was nothing like Cain's slow savoring reaction to her body, yet she felt the lingering scars which made her want to hide herself.

He did nothing to discourage her nervous modesty. Instead he stood up and shrugged off his jacket, then began removing the sapphire studs from his shirt and cuffs, knowing she was watching him. With his back still turned to her, he said, "I like the feel of those turquoise eyes on me."

Roxanna flushed and squeezed them closed. He chuckled, a rich, low sound. She could not resist peeping.

"You wanted to watch me undress at the river. Now it's legal." Cain turned to give her a view of his dark chest as he slipped his shirt off and tossed it after his jacket and the jewelry. He started to reach for his fly and her lashes fluttered down once more. "You weren't this shy when I was naked and unconscious in Sees Much's lodge."

"That was different," she replied, staring at the ceiling. "You were injured . . . you weren't watching me . . ."

"Watching you?" he supplied with a smile. "Yeah, I remember how you took off when I woke up." He changed his mind about taking off his pants just yet. Instead he sat down on the bed beside her once more.

She turned to him, determined not to act like a vaporing virgin when she was nothing of the sort. But the fear was no act. She was afraid of what she felt for this enigmatic man who had wed her for his own mysterious reasons. And afraid of what he would learn about her all too soon.

Cain reached for her hand that clutched the sheet and lifted it to his chest, pressing it against the solid thud of his heart, which accelerated at her touch. "A woman has a great deal of power over a man, Alexa, if she learns how to use it."

Not the way I was initiated, she wanted to cry, but did

not. This would be completely different. He had promised to try to make it good for her. She believed he would. "Teach me what to do," she said, wanting to learn all there was to learn about the mystery of husbands and wives . . . and love.

Chapter 10

"Just be yourself, Alexa . . ." he murmured, bending down to press his lips to her throat, then to her ear, teasing the lobe between his teeth gently and flicking his tongue inside the delicate interior. "You have passion. I can sense it inside you . . . deeply buried . . . just waiting to be set free. . . . Trust me, don't be afraid." His low mesmerizing words were punctuated by soft brushing kisses along her neck to the frantically fluttering pulse at the base of her throat.

Roxanna felt soothed by the melodic cadence of his voice, the solid thud of his heartbeat, the warm hard pressure of his body. Of their own volition her arms wound around his neck, pulling him closer. She remembered the feel of his mouth on her breasts, suckling, teasing, making them ache. Would he do that again? Her body arched in anticipation when his lips trailed kisses to the lacy edge of her chemise, brushing the sheer fabric lower, pulling the drawstring so the neckline gaped open. The air touched her bare breasts and her nipples shrank into sharp points as if crying out for the heat of his mouth.

Cain too remembered touching her breasts, feasting on their pale creamy beauty. He raised his head and pulled away the opened chemise, cupping one small perfect globe in his hand, teasing the tip with thumb and finger, watching her body arch convulsively. "You like this, don't you, Alexa?'' She whimpered, turning her head into the pillow and digging her nails into his shoulders, urging him to suckle her. He needed no further invitation, taking one nipple in his mouth and gently massaging the other one with his thumb.

After pleasuring both of them, he said raggedly, ''I never saw breasts so lovely.'' His intent gaze swept up to her flushed face with thick pale lashes shielding her eyes. She was strung out tight, frightened and hungry all at once. He knew because he felt the same way—for completely different reasons. Sexual pleasure was as familiar to him as breathing, yet coupling with this woman would be different. He had desired her the first moment he had laid eyes on her, that had been no lie. But he feared how much, how intensely that desire drove him to need this—to need her. Desire was familiar, yes, but need was not.

She moved restlessly beneath him, tossing her head. Her hair slid across the pillows like shimmering quicksilver. He gave up trying to read more from her face and turned his attention back to her body. With a few deft motions, he unfastened the drawstring to her pantalets and pulled the frilly underwear low on her hips, then kissed and nipped a soft wet trail down to her navel. When the tip of his tongue dipped inside the tiny indentation, he could feel her quiver like a finely tuned violin string. Smiling against the silk of her belly he raised his head, retracing the path back to her breasts, then up to take her mouth once more in a deep slow kiss.

Roxanna let her tongue dart out to touch his, timidly at first, then with increasing boldness when he growled his approval deep inside her mouth. The shocking tantalizing things he had done to her body set her senses clamoring for more in spite of her fear. She was on fire, filled with an inexplicable longing she could never have imagined before.

When her tongue twined with his, sensuously sliding into his mouth, Cain was almost undone. His body, held under such rigid restraint as he slowly wooed her, now demanded surcease. He knew nothing about virgins but a great deal about women. She was ready . . . yet not. He could still sense a reticence in her. The residue of virginal fright? She did not know what went on between men and women. He would teach her. The thought gave him pause, for implicit in the pride of possession was the responsibility to care for a woman such as this. *Go slow. Don't frighten her with your passion until you can make her share it.*

Roxanna felt the loss of his warm body when he suddenly stood up and turned away from her. Had she done something wrong? Been too bold and forward returning his kisses? She longed to be held and caressed again, to feel cherished and desired. "Cain," she ventured softly, daring to keep her eyes open.

He jerked his head up but did not turn as he stood with his hands on the waistband of his pants. He could feel her eyes on his back, picture her softly parted lips as she spoke his name. He felt his shaft straining to be free of the constraining misery of his trousers. Would the sight of his erection frighten her? Once he turned back to her could he keep from falling on her like some wild randy boy? Never in his life had a woman affected him this way! Slowly, carefully he unfastened his pants and pulled them off, fighting all the while for control.

Roxanna stared at the rippling symmetry of muscles across his broad shoulders and back, then skimmed lower to the small hard buttocks and long sinuous muscles in his legs. She waited for him to turn back to her, but he did not.

Instead he stood still, completely naked in the dim light. His fists were clenched at his sides, his head thrown back. The only sound in the silent room was the deep shuddering sound of his breathing.

She sat up, oblivious to the chemise which hung around her waist, baring her breasts. "Cain . . . what's wrong?" *Come back to me.*

Slowly he turned to face her, his features contorted with the anguish of fierce desire. He watched her eyes drop to his swollen, straining phallus, then lift quickly. "Nothing's wrong, Alexa." *Except I want you too much.*

Roxanna took in the maleness of him, big and hard and hurtful looking. That was all a man's sex had been to her before. But this was Cain, her husband, and there was beauty in his desire, tempering it into something far different than the ugly violence of the past. *Don't think about that!* She watched the fluid grace of his movements as he stepped up to the bed and placed his knee on the edge of the mattress. His skin was bronzed, lightly furred with black hair across his chest, arrowing into a narrow vee on his washboard belly, then blooming into a thick tuft surrounding his male member.

Cain gave her little time for virginal panic, reaching out one hand to take hers. He pulled her up into a kneeling position facing him, then drew her into his arms. She came unresistingly, sliding her arms over his shoulders as he took her mouth in a soft deepening kiss. His arms enveloped her, pressing her tighter against him, tilting her hips to cradle his sex at the juncture of her thighs, then gently rocking back and forth against her.

She could feel the pressure of his engorged shaft almost thrusting through the thin barrier of her lace underdrawers. The size and heat seemed magnified as his hips moved against hers subtly while his hands finished the job of unfastening her pantalets and pushing them the rest of the way down her thighs, along with the loose chemise bunched at her waist.

"Lie down," he commanded, releasing her and lowering her to the bed and then following her, partially reclining on his side. He pulled her underwear completely off and tossed it from the bed. She lay completely naked now, her skin pale as cream in the gathering darkness. His fingers stroked the silkiness of her belly, skimming down her thigh and over the curve of her calf, then trailing back up the other leg, pausing to caress the slight swell of her hip.

She arched and preened instinctively, like a sunning kitten under the delicate ministrations, forgetting the utter vulnerability of her nakedness and the intimidating size of his phallus. Instead she simply soaked up the tender magic of his touch and his kisses raining soft as butterfly wings across her breasts and belly. But then his knee somehow insinuated itself between her thighs, spreading them, and his hand feathered over the soft curls at the juncture of her thighs. Involuntarily her muscles tightened.

"No, open to me, Alexa," he murmured low, feeling her resistance. "I won't hurt you." *Liar,* his conscience chided, but his body, so long denied surcease, could wait no longer to have her. The creamy moisture he felt when his fingers parted her soft petals told him she would never be more prepared to lose her virginity.

Roxanna surrendered to his soft urgent voice and let his hand find her. A sharp frisson of pleasure darted from where he was touching her so intimately, dancing along every nerve ending in her body, seeming to radiate right down to her toes. This had never been a part of her ugly past! She heard a low breathy sob and realized that it was her own voice, urging him to take more. *Now . . . now!*

Cain poised at the brink, so eager to plunge inside of her, yet unwilling to tear her delicate flesh. He moved his staff back and forth at her portal, lubricating his way with her generous moisture, then slowly, ever so gently he pushed forward. She was tight, incredibly tight and small, but he felt no other impediment as his thrust deepened bit by tiny bit. He waited for her cry of pain, bracing himself to stop if he hurt her, telling himself that he had the willpower to do it. But she made no sound other than soft breathless little pants as she clung to him.

Roxanna waited for the raw burning pain, fully expecting any second to have the hazy veil of heat and pleasure rent asunder. His phallus was large and hard, stretching her as he filled her. There was tightness and discomfort but no pain, only a compelling sense of completion when he seated himself full length inside of her. Her hips arched against his and her nails dug into his shoulders. She could feel his hesitation, as if he was testing her readiness, his body bowstring-taut, ready to explode. Suddenly, she too felt that tension.

Cain gritted his teeth to keep from spilling himself when he felt her hot velvet sheath completely envelop him. Then she moved and he was lost. With a guttural oath he rocked up and back, stroking slowly as his mouth sought out hers. He kissed her with far more fierce abandon than he allowed his lower body to exhibit . . . at first. But then she caught his rhythm, matching his thrusts, holding him with her legs tightly pressing around his hips. Cain could go slow no longer. His strokes grew swifter and fiercer, higher and harder.

Roxanna was spiraling out of control, bucking and arching, eager, no, desperate to have him drive even deeper . . . faster. She squeezed her eyes tighter and concentrated on the ever-widening waves of pleasure that washed over her, wondrously satisfying yet leaving her craving more.

More. Had she breathed the word aloud? She did not know, only rode with him, responding to each subtle shift in rhythm, reveling in the hardness of his muscled body pressing against her softness, coarse chest hair tickling sensitive breasts, faint bristles of a whiskered jaw abrading the delicate skin of her throat and face.

Then he stiffened suddenly and began to shudder uncontrollably, swelling and pulsing deep, oh, so deep inside of her, and she followed him over the top, unknowing, into a whole new world of such wonder it numbed her mind—but oh, her body! Her body soared with a blissful shattering pleasure that left her at last limp and utterly at peace with satiation.

Cain lay over her, his body still pressing hers into the soft mattress as he struggled to regain his breath after the glory of what they had shared. At least he hoped they had shared it. He could feel her arms, still holding him, the pads of her fingers now softly massaging where before her nails had dug in fiercely. He knew female contentment when he saw it . . . but he was suddenly afraid to look in her eyes. Would they mirror his soul, bare truths to him that he did not want to face?

He should harden his heart and pull away from her, roll

over and go to sleep, ask nothing, explain nothing. But then her fingertips glided up to his face where it lay buried in the silken nest of her hair and she touched the scar on his cheek, tracing the long narrow path the bullet had taken on that fateful day.

"How did you get this?" The question was not the one she longed to ask, but it popped suddenly into her mind. He pulled away from her, leaving an empty void that only he could fill. For an instant she feared he would get out of bed and walk away, but he only rolled onto his back beside her and stared at the ceiling above them. Suddenly an icy dread seized her. *Does he know?*

Instead of accusing her, he simply replied to her spoken question. "High-Backed Bear shot me before I killed him."

She shivered and reached out to him. "You could've been killed."

His arm drew her to his side. She fit so naturally that it terrified him. "Not the first time, not the last," he answered dismissively.

Roxanna's arms tightened around him. *I love you, Cain.* She longed to speak the words but did not dare. What would he say in return? Somehow she intuited that it would not be the answer she wanted. "I . . . I couldn't bear it if you were killed."

"I wouldn't be real happy about it myself," he replied lightly, raising up on his elbow to gaze down at her face. "Don't look so worried. I've survived this far. I don't plan on dying anytime soon."

She caressed his jaw, letting the faint bristle of his whiskers tease the sensitive skin of her fingertips, and was rewarded by his sharp intake of breath.

"I want you again."

The words seemed forced out of him, but she smiled anyway, reaching up with both arms to pull him to her in a deep, fierce kiss.

Cain was gone. Roxanna felt the absence of his body heat the moment she awakened with her arm reaching across the big wide bed for him. His pillow was cold, although it still held the indentation left by his head. When she rolled up, a slight ache reminded her of the past night's unaccustomed exertions. Her body was sore, but considering the fierce way her husband had made love to her, she was amazed there was no real pain.

The long ride from Vicksburg had been a nightmare of blood and agony. She had believed then that she could never again endure a man's embrace, let one invade her body in such a painful and degrading manner. Yet from the first moment Cain had touched her, she had desired him in spite of her fear, letting go of all past shame and guilt and misery. She lay back and closed her eyes blissfully, remembering the night, the urgency of his passion and her own answering passion.

He had not sensed her lack of virginity—or at least she assumed he had not. Surely not, or he would have questioned her . . . wouldn't he? She sat up and looked around the room. Clothing lay scattered across the carpet. Her beautiful wedding dress was crumpled in a silken heap by the mirror. Various other lacy undergarments and petticoats decorated the floor and chairs. One silk stocking even hung from a lampshade!

Then she saw the note, folded and sitting on the dresser by the window. Trembling, she threw back the covers and slipped from the bed, only to realize she wore not a stitch of clothing! Grabbing the bedsheet, she yanked it free and wrapped herself in it, then walked over to the dresser and picked up the note, her heart pounding with dread.

> My dearest Alexa,
>   You looked so peaceful sleeping and you had such a need of your rest, that I did not disturb you.

She felt the heat of a blush radiate from deep inside her, remembering why he was so certain that she was exhausted. Steadying the paper, she read the rest.

I have to check the progress of the grading crews west of Laramie and should be back in three or four days. In the meanwhile, Jubal will be in Cheyenne if you need anything. Be ready to leave when I return. We will live on the construction line until the Union Pacific finishes its contract.

Cain

No words of love, just the bold slash of his signature. But he did indicate that her place was with him. Surely that meant something. And the terse message had been addressed to "My dearest" Alexa. She felt a renewed sense of hope as she folded the note and prepared to face her first morning as Mrs. Cain.

After she had bathed and dressed, she sent a message to Jubal asking to have dinner with him if he had no meetings scheduled. Shortly, a knock sounded at the sitting room door. Assuming it was his reply, she put down the clothing she had begun packing for the trip to Laramie and went to answer it. Her smile froze when she opened the door.

"Good morning, Mrs. Cain." Isobel Darby's voice was ice-cold, but the hot light of triumph glowed in her dark eyes.

"What do you want?" The question was automatic even though Roxanna knew the answer. *To ruin me.*

Isobel's eyes swept over her hated enemy with insolent amusement, like a cat studying a cricket before swatting the life from it. "My, you do look . . . satiated, I suppose is the right word. Your half-breed buck must have pleased you in bed—but then a slut like you would sleep with any low sort, I imagine."

"You ought to know, since I slept with your husband." The false smile on Isobel's face vanished and for one moment Roxanna thought the other woman was going to claw at her, but instead Isobel regained her poise.

"This really isn't a conversation best held in a public hallway." She nodded regally to the sitting room behind Roxanna.

Roxanna stepped aside, admitting her, while her mind raced. In the past five years the woman had confronted her in person only once, although she had made sure Roxanna knew exactly who had smeared her reputation on every occasion. What was Nathaniel Darby's obsessed widow up to now? "Speak your piece and leave," she said tonelessly.

One black eyebrow rose sardonically. "Very well. You always seem to land on your feet, Roxanna. Surviving captivity with savages, the scandal of all the gossip about it—"

"You were the one who started the rumors in Denver."

"A pity your San Francisco railroad baron was so squeamish and broke your engagement."

Isobel looked anything but sorry. Roxanna waited, hating the dampness forming on her palms and trickling down between her breasts. She would volunteer nothing more.

"But you captured yourself a husband anyway—or was that the old Scot's doing? Getting rid of the embarrassment of a ruined granddaughter by marrying her off to his hired gunman?" She studied Roxanna from beneath lowered lashes as she examined the furnishings in the parlor, touching the lampshade sitting on the side table by the sofa.

"Stop trying to make me squirm, Mrs. Darby. If you intend to go to Jubal with your story, I can't stop you," she said, revealing nothing of the agony she felt, not so much for Jubal as for Cain. She had lied to her own husband, deceived him. He would leave her.

"Very well," Isobel said. "Distasteful as such tawdry matters are for a lady, I must confess that my finances are exhausted. In uncovering your rather circuitous travel west I spent the last of Nathaniel's inheritance."

"You mean the money he stole from his beloved Confederacy," Roxanna corrected, quickly intuiting where this confrontation was headed.

Isobel reacted as if Roxanna had emptied a chamber pot in her face. Crimson rage flushed her cheeks and her eyes turned from light brown to soulless inky pools glittering venomously. "Nathaniel was not a thief! He was a Southern gentleman. Your lies about him caused his death.''

''I told the truth. He was a war profiteer, selling army supplies to the highest bidder, supplies desperately needed by the Confederates. I only sent a letter to General Johnston informing him where to look in the colonel's own records. He killed himself rather than face the disgrace of a court-martial.''

Isobel flinched with each word Roxanna spoke, yet eerily held her peace. Only the chalky pallor leaching away the red flush of fury indicated how bitterly she fought to deny the truth. ''You murdered him,'' she insisted stubbornly. ''It was your fault he died.''

''And you've made me pay for it over and over.''

''And bringing you to justice has exhausted my resources,'' she replied, her composure once more in place as she tugged on one snowy lace glove. ''Fortunately, at the same time I was running out of money, you—scheming little fraud that you are—succeeded in posing as Jubal Mac-Kenzie's only heir. One day you'll have all his wealth—if he doesn't learn that his real granddaughter died back in St. Louis.''

''Do you really believe I'll pay you blackmail?''

''Of course you will if you want to continue your little charade as Alexa Hunt . . . and be that Indian's wife.'' The last words dropped like stones.

Under Isobel's piercing stare, Roxanna tried not to betray her fear—but knew she was failing as miserably as an understudy for Polonius suddenly being thrust into the spotlight to play Hamlet. . . . ''You'll only go to Jubal anyway. Why should I pay you to destroy me?''

A cold cruel smile touched Isobel's thin mouth, then crumbled into a grimace as if her muscles were unaccustomed to the activity. ''Oh, in time no doubt I shall, but for now I need money. You can pay me in installments and hope for sufficient time to work your wiles on that old man and the half-breed. Who knows, you might just be able to win them over so the truth won't matter. Then you'd have the sweetest revenge of all.''

Alexa had always been given a more-than-generous allowance by Jubal. When Roxanna closed down the house in St. Louis, several thousand remained unused in her account. Rather than leave it there and risk having the bank contact him, she had closed out the account and transferred all Alexa's funds to a bank in Denver. "It will take me a few days to wire for the money. Will two thousand do for now?" There was a good deal more, but Roxanna was not about to volunteer that. She needed time to think, to plan.

Isobel nodded brusquely, wanting to get past the vulgar discussion of dollars and cents. "I shall expect the deposit in my account at Blankenship's Bank on Seventeenth Street in Denver." She walked swiftly to the door. With her hand on the knob, she turned to say, "I trust you'll be resourceful in finding ways to extract more cash from MacKenzie, since I'm certain your Indian hasn't a sou."

With that she was gone, leaving Roxanna shivering in the warm room. She turned and walked to the window, looking out on the midday street, which teamed with life. A pair of bawdyhouse women resplendent in garish satins strolled past a grubby prospector down on his luck while a cursing driver lashed his mules. Roxanna saw and heard nothing, only stood rubbing her temples. Her mind churned frantically, but she could not come up with a way out. Isobel would win again unless . . .

Dare she tell Cain the truth? It would mean far more than confessing that she was not Jubal's granddaughter. She would have to tell him the whole ugly story of that night in Vicksburg. Would he still want her after that? She rang the bellpull, frantic to have a steamy hot bath as quickly as possible even though she had bathed only an hour earlier.

Cain squatted on the muddy ground examining the tracks of what he estimated to be a dozen or so horses. He looked around the wreckage of the camp. Only yesterday it had held a crew of fifteen graders and enough supplies to complete another twenty miles of track. Now all that remained were ashes and corpses. "This smells wrong for Indians, Finny."

The rawboned Irish surveyor riding with him leaned over his saddle and spat a wad of tobacco before replying, "And who might ye be thinkin' this is—old Queen Victoria's Royal Lancers?"

"About as likely as Cheyenne raiders. Some of the horses were shod," Cain replied, standing up and dusting the muck off his trousers.

Finny snorted. "Them heathens are divlish clever. Prob'ly stole the horses from the army. Sure and it wouldn't be the first time."

Cain shook his head. "A handful, maybe, but not this many. A lot of warriors refuse to ride ponies broken to saddle. Indians steal white men's horses to count coup and to trade, not to ride. Besides, the way that fire was set was too calculated for a hit-and-run raid. Every tie was burned to cinders. Looks as if they dug a trench around the dump and poured something flammable on it. Deliberate sabotage."

Finny tugged at one greasy lock of long hair, then shoved it back under the battered felt hat covering his head. "They got plenty reasons 'n more for wantin' the Iron Horse stopped. Look what old Turkey Leg did over on Plum Creek."

"He derailed a train, but then his warriors ransacked the cars and took off with all the supplies and gewgaws that took their fancy."

"Sure and they can't be carryin' off thousands of oak rail ties," Finny scoffed.

"But they could have taken food. Hunting is poor—their people hungry. Yet these raiders burned up the mess tent with every sack of flour and can of beans in it. Near as I can tell, they took nothing—and they veered off to the south. The hostiles are mostly north and east of here."

Finny shrugged. "Who would you be figgerin' it is, then?"

"At forty-eight thousand dollars' federal subsidy for each mile of track laid, this race to link up the Central Pacific and the Union Pacific could turn pretty ugly. MacKenzie's already found out Powell was sniffing around Salt Lake a few weeks ago, trying to interest Brigham Young in a grading contract with the Central Pacific.''

"But Young's already signed a contract with the Union Pacific,'' Finny said in righteous anger. Then comprehension dawned. ''And yer thinkin' himself it was sendin' men to raid our camps and kill our crews?''

''That or your queen's lancers.''

"That dumpy little Sassenach is *not* my queen!'' Patrick Aloysious Finny drew himself up indignantly and emptied the contents of his mouth. It landed with a loud splat between the horses' hooves, creating a small brown crater in the dirt.

Chuckling, Cain remounted. ''You'd better catch up with the rest of the crew headed back to the construction camp. Wire the bad news to Jubal for me. He'll have to send woodcutters into the Medicine Bows for more timber. You get a burying party up here. I'm going to follow these tracks and see what I can figure out before the trail goes cold.''

''Have a care, boyo. This is divlish mean country out here—one hundred miles to water, twenty miles to wood, six inches to hell,'' Finny cautioned as the Scot's Injun rode away.

Cain followed the trail along the Little Laramie River, then traveled south to the North Platte. This rocky ground had received no rain for weeks and yielded scant indication of where the raiders had gone. Probably down the North Platte to the trading posts and settlements farther south. He was certain they had not split up the way raiding parties from a warrior society would as a precaution against leading their enemy back to their villages. This group of killers had stuck together . . . like white men would.

He puzzled over who they were as he rode deeper into Colorado Territory. Renegades for hire to the highest bidder, maybe half-breed gunmen like himself, pushed outside the law—just the sort Andrew Powell liked to hire. *You son of a bitch, I won't let you beat us,* he thought grimly. Now he had a stake in the Union Pacific along with Jubal.

Thoughts of Jubal brought thoughts of his wife. "My wife." It still sounded strange to say it aloud. He had married Alexa Hunt to become MacKenzie's chief of operations. He had not planned to have her intrude in his thoughts and disrupt his sleep the way she had since they had consummated their vows.

Just thinking about that consummation made his body respond, hardening uncomfortably against the unyielding leather saddle. He could abandon this chase and push for Cheyenne tonight. It would strain his mount, but the big chestnut was used to such demands.

"Damned if I will," he muttered to the stallion. He would play out his hand here and see if any of the garrulous traders along the way could give him bits of information linking the renegades to Powell.

"He said he'd be back in three or four days. It's been over a week, Grandfather." Roxanna sat in Jubal's opulent railcar sipping a cup of rich black coffee, the remains of his private cook's fluffy omelet mostly untouched on her plate.

Jubal studied the dark circles beneath her eyes. "Do na' worry, lass. You know he wired me two days ago. This is part of his job and he's damn good at it."

"But he's only one man, alone in that wilderness chasing after a whole party of renegades who murdered over a dozen men already." Roxanna bit her lip and stared down at the linen napkin clenched in her hands.

"You love him, do you not, Alexa?" the old man asked gently.

Her head jerked up. "He's my husband. Of course I do," she answered a bit too quickly.

Jubal studied her with shrewd gray eyes. "Then why are you so defensive about it?" He shushed her protest with a wave of one big freckled paw. "When I arranged yer betrothal with that spineless Powell whelp I had misgivings about giving you to a stranger . . . but he was from impeccable bloodlines, seemed decent enough at the time. Besides, you were twenty-one and still unwed, a wealthy woman all alone. I convinced myself I was doing it for yer own good.''

Roxanna flushed. If he thought twenty-one was an old maid, what would Jubal say if he knew she was really twenty-three? And a fraud to boot? She shivered and pushed thoughts about Isobel Darby to the back of her mind. Her husband's absence was more worrisome even than that hateful woman.

"When Powell broke the engagement," Jubal continued awkwardly, "I . . . I was worried about you with Cain."

"You mean because of his mixed blood?"

He could see the anger sparkling in her eyes. Damned if she wasn't well and truly smitten with Cain. The idea disturbed him, for he was not sure if her husband returned her regard in equal measure. "No," he began carefully, choosing his words slowly. "But you saw firsthand how most people out West feel about Indians—and half-breeds."

"And women who've consorted with them. Damn their eyes—hypocrites all of them," she said indignantly, then added with scorn, "Those Cheyenne who captured me had a lot more honor—and honesty. . . ."

"Not exactly popular sentiments, lass," he said gently. Never known for being a diplomat, MacKenzie was usually blunt-spoken. In business it served him well, but not with females, especially this one, whose spunk and loyalty he was coming to admire. "I do na' hold his Indian blood against him half so much as he holds it against himself."

She nodded. "He wants to be white. He's educated, hardworking—everything he should be, and yet our fine Christian society won't give him a chance."

She did wear her heart on her sleeve. "Aye. He is all that. I've come to rely on him this past year. The men may resent his blood, but they respect him and follow his orders. That's why I've decided to give him a promotion. He's done a lot more than round up drunken workers and stop their brawls. I've decided to make him my chief of operations."

Roxanna was stunned. "Are you doing this because I'm your granddaughter and I married him?"

What she said struck too close to home. He cleared his

throat, wondering if he would have eventually given Cain the job even if he had not married Alexa. "I did it because I believe he can perform the job—and it isna' an easy one." That much was true. "Now that the peace with the Central Pacific's been broken, we'll have a real cutthroat race on."

"You mean to reach Salt Lake before they do so the Union Pacific gets more federal subsidy?"

"Aye. Yer a quick one, lass," he said with a twinkle, relieved that she did not take Cain's sudden promotion amiss.

She smiled for the first time. "I've been listening to you and Cain and other men. Everyone between Cheyenne and Laramie is talking about the competition to lay the most track." Then her expression shifted as she stared out the window at the distant mountains. "I only hope he'll return safely in time for the welcome party in Laramie Saturday."

"Cain will be in Laramie right enough, but if we do na' finish our breakfast and get a move on, we'll be the ones late." He checked his heavy gold pocket watch and added, "The trains pull out for Laramie in two hours."

Chapter 11

Isobel Darby's account was credited with two thousand dollars two days after her confrontation with Roxanna. The widow relished the idea of her enemy spending the past week in nervous apprehension, wondering when she would be unmasked. But Isobel had other plans. Smiling serenely, she stepped from the Central Pacific train just arrived from Sacramento. The ride through the mountains to San Francisco had been nerve-wracking, but even the sooty chugging locomotive was better than being slammed about in a cramped stagecoach as she had on the first leg of the journey.

She checked the address on the card and signaled a hackney, issuing crisp instructions for her destination. A quarter hour later the Widow Darby was ushered into Andrew Powell's ornate offices. "Mr. Powell has been expecting you, Mrs. Darby," Ezra Harker said respectfully, curious in spite of his professional mien as to why a busy man such as his employer would deign to interrupt a tight schedule to confer with a mere female, even if she was a handsome-looking one.

Andrew Powell rose and rounded his heavy cherrywood desk to greet her. The room, large and expensively furnished in muted dark colors, suited him perfectly. She felt startled by a spark of attraction. He radiated power as he crossed the Aubusson carpet and took her hand, fixing her with cool blue eyes.

"Mrs. Darby. A pleasure, madam." Powell bowed over her hand, applying just the right amount of pressure as he touched his lips to her gloved fingertips, then escorted her to one of a set of bergère chairs. They took their seats facing each other. Then he spoke. "I understand from your wire that you have some valuable information for me concerning Jubal MacKenzie's granddaughter."

"First let me set some ground rules, Mr. Powell," she said briskly, ignoring his charm. "If the information proves useful to you, I trust the sum I named in compensation will be acceptable."

"Ten thousand dollars is a great deal of money, Mrs. Darby."

Her expression was glacial as the Sierras. "For a man who receives five times that much for every mile of track he lays between here and the Rockies, I should think it quite modest indeed."

Powell studied the determined-looking widow for a moment. She was cold as a well digger's ass in spite of the syrupy drawl in her voice, yet something about her naked avarice excited him. He nodded at length. "Point well taken, Mrs. Darby. I shall pay you the ten thousand . . . *if* the information is useful."

Isobel Darby's thin lips widened in a sly smile, revealing small perfect white teeth. "In that case, let me tell you all about Alexa Hunt and Roxanna Fallon. . . ."

As the widow spun her incredible tale, neither she nor Powell noticed the door to the adjoining office had been left ajar. Inside it, working quietly at his desk, Lawrence let his pen drop, spilling a large blotch of ink onto the account ledger while he listened.

Cain rode into Laramie in the late afternoon, frustrated, exhausted and filthy from eight days on the trail without even the simple amenities of a drink of whiskey or a shave. He headed the chestnut down A Street to the railroad depot where Jubal's private car should be, ignoring the raucous Saturday night crowd of railroad laborers, miners, gamblers and floozies. He was all too familiar with the hostile uneasy whispers of the men and the speculative come-hither looks of the women.

His wife was waiting for him. He hoped Jubal had been able to secure the extra car for them as he had promised. Bedrolling out on the ground held little more appeal than sleeping under the same roof as the keen-eared old Scot, not that he planned to do a great deal of sleeping once he had Alexa in bed with him. He had spent the past week dreaming of her at night, thinking of her far too much during the day. That was a dangerous flaw for a man in his business. He decided the best way to deal with his obsession was to make love to her every night until the fascination wore off. Surely it would with time.

Meanwhile, he had enough railroad business on his plate to keep three men busy. MacKenzie wasn't going to like what he had to tell him about the raiders. He was deep in thought when a low feminine voiced called his name.

"Cain, it's about time you're back!" Roxanna scampered down the steep steps from the railcar and dashed over to where he was dismounting. She threw her arms around his neck, heedless of the gawking workers passing by. He smelled of sweat and horse and a week's growth of thick black beard scratched her face, but she did not care.

Cain inhaled the scent of lilacs and felt the sweet softness of her mouth as she feathered swift excited kisses across his face. He knew half of Laramie was watching them avidly, appalled at the slender blond woman throwing herself at a dirty breed. Damning them all, he crushed her in his arms and kissed her deeply, unleashing the hunger that had frustrated and angered him all week.

Let them look.

His mouth was fierce and possessive, slanted over hers, demanding her submission. She opened to his tongue, letting it plunge, greeting it with her own eagerly, until at last he broke off the heady caress and stared into her eyes. She ran her hands over his dusty wrinkled shirt, feeling that he was whole, safe and once more in her arms.

"I missed you," he said in a low growl, the admission surprising him.

Roxanna beamed, forgetting all her fears, even the threat of Isobel Darby. "And I missed you," she said shyly, realizing what a spectacle she had just made of herself. What must he think of her? "I was so worried when Grandfather told me you were tracking a bunch of renegades who'd killed a whole grading crew." She could not restrain herself from running her hands down his arms and across his chest. "You're alive and in one piece."

"I'm filthy and I need a shave," he replied, trying to step back from the naked longing that shone from her eyes. Did his own reveal the same thing? "No time to clean up out on the trail," he added, seeing the faint pink abrasions his whiskers had left on her delicate skin. "I've marked you." His hand raised to touch her cheek before he could stop himself. She took it in both of hers, pressing the palm to her lips.

"In more ways than one, but I don't care if you're dirty—only that you're safe." Still holding his hand, she turned back toward the train. "Come. We have a private car of our very own. It's not so opulent as Grandfather's, but I absolutely love it. I've been fixing it up while I was waiting for you to return. The striker can draw you a bath." Roxanna knew she was babbling. Nerves. The awful lonely days of waiting for his return and worrying that some renegade might shoot him in the back were over. If only the threat of Isobel Darby was over as well.

Tell him the truth. Could she dare? If he learned of her deception, how would he react? In many ways he was as much of an enigma to her as she would be to him as Roxanna Fallon. She could not be sure if he cared for her enough to forgive her past. Perhaps with time she could bend him to her as their love grew. Her tumbling thoughts were interrupted when they reached the railcar and he scooped her up in his arms and climbed aboard. She clung to him as he carried her inside the door she had left standing ajar in her headlong rush to greet him.

He looked around the room, which had been furnished with a settee and a pair of chairs, various small tables and lamps. Lace curtains hung on the windows and heavy velvet Austrian shades were pulled up to admit the late afternoon light. Several Turkish prayer rugs were spread across the floor and a large bouquet of spring wildflowers filled a crystal bowl sitting on the round oak dining table in the far corner.

It was the most elegant place he had ever called home—and he owed it to his wife's grandfather. "Mighty fancy," he said, placing her once more on her feet.

"Grandfather's cook prepares our meals and Li Chen brings them over and serves. The bedroom—" she paused, blushing furiously as she stood in the doorway "—er, is here," she finished, lamely. "I'll have Li Chen prepare you a bath if you wish." He was grinning at her! The return of this more familiar high-handed manner was welcome, but she still blushed to the roots of her hair.

"You do that. Tell him to bring lots of hot water. The first tubful will probably turn to mud before I'm done." When she passed by him to ring the bell summoning the Chinese servant, he reached out one arm and pulled her back into his embrace. "After I get cleaned up . . . we'll see about that bedroom."

His voice was low and intimate and its resonance made her tingle all the way down to the pit of her stomach. Memories of their wedding night had heated her dreams since he went away. She decided to seize every moment she was given with her husband and banish all thoughts of Isobel Darby. If—no—when the charade was over she would have memories no one could take away from her. "Take off your clothes . . . and I'll see you have all the . . . bath water you want."

He lowered his mouth and kissed her again with the same pent-up hunger, then broke away. "If I take off my clothes, I'm not sure I'll wait for a bath."

"You don't have to wait, Cain," she answered boldly.

He cursed, then said, "Fetch the damn bath if you don't want your satin bedcovers fowled with prairie dust."

Roxanna's hands curved around his broad shoulders, then moved up, pulling his head down to hers once more. "We can always buy new bedcovers," she said against his mouth as he took her lips once more.

"You'll be . . . as smelly . . . as I am . . . by the time . . . we're through," he said between kisses.

"Then I'll order . . . enough bathwater . . . for both of us," she finally managed before he carried her into the bedroom, kicking the door closed with one foot. He let her slide down the length of his body, still pressing her close. Their hands were as busy as their mouths, pulling and unfastening, eager for the contact of bare flesh to bare flesh.

Finally they broke apart so he could fling the buckskin shirt over his head after she had tugged it loose from his waistband. The back of her dress gaped open where he had unhooked it and he peeled it down her arms, shoving it lower. It pooled around her ankles with her petticoats. His eyes lit with appreciation. "I see you took my advice. No more corsets."

"I'm a dutiful wife, Cain." Her fingers worked clumsily on the unfamiliar belt buckle at his waist, then fumbled, hesitating at his fly. He stood with his palms cupping her breasts, doing magical things to her nipples through the thin lawn of her chemise. Feeling her stop, he reached down and quickly opened his breeches. His sex, hot and turgid, sprang free. He lowered her hand toward it. When she clasped the pulsing staff, he let out a ragged oath and pulled her to him, burying his fists in her hair and molding his mouth to the curve where her neck and shoulder met.

Roxanna closed her eyes and reveled in the salty taste of perspiration on his skin combined with the faint aroma of horse and tobacco and man as she nuzzled his throat and ran her fingers through the damp springy hair on his chest.

"I told you I needed a bath," he said with a husky laugh as he pulled her chemise off and his mouth closed over the hard aching point of her breast. His hands swept down over her ribs, fingers splayed, feeling the intense vibrations of her wildly beating heart, then moved lower to rip open the waistband of her pantalets and push them over her hips. "Kick them off," he commanded, and she obeyed.

Roxanna felt his big calloused hands cupping her bare buttocks, lifting her up against him. Her legs wrapped around his waist as he backed against the wall, positioning her over his rigid staff. Her eyes met his in startled inquiry as she intuited what he was going to do.

With a feral grimace of intense pleasure he slid deep inside of her, murmuring raggedly, "One way to keep the bedcovers clean."

After that neither of them could speak again for some moments. She held on to him, letting his hands direct her hips for his thrusts, long, slow strokes that sent wild heady frissons of pleasure shooting throughout her body. Their frenzied ride grew swifter and harder as the passion built until all that broke the silence on the warm still air was the rasping of their breath.

Cain felt his climax roaring down on him and braced himself against the wall. But his knees nearly buckled when she cried out as her tight sheath contracted around him draining him dry. Her nails raked his back and dug into his shoulders as she trembled so sweetly, so fiercely in his arms. He felt the tangled silk of her hair spilling over his arm as her head dropped limply against his chest. Still she held her thighs clamped tightly around his hips.

He slid slowly down to the floor and they sat facing each other when she finally dared to raise her head. Dear God, she still had her stockings and garters on, even her shoes! His trousers were halfway down his legs, caught on the top of his boots! Roxanna bit her lips, feeling her embarrassment rise. She had thrown herself at him like some Hell on Wheels calico cat. And he had responded like a randy track layer. But it had been so glorious that she could not regret it. Did he?

He sensed the wary uncertainty darkening those luminous

turquoise eyes. When they fluttered shut, he bracketed her face between his hands and pressed his lips against one, then the other. "It was good, Alexa."

"Even if I behaved like a wanton hussy?" she could not help but ask.

A crooked smile touched his mouth. "I don't think there's any other kind of hussy—but you aren't one, Alexa. As to being wanton . . ." He skimmed his fingertips across the swell of her breasts, then raised her chin with his hand and kissed her lips softly. "I like it—as long as it's just for me."

"Only for you, Cain," she whispered, returning the gentle kiss.

They held each other in contentment for several moments. Then he chuckled as he lifted her off him. "I think I have splinters in my butt."

"I could examine it—let me fetch my sewing kit," she teased back. "Or would a tweezers be better than a needle?"

"Flippant little vixen. Just order that bathwater." He watched with keen appreciation as she scrambled up wearing only silk stockings and high-heeled slippers. The rosy flush of embarrassment staining her pale skin was endearingly innocent in spite of the provocative manner in which she was dressed—or undressed.

Li Chen fetched buckets of steaming water, filling the huge copper tub in the dressing room of their car. Roxanna was fascinated when Cain conversed in fluent Chinese with the servant. When Chen departed, she remembered Enoch Sterling's tutelage as they climbed into the water together. After a long soapy interlude and languid lovemaking, she watched him shave as she dried her hair, brushing it until it glowed like moonbeams.

Roxanna listened to the soft rasp of the razor against his thick beard, watching as each long clean stroke revealed more of his harshly beautiful face. She had never seen a man shave before, never would have imagined it was an erotic act. But that was before Cain, sitting naked in a bathtub with a small oval mirror facing him on the dressing table as he wielded the strait-edged blade with keen precision.

Cain could hear the steady cadence of brushstrokes crackling through her hair. She'd dried herself off and slipped on a filmy nothing of a robe. The pale aquamarine silk clung to every slender curve of her body. He felt himself growing hard again in the cool bathwater. "I can't get enough of you, Alexa," he said in a low voice.

He sounded almost desperate as she watched him climb from the tub. His long powerful arms and legs rippled sinuously with sleek bronzed muscles. Droplets of water caught in the dense pelt on his chest, glistening like diamonds in the flickering lamplight. She put down her brush and picked up a towel to dry him, walking over to where he stood. After she rubbed his chest and arms, she knelt and started to run the towel down the lean hard muscles of his legs until he pulled it away and tossed it onto the scattered piles of discarded clothing littering the floor. He lifted her to stand before him, studying her face with dark, almost haunted eyes. "If I'm taking too much, Alexa . . ."

She shook her head vehemently, moving into his arms. If they didn't hurry, they'd be late for the welcome party. Jubal would be waiting. . . . "Love me again, Cain." *Love me. . . .*

"It's Powell. I know it is. Old George Willis down on the North Platte knows the renegades. Some white, a few half-breeds with them. Trouble for hire. One of them is a real snake, Johnny Lame Pony. He's worked for Powell in the past."

"But he couldna' tell you for sure that the Central Pacific hired them or where this Lame Pony disappeared to after you lost their trail?" Jubal asked, shoving away the lukewarm cup of coffee and empty breakfast plate.

Cain paced over to the window, looking across the rails to where the other private car sat. *With Alexa inside it.* "No. But we can be prepared for them the next time they strike."

Jubal observed the direction of Cain's gaze but did not mention Alexa. "You mean the army?"

"Dillon's command has been beefed up since your old

friend Sherman agreed to protect the Union Pacific this summer. I'll ride to Fort Russell and tell the colonel everything I've learned. Then we'll see what those bluebellies can do.'' He started toward the door, but MacKenzie's voice halted him just as he pulled it open.

"Yer sure Alexa willna' mind yer being gone so much while yer just newlyweds?''

"She likes the homecomings well enough,'' he replied, storming out the door, slamming it behind him.

"Weel, now, laddie, what was that all aboot?'' he chortled to himself in a thickened Scot's burr.

On the long hard ride to Fort Russell, Cain mulled over his relationship with Alexa. She was everything he, or any man, could ever have dreamed of in a wife—head-turningly beautiful, a well-bred lady and at the same time a passionate woman who possessed keen intelligence, even a sense of humor. The problem was that a man like him had never allowed himself to have that sort of dream. He had burned with ambition, yes, but using Alexa as the means to achieve it had been done on sudden impulse. The situation had been dropped in front of him and he had taken advantage of it.

Had he also taken advantage of her? No. He vehemently denied that. Her reputation was ruined and no white man would have her, unless Jubal had paid some worthless eastern fop to marry her—a man who would never have let her forget how tainted she was. Cain could never accuse her. He knew that she had never been touched by any of Leather Shirt's warriors or even himself before their wedding night.

Yet he could not quit worrying it, like a tongue probing a sore tooth. On their wedding night her fearful shyness had touched a chord of tenderness he never knew he possessed. Then her quick passion yesterday had ignited a fire in him that might never be quenched. She kept him off balance, unsure of how he should feel about her—or how *much* he should feel.

When they awakened this morning she had been reticent again, perhaps embarrassed by the way she had responded to him the previous day. He always seemed to sense an undercurrent of nervousness in her beneath the exterior of self-possessed St. Louis socialite. Even in his grandfather's village, she seemed afraid of something—not the Cheyenne, not even him, although he had given her plenty of reasons. Something else. But what?

Perhaps he was imagining things. He had spent entirely too much time mooning over Alexa Hunt—no, he was forced to amend that, Alexa Cain. His lips twisted in a wry grimace, thinking of her claim on the name that he had chosen as a badge of his solitary life. He pushed that and other disquieting thoughts from his mind and considered what he would say to Dillon when he reached Fort Russell.

Summer came to the High Plains fierce and sudden as a train wreck. The heat gripped men and livestock like a vice and the relentless searing wind choked them with alkaline dust. Track layers left a trail of sweat pouring off their bodies as they toiled in tandem under the broiling sun, five men to nearly a thousand pounds of iron. From the wagon bed they carried the rail to track end, then on command of the foreman dropped it in place for the spikers with their powerful sledges to go to work. Sparks flew off their hammers as they smashed the spikes, driving them through the rail, biting deep into the wooden ties below.

Cain was ever-present, watching for trouble. It was not uncommon for him to ride a hundred miles in one day, changing mounts at each stop as he oversaw work crews of graders, tie setters and track layers. By midsummer, they had perfected a rhythm. When supplies were available—and Jubal made certain ties, rails, fishplates and bolts never ran short—the crews laid over two miles of track each long summer day.

The high elevation of Laramie was left far behind as they entered the killing heat of alkali basin lands cross-sectioned by river gorges. To add to the misery of the weather, the dust and the mind-numbing drudgery, there was constant danger lurking in a deadly host of forms—Indian attacks, outbreaks of dysentery and even cholera which killed more men than the hostiles, as well as the explosive eruptions when cuts were blasted, causing two-hundred-pound pieces of granite to whistle through the air.

At first Roxanna had watched the progress of the rails and waited fearfully for word from Isobel Darby. Now that they were isolated in the wilderness with the Union Pacific work crews, Roxanna knew that the widow could not blackmail her or expose her until they reached Salt Lake, which was some months away. Given that reprieve, she immersed herself in being a railroader's wife. There were not many respectable women on the line, although scarlet poppies abounded in every saloon and bordello along the way. The laborers could not afford to have wives or children with them, nor were there any provisions for housing them. But a few of the higher-paid professional men, the chief engineers and crew supervisors, were given space for their families in extra work cars.

Roxanna was set apart from them not only by virtue of her position as a director's granddaughter, but also by the gossip that followed her from Cheyenne. After all, she had been a captive of the very savages who continually killed and mutilated railroad workers. If that was not enough, she had gone and married the "Scot's Injun," that fearful halfbreed gunman who now lorded it over his betters. It created resentment that Jubal relied more and more on Cain, no longer just as a gunman who could protect the crews, but as a businessman who negotiated contracts and planned strategies.

Since she was cut off from the limited social life on the trail, Roxanna decided to carve out a useful place for herself. She had learned valuable nursing skills from Sees Much. Now she worked with the company doctor to treat injuries and nurse the men who fell ill.

"If we could just get you damn fools to stop drinking ditch water, maybe you'd stop coming down with dysentery every week," Dr. Milborne said sourly to the big spiker who sat doubled up in misery on the edge of the examining table.

The physician's traveling office was set up in an infirmary car at the head of the Union Pacific work train, close to where accidents were likely to happen.

"Aw, Doc, I ain't drunk no ditch water, jest what's in them barrels," the man averred, then smothered an oath of pain because Mrs. Cain was present.

"The Chinese on the Central Pacific never get stomach complaints. My husband said it's because they drink only tea made with boiled water. That would help with the contamination problem," Roxanna said to Milborne.

"Beggin' yer pardon, ma'am, but me'n the other boys ain't gonna drink no Chink tea. Afore yew knowed it, we'd be shrinkin' and gettin' slanty eyes," the spiker said.

The doctor rolled his eyes in exasperation as he handed her a dose of calomel to give to their patient. "You see how hopeless it is? I can't even get the water boys to scrub the muck out of the barrels before they refill them."

She watched as the spiker downed the noisome liquid, then helped him from the table and onto a cot in the adjoining room, where several of his fellows lay with various complaints—one broken arm, two powder burns from a blasting accident, one infected foot and six other cases of dysentery. This was only Thursday. Business picked up quite a bit after Saturday nights in the saloons.

Roxanna returned to the office just as two track layers struggled through the car door dragging a third by his arms. He slumped onto the table and his fellows waited, hats in hand, saying only that he'd stumbled on a tie and fallen into the path of a sledge, which had clipped his eye.

"Let me have a look," the doctor said to him. As soon as the patient raised his head, the physician swore, then looked apologetically at Roxanna, who only smiled dismissively. After the past month working around railroad laborers, she had heard far worse.

Fumes of "pop skull" whiskey rose off the man's sweaty body like swamp gas in a Louisiana bayou. "Danny Deeken again. I should've known. One of these days you're going to kill yourself, but it won't be on Union Pacific time. Cain told you if you ever sneaked a bottle to work again, you'd be fired,'' he said as he examined a bump the size of a buzzard's egg forming around Deeken's left eye.

"Sure'n I know it," the patient wheezed. "The trouble began when Zigler started throwin' punches. Got meself in the way of one."

Milborne scowled. "Zigler's a foot taller and weighs three stone more than you. You were drunk or crazy to provoke him."

"Ah, but the whiskey was so good I fergot meself, I did. It was strong enough to make a hummingbird spit in a rattler's eye!"

Roxanna was appalled when the doctor pried open Deeken's injured eye, revealing the bloodshot damage. "Will I lose me eye?" he asked, still too drunk to be all that concerned.

Milborne shrugged. "No. You'll survive until your liver ossifies, which shouldn't be all that long. It ought to be the consistency of a mastodon tusk by now." The dour little physician shook his balding head in frustration as he worked, carefully placing a pad on the injury, then wrapping Deeken's head to hold the pad in place.

"When you've had enough, why can't you simply ask for a sarsaparilla?" the physician asked in exasperation as he helped Deeken down from the table.

"Doc, when I've had enough I can't *say* sarsaparilla," was the slurred reply.

Roxanna shared a laugh with the physician as they helped Deeken reach his friend's arms. "Haul him into the back and let him sleep it off," he instructed them. "He's gonna wake up with an elephant-sized headache."

Late that afternoon when things were quiet, Roxanna sat sponging off one of the dysentery patients, who moaned feverishly in his sleep.

"You have a healer's touch, Mrs. Cain," the doctor said gently, pausing beside the foot of the cot.

"Another medicine man once told me that not too long ago. I would never have thought it before then." She shrugged. "I like to be useful. My husband's away a great deal and this keeps me busy. I'm not exactly welcome in the small social circle here," she said without rancor.

Milborne's kindly brown eyes studied her for a moment as he cleared his throat awkwardly. "I'll be honest, Mrs. Cain—when you first volunteered, I had my doubts. Gossip is an ugly thing. I shouldn't have believed a word of it, but I did and I owe you an apology for that. You're a fine woman and a real lady."

"No matter that I lived with Indians and married a half-breed?" Her voice held no censure, just a gentle sadness more for Cain than for herself.

Milborne's sallow complexion reddened. "You do believe in calling a spade a spade, don't you, Mrs. Cain? I can see that you're Jubal MacKenzie's granddaughter."

Roxanna smiled. "That's the best compliment you could give me. Thank you, Doctor."

"Yer missing him, are you not?" Jubal asked Roxanna that night at dinner.

The two of them dined alone in his car since Cain was in Salt Lake making arrangements for the Mormon grading crews to start work on the route the Union Pacific surveyors had set up. He had been gone for over a week and their big bed was cold and lonely without him. "Yes, I miss him terribly, Grandfather." She shoved a forkful of creamed potatoes around on her plate. "Will he always have to travel this way—did you when you were young?"

"Aye, I did. And there are times, seeing you now, that I regret it, lass. Ambition's a fine thing in a man if it doesna' cost him his family."

"I'd never blame Cain—or leave him because he works too hard," she said quickly.

"But you do na' like being apart. And it isna' fair to you. My Abbie never complained either. Looking back, I wish she had. I took her for granted. Then when she was gone . . ." His voice faded and a misty look came into his eyes. He blinked and looked out the window at the distant mountains.

Roxanna reached out and placed her hand over his big gnarled paw. "You must've loved her very much."

"Aye, but I wasted all those precious years we had together—years when Annabelle was growing up. Abbie raised yer mother almost single-handed. Perhaps if I'd taken a hand sooner after Abbie died, Annie wouldna' have married Terrence Hunt."

"You never approved of my father, did you?" Roxanna asked intuitively. Alexa had never mentioned it, but she had spoken little of her father.

"He wasna' worthy of Annie. But he was there and I was off, studying steel processing in Manchester, buying timberlands in Canada or poring over account books in Pittsburgh. I suppose I buried myself in work to escape the grief of losing Abbie. I ended up losing them both—and you, when yer father took you off to St. Louis."

His melancholy look touched still-raw memories of her beloved father, lynched by night riders, the numb grief of her mother, compounded when their only son Rexford was killed in the war. Roxanna blinked back her own tears. She had lost all her family the same as Jubal. *I'm all he has left and I'm a fraud. Please God, don't let Isobel Darby destroy Jubal too.* She had come to admire and respect this gruff old man. He would be devastated to learn that his last living descendant was dead and that he had been taken in by an impostor. "You mustn't blame yourself for what's in the past," she reassured him. But she would always blame herself . . . for so many things.

"I'm sorry, lass. An old man's regrets about the past are poor dinner table conversation."

"I love you, Jubal MacKenzie. You must always believe that," she said solemnly.

"I will, lass, I will," he replied gently.

They sat across from one another, his big freckled hands holding her small pale ones, both blinking back the betraying moisture in their eyes.

At length Jubal broke the silence. "I'm happy things are working out between you and Cain. He'll be back in a day or two. Best you get yer rest tonight while you still can sleep," he teased.

She blushed. "Grandfather, you are an old rascal!"

"Aye, but I was a young rogue once. Enjoy yer time together, lass. I'll see what I can do to keep yer husband closer to camp for a while."

"You depend on him and he loves the challenge of new responsibility."

"He's the best operations chief I've ever had," he agreed. "I canna' wait to present him to the Union Pacific directors and all the Washington muckety-mucks." He chuckled.

"Will they mind his being part Indian?" A worried frown crossed her forehead.

"I dare any of them to say so to his face," Jubal said with a sardonic chuckle.

"No, I don't imagine they would dare," she replied thoughtfully.

"Aye. Cain isna' a man to cross," Jubal agreed heartily, walking over to his liquor cabinet.

Roxanna could imagine his fury if he learned how she had deceived him, and suppressed a shudder. *Don't think about it.*

Jubal waited while Li Chen removed the remains of their dinner, then poured some aged bourbon into two glasses and handed the smaller one to her.

She raised her glass to his. "To America, the land of opportunity—and damn good whiskey!"

He returned the salute. "That's my lassie!"

Chapter 12

"I don't see why you can't handle this. My job is moving the men out on the line."

"Yer job is also learning to move among the muckety-mucks who control the Union Pacific purse strings. If I learned to dance their jigs, so can you. Besides," Jubal said slyly, "maybe yer wife would enjoy a wee bit of socializing with the sort of nobs she knew back in St. Louis. She's worked hard with Doc Milborne. It would do her good to get away from the camp here, go back to Chicago, get dressed up in her finest and have some fun."

"She says she enjoys tending the sick and injured. But I know she isn't accepted by the other respectable ladies. Working with doc has given her something to do, to feel useful while I'm away."

"Aye, and yer away too much for being newly married." Jubal threw up his hands before Cain could answer back. "I know, laddie, I know it's me who gave you the job that takes you away. But you see, that's why hosting this delegation of Union Pacific directors is so perfect. You can get to know Durant and his oily cronies from back East and at the same time give Alexa a week for socializing and female fripperies."

Cain grunted in capitulation. "All right. I'll do it. Just as long as they don't expect me to put on a Wild West show with those damned Pawnee."

"They wouldna' ask. When Durant arranged that exhibition last year it fair scared half the ladies into a swoon," Jubal said, chuckling.

Cain was surprised at Alexa's reaction when he gave her the news. Rather than bubbling female excitement over glittering social events in the big city, she seemed reticent, as if worried about something. "What's wrong, Alexa? Jubal thought you'd be excited at the chance for parties and shopping, the trip back East."

"Oh, I am, but . . . you don't want to go, do you? I mean, your work is here."

"As your grandfather reminded me, my new duties include learning my way around the 'muckety-mucks' who hold the purse strings for the Union Pacific." He studied her, sensing there was more to her reluctance. "You're afraid of what they might think because you married an Indian."

She gasped, hurt at first that he would think so poorly of her, but then she reminded herself of how painful his life had been growing up half red in a white world. She reached up to touch his face with her hand, willing him to look into her eyes, to see her heart. "I don't give a damn what Dr. Durant or the whole Union Pacific thinks," she said fiercely. "I grew up in polite society, and believe me when I say I much prefer the friends I made in Leather Shirt's village to anyone I know in St. Louis—or might meet in Chicago."

"I don't think a return trip to visit the Cheyenne is feasible right now," he replied dryly. "You'll just have to settle for the snobby muckety-mucks. Besides," he added, taking her hand and planting a moist kiss on the palm, "we'll have the car all to ourselves for three days before we reach Chicago."

The journey to Chicago was an idyll of lovemaking and an opportunity for them to spend uninterrupted time together, a luxury never afforded them in the big rail camp. As the private train made its way east to pick up its august passengers, Roxanna discovered that Cain's education was far more extensive than she had ever imagined.

"I knew you spoke Chinese, but you mean you've actually read these?" she asked, kneeling beside his old trunk, which had been delivered to their private car the day after their marriage. Until now it had remained unpacked, shoved hastily into a corner of the storage room. At her urging, he had dug out his small cache of personal possessions, adding them to the things she had brought from the Hunt household in St. Louis.

He picked up a slim volume of Greek, the pages well thumbed and yellowed with age. *The Plays of Aristophanes.* "Too bad you can't read Greek. You might enjoy *Lysistrata*. But then, come to think of it, it might give you some bad ideas," he added as she took the book and gently opened it.

"You mean about withholding my favors from you until you did what I wanted?" she asked sweetly. "I can't read the original Greek, but I have read translations of Aristophanes."

"Not exactly a conventional education. Does Jubal know what sort of teachers you had?" he asked, intrigued, trying to imagine Alexa as a girl.

"My father taught me to love literature," she began, then stopped abruptly, realizing that she had no idea if Terrence Hunt had ever read a book in his life. Quickly she shifted the subject back to Cain. "Tell me about growing up at the mission."

At first Cain was not certain he could talk about Enoch, but once he began, it was as if a whole floodgate of memories was opened. Rather than the unbearable pain he had always experienced before, now it felt right to speak of his mentor's life. "He was an amazing man. By turns stern, pious, yet gentle, humorous. Always endlessly patient. And I gave him ample reason to exercise that virtue.

"He was a missionary among the Cantonese for over a decade. Then when civil war in the Chinese provinces forced him to leave, the Methodist Missionary Society sent him to Colorado to bring the Gospel to the Indians.'' He laughed bitterly. ''Quite a change—from one of the most civilized people on earth to one of the most savage. A less adaptable man would have failed.''

''Did he make you feel your Cheyenne blood was savage?'' She intuited the answer and wanted to draw him into thinking about it.

''No. He found much to admire among all the plains tribes—their morality, their sense of honor, the way they care for children and the elderly, even some of their religious beliefs.''

''Then why do you feel your mother's people are savages?''

His expression darkened. ''You don't know what it's like growing up in an Indian camp. You only spent a few weeks with them as a guest. But you saw what Weasel Bear did to me.''

''And I also saw how the rest of the people felt about his treachery too. He broke their laws and he was forced to flee in disgrace.''

''Could you live like a squaw—dress game and scrape hides, haul water and dig roots, perform all the heavy, endless chores a Cheyenne woman must?'' he asked scornfully. ''You'd have to survive on the thin edge of danger, where a Pawnee raid could mean kidnapping or death. Could you live with people who believe coyotes talk? Who recoil in terror from the ticking of a timepiece? Quake in fear at an eclipse of the sun?''

Scorn turned to anguish now, as he recalled the ten-year-old boy at the mission who threw Enoch's timepiece across the floor when the sound of the mechanism made him believe that it was alive with white-eyes magic. All the other children had laughed at him until the headmaster had stopped them and taken the frightened new boy under his wing.

''The way they live is hard and dangerous,'' Roxanna conceded. ''I know I wouldn't choose that life, yet there is much to admire in it and in those people. I admit they sometimes seem superstitious, even childlike regarding things they don't understand . . . but there are things whites don't understand either.'' She struggled to explain the feelings she had about Sees Much and his visions. ''Sees Much has an understanding of people that is beyond perception . . . almost magical. There. Does that sound superstitious? He knew we were going to marry while we were first in their camp.'' *He told me to love you. And I did.*

Cain remembered the old man's uncanny knack for knowing what others thought, disconcertingly often before they thought it. ''Sees Much is perceptive, shrewd,'' he said dismissively. ''He understood that I didn't fit in, never would. When my grandfather insisted I join in the Sun Dance ceremonies at puberty, Sees Much said I was not ready. Luckily my father came along and took me to the mission before I reached the vision quest age.''

Roxanna had become all too aware that her husband rejected his Cheyenne blood. It would do no good to argue about the Indians or Cain's place with them. Instead she focused on the life he had assumed at Enoch Sterling's mission. ''It must have been hard being torn from one world, then left rootless in another.''

He reminisced about growing up at the mission, adolescent pranks, the rigorous curriculum he followed, his quest to find a niche for himself as a mixed-blood among whites. How different his life might have turned out if not for the hatred of High-Backed Wolf and the death of Enoch Sterling. One day she would get him to explain more about that awful tragedy, but not yet. First he must learn to trust and, in that trusting, to heal.

Of course if he learned of her secrets, could he ever again trust her? Or would he become even more the bitter loner who never let love touch him? Roxanna clung to Sees Much's dream that had brought them together. Surely it must mean that Cain was fated to return her love.

The group of Union Pacific directors and influential politicians the young couple were to escort west on the sightseeing junket had all assembled at the elegant Tremont House in Chicago. When Cain and Roxanna arrived, the illustrious—or infamous, depending on whom one asked—Dr. Thomas C. Durant sent his personal carriage to transport them from the train to the hotel. That night there would be a lavish dinner party, then in the morning the entourage would embark on their grand adventure.

Roxanna took special care with her toilette, using the services of a well-trained hotel maid who pressed her pale blue satin gown and assisted her in arranging her hair in a fashionable chignon, smoothed high atop her head with a few delicate curls escaping in wispy corkscrews around her temples.

Cain entered the room after a perfunctory knock just as she was dismissing the maid. The large Polish woman sidled past him with a nervous curtsy, then made a hasty exit. He ignored her and turned his attention to his wife. "You look delectable," he said hoarsely, drinking in the way the low-cut satin gown shimmered in the light, molding sensuously to the subtle curves of her body. The royal blue lace trim on the bodice and hem matched the rich twinkle of sapphires at her throat and ears.

Roxanna smiled and returned his perusal, stepping closer to adjust the charcoal silk tie at his neck with wifely propriety. "I see you're wearing my little gift," she said, pleased, ever amazed at how startling his elegant transformation was each time she saw him in formal clothing.

"I'd scarcely call a set of diamond shirt studs a 'little gift,'" he replied with a lazy drawl, tilting her chin up for a soft brushing kiss. "You must've used up half the trust money buying them."

"There is much more," she said airily, although she had about exhausted what funds were left in Alexa's account on the purchase. "You'll be the handsomest man at the party tonight."

He chuckled. "Hardly difficult considering that Durant is a dried-up old piece of rawhide and Seymour is hog fat and combs his hair in a swirled pompadour to hide his bald spot."

Roxanna burst into laughter. "I take it you've met them before."

"Not really. I've been in the background when the vice president and his consulting engineer came to do battle with Jubal over surveys and building plans. They're a pair of highbinders who'll milk the Union Pacific for every cent of profit they can squeeze out of it."

Roxanna digested this, fitting it into the information about railroad politics she was accumulating in her mind. "I take it my grandfather doesn't care for them. What about Oliver Ames? As president of the Union Pacific, is he above profiteering?"

"He's not as blatant about it as Durant and Seymour, but yes, he and his brother Oakes have made a few million on construction contracts. He's a glib New England charmer, though, in a grandfatherly sort of way."

She sniffed. "Then there'll be no man worthy of working my wiles on but you."

"I'm certain you'll find some men to charm," he replied dryly. "Between the factions of Durant and Ames, they've invited half the Congress on this little junket. Jubal wants me to feel them out about subsidy increases, more rigorous inspection standards, and government intervention to set a meeting site for the Central Pacific and Union Pacific."

He obviously did not relish the assignment, she thought with a wry smile. How ironic that this was precisely the sort of dinner table intrigue at which she excelled. "Perhaps I'll overhear something of value. I shall keep my ears open," she said, gliding out the door on his arm.

By the time they were halfway through the interminable dinner's sixth course, Cain realized Alexa had made no idle promise. Sitting between the garrulous old fool Seymour and the chairman of the Senate Railroad Oversight Committee, she extracted useful tidbits of information with such effortless ease that the two were completely unaware they were being "milked."

Burke Remington, the senator from Massachusetts, leaned back after the poached salmon course was served and observed her with unsettling blue eyes. He was of middle years, tall and well built with a thick head of graying blond hair and enough vanity to believe himself irresistible when he turned on his charm. "As consulting engineer, Silas, you're most informative about survey plans through Wyoming, but I suspect the lady would rather discuss something a bit less technical," Remington interjected just as Seymour finished describing his plans to circle around the Dale Creek Canyon area instead of building across it. Although he did not say it, this would add nearly fifty miles to the route and over two million dollars in federal subsidies.

Roxanna realized Remington was too shrewd for open flattery and decided it was best to try another tack. Smiling, she nodded. "Although some ladies do have a difficult time comprehending gradient quotients and soil density, as the granddaughter of a railroad builder, I confess to a rather unfeminine interest in how the transcontinental is being constructed."

"For myself, I find all this talk of routes and subsidies a crashing bore," the senator's young wife Sabrina said in her whispery Southern drawl. "Do let's change the subject." She leaned closer to Cain, affording him an ample view of large milky white breasts barely concealed in raspberry velvet. "Tell us about the West, Mr. Cain. Will we see a buffalo stampede . . . or wild Indians?"

She was a beauty with lustrous sable hair and a magnolia complexion, but there was a brittleness in her smile and an avid gleam of hunger in her china-blue eyes that set his teeth on edge. He'd seen it all too often before. "Sorry to disappoint, Mrs. Remington, but the buffalo are all pretty much to the north of our route this time of year. We might encounter a few, but believe me, you wouldn't want to be caught in a stampede any more than you'd want to meet any wild Indians."

"I should hope not!" Horace Scoville, an Ohio congressman, said with a shudder. "I hear the savages torture and kill decent God-fearing surveyors and workmen whenever they can slip through the army patrols.''

''And abduct innocent white women for their fiendish debaucheries,'' Hillary Seymour added, shaking her triple chins, as the horror of such ''debaucheries'' reddened her already florid complexion.

''You wouldn't know anything about those fiendish debaucheries, would you, sugar?'' Sabrina Remington whispered so low no one but Cain could hear her. Her foot, free of its slipper, caressed his leg in a swift, unsubtle gesture.

Cain felt an urge to grab her by the ankle and haul her over to her husband, who seemed, for all his shrewd political instincts, to be oblivious to his much younger wife's sexual overtures. Or perhaps he simply did not care. Worse yet, was he using her in the hope of obtaining some information? Regardless, her expectations would be dashed, Cain thought grimly.

Once he might have cynically taken what she offered, telling himself that he didn't care that he was an exotic forbidden curiosity to her. To him, women like her had also been trophies, wives and daughters of rich white men, creatures of the world which had shut him out. But all that had changed. Sabrina Remington's little games were repellent. He was a married man now. The realization that he desired no woman but Alexa shocked him right down to the soles of his shoes.

Roxanna observed the subtle interchange between her husband and Remington's wife with seething fury, which she managed to conceal with great difficulty. If the oblivious senator was not so busy interfering in her attempts to ferret information from the railroad barons, he might have noticed what the little hussy was about! By the time the ladies excused themselves from the dining table, leaving the gentlemen to port and cigars, Roxanna was ready to dump the crystal vase filled with roses over Sabrina Remington's head. She pleaded a migraine to escape their dreary company and went in search of some headache powder.

''It was really surprising Mr. MacKenzie did not make

this trip,'' Hillary Seymour said, testing the waters as the ladies filed down the hallway into a parlor for their coffee.

"I confess I was shocked that he sent this Cain fellow," Cordelia Scoville whispered, taking the bait.

"Not half as shocked as I was that he permitted his granddaughter to marry such a person—why, he's no more than a savage in evening clothes, a gunman of mixed blood," Congressman Kittery's wife intoned in a scandalized voice.

"I heard rumors that she'd been ruined and no man of good family would marry her," Mrs. Seymour said. "Carried off by the savages, then escaped somehow."

Roxanna was not the only one bored with the women's backbiting gossip. Sabrina Remington was far more interested in meeting the mysterious Mr. Cain face-to-face than she was in talking about him—or his washed-out skinny stick of a wife. After enduring fifteen minutes or so of catty exchange about Cain and his wife, the garish ball gown General Grant's wife wore to President Johnson's gala and other tedious eastern society topics, Sabrina slipped out.

Burke would be closeted with Dr. Durant discussing Credit Mobilier affairs for hours. She smiled ferally and began her search. A pity Cain's wife had a headache. *I feel perfectly marvelous.* She intended to make Cain feel equally good.

Her prey had gone to the bar downstairs and ordered a whiskey on ice, a taste he'd acquired while living in San Francisco and seldom had the opportunity to indulge. The men had broken up into cliques quickly enough. Thoughts of Alexa in that blue satin concoction she had worn tonight played in his head, or rather thoughts concerning how delicious it would be to get her *out* of it.

He pulled his gold watch from his vest and checked the time, hoping the ladies had called it a night. His eagerness to bed his wife still worried him occasionally, but he was growing resigned to the marriage. She was beautiful and responsive. He'd be a fool not to desire her, he reminded himself as he polished off the last of his drink and made his way out of the bar.

The Remington woman was waiting for him as he crossed the lobby, heading toward the stairs. She materialized from behind a tall potted palm and placed one small hand sparkling with rings on his chest. "How delightful that we meet again, sugar. I know you couldn't tell me about wild Indians at table . . . but now we can be alone . . . and I am insatiably curious."

She drew closer and he could smell her musky perfume, heavy and sweet. After his rebuff of her at the dinner table, her boldness startled him. "You'll have to find another tour guide to satisfy that curiosity," he said in the soft deadly voice that made men tremble with fear.

She trembled another way altogether, licking her lips in that practiced sexual gesture. When he tried to brush her hand away, she slid her fingers in the front of his shirt, anchoring them in the crisp black hair, pulling until he cursed in annoyance at the discomfort. "My lands, what a shame your poor little wife is ill with a migraine."

"Why, Mrs. Remington, thank you so much for your concern. But I experienced a remarkable recovery as soon as I learned you'd left the ladies to their gossip," Roxanna purred. She glided up to them as Sabrina hissed in shock and stepped back. Placing one hand proprietarily on Cain's shoulder, Roxanna added with an arch smile, "This wild Indian is already taken. I suggest you look for another—or perhaps content yourself with the man you married, even if he does seem a bit old for wildness . . . of any sort."

For one instant Cain thought Sabrina was going to launch herself at Alexa. His wife did not even flinch but stood calmly, staring down at the shorter woman as if daring her. Sabrina Remington drew herself up with a nasty smirk. "I heard you lived with savages out West. Now I know it isn't just idle gossip."

After she stalked away, Roxanna turned to Cain, smoothing his shirt where Sabrina had wrinkled it. "It looks as if I saved you from having your chest scalped."

He scowled down at her possessive gesture. "I could've gotten rid of her without help. Hell, Alexa, all I need is to try explaining to Jubal how you got both eyes blacked in a catfight with a senator's wife.''

''You act as if I'd lose,'' she replied, affronted before she realized how boldly she had behaved. Was he displeased by her forwardness—or worse yet, angry because she interrupted a tryst?

Before she could turn away, he reached out and pulled her tightly into his arms. ''I'd bet on you every time, Her Back Is Straight,'' he murmured, inhaling the subtle lilac scent of her hair. ''This is our one night in a bed that isn't rolling over the rails. Let's take advantage of it.''

Breathless, she looked up into his eyes and read the hot raw hunger in them. Without another word, he scooped her up into his arms and strode to the deserted back stairs. In moments they entered their suite. The maid took one look at the way Cain held his wife and mumbled her excuses.

''You're awfully hard on help,'' she murmured against his throat, not sounding particularly concerned as he set her down in front of him and began unfastening the row of tiny satin-covered button loops running down the back of her gown. With his arms around her, he was working blind, but he was exceedingly deft at the task. ''You've had lots of practice disrobing ladies,'' she said with a hint of crossness in her voice.

He smiled against her hair. ''Not exactly ladies . . . but there was this dancer on the Barbary Coast who wore satin costumes with buttons—''

She gave him a playful punch in the stomach. ''I don't want to hear about your other women. . . . Were there terribly many of them?'' She chewed her lip in vexation.

''As many as leaves on the trees, as plentiful as buffalo on the prairie,'' he replied with a mock accent as he peeled the heavy dress from her shoulders and began tugging it down her arms.

In spite of herself, Roxanna giggled. ''All right, great chief. Be serious. They were sporting women who knew . . .'' She felt her courage evaporate as his hands stilled on her arms. "That is . . . they knew how to please you."

"Not half as much as you please me," he admitted.

"But I don't really *do* that much. You do it all." Her face reddened in mortification. Whatever had she blurted out now? The encounter with the beauteous and sophisticated Sabrina Remington must have unhinged her mind—it certainly had her tongue!

One black eyebrow raised in amusement. She had such natural passion, all the right instincts in spite of the repression of her upbringing. He could teach her much and he knew she'd prove an apt pupil. He chuckled. "Oh, so you want to *do* more?"

His hands had continued their swift efficient task as they spoke until she was standing before him in nothing but high-heeled slippers, stockings and filmy undergarments. Dress and petticoats were pooled at her feet. He was still fully clothed. He raised her hands to his chest, willing her to continue. "Lesson one—a man likes a woman to undress him sometimes." With trembling, clumsy fingers she began removing the diamond studs as he shrugged out of the jacket. He held one palm out for her to deposit the sparkling jewelry.

When she had completed the task, he stood still, arms down until she peeled the shirt off his broad shoulders and discarded it. In so doing, her face moved close to his chest. The male scent of him filled her nostrils. Looking up into his eyes, she inhaled the heady aroma and he smiled, as if knowing how his nearness affected her.

"Don't stop now." His voice rumbled low, breaking the silence.

Working up her courage, she reached for his fly and began to unfasten the buttons. Then, feeling his shaft press against her fingers, she hesitated, biting her lip. His low wicked chuckle added more heat to her already flaming face. He stilled her hands and pulled away, whispering hoarsely, "Let me."

Roxanna watched as he quickly pulled off his shoes, then

yanked off his trousers and underwear. Her breath caught at the sheer male beauty of him, tall, lean, bronzed skin covering hard sinuous muscles. She stood still, entranced as he took her hand, expecting him to finish removing the rest of her clothes now that he was completely naked.

He surprised her. When they reached the bed, he stretched out on it, looking up at her and saying, "Lesson two— sometimes a man also likes a woman to undress for him while he watches. Real slow." The words were lazily drawled. A dare.

Roxanna had from her earliest successes as a spy considered herself a consummate actress who could assume any sort of role. But could she do this? Act the part of a bold, wanton woman using her body to entice, seduce, enslave? She studied his languorous pose, noting his rock-hard straining staff. He was certainly moved by her initial ministrations. A slow smile began to work its way across her face. Perhaps she could do some teaching.

Watching her from beneath hooded eyelids, he sensed the change immediately. A subtle shift from blushes and reticence to a new realization of her power. When he had told her before that a woman had power over a man, he knew she had not believed him. But she did now. *What have I done?* he thought uneasily as Alexa began to tug ever so slowly at the drawstring of her chemise. When it came loose, she wriggled her shoulders, provocative as Lilith. The wispy silk fell over a creamy expanse of flesh and caught, just barely caught, on the hardened tip of one nipple.

He almost jumped straight off the bed. Only by a sheer act of will, clenching his fists in the sheets, did he remain recumbent. She let the chemise cling, turning her attention to her earrings, removing one sapphire pendulum, then the other. Her fingers toyed with the heavy necklace nestling between her breasts, then glided past it, ignoring the chemise, moving to the tapes holding up her lacy pantalets. She unfastened them with mind-bendingly delicious hesitation. "You might hurry just a bit," he urged, alarmed at how hoarse he was. Damn, he was on fire!

Roxanna could see the effect she was having on him, hear it in his voice. She slid her hands around her waist and began to slide the lacy underdrawers down, pausing at her navel, then moving lower to the curve of her hips. When his breathing hitched again, she stopped, gliding her splayed fingers back up to the edge of the chemise, tugging on the bottom while shrugging her covered shoulder free of the silk. This time it slithered past both rigid nipples, baring her breasts.

The silk bunched around her waist. She gathered it in her hands and stretched her arms up, pulling it slowly over her head, then tossed it to him. The gauzy white silk seemed to float across the space between them. He reached out his hand and caught it, bringing it to his lips, inhaling. "Lilacs," he murmured, his eyes riveted to the pale pink rosettes crowning her breasts. They seemed to tighten even more as he stared, fueling the low fire building deep inside her belly.

The slower I go, the hotter I feel, she thought ruefully. She was desperate for him to touch her, to take her this very moment! She undulated her hips in an unmistakable roll and the lacy drawers dropped to her knees. She kicked them away and stood for a moment. Clad only in high-heeled slippers and silk stockings held up by pale blue satin garters, she remembered the way they had made such wild love against the wall in their railcar and wondered if he too was thinking of it.

He was. His reckless hunger that day had worried him, not just the fear that he would frighten his bride with his lust, but also that he was so uncontrollably enthralled by this slim blond woman. His throat closed up when she placed one small foot on the edge of the mattress and worked it free of the dark blue satin slipper. He could smell the sweet musk of her body, ready, eager for him. She flexed her knee provocatively. He never realized just how long, how slender her legs were until she began to roll down the garter, peeling the silk stocking along with it. She tossed the first stocking on the floor, then reached up for the heavy gold clasp of the sapphire necklace.

"Hmmm. I think I'll leave this on . . . for modesty's sake." She turned her attention to her remaining shoe and removed it and her last stocking, even more slowly.

Just as she started to toss away the stocking, he encircled her slender ankle with his hand and tumbled her onto the bed. He caught the stocking as he rolled her across him and onto her back in the center of the big mattress. When he raised up over her and looked down into her eyes, he could not mistake the feline satisfaction and triumph. Her arms encircled his shoulders, pulling him closer.

"Was that something like you had in mind?" she asked innocently. All the while her heart beat frantically and need for him clawed deep in her belly.

"Something like," he echoed, obliging her with a deep hungry kiss, opening his mouth and molding his lips on hers, hot as a furnace. His tongue swept across the seam of her lips and plunged inside when she opened, drawing her tongue to mate with it, sucking, then thrusting his tongue in swift sweet strokes until she was breathless.

Her fingers burrowed through his hair, holding on to his head as he savaged her mouth with rapacious kisses. When he moved lower to her throat, pausing at one ear to flick the tip of his tongue inside, she shivered with pleasure. Smiling, he ran his mouth over the furiously thrumming pulse in her throat. His hand cupped one pearly breast with its pale pink crest standing erect, begging to be caressed. He tweaked it between finger and thumb until she whimpered, then slid down to place his mouth on it. She arched up, digging her nails into the banded muscles of his back. As he suckled one breast, his hand readied the other for the sweet ministration of his mouth.

He felt her quiver as tiny moans of pleasure escaped her lips. At length, he moved away from the feast of her breasts, tracing a wet trail with his tongue down to her navel. His hands spanned her slim waist, then slid over the curve of her hips, as his face pressed into the concave softness of her belly. Her head tossed from side to side on the pillows, spilling pale hair like a silvery waterfall about her shoulders. She writhed, still emitting the little sounds of pleasure until his mouth brushed the soft curls at the apex of her thighs.

Roxanna stiffened and raised her head. "Cain, what are you doing?"

Chapter 13

"Making love to my wife," he paused long enough to reply raggedly. "Lie back." He cupped the round smoothness of her buttocks in his hands and lifted her hips like an offering on a pagan altar.

"You can't—"

"I can," he murmured, nuzzling her moist pink petals with his lips, then letting his tongue flick out, seeking the swollen little bud at the core of her body. The instant he touched it, he could feel her response. A low keening cry issued from her lips. She grew very still, terrified with this strange new and intense loving.

Hearing her moans of helpless ecstasy, he applied himself to the unfamiliar exercise. He had mostly used whores when he needed sex and this was not an act he would perform on them. This was a special gift for a sensuous, passionate woman who enjoyed lovemaking as much as her man did. Alexa was made to be loved this way and he was enjoying teaching her more than he would ever have imagined possible.

Feeling the heat of his mouth on her, her mind simply shut down and her body took over. She should be shocked, horrified. This was depraved, sinful . . . unimaginable, delicious. . . .

Cherishing and coaxing, he stroked new, more intense

sensations from the core of her femininity. Her hips were motionless, cupped in his hands; her heels dug into the mattress on either side of his torso, her thighs spread wide. She was offering herself to him. And it was glorious beyond anything she had ever felt before. The starburst of orgasm came so swiftly, so intensely that it left her panting, too breathless to cry out.

Cain felt her arch up taut as a bowstring. Then the pulsing contractions began. He kept his mouth on her, firm and hot, until they began to fade. Swiftly, before she could recover from the lethargy of culmination, he slid up her body, covering her as his hand guided the thick aching length of his staff to the sweet portal it craved so desperately. He plunged swiftly inside with a guttural oath that was endearment.

Roxanna floated on a wave of blissful satiety an instant before she felt the steel power of his body lay claim to hers. His first thrust seemed as if it should have sundered her body in two. But it did not. She could feel the desperate, long-denied hunger in him and gloried in it. He had loved her thoroughly and deserved his own release. Eagerly she tightened her legs around his hips, arching up to meet his slick heavy plunging, only to feel the old familiar heat beginning to spread across her belly, centering where he was joined to her.

"Yes," he whispered to the silent question in her passion-glazed eyes when they opened in wonder, then fluttered closed once more as she joined in the ever-quickening rhythm. He braced his arms on either side of her, raising his upper body so he could thrust deeper, harder. His teeth were clenched as he struggled to hold back, prolonging the incredible soul-engulfing pleasure, feeling her sweet tight sheath squeeze him. Finally, he could withstand the exquisite torture not a moment longer. Crying her name, he spun out of control, pulsing semen deep and high against her womb, as great shuddering waves of climax seared him, drained him.

Roxanna felt his body tense and his shaft swell even more deeply inside of her, filling her with the sweet liquid heat of his seed. Her own passion crested with his, each intensifying the other. Cain trembled as he collapsed on top of her. She welcomed the weight of his big sweat-slicked body, enfolding him in her arms, her legs entwining with his, murmuring a soft declaration of love low against his chest. He could not hear it over the ragged sounds of their breathing and the thundering of their hearts.

The sightseeing trip west began early the next morning. The small group, hand-selected by Dr. Durant, assembled on the platform of the train station. Unfortunately, from Roxanna's point of view, the Remingtons were among them. So were Silas Seymour and his garrulous wife and the odious Scovilles. She did not tell Cain that the rumors regarding her captivity had been spread through the upper echelons of railroad social circles. It would serve nothing, except to make him brood more about his Cheyenne blood tainting her. One benefit of this junket was that the scandalized curiosity and veiled hostility of their guests drew the two of them closer together. With no assignment to take him from her side, they slept and awakened together more days in a row than they had in all the preceding months of their marriage.

Roxanna adored waking up each morning to feel his big body curved around hers, an arm or leg thrown possessively across her. Often she would lie quietly just inhaling the scent of him, sometimes raising her head to watch him sleep, studying the magnificence of his long limbs and broad muscular chest, the cunning patterns of black hair on his skin. Occasionally she would reach out and touch the raspy bristle of his night's growth of whiskers. Of course that often awakened him. Then he would roll over and pull her beneath him, his quick passion igniting hers.

How different it was to live with a husband, to love him and laugh with him, to share his dreams as well as his body when he made love to her. Roxanna treasured every moment. Since Vicksburg she had never imagined that this wonderful life, the hope of every other young woman, would ever be possible for her. But the shadow of Isobel

Darby still haunted her dreams, making the time spent loving Cain doubly precious.

The first few days of the trip were uneventful as the prosaic flat farmlands of Illinois and Iowa were traversed. Indeed the only breaks in the monotony were the lavish meals served by Durant's private chef, brought with him from New York. The second day out as everyone shared a breakfast of sweet pink ham, then lacy crepes and fresh strawberries, Ralph Benner, a native New Yorker, commented on the monotony of the scenery.

Mrs. Scoville took umbrage on behalf of her husband's agricultural constituents from central Ohio. Drawing herself up, she said glacially, "You can keep all your high and mighty Rocky Mountains, even the fancy European Alps. I for one would far prefer to gaze out over a fertile American cornfield any day."

"So would a hog," Sabrina Remington drawled just loud enough to carry across the aisle to the Scovilles' table.

"Well, I never!" Cordelia Scoville huffed, turning as fuchsia as her dress.

Roxanna almost liked Sabrina for a moment . . . but it passed. Even Cain smothered a smile behind his hand as Dr. Durant quickly changed the subject.

When the train rolled into Nebraska, the terrain began to change dramatically. Rich cultivated fields gave way to vast tractless stretches of wilderness where tall stands of wild grasses dipped their gold and russet blades against the fierce plains winds.

"It's so desolate out here. Whyever would anyone want to come west?" Cordelia Scoville asked pettishly, gazing out the dining car window at luncheon one day.

"What is the railroad going to transport? It seems to me there's not a cash crop that would grow between the Missouri River and California," the congressman chimed in.

Thomas Durant's deep-set eyes narrowed on Scoville, but his smile was politic as he replied in his smooth manner, "The wealth of the Orient, for openers, Congressman. Just think of it, gentlemen—and ladies—the riches of China and

India brought to California by American clipper ships, loaded on rails across America, then sent by American sail to the rich markets of Europe.'' He steepled his hands and looked over well-manicured fingers at the people surrounding him. Durant loved to pontificate. ''Why, the route across this continent will revolutionize world trade, eliminating the lengthy and dangerous passage around the Cape of Africa.''

''What about that canal Napoleon III is building at Suez?'' Burke Remington asked. ''A pathway between the Mediterranean and the Indian Ocean would revolutionize world trade even more.''

Silas Seymour harrumphed, then spoke in his pompous deliberate way as if on cue from Durant. ''Ferdinand de Lesseps's Frenchmen have been attempting to complete that Promethean endeavor for nearly a decade. It's an engineering fantasy which will never be translated into reality,'' he pronounced.

Not wanting to dispute Seymour's blithe dismissal of the Suez project, Cain shifted the topic. ''The real reason for the transcontinental lies here in the United States, most particularly in the West. Rails will link this country together and enable stockmen and farmers to develop the land the way mining interests have already tapped into mineral wealth.''

''You sound positively idealistic, Cain,'' Remington said cynically.

''What will happen to your Indians when all this civilization comes with the completion of the rails?'' Scoville asked. His narrow little weasel face squinted in concentration as he leaned forward, verbally daring Cain to respond.

''They're not *my* Indians, Congressman,'' Cain replied in a level voice. His eyes bored into Scoville's.

The little man quickly subsided. ''I only thought . . . that is, since you're part Indian, I assumed you had an opinion on the issue.''

''I do. The Indians will lose . . . everything,'' Cain replied flatly, then dismissed Scoville coldly, turning to stare out the window at the tractless rolling hills of western Nebraska.

Roxanna interjected a comment, and conversation shifted away from the ugly insinuations of Scoville. She could feel that Remington woman's lascivious gaze on Cain as she placed her hand on her husband's arm. He turned, giving her a look which indicated he was used to such innuendos. But she knew they still hurt.

The next morning they sighted their first buffalo, a small scattered herd that had wandered south. Several of the men seized guns, all jabbering excitedly.

"Haven't had a shot at one of the old beasts from a running train all year," Silas Seymour said, carefully arranging a hat on his windblown pompadour.

"A hundred dollars says I down the first one." Ralph Benner, one of the directors, waved a Winchester around as carelessly as if it were a child's toy.

"Ooh, I'd love to try my hand, Burke. Could I shoot one?" Sabrina Remington cooed to the senator, who sat back in bored amusement as the other easterners bounded around like children.

"Really, Mrs. Remington, fire a weapon?" Hillary Seymour said, raised eyebrows indicating how uncouth she considered the idea.

"I say, Cain, have the trainmen slow the engines so we can get a better shot," Durant directed imperiously when Cain entered the parlor car.

"No one's going to shoot buffalo from this train," he said to a chorus of angry exclamations.

"Whyever not? I always allow my guests a little target practice. It's quite the sporting thing," Durant said in frosty affront, glaring at Cain.

"I'll arrange a shoot when we reach North Platte. The *sportsmen*"—he emphasized the word scornfully—"will have better luck on solid ground."

"But what harm to pop a few as we ride by?" Scoville asked in affront.

"That's just it—you ride by. You leave the carcass to rot, hides, meat and all. There are hungry people who can use the buffalo you shoot."

"Hungry Indians?" Burke Remington taunted.

"They were still people the last time I checked," Roxanna snapped, thoroughly disliking the arrogant and cynical senator as much as she detested his sluttish young wife.

"Phil Sheridan's policy is to decimate the buffalo so the hostiles will starve. I understand Grant agrees and he'll be president soon," Remington said, looking over at Cain. "What do you think of such an idea?"

Cain shrugged. "Barbarous but effective. Inevitably whites will win. What starvation and soldiers don't kill, smallpox and measles will."

"What a ghoulish plan," Hillary Seymour said. "Surely an enlightened, civilized society can think of a better way to deal with savages."

"This is men's business, Hillary," Silas said peremptorily to his wife, then turned to Cain, red-faced and blustering. "We want to have a bit of sport. You can't—"

"Jubal MacKenzie put me in charge of this little junket, gentlemen, and I don't intend to have a bunch of greenhorns shooting their own feet off, not to mention each other." He reached over and relieved Seymour of his shotgun. "And what do you think you can do with this? That game is so far out of range for this weapon you'd stand a better chance of throwing rocks and hitting a buffalo."

Seymour's face turned an even brighter cherry red as he harrumphed angrily, but he made no attempt to retrieve the weapon from Cain. Then the sharp report of a rifle echoed from the rear car. With an angry oath, Cain stormed for the door between cars, pausing long enough to order, "If anyone else fires a weapon on this train, they will shortly thereafter be walking to North Platte."

Just as he reached the car and jerked open the door, another shot rang out and a young buffalo bull standing outside the shelter of the herd went partway down, then staggered back onto its feet and moved slowly toward its fellows. "Scoville, you son of a bitch, I told everyone no shooting from the train."

The congressman smirked. "I hit one. That's all I intended to do."

"And you didn't kill it," Cain said savagely, seizing the carbine from the little man's hands as Scoville backed away.

The others in the party had filed after Cain in curiosity. He stormed past them, shoving the weapon into Durant's hands. "Put this and all the others away after the train stops."

"Stops? I thought you said we weren't to have a shoot until North Platte," Ralph Benner said.

"We aren't. I have to finish that bull. No hunter worth his salt leaves a wounded animal to suffer." He made his way through them and vanished into the next car. En route he encountered Mrs. Durant with several of the other women. "Tell all the ladies to be prepared for a stop."

She nodded as he continued forward. Shortly the train slowed to a halt and a livestock car was rolled open. The passengers disembarked to watch as a bay gelding was led down a ramp, bridled but not saddled.

"Just like the dime novels," Sabrina said with a wicked chuckle as she watched Cain swing up and ride off bareback.

"I say, perhaps this will be a better show than just popping off the guns in front of the ladies," one of the directors interjected. Eager to watch Cain dispatch the quarry, several others brought out pairs of field glasses, far safer for them to operate than firearms.

"He looks like one of those savages, no matter the civilized clothing," Cordelia Scoville whispered to her companion. Her voice carried to Roxanna on the clear dry air.

Cain approached the herd, which so far had not stampeded. Seeing the wounded bull, he slid down from his horse and raised his .52 caliber Spencer. The buffalo stood still, its bloodied rear shank trembling, staring at the man. Then, without warning, it began a ponderous charge in spite of its injury.

Watching from a distance, Roxanna bit down on her

knuckles when the bull charged at her husband. "He's on foot—if he misses—"

A shot rang out. The great beast went down cleanly, but the wind shifted suddenly and the herd caught the blood scent. In seconds, scores of placidly grazing animals thundered in a mass, billowing up thick clouds of dust.

Roxanna screamed out Cain's name and began to run toward him. Everyone around her raced the opposite direction for the cars, over a hundred yards distant.

As Cain remounted, he heard Alexa's voice, faint over the pounding roar of the stampede. He kicked his horse into a gallop, yelling for her. What was the fool woman doing out here?

The herd ran instinctively from the scent of death, heading straight for the train. Cain followed the sound of Alexa's voice through the clouds of dust, praying he would reach her before they did. Suddenly she materialized, her once-vivid rose morning dress now coated tan, almost blending with the air.

"Alexa," he yelled, leaning down to scoop her up across the horse's withers as he reined the animal to the left, cutting away from the approaching buffalo.

Roxanna clung to his leg as they galloped furiously over the sun-baked earth. Beneath her the horse's hooves churned. If she fell off, she would be mangled beneath sharp iron shoes! She felt Cain's hand gripping her rucked-up skirts tightly, closed her eyes and prayed. Finally, after what seemed hours but could only have been minutes, he pulled the horse to a stop.

The ground still vibrated from the stampeding beasts that had swept around the front of the train, but the sound was growing fainter now and the air was beginning to clear. He released his desperate hold on her and lowered her from the horse, then slid down after her. She coughed until her eyes teared, trying to drag air into her lungs as he held her, soothing her. "Take slow, even breaths, don't clench up."

At last she gasped, "Thank God you're all right."

"Me? I was mounted! What the hell possessed you to run

into the middle of a stampede on foot? Were you going to shoo the buffalo away like they were chickens?" His fingers bit into her arms, then he pressed her against his chest as she sobbed.

"I watched as you almost died that way once. I couldn't do it again. I . . . I just didn't think. You were dismounted when they turned to run and then I couldn't see you." She could feel the pads of his thumbs rubbing the trail of tears from her eyes.

"Alexa, I'm sorry." He tilted her chin up and looked into her eyes, red-rimmed and bloodshot from the stinging dust. Two muddy rivulets had cut a pathway through the caked grime on her cheeks. Her hair looked as if it were a powdered wig. A woman had never seemed more beautiful to him than his wife did at that moment. What if he had lost her? He squeezed the frightening consideration from his mind and crushed her to his chest. "Don't ever do anything like that again or I'll tan that lovely little backside pink. Why didn't any of those so-called men try to stop you?"

Snuggled securely against his chest, she felt giddy with relief. "I suppose because they were too busy stampeding back to the train themselves."

"Jubal didn't realize what he was asking when he gave me this assignment," he said grimly.

She grinned through her grime at his harsh dirty face. "Oh, I rather imagine he knew exactly what he was asking. No harm's been done, Cain. It would be most politic to put the whole foolish incident behind us rather than alienate the directors and their political backers any more."

He could hear the cautioning tone in her voice and knew she was right. "Damn, but I want to take that little weasel Scoville and throw him in front of a rutting bull buffalo to be stomped into mush! But I guess I won't," he added reluctantly as he swung back up onto his mount and pulled her into his lap.

"We were supposed to have enough bathwater aboard to last two more days. After we get through scrubbing all this off, I bet the others will have to make do with cat washes until North Platte,'' Roxanna said as they rode back to the train.

The staged buffalo hunt in North Platte went off smoothly, as did several stops en route to Cheyenne for sightseeing on horseback. Horace Scoville had subsided into sullen quiet and Burke Remington's attempts to provoke a fight between various members of the party had ceased. Although the women were superficially polite to her, Roxanna knew they considered her little better than a calico cat. The men, however, were fascinated by her beauty and charm in spite of— or perhaps because of—the curiosity of her having survived the infamous ''fate worse than death'' only to wed the equally infamous Scot's Injun.

After two days of political speeches, banquets and baby kissing in the new territorial capital of Cheyenne, the excursion continued in the mountainous grades to the west. As they approached the high bridge near the summit in the Medicine Bows, the train chugged laboriously on the long inclines.

''Why is the train going so slowly?'' Ralph Benner complained, peering out at the mountains.

''We've been climbing steadily uphill for the past day. The boilers can only stand so much pressure pulling a long heavily laden string of cars like these,'' Cain explained. ''We'll hit the crest just a few miles before the bridge. After that we'll pick up speed into Laramie.''

By late afternoon the scenery grew increasingly more spectacular, with snowcapped peaks glistening on the far horizon and summer field flowers blazing in purple, russet and white splendor. When the silly chatter of the women and bombastic posturing of the railroad barons became too much for her, Roxanna slipped away to search for Cain, who in response to a message had gone to the car where the horses were kept at the rear of the train. It was tricky negotiating between the last of the parlor cars and the freight cars. She waited for him in a deserted smoking car, hoping for a few moments alone. When he entered the car, she smiled mischievously and said, "I couldn't stand Dr. Durant's pontificating about the Union Pacific linking the Levant to London another minute. I don't think he really believes it."

"Not according to Jubal. The good doctor is just in this to milk all the money he can from the government, then pull out and the Union Pacific be damned."

"Why—" She stopped speaking when the train gave a sudden lurch forward. "What was that?"

He frowned. "I don't know." He glanced out the side window, then opened the door through which he had just come and stepped out onto the platform.

Roxanna heard his oath before he returned, grim-faced. "What's happened?"

"The freight cars have come uncoupled."

"But how?"

"I'm not certain. It's been a long hard pull up the divide. Maybe the strain caused a coupling pin to give way when we crested the hill and started downward, or the yardmen in Cheyenne didn't check the couplings carefully enough."

"We'll be in Laramie in a few hours. Surely they can send an engine out to pull the freight cars in," she said reasonably.

His eyes narrowed on the slow decline of topography outside the window. "We may not have to pick them up. They may just pick us up," he replied grimly.

"What do you mean? Oh!" she gasped, realizing they were curving around a series of low dips and rises in their descent into Laramie. If the loose cars behind them gained momentum over the next few downhill turns, they might just crash into the passenger cars from the rear.

"Yeah. It could be a pretty tight race. We've got to put on some real steam and pull enough ahead to reach the switching tracks at the railhead." He held her by her arms and looked into her eyes. "I need your help, Alexa. Go forward and start rounding up all the passengers. Get them into the front Pullman next to the engine. Have everyone lie on the floor. I'm going to tell the engineer. Then I'll be back to help you." He studied her face. "Will you be all right until I return?"

"You're wasting time, Cain," she replied, trying to appear as calm as possible.

He nodded, then ran past her, racing to reach the engineer.

Train wreck! Roxanna tried not to panic as she made her way back through the cars. She approached the men smoking and playing cards in the next car. "There's an emergency. We need to get everyone up front." She quickly explained what had happened.

"You mean the train might crash?" Scoville squeaked.

Seymour huffed and Durant paled but nodded. "We should get everyone to the first car. It would be safest."

They set out through the train, gathering up all the passengers. Surprisingly enough, when Cordelia Scoville and even old Mrs. Seymour grew hysterical, fainting and sobbing, Sabrina Remington, in a no-nonsense manner at odds with her usual syrupy drawl, told the older women to pull themselves together and move to the front of the train. Seizing hold of the blubbering Cordelia, Sabrina practically dragged her forward to the front car. The others followed docilely.

Over the rhythmic roar of the steam locomotive, Cain quickly explained to the engineer what had happened. "Maybe we can get the attention of the crew on those freight cars. Hit the whistle a loud blast—distress call. The cook and several of his helpers are on the food car, plus stock handlers in the back. If they look out and see what's happened, they can try to set the hand brakes."

"Not easy, but it could work," the engineer, Paul "Jingles" Pringles, replied. The big blond Swede blew a mighty blast on the whistle, followed by several more as Cain climbed out of the cabin to watch for a response. Nothing.

He cursed, finally climbing back down into the cabin. "It's as if they're all gone, but I know they can't be."

"How close are the cars?" Jingles asked.

"Close!"

The engineer paled, opening the throttle wide while his

stoker fed the voracious boiler. Cain helped the fireman haul wood from the bin across the floor, tossing it into the maw of the furnace until it was fed as much as it could hold.

The engineer had never run this far west before, but Cain was familiar with every mile of treacherous curves on this run, having supervised the grading and laying of track. The heavily laden livestock and supply cars might catch up on any of several curves, literally knocking the passenger cars off the rails and down steep rock embankments.

"There's a sharply dropping turn coming up around that outcrop of shale about a mile ahead," he said, pointing to the left. "Can the train hold the track?"

Jingles wiped the sweat from his face with a greasy red bandanna. "Your guess is good as mine, Mr. Cain. I ain't never run a train wide-open throttle downhill on curves like that last one we just took, but if we made that, hell, I reckon we'll make the rest."

Cain climbed out of the cabin again and leaned over, looking for the uncoupled freight cars. "We gained a couple hundred yards on them on that last incline. I'm going to lighten up these passenger cars, see if we can increase our speed. You keep on that whistle. What the hell's happened to those men?"

Jingles nodded. "Send me a man to keep watch on the runaway cars. If anyone aboard applies the hand brakes, I'll need to slow this baby down—quick."

"Right." He walked into the first car, now filled with passengers, and sent Benner forward, then said to the others, "I need able-bodied men." He selected four Union Pacific employees and Remington, Argyle and Schmidt, all chosen because they were larger men who could lift and carry. "We're going to throw anything we can overboard to lighten the load on the engine."

He directed the men to disperse through the cars, tossing out the doors and windows all the trunks of clothing and linens, furniture, weapons and ammunition, everything not nailed down. At one point a hysterically screeching Cordelia Scoville came storming into the car that several of the men with Cain had just finished cleaning out.

"How dare you!" she accused, red-faced with fury, glaring at Cain. "I just saw my trunks—all my jewels, my new Worth ball gown—everything thrown down a ravine in this desolate wilderness!"

"Unless you want to be thrown down a ravine right after it, I suggest you get out of our way," he replied.

"He'll do it too," Sabrina Remington said cheerfully, coming up behind them.

"I'll have you know Mr. Ames is a personal friend of the congressman's. I'll see you fired from the Union Pacific, you—you red savage, you!"

"If we crash, we'll all be fired, literally," Sabrina said. "Come along, Cordelia." She pulled the huffing, teary-eyed congressman's wife back through the door.

Dismissing her, Cain scanned the car for anything metal that could be used as a crowbar, ordering the others to do likewise. Soon they had seized whatever would serve and began loosening beds, heavy brass fixtures, even the seats fastened to the floor. Within twenty minutes the last three cars were totally stripped and the rugged rocky earth they sped past was littered with the opulence of the Union Pacific, right down to its brass cuspidors.

The shrill screech of the whistle still failed to rouse anyone on the freight cars, which kept bobbing back into view every time they crested a slight rise on a heavy grade spiraling down into Laramie. The train bounded from the rough tracks at every bump. Surely it would jump the rails at any second! On they sped past ravines, with the desperate cry of the whistle echoing after them.

Some of the women sobbed, a few cried frantically. Roxanna did what she could to comfort them, then went in search of Cain. If they were all going to die, at least she would do so at his side. *Perhaps he'll tell me he loves me.* It would almost be worth it to hear those words.

With terror clogging her throat, she made her way through the stripped cars, stumbling and losing her footing with every lurch and bump. Crossing the platforms between cars was particularly dangerous, but she persevered, with white knuckles gripping the railing past the first coupling. Then at the second, the wind whipped her hair free of its pins and sent it flying across her face, obscuring her vision. She reached up with one hand and brushed it away just as the cars bounced hard against the iron rails. Her grip on the railing was torn loose by the impact and she screamed, clawing frantically for something to hold on to as she fell.

The earth flew by in a sickening blur beneath her as she hung suspended between the two platforms. She struggled to gain purchase for her feet on the coupling while clawing hand over hand on the railing so that she could climb back up. Her long skirts whipped in the wind, wrapping around her legs like a coffin shroud. The soft-soled slippers on her feet slipped from the greasy surface of the coupling and she almost went down. Arching her back frantically, she regained a foothold and started to pull herself up once more.

Cain opened the door and stepped onto the platform, ready to jump across the cars when he saw Alexa. Her hands were just about to give way as he threw himself to the platform floor and seized a fistful of her silvery hair, the first thing he could grab as it streamed out like a flag behind her. Then he grabbed her arm and began to lift her up very carefully until he had her completely back onto the platform. Kneeling, he pulled her into his arms and fell back against the car door, holding her tightly.

"What the hell are you doing back here?" he yelled over the deafening clank and screaming whistle.

Roxanna looked up into his face, pale in spite of his bronzed skin. The ground rushed by them in a blur of sickening speed, but she saw nothing but the expression in her husband's eyes: fear . . . love?

Before she could say anything, they were pitched into a hard roll when the cars were whipped around another bend in the track cut through solid walls of granite, the sharpest on the downhill grade yet. Cain could feel the wheels on the left side leave the track as the train tilted precariously. Would it hold? Or would they career into the granite wall of the cut? He held tight to his wife and prayed.

They cleared the curve—barely. Cain struggled to his feet with Alexa as the men helping him dismantle the cars appeared in the door behind them. "Go on forward. There's nothing more we can do," he said, steadying her with his arm as the others crossed the platforms and filed ahead. Carefully Cain helped Alexa across.

They reached the opposite door just as the deafening scream of metal skidding on metal was followed by the sharp crack of wood splintering. The sound of the freight and kitchen cars smashing into the rocky wall of the cut was deafening. Dust and debris shot up with the impact of a charge of patent blasting oil. She burrowed her head against his shoulder, shuddering. Almost at once the train began to slow.

"Oh, Cain, those men! The cooks, the stock handlers—the horses."

"Christ! I'll see what happened. We need to keep the others together until I find out."

He started to turn away, intent on getting his Spencer in case any of the horses were still alive and injured, but she pulled his head down for a swift life-affirming kiss.

"Thank you again for my life."

"Please, take better care of it from now on," he replied gruffly, jumping off the train, which had now all but stopped.

Everyone piled out of the cars, all talking at once. Cain issued curt orders to the stewards, secured weapons and began to walk back up the grade to the site of the crash. Roxanna stood staring after him, wondering if she had read too much into the look in his eyes when he pulled her from the wheels.

When he returned, Cain's expression was stony. "It was sabotage," he said coldly. "One of the cook's helpers jumped the train just as we crested the divide. He pulled the pin to uncouple, timing it so the cars' momentum would carry them to catch up with us on the downhill curves. The pin was greased, or he would never have gotten it out. Still, it must've been a bitch getting it free at just the right moment. One of the stock handlers caught him after he did it and got his head bashed in for his trouble. He was able to talk. It's a miracle he lived.''

"What about the others?" Roxanna asked.

"Three dead from the crash. The other two are pretty banged up, but they'll survive—when whatever they were drugged with wears off.''

"Drugged?" Durant's eyebrows rose over his deep-set eyes. "Then there's no doubt this was a deliberate attempt by the Central Pacific hooligans to kill me."

"You and all the other directors aboard," Cain said dryly.

"Dastardly business, dastardly," Seymour huffed.

"If the plan had worked and the heavier freight cars had barreled into us on one of the curves, there wouldn't have been so much as two splinters left joined together after the dust settled. Ladies and gentlemen, we are very lucky,'' Cain said levelly.

"Are you certain the Central Pacific directors would countenance such ghastly carnage?" Burke Remington asked skeptically.

"Andrew Powell would," Cain replied levelly.

Chapter 14

"I don't see what you're waiting for," Isobel Darby snapped angrily, then took a calming sip from her glass of champagne. Andrew always imported Dom Perignon from France. "I want Roxanna Fallon destroyed."

Powell watched her agitated pacing from his chair by the window. This house had a splendid view of the bay—almost as fine as the one he had shared with his wife before her death. Now he and his son lived there alone. Lawrence was no doubt curious about Andrew's relationship with the chilly Southern belle. That was one reason Andrew ensconced her here, where Lawrence knew he had always kept his mistresses. Best if his son did not know the exact nature of his dealings with Isobel.

Not that bedding her hadn't been briefly diverting. Her very coldness had been a challenge. At first she had lain in icy resignation when he took her—until her body overrode her will. She hated herself because of the way she responded to him. After the first time, she had cried and thrown a Sevres vase at him, spitting and clawing when he finally subdued her. Isobel liked to be forced. Then she could pretend that she did not enjoy it, that she was still loyal to her poor dead husband. Andrew smiled sardonically for a moment, speculating whether her beloved colonel had ever tied her to a bed.

The widow paused in midstride, looking at the bemused heavy-lidded expression on Powell's face. She subdued the urge to claw it off. "You haven't been attending a word I've said, Andrew." She smoothed one pale elegant hand over the skirt of her violet silk evening gown. Although she could never give up the conceit of wearing mourning colors for Nathaniel, she did enjoy beautiful clothes . . . and black, gray and purple shades were her most becoming colors. "I had hoped by now that you understood what destroying that Fallon hussy means to me."

Her voice was syrupy and entreating, but her brittle body language and the hardness of her facial expression made the plea into a command. "I'll unmask your clever little impostor . . . when it suits me. Never fear, Miss Fallon will go down right along with Jubal MacKenzie. I have plans . . . elaborate, long-range plans that I do not intend to share with you."

"It has been two months. I'm growing tired of all the silly railroad politics."

"I told you when we first met, my dear, that this would be a matter of some delicacy, especially considering that MacKenzie married off the girl to his breed gunman. Cain is another chess piece I need to consider."

"Are you afraid of him?" She could not resist the snide remark.

Powell's expression darkened, but he did not raise his voice. "I'm not one of your silly Southern cavaliers who will leap to defend my honor, my dear. Frankly, you're beginning to bore me with your tiresome theatrics. Even your novelty in bed is wearing thin."

She stormed across the room, ready to fly at him, hands curved into claws, but at the last moment she stopped, struggling to regain her composure. A slow vitriolic smile spread across her face. "No, that is precisely what you wish me to do, isn't it, Andrew?"

He stood up and reached out to her, wrapping one large

hand brutally around her slender wrist and pulling her to him. "What I want you to do right now is shut up and leave MacKenzie and his supposed granddaughter to me. Is that quite clear, my dear?"

The pressure of his fist tightening around her wrist would leave an ugly bruise. She looked down at the effortless way he held the slender bones, knowing he could snap them with ease, and felt that dark thrum beginning to pound through her blood once more. "Damn you, Andrew," she cursed, but her voice was breathless with excitement she could not conceal.

As he lowered her to the floor and methodically began to tear open the front of her dress, she lay rigidly under him, willing herself to think only of the woman she hated above everything. Coming to Andrew Powell had been a mistake. She must get away from him . . . while she still could. Against her will, her body began to betray her yet again.

BEAR RIVER, IN THE NEWLY FORMED TERRITORY OF WYOMING

"I couldna' get Huntington to set a fixed meeting point," Jubal said wearily. "He still believes Powell can push the Central Pacific tracks past Salt Lake all the way to the Wyoming territorial line."

Cain pushed his hat back on his head and shed his buckskin jacket. It was warm in Jubal's railcar. "Now that Powell's got the Mormons grading track for him, Huntington could be right. We'll be up against tunneling through granite in a few weeks, Jubal. I know what that cost the Central Pacific in the Sierras."

"Then, by damn, we make no winter camp this year!" MacKenzie said, pounding on his desktop. "Can you keep the men working straight through till spring?"

Cain considered. "Depends on a number of things. As long as snow doesn't stop the supply trains, the men can work in the cold. Hell, the Chinese did it. We could reach the territorial line by December. They can survive the weather, but we're losing too many of them in those renegade attacks.''

"Dillon hasna' been able to catch them while I was in Washington, I take it," MacKenzie said sourly.

"A few narrow misses, but they always slip away. Johnny Lame Pony is nobody's fool. He's just as crafty as that cook's helper Powell planted on the train."

"I take it no link between that crash and Powell has turned up either." Jubal knew it was hopeless. "Damn but the man has his nerve, trying to kill half the Union Pacific directors and a good number of our political friends in Congress in the bargain!"

Cain grimaced. "With men like Scoville and Remington as friends, we just might be better off facing an honest enemy."

MacKenzie snorted angrily. "Honest and deadly. When I think he could've killed the lass and all those other women . . .''

"I'll pin that on him yet—and deal with his renegade raiders," Cain replied with determination. "Regular army patrols keep their attacks to a minimum, but our men are getting frightened—and the sabotage to tracks has been escalating. We have a real problem with supplies for our grading crews right now."

"Speaking of supplies, I picked up some interesting news while I was in Washington. Rumors swirl around Collis Huntington like maggots on putrid meat."

Cain looked up from the reports he was perusing. "What sort of rumors?" Jubal never concerned himself with petty gossip.

MacKenzie rubbed his hands over the one bit of heartening news with which he'd returned. "It seems, laddie, that Huntington's upset over some irregularities in the shipments of Central Pacific material. He and old Mark Hopkins have been comparing notes between what's listed on the cargo manifests on the East Coast and what arrives in San Francisco harbor. Someone's skimming . . . to the tune of several million dollars. And if you think I have a tight-fisted Scot's soul, you havena' seen the likes of Mark Hopkins.''

"A falling out between the Central Pacific directors in the offing,'' Cain mused. ''Do you think Powell is involved in the theft? It isn't like him to be careless—or to chance messing with Huntington or Hopkins.''

Jubal's brow wrinkled. ''Aye, it isna', but I plan to look into it further. No matter who's behind it, it can work to the Union Pacific's benefit. Meanwhile, you just keep the crews working in spite of the wrath of winter storms and raiding renegades.''

"Anything else you want me to handle?'' Cain asked sardonically.

Jubal laughed and placed one hamlike hand on Cain's back. "For now, go home to yer wife, laddie. It's late and I know she has yer dinner waiting.''

"You're positive, Dr. Milborne?'' Roxanna's eyes glowed with joy. She had been so frightened the past week that she was coming down with some terrible malady. Last night she'd actually fallen asleep while waiting for Cain to come home for dinner. But now she understood why.

"Yes, you are most certainly in a family way, Mrs. Cain. I should say the child is due in the spring.'' He hesitated for a second, then stated, ''I wouldn't think it wise to remain with the work train, especially over the winter months. I understand there'll be no permanent camp this year and we're headed into mountainous country.''

Roxanna shook her head. ''No, Dr. Milborne, I want to be with my husband. Our railcar is very comfortable. I'm certain I'll be fine.''

Milborne took one look at her determined expression and knew further argument was useless. Cain had been away far more than he had been with his wife over the months of their highly irregular marriage. He wondered if old Jubal might decide to send his granddaughter to safety in Denver when he learned of her delicate condition, but decided it prudent not to mention that possibility.

On her walk back to the car, Roxanna was wrapped in a

euphoric haze, thinking of a small black-haired child, a miniature version of Cain. He would want a son, of course. All men did. *Or would he?* The thought struck without warning. They had never talked about children. In truth she had never given it much thought because after the horror of Vicksburg, she had come to believe she might be barren. A child, a gift of love from her husband, was something so beautiful, precious, unimaginable that soiled and unworthy Roxanna had never dared to hope for it. But now a miracle had been granted her.

She desperately wanted to build a family with Cain, to surround him with unconditional love, to make up for the bitter loneliness of his earlier life. He had never spoken of love, making her reticent to confess how desperately she had come to need those words, for she loved him with her whole heart. Each time he lay with her she tried to tell him with her body what she could not say. She hoped from the hunger with which he took her that he was coming to love her, but sensed at times that he was angry with himself for wanting her so. Certainly he did desire her. She had tried to tell herself that it was enough. Would she lose even that when she began to grow fat and shapeless carrying his child? He was gone too much anyway on Union Pacific business. There could be other women in the camps. . . .

"No," she murmured resolutely to herself, hurrying across the muddy ground, stepping across puddles glassy with a fine film of ice in the twilight chill. The other specter haunting her relentlessly was exposure of her identity. If Cain wanted Alexa Hunt's children, would he want Roxanna Fallon's—once he knew the whole ugly truth about who she was and what she had done . . . what had been done to her? Would he see this baby as her way of binding him to her when her deceit was revealed? And surely it would sooner or later be revealed.

Perhaps if Isobel is desperate enough for more money . . . No, she let the thought fade, knowing she was only deluding herself. The woman's sick hatred would never allow that. The blackmail was only another means of toying with her.

"I'll have to tell Cain the truth. Now. Tonight," she vowed. *Before your courage deserts you,* an inner voice murmured. If he accepted her as Roxanna, then she would tell him about the baby. And Jubal. How would he take the shocking news? She pushed the thought aside, concentrating on working up her courage to tell her husband first.

Here and there workers she had helped at the infirmary called out greetings. She returned their hellos absently, intent on reaching the car. Cain might already be waiting for her. Should she tell him at once?

Yes, she would. Climbing up the stairs to their railcar, she pushed open the door and stepped breathlessly into the parlor. Taking a deep breath, she called out, "Cain? Are you home?"

Receiving no answer, she flung her cape across the settee and headed for the bedroom to freshen up. Li Chen would be here soon with their supper. Then she saw the envelope propped up on the dining table. Her husband's bold, careless scrawl was unmistakable. With a sinking heart she tore it open and read.

Alexa,
    I've gone to check on the grading crew to the west. I'll be gone for a week or so.

                                                    Cain

No apologies, no real explanation of why *he* had to do everything on this accursed railroad! All her resolve began to ebb as anger and disappointment brought tears brimming over. She wiped them away with the back of her hand, blinking at the harshly scrawled message. He could not even close it with "love"! She sank down onto a chair and lay her head on the table, suddenly too weary to do more.

NEAR THE UTAH-WYOMING BORDER

Huge chunks of granite, some weighing more than one hundred pounds, flew through the air like the eruption of a giant volcano. Smoke billowed out and the reverberations of the roaring blast almost deafened the two men lying on the ground.

"Damn, sure and that was a close one," Patrick Finny said, dusting himself off, checking his person for injuries from the explosion.

"Too close," Cain said, still crouched behind the shelter of the boulder where he had thrown himself when the unexpected blasting began.

"Those Mormon graders have a right sour outlook. What else might they be doin' to us just because the Union Pacific lordships are slow payin' their wages?" Finny groused, starting to rise to his feet.

Cain grabbed him by his shirttail and pulled him back just before another blast shook the ground beneath their feet.

Finny tumbled down beside his benefactor and groaned. "Sure and every bone in me bloody body is broke. What the divil's *wrong* with those fellows? This isn't the section of rock they're supposed to cut."

"You know that and I know that, but they don't seem to," Cain replied, studying the lay of the land. They had walked out from the camp and climbed this rocky hill to check the course through the draw where the grade was to be cut. The survey called for the blasting hundreds of yards to the south of them. Just as he ruminated on that mystery, another blast erupted, but this time it was much farther distant, where they expected it to be.

"Glory to the blessed Mither and all her saints, they finally got it right."

"Don't leap up too quickly. There could still be another blast rigged to go off close by," Cain cautioned. "I'm going to circle back through that brush." He motioned to the left. "You go around the other direction, and for God's sake keep low and look for signs of a charge."

"Sure and I can be smellin' it, the way that stuff stinks," Finny said, spitting a wad of brown tobacco juice from his mouth, which smelled little better than the acrid burn of blasting oil.

They set out down the hill, gingerly picking their way, listening and sniffing the air as they went. When using patent blasting oil to cut the grade, workers normally dug a deep narrow channel into the large rock surface, then placed the explosive inside and lit a fuse—a long slow-burning fuse.

No hiss of a fuse, no pungent stink of oil. They reached the bottom of the hill and rejoined forces. "I didn't see any sign of a blast being set. Did you?" Cain asked Finny.

The Irishman shook his head. "Just a couple of holes in the good mither earth the size of an Englishman's greed."

"Almost as if someone deliberately threw vials of oil directly at us."

"You're meanin' they wanted to kill us?" Finny replied nervously, glancing around him. They were out in the open now where it would be difficult to get close enough to repeat the trick. The camp could be seen in the distance. Several of the graders were running in their direction, yelling.

The grading camp was run in such a slipshod fashion that the supervisor could not even account for whether or not any of his men had set charges on the wrong hill. Nor did he keep good enough records to verify the theft of any blasting oil. Cain detected whiskey fumes on his breath and that of several of the others. He fired the lot of them and sent Finny back to inform Jubal that they would need a new supervisor and half a dozen blasters on the forward grading crew. Then he rallied the rest of the men and put them back to work. He kept a close count on the cases of blasting oil.

The week dragged interminably as Roxanna waited for Cain to return. She struggled to hold fast to her vow, but the passage of each day made it more difficult. Sleep eluded her in spite of the exhaustion Dr. Milborne had explained was normal in the first months of pregnancy. She hated lying alone in the big empty bed, aching to feel the warm reassuring presence of her husband's big powerful body spooned around hers.

Please, God, don't let me lose him! Roxanna lay huddled

on her side with one hand protectively over her abdomen. She had just awakened from another nightmare in which Isobel told Cain that his wife was a harlot, a spy and an infamous stage actress. Something had awakened her, thank goodness.

Then she heard the sound again—the faint squeaking noise of a window being raised—the rusty one in the storage compartment of their railcar. Someone was climbing inside!

Everyone knew she slept alone in the railcar while Cain was away, but who would accost Jubal's granddaughter, no matter her tarnished reputation? And only a madman would risk Cain's rage. Silently she slipped from the bed, trembling with terror. A thin shaft of moonlight sliced across the room. Using it to gain her bearings, she moved carefully to the dressing chest in the corner and slipped open the bottom drawer. Where was her Sharps pepperbox? She had concealed it beneath her lingerie, where Cain would not find it and ask embarrassing questions.

The footsteps were slow and stealthy as the intruder worked his way through the dark crowded storage room to her bedroom door. She clawed through filmy silk garments in the drawer. At last her fingers seized upon cold metal. Was it loaded? She could not remember, nor was there time to check, for the door swung open with a sudden swish and a squat burly silhouette stepped into the room. Peering at the empty bed, he muttered a curse and turned to scan the rest of the large room.

Knowing that she had nowhere to run, Roxanna huddled motionless in the corner, clutching the gun in both hands. His eyes were already accustomed to the dark and she was wearing a white nightrail. Little chance he would miss her. He did not.

"A light sleeper, eh?" he muttered. Moonlight danced on the steel blade clutched in his left hand when he moved toward her.

"I have a gun. Stay back," Roxanna managed to say in spite of the fear squeezing her throat closed.

The intruder laughed, low and ugly. "You got some nerve, honey," he said, undeterred.

Roxanna fired point-blank. The small pistol's sharp report was followed by a bellowed oath as her assailant was knocked backward but not off his feet by the .32-caliber bullet. She quickly cocked it to fire again, but the figure lurched into the shadows. She heard the clatter of his knife hitting the floor as he yanked open the parlor door. She fired again, but was instantly sure she had missed. Before she could fire a third shot, he was out the door.

She heard the sound of footsteps pounding across the muddy earth along the work cars. By the time she reached the window and looked outside, he had vanished in the darkness. She stood with her back against the wall, clutching the pistol as she shivered in the aftermath of pure terror. In moments Li Chen dashed across the tracks, with Jubal close behind. The whole camp would soon be awakened. Roxanna sat down on the edge of her bed, trembling with the sudden overwhelming need for a bath.

By morning word spread that someone had broken into the railcar of MacKenzie's granddaughter, intent on dishonoring her. Jubal posted a five-thousand-dollar reward dead or alive for a large thick-set man with a bullet wound somewhere on his upper body. The whole camp was searched and every man on the work crew summoned for a roll call. Whoever her attacker was, he was not on the Union Pacific payroll.

Jubal stormed furiously about the sort of lowlife scum who would attempt to rape a sleeping woman in the sanctity of her own bed. He posted two guards on the railcar until Cain's return. Everyone believed the attacker was motivated by the scandal over Alexa Hunt's Indian captivity and subsequent marriage to a breed gunman.

Only Roxanna feared the truth. Had that calm methodical hulk who stalked up to her raising his knife blade been a lust-crazed rapist intent on sampling what she was giving to the "Scot's Injun"? Or had he been hired to rape and murder her? If so, she knew who had paid the man for the job.

She dared tell no one, least of all Jubal, who was in a killing rage already. Perhaps Jubal was right and the man was only a drunken drifter who attempted to rape an unprotected female. Perhaps Isobel Darby would forgive her and enter a convent!

No matter. First she had to work up her courage and confess her identity to Cain. She owed her husband the truth before anyone revealed it to him.

But Cain did not return from his work with the grading crews. En route he had received word that Indians had raided a timber camp to the west and killed several of the workers. He sent a terse wire to Jubal and went riding off, unaware of what had almost happened to his wife.

Roxanna lived in a misery of nervous apprehension, rehearsing ways to tell her husband who she really was, while at the same time looking over her shoulder for another assassin. Jubal insisted she go nowhere without an armed escort. In spite of the embarrassment, she agreed.

A week later Patrick Finny, who had just returned from surveying with Cain, drew that task one afternoon. Accompanying her from the infirmary to Jubal's railcar for dinner, he attempted to cheer her. "Sure'n himself will be ridin' in any day now, don't you fret, ma'am."

"It's dangerous enough, Mr. Finny, ahead with the surveyors and grading crews. But now my husband has gone alone after the renegades who've been attacking our men."

Finny grinned. "Cain has more lives than a Wyoming wildcat. Why, he's tougher than yer granda'n I don't mind sayin' meself, that's fair near indestructible."

"You've worked for Grandfather for a long time, haven't you, Mr. Finny?"

"Sure'n it's been over a dozen years now. Niver dreamed I'd follow himself to this godforsaken wilderness, though. We started back in Pennsylvania, we did," he said with a merry twinkle in his eye. "Met at me former employer's funeral. He'n yer granda owned a business together."

"And a cheeky bastard you were then too," Jubal said,

scowling down from the deck of his railcar as they walked up to the steps.

"Ya wouldn't be rememberin' about the headstone, now, would ye?" Finny said with a chuckle.

Jubal harrumphed. In spite of his gruff tone of voice, it was apparent MacKenzie was enjoying the exchange. "You mean, 'Here lies Lachan Bruce Campbell, a good father and a pious man'?"

"And to that I replied, 'Just like the Scots, ta be buryin' three men in one grave.' " He turned to Roxanna grinning. " 'N so this one hired me on the spot."

"Did you really, Grandfather?" She caught their infectious humor, a pleasant relief after the tensions of the past week.

"Indeed I did. I always appreciate a surveyor who recognizes good use for a piece of land when he sees it."

"If yer worship has no further need of me, I'll be takin' me leave now. Old Weevily Joe's been clangin' the dinner bell'n he doesn't serve after the last table's been cleared." He bowed gallantly to Roxanna, doffing his battered cap so strings of greasy hair fell across his forehead, then assisted her in stepping aboard the railcar. "Anytime you're in need of a bodyguard, I'd be honored, Mrs. Cain,'n don't ye be worryin' about the mister. He can take care of himself."

"Damned rascal," Jubal groused fondly as the Irishman sauntered off toward the dining cars. Then, turning to Roxanna, he smiled and held out a wire. "Just delivered three minutes ago."

She tore it open and read eagerly. "Cain will be home tomorrow!"

"Aye, lass. He's safe. For all yer fretting over him, yer the one we need to worry about," he said as they entered the door.

Chen had dinner ready to be served. Roxanna was too excited and nervous to do justice to the succulent roast pork and wild rice, but she tried, knowing Jubal would ask what was wrong if she did not eat. Anyway, the baby needed good nourishment. Part of her was overwhelmed with joy and relief that her husband was safe and would at last be returning. And part was filled with dread for the confession she had to make to him.

By the time the fragrant steamed pudding and hard sauce was served, Roxanna was feeling a bit ill. She decided she must speak to Chen about the rich menus, which weren't good for Jubal's weight problem either.

"You look a bit peaked, Alexa."

"It's just the heavy food. I fear I've overeaten," she said, shoving away the sugary dessert.

He snorted. "You hardly eat enough to keep prairie dog pups alive," he said, studying her as he trimmed and lit one of his cigars.

"I suppose I'm excited about Cain's return," she confessed, unable to prevent a pink flush from heating her cheeks.

"You wouldna' have some news to share with the laddie, now, would you?" he asked gently.

Roxanna's teaspoon clattered against her saucer as she jerked her hand reflexively. "What do you mean?" *He can't know!* Unless Isobel Darby had wired him this very afternoon!

A wistful smile touched the Scot's lips. "Do na' be upset with an old man's dream, lass. I only thought there might be a wee little Cain coming."

His expression was eager yet almost shy, like nothing she had ever expected to see on Jubal MacKenzie's face. The icy clutch of dread squeezing her heart eased. "How . . . how did you guess? Dr. Milborne only confirmed it for me a week ago."

"After all the years of living without my family, I suppose I'm making up for lost time by learning yer moods and manners, lass," he said, patting her hand affectionately. Then, chuckling, he continued, "No wonder you were disappointed when Cain dinna' come back with Patrick Finny." His mood suddenly turned sober. "You are happy about this bairn?"

"More than anything, Grandfather. . . ."

Jubal sensed the hesitation in her voice. "But?" he prompted.

She shrugged. "Only the usual silly things women worry about—getting fat and unattractive to my husband." *Chaining him to me with this child if he hates me when he finds out what I am.* She squeezed Jubal's hand impulsively. "Don't tell him. I . . . I need time to break the news in my own way."

A troubled expression settled on his face. "Alexa, is everything all right between you and Cain—not"—he put up his hand quickly—"that I'd ever breathe a word to him'n spoil yer surprise, mind."

"Everything is fine, Grandfather, really. I just miss him when he's gone, that's all."

"I told you I could—"

She shook her head. "No, I know how much you depend on him and he loves the work." *But does he love you?* a voice taunted her. Worse yet, what if he truly had come to love Alexa but turned away from Roxanna?

"I'll keep mum about the bairn . . . er, after a wee bit of discreet celebratin' on my own. But I just want you to know how happy you've made an old man with this news. Now," he said, his mood shifting to businesslike efficiency, "it's time you were safe in bed. You need yer rest."

Roxanna's eyes filled with tears. How could she bear to hurt this dear man by telling him his last blood heir was long dead back in St. Louis? Her troubling thoughts were interrupted by the sound of hoofbeats and voices outside.

"Cain!" she cried, dashing to the door. In spite of her fears, she was unable to stop the wild burst of elation that rose at the sight of him. The dim light from inside the car shadowed his face, which looked harsh and piratical with a week's worth of beard covering it. His eyes glowed in the darkness, black as ink, fixed on her slender form.

"Alexa," he said softly as she ran into his arms on the platform of the car. The soft smell of lilacs blended with the sweet silky essence that was hers as he enveloped her in his arms.

"I'll talk to you in the morning, lad. Take yer wife home now," Jubal said, turning back to the door with a smile.

A chill wind was soughing down from the mountains to the west. No one was out, although the dim sound of the men's voices echoed from the sleeping cars in the distance, along with the frail notes of a harmonica. "I ran into Pat Finny on my way in. What's this about you receiving a bodyguard around camp?" he asked as they walked past a cluster of empty supply wagons.

"Someone broke into our car while you were gone. He had a knife." She could feel the arm he had around her stiffen.

He stopped and looked down into her face. "Did he touch you? Are you hurt?"

His expression was concealed by darkness, but she could feel the thunderous anger leashed inside him. "No. I shot him—with my pepperbox."

His chuckle was half a sigh of relief. "You're full of surprises, Alexa. I never realized that you knew which end of a gun the bullets came out of."

"Well, I guess I'm not such a great shot, considering he was able to escape afterwards," she said with asperity. Her nerves were strung so tightly she began to tremble.

Misinterpreting her shivering, Cain pulled off his coat and placed it around her shoulders, then resumed walking. "And you have no idea who he was—did you get a look at him?"

"It was dark. I only saw a silhouette," she evaded. This was something she must tell him in the privacy of their own quarters. She kept walking.

Just as they stepped over the tracks crossing into the long shadow of a deserted supply car, Roxanna's high heel caught on the edge of a tie and she stumbled. As Cain reached out to catch her, there was the sharp crack of a rifle and a bullet passed within inches of them.

"Down," Cain whispered, dropping to the ground with her in his arms and rolling beneath the wheels of the car. He shoved her behind him, pressing her to the splintery oak ties as he drew his pistol and peered out into the blackness.

The soft scudding sound of boots running across the hard-packed earth gave away their attacker's position. "Stay on the ground and don't move," Cain commanded, then rolled out from beneath the car and took off after the retreating assassin.

Her heart hammering in her chest, Roxanna lay on the cold ground, watching as Cain vanished into the shadows between some supply wagons. If she had not tripped—if Cain had not caught her—the shot intended for her could have hit him by mistake. Now she had not only endangered her unborn child but her husband as well!

Two shots rang out in rapid succession near the corral. Heedless of Cain's command, Roxanna scrambled up from beneath the car and ran toward the sounds of whickering horses and braying mules. Voices were raised in the cars where the men slept, but there was no more shooting. Then she saw him, kneeling in the moonlight beside a prone figure. "Cain!"

Alexa's frantic voice made him turn as she dashed up. Holstering his gun, he grabbed her arms. "I told you to stay put."

"I heard the shots and I was afraid—" She broke off and threw her arms around his neck, sobbing uncontrollably against his chest.

He held her in his arms, gently caressing the shiny hair which had come free from its pins and tumbled down her back. "I'm all right, Alexa. It's over," he said when she subsided.

By now a crowd of rumpled men had assembled. Some rubbing sleep from their eyes, others clutching rifles or pistols, most half dressed in only britches, a few in nothing but long johns. Cain ignored their questions and kicked the would-be assassin over onto his back. "Can you tell if he was your attacker?"

She looked at the tall thin body stretched grotesquely in the dirt. "I don't think so. He's too tall, not thick enough. Has he been shot with a pepperbox?"

"No. Only one bullet in him—mine, right through his

heart." Cain had already examined the man, cursing the bad luck that forced him to shoot, but the man had turned and fired just before he had the chance to tackle him. It was kill or be killed. Now he could not question the bastard.

Puffing with exertion, Jubal arrived. Once he had ascertained that Roxanna and Cain were all right, he took charge of dispersing the men and disposing of the body, admonishing Cain to take his wife to safety.

After they reached their car, Cain lit the lamp as Roxanna sank onto the settee, white-faced. He poured a small glass of whiskey and pressed it into her cold hands. She clutched it to her chest, sitting frozen as a statue.

"Drink it, Alexa," he said gently, brushing the thick curtain of silvery hair away from her face with one hand. There were a lot of questions he wanted her to answer, but she looked so pale and distraught that he decided they could wait until morning. He sat down beside her and started to take her in his arms, but her words froze him.

"My name isn't Alexa, Cain. It's Roxanna. Roxanna Fallon and someone sent those men to kill me."

Chapter 15

If she had punched him in the gut with a singletree he could not have felt more shock. He reached over and took the glass from her white-knuckled hand, setting it on the table. Neither one of them needed to be muzzy-headed at a time like this—if they weren't both addled already. "Would you mind explaining that?" he said quietly.

Roxanna took a deep breath. The tight incredulity in his voice was not reassuring, nor was the intent way his black eyes studied her. "I went to school with Alexa. We were friends."

"Past tense? I imagine impersonating her so you could marry her rich San Francisco fiancé might put a strain on the friendship." His whole body felt numb. This was no joke! He had not misunderstood her disclaimer.

His sarcasm stung. "Alexa's dead," Roxanna said as the painful memories of her friend's last days washed over her again. Since marrying Cain, she had given so little thought to the tragedy of Alexa's brief life. "I was living with her in St. Louis. Jubal's letter came just before she died of consumption."

"And you decided to take her place—marry a millionaire and live happily ever after." The shock was beginning to wear off, replaced by a killing anger. He had fallen under the spell of a cheap fortune hunter! "How in the hell could Jubal believe your impersonation?"

Roxanna rubbed her temples, looking down at the carpet, unable to meet his cold black eyes. "Jubal hadn't seen Alexa since she was little more than a child. We had the same unusual coloring . . . and I knew all about her family."

"How convenient, Miss—what did you say your name was, wife?"

A flicker of anger broke through her numb lethargy. *This isn't fair!* she wanted to cry, but deep in her heart she knew he had a right to feel betrayed. "Roxanna Fallon," she repeated dully.

"I assume you have no family, Roxanna—or was the assassin I shot hired by your father to kill me for daring to touch his lily-white daughter?"

"No, Cain. My family are all dead . . . in the war. And that man wasn't trying to kill you. He was hired to kill me. So was the one who broke in here last week."

Tears leaked in crystalline rivulets down her cheeks as she huddled on the chair, looking small and forlorn . . . and still so lovely. He almost reached out to touch her cheeks but stopped himself with an angry jerk of his hand and leaned back, scowling instead. "Why?" he demanded flatly.

"A woman named Isobel Darby hired them."

"I assume she had a reason."

"She believes I'm responsible for the suicide of her husband. He was a colonel in the Confederate army . . . and I was a Federal agent." Roxanna could never tell him about her obscene bargain with Darby, that horrible degrading night, the shame which had haunted her every day of her life since. She could not bear for anyone to know— especially her husband.

"A spy. No wonder you're such an accomplished little actress. It must have galled you when the betrothal with Powell fell through and you had to settle for hired help—a half-breed at that," he added bitterly.

"That's not true! I wouldn't have been able to go through with marrying Larry—not after I met you." She would have thrown away everything—respectability, wealth, security— just to have this man love her. His expression was shuttered now, the raw fury banked, but she knew he did not believe her.

Her eyes shimmered with tears as they met his beseechingly. He could smell the scent of lilacs as she leaned closer, reaching out her hand to him, a pale soft little hand with his heavy gold wedding band shining on the third finger. Roxanna Fallon was his wife. He enveloped her hand in both of his big ones, pressing tightly, pulling her closer until their faces were inches apart.

"I don't know what to believe, Roxanna. You've lied to me and used me. You weren't a sheltered young virgin raised in genteel society, that's for damn sure. Was I your first lover?" He felt her flinch and try to pull away from him, but he only tightened his grip. "Damn, even that! I'd always heard virgins bled on their wedding night. It never even occurred to me to question why you didn't," he said with self-disgust at his gullibility, throwing her hand back to her as if it were an adder. He got up and paced across the room, standing with his back to her.

"I've loved no one but you, Cain. Given myself to no one but you." That was true—what she had lost in Vicksburg was not given—it certainly was not love. But how could she expect him to believe her? "I'll go to Jubal in the morning and tell him the truth myself," she said in defeat, rising on rubbery legs that somehow supported her leaden body.

"No." If Jubal ever found out . . . what would the old man do? God knew MacKenzie had fallen for Roxanna's act hook, line and sinker, the same way he had. Jubal wanted to believe she was Alexa. He'd grown amazingly fond of her over the past months. Would the truth make him fire Cain as well as denounce Roxanna? Damn if Cain intended to find out!

His voice cut like the slice of a whip. In an instant he crossed the room and seized her by her shoulders. "You won't tell Jubal anything. What's done is done. From this day on, you *are* Alexa. You dealt yourself this hand, sugar. Now you are damn well not going to fold."

She felt his fingers digging into her flesh like steel talons. Why did he want to continue this farce? "But what about Isobel Darby? She's followed me ever since her husband's death. Even blackmailed me in Cheyenne."

"How convenient you had the MacKenzie millions at your disposal," he said curtly. "I'll handle this Darby woman. After two failed attempts on your life, she'll reconsider. I'll damn well see to it that she does."

If Roxanna hoped there was some spark of compassion left, the cold finality of his last words settled the matter. She needed time alone to think, to figure out what to do, but not tonight. She was so tired, so confused and shaken. Her first impulse was to tell Cain she was finished with deception. If he could not forgive her and love her for who she was, she was going to tell Jubal the truth and pack up and leave. But she had the baby to consider, not just herself anymore. How could she care for a child if she was cast adrift penniless again with Isobel still trying to kill her?

She turned to tell him he was going to be a father but could not form the words. The way he felt right now, he might question whether this child was even his. She must play out the charade and let him deal with Isobel Darby.

"Do you understand me . . . Alexa?"

His question broke into her chaotic thoughts. "Yes, I understand, Cain." With that she turned and walked into their bedroom. She fell face down onto the big wide bed and closed her eyes. Just as exhausted sleep started to descend on her, she heard the outside door slam and Cain's footsteps fading in the stillness of the night.

He tried to get drunk. When that didn't work, he found several miners passing through who had been more successful. When their slurred epithets about his parentage carried across the tent, he was grateful. With a savage joy he beat them senseless, then rode away from camp headed for nowhere in particular.

When the sun began its abrupt climb heavenward, spilling amber and orange against the lightening canopy of eastern sky, he reined in his horse and surveyed the vast emptiness of the Red Desert, one of the most desolate stretches of land on the Union Pacific trail. Right now his life seemed even emptier and as insubstantial and transitory as the wind moving across the sand dunes. He could lose it all—Jubal's trust, his job as operations chief, the money and power it would have brought him, the vindication of succeeding in a world that scorned his kind.

And all he could think of was Roxanna Fallon. His wife. He leaned on the saddle horn and stared at the molten golden ball of the sun . . . and saw her face, wide turquoise eyes brimming with tears, soft pink lips trembling, so vulnerable-looking as she assured him that she loved him. An assertion he was afraid to trust. Why should he? After all, by her own admission she had been a spy. He imagined she had been damn good at it. He and that canny old Scot had sure fallen for her lies. So had everyone else, from Doc Milborne to Sees Much.

Then again, maybe the old shaman knew the truth, or some part of it. He had always pursued his own mysterious course. Even as a boy Cain had been discomfited by Sees Much, who seemed to understand the innermost secrets of his heart. He laughed to himself at the irony of it all. He had felt so guilty about using Alexa to get what he wanted from Jubal MacKenzie, and all the while she had been using them both.

How many other fools had fallen for her sweet deceptions? How many men had she lied to—or lain with? "At least I can absolve myself of the guilt of deflowering an innocent under false pretenses," he muttered aloud, hating the idea that his doubts about her past lovers bothered him as much as the possibility of losing everything he had worked to achieve on the Union Pacific.

The best thing he could do, he decided as he retraced his path back to the rail camp, was to track down this Isobel Darby and deal with her before she went to Jubal and exposed Roxanna Fallon for the fraud that she was. What the hell had his wife done to cause such hatred? Cain was not certain he ever wished to know.

When he returned, Jubal was waiting with questions about the attack, highly agitated that some maniac had tried to murder his granddaughter. "I tell you, lad, if I'd had the son of a bitch in these hands"—he held up his great gnarled paws—"I'd have made him die far slower than a clean shot in his heart. But I'm grateful that you finished him. I couldna' find out anything aboot him. As if he and the other one dropped out of the sky just to terrorize the lass."

"This one's dead, Jubal. Whatever his motives, it's over. But I think it might be best if Alexa went to Denver with you when you meet with Powell. The rest and divertissement of civilization will be good for her."

MacKenzie studied Cain for some sign that Alexa had told him about her condition but could read nothing behind that inscrutable Indian facade of his. *No wonder he has such an affinity for the celestials,* he thought wryly. "Aye. I'll take her to Denver. But as to the great man, he isna' coming. And just when I was almost ready to expose him with his hand in the Central Pacific till."

Cain blinked. "I take it you've uncovered something about those missing shiploads of supplies?"

"Aye." He shoved a sheaf of papers across his desk. "Take a look at what my agents in New York just found."

Cain perused the report which connected Andrew Powell with an eastern holding company that contracted with Collis Huntington to ship two hundred tons of bolts and fishplates to the Central Pacific warehouses in San Francisco. "He not only owns the supplier, he owns an interest in the shipping firm as well. Not surprising but rather clumsy."

Jubal stroked his beard. "Aye, I thought so too. A dangerous thing to cross Mark Hopkins, not to mention old Collis himself. But there you have it in black and white. The only thing left to do is verify some money transactions in San Francisco banks and we'll have him nailed to the cross—or rather the rest of his cronies on the Central Pacific board will," Jubal said with relish.

"I'd like to go to San Francisco and count coup on the bastard in person, Jubal," Cain said coolly.

MacKenzie could sense an edge in his protégé's voice. "Still hate his guts for the way he endangered Alexa in that train wreck, eh?"

"That and the way he's sabotaged our operation and caught the Cheyenne in the middle."

"I suppose you have a right, lad. Aye, after we settle in Denver, go and beard the lion in his den."

Keeping the keen edge of satisfaction out of his voice, Cain asked, "Isn't the meeting in Denver off?"

"No. I said Andrew Powell wasna' coming. He's sending his son," Jubal replied, curling his lip as if he'd just sucked on a persimmon.

Cain smiled coldly. "Good. You certainly don't need me, then. I have enough trouble to occupy myself here with renegade raids, sabotage and workers threatening to strike for pay in arrears. You can browbeat Larry into agreeing to stop at the Nevada line if the old man isn't there."

"Maybe," Jubal equivocated, "but I think you should go too, get yer wife settled in Denver first." He hesitated when Cain made no response, then said, "I heard aboot that fight in the big tent last night."

"A couple of miners looking for trouble with a breed. Nothing new in that."

"Aye, except that you were drinking. You and Alexa have a fight?"

"That's between me and my wife, Jubal."

Cain's voice was as cold and clipped as the old man had ever heard it facing down a gun sharp or a room full of drunken trackmen. MacKenzie watched his operations chief storm out the door. "And what exactly was all of that aboot, laddie?" he murmured on the empty air.

While Cain set about tracking down the elusive Isobel Darby, Colonel Riccard Dillon was doing some tracking of his own several hundred miles to the northeast. As the column of Blue Coats rode toward the Cheyenne village,

Johnny Lame Pony sat on a wooded ridge, watching them from a distance.

"Working like a medicine man's magic," he muttered with a feral smile, revealing several blackened teeth. His large flat face was deeply grooved by a lifetime spent on the plains. A narrow slash of a mouth turned down harshly as soon as the brief smile erased itself. The shadowy beard and heavy eyebrows, inherited from his white father, added to the look of menace. Slitted black eyes darted furtively, studying the approaching soldiers. Everything should go according to plan if Weasel Bear had done as he was told. The Iron Horse man should be pleased. With dreams of whiskey and whores filling his mind, Johnny Lame Pony observed the scene unfolding below.

Sees Much sat serenely, smoking his pipe when Leather Shirt entered the lodge. "The Blue Coats are coming," the chief announced.

"I have said," his brother replied. "Have you found Weasel Bear?"

Leather Shirt's face darkened with fury. "He has escaped, but two of the young Dog Soldiers who rode with him have been caught. I will not turn them over to white eyes' justice. It is for us to mete out their punishment."

Sees Much nodded. That was the Cheyenne way. "It would be wise to hide them and their ponies. They will be banished by the council for joining the raiders. What then, when the Pony Soldier Dillon captures them?"

"They will no longer be Cheyenne after the council speaks. The soldiers may do as they will with them."

Sees Much nodded again. "Banishing young troublemakers whose hearts are bad against the whites will not protect us when the soldiers come. To them one red man is much the same as another."

"What would you have me do to protect our people?" Leather Shirt asked.

"That is out of our hands now, I think. The Powers do

not show me all. But the Lone Bull will return to us for a while. I do not yet know why.''

"He is Not Cheyenne," Leather Shirt said sharply.

A strange look infused the older man's face. "His heart is in his father's world, but it is not his father's heart," was all the old seer would say.

Outside in the autumn heat, Riccard Dillon rode between the rows of lodges as the Cheyenne stood quietly, watching them. Women quieted frightened little children and pulled older ones back, letting the men line the route of the enemy into the heart of their camp.

Damn unreadable faces, Dillon thought in irritation, knowing they would love nothing more than to put a bullet in his back if they thought they could get away with it. "My scouts had better be right about this," he muttered to himself as he dismounted in front of old Leather Shirt's lodge and faced the tough old buzzard.

"I am looking for raiders—warriors who killed peaceful workmen down on the trail of the Iron Horse to the south. The White Father is greatly displeased. They have broken the Treaty of Medicine Lodge and must be punished."

"If Cheyenne break our law, we punish," Leather Shirt said.

Dillon swore silently. "I followed those men here to this camp. They ride shod horses and have new Winchesters— Yellow Boys. Will you let me search for them?" It was not quite a request. Dillon's eyes scanned the warriors around the camp and figured he had them outnumbered almost two to one. Not bad odds with all the women and children in the way. Hell, he hoped this wouldn't turn into a slaughter of civilians. He'd had a belly full of that already.

Leather Shirt waited a beat, then nodded. "Search." As the Iron Horse soldier ordered his men to check the lodges and the horses grazing outside the camp, the chief hoped his warriors had hidden Weasel Bear's followers in the caves without leaving a trace. Still, it was a strange thing that the renegade had returned home after his disgrace last spring, knowing he was not welcome. It was almost as if he had wished to lead the Blue Coats down on his own people.

Dillon waited stoically, never relaxing his vigilance. The old chief made no attempt at hospitality. *At least he's no hypocrite,* he thought wryly. The soldiers found no trace of the horses but one brought back two Yellow Boys.

"Found 'em in them lodges," the trooper said, pointing to a couple of teepees near the edge of camp.

Dillon turned back to Leather Shirt, who scanned the weapons impassively. "We have more." At his hand signal, several of the warriors in the crowd raised their arms, revealing the shiny brass magazines on their weapons. "Not raid Iron Horse. We hunt buffalo."

"Where did you get the Winchesters?" the colonel asked, cursing over the number of new weapons.

"Trade for them. Ask the one you call Cain." A half smile touched the weathered face at Dillon's look of incredulity.

"You know Cain?"

"Here he was called the Lone Bull. We were his people," Sees Much said, materializing beside his brother.

Dillon scratched his head. He knew Cain was born in a Cheyenne camp even if he was raised white. Nobody seemed to know much more than that. They had worked together the past year on railroad jobs, pacifying Hell on Wheels towns, chasing raiders, all the usual dirty business the army was assigned to do for the Union Pacific. He did not think Cain would cover for Indians who attacked his workers and sabotaged their camps.

Still, this would bear more looking into. He had a sneaking hunch those renegades had been here, at least for a while. Maybe he and Cain should have another talk—if he could reach him now that Cain had become such a bigwig on the Union Pacific.

When the Blue Coats rode away from Leather Shirt's camp, Johnny Lame Pony watched in satisfaction. Soon Weasel Bear and the others would join him and they would meet up with the rest of the renegades. His job was done

here. The soldiers had been led to Leather Shirt's camp and
their leader believed that this band was involved with the
attacks on the railroad. That was what the Iron Horse man
had paid him to do.

DENVER

Roxanna sat staring at her reflection in the mirror. In spite
of riding frequently in the bright autumn sunshine, she
looked wan and pale with dark smudges beneath her eyes.
She had not been sleeping well the past weeks, her appetite
had fled and she was constantly fighting the urge to burst
into tears. Doc Milborne was concerned about her health.
So was Jubal. Both were afraid she was not suited to carrying a baby, but she knew that was not the cause of her
symptoms.

Her husband's cold neglect was destroying her inch by
inch. After their terrible confrontation when she revealed her
identity, he had not touched her. That night he had not come
home at all! The second night they lay in bed side by side,
acutely aware of one another, both careful to stay far to their
respective sides of the mattress. After two more days of such
torture, he rode off with a company of soldiers to chase
renegades, leaving her to make the trip to Denver with a
fretful Jubal, who insisted she remain in the city for the
duration of her confinement.

"How can I endure seven more months like this?" she
asked her reflection.

"What did ye say, mum?" the little Irish maid asked as
she fussed with Roxanna's ball gown.

Jubal had insisted she have a lady's maid now that she
was to be ensconced in civilization. Eileen was sweet and
cheerful, the daughter of a spiker for the Union Pacific. Roxanna smiled and shook her head. "Nothing, Eileen. I was
just mumbling to myself," she replied, taking up her powder
puff to apply some cover around her eyes.

It was a good thing she had theater training in applying
makeup, she thought grimly, setting to work to eliminate the

visible evidence of the stress she had endured in past weeks. When she was satisfied that she'd done all she could, she let the maid work with her hair, piling it high on top of her head in heavy gleaming coils, set with jeweled combs. Amethysts winked brilliantly through the silver gilt curls, and a matching necklace of square-cut stones set in delicate silver filigree lay around her slender throat. When she had put the long dangling earrings in her ears, she let Eileen help her with the pale smoky lavender gown of watered silk.

The jewelry and the silk had been waiting for her when she arrived at the hotel two days earlier. A terse note in Cain's bold scrawl accompanied them, indicating they were a wedding gift. No sweet sentiment or words of reconciliation, just the simple declaration:

We didn't have a fancy wedding. I thought the colors would suit you.

How he had managed to select such beautiful things when he'd been traveling almost constantly, she was uncertain. Perhaps he'd wired someone here in Denver to make the purchases for him. However he had accomplished it, the changeable shades of purple were perfect on her. She regretted he would not be here to see the finished product.

She turned in front of the mirror and admired the seamstress's handiwork. Mrs. Ebermann had toiled long hours to complete the creation in time for the gala tonight, an elegant affair to honor the bigwigs from the Central Pacific and the Union Pacific. The dignitaries had assembled to negotiate a final meeting place on the twisting fifteen-hundred-mile trail between Omaha and Sacramento.

Roxanna dreaded another appearance in Denver after the horrid debacle last spring, but Jubal had shored up her courage by asking her if she cared for the good opinion of a pack of vicious backbiting old harridans. When she replied no, he challenged her to prove it, saying, "Thumb yer nose at them, lass, and dance with yer husband in front of the whole lot. Dr. Durant, General Dodge, even old Collis Huntington will dance with you.''

She had laughed. ''Grandfather, is that a promise or a threat?''

But her husband was not even in Denver. Cain had responded to Jubal's wires noncommittally, saying he had too much work at the construction site to come for what he feared would be a useless meeting. What exactly—if anything—he said about escorting his wife to the gala, Jubal did not mention, although she knew the old man was furious with his young protégé.

Roxanna felt terrible about coming between Cain and Jubal, who had enjoyed such a splendid relationship before she entered the picture. In many ways the old Scot had become a surrogate father for Cain, taking the place of Enoch Sterling. Now that too was unraveling because of her deception.

A tap at the door brought her out of the despondent train of thought. If she had not come west, she would not have fallen in love with the man who had given her this child and who was worth everything to her now. She turned and smiled as Jubal entered the room, already tugging at the tight silk tie around his throat, trying to loosen it.

''Here, you've pulled it crooked,'' she said, walking over to adjust his uncomfortable finery.

''I'd like to pull it off entirely,'' he groused, then studied her with warm appreciation. ''Just look at you, lassie!'' he said, motioning for her to pirouette for him so he could see the effect of Mrs. Ebermann's handiwork.

She turned in a circle, pleased that he was proud of the way she looked, trying not to think of her absent husband. ''You look quite resplendent yourself, sir,'' she replied warmly as he gallantly offered her his arm and they swept from the room.

The orchestra was playing a lively quadrille when they entered the ballroom. Many of the social arbiters who had been present at her debut in Denver were here once more, perhaps to gossip or gloat about the scandalous MacKenzie heiress—or because they dared not boycott a gala honoring the titans of the transcontinental railroad. Either way, Roxanna felt uncomfortable as they made their way through the glittering assembly.

Jubal watched in satisfaction the proud way she held up her head and defiantly walked past the catty females who whispered rudely. He also noted with a pang that her eyes returned to scan the mezzanine several times, as if hoping to catch a glimpse of Cain in his old job. Instead, Williams and Cates, two of the hand-picked security men Cain had trained, walked the premises in his place. MacKenzie cursed his protégé for a fool. It was painfully obvious that she loved him to distraction. His place was by her side. As the old man turned her over to a younger dance partner, he vowed to take a hand in matters the next day. Cain would make up with his wife if Jubal MacKenzie had to drag him to Denver tied behind a Union Pacific freight wagon!

After dancing with numerous high-ranking railroad officials, including General Grenville Dodge himself, Roxanna began to relax a bit. Jubal was right. She could do this. *I'm just playing another part, after all.* The general, an intense man, danced the same way he had led men during the war, carefully and methodically, with a starched military manner. All he could talk about was the way Dr. Durant and his New York faction were ruining the Union Pacific. When Roxanna spied Lawrence Powell making his way across the crowded floor toward them, she sighed inwardly in relief.

"I hope you don't mind my cutting in," Lawrence said after the general excused himself.

"Not at all. I'm growing weary of discussing nothing but railroad politics," she replied as he swept her into a polka.

"Then I shall talk only of how lovely you look, how well you dance and how salubrious the autumn weather has been," he replied with a boyish grin.

They danced until they were breathless, then strolled to the refreshment table, where he fetched her a lemonade and himself a whiskey punch.

As they walked away, Cain observed Roxanna in her ballroom finery. He'd chosen the color well. The subtle shades of lavender and deeper violet constantly shifted under the gaslights, accenting her unusual hair, turning her turquoise eyes almost smoky. She was so breathtaking that it hurt his heart to look at her.

He'd been a fool to answer Jubal's summons. Poor Alexa, the bereft victim of the city's censure. She certainly didn't look bereft to him. He'd watched her dance every dance, laughing and chatting, working her charms on every male who came near her. Until Powell approached her, Cain had stayed hidden, observing like a boy with his nose pressed to the glass window of a candy store. Damn the bastard, he had no right to dance with her! Cain was amazed Larry possessed the temerity to even face her after what he'd let old Andrew do. He agonized about going after her. He would look like a jealous fool. Well, what the hell! He was.

The fall evening was warm and the ballroom crowded. Roxanna and Lawrence wended their way through the press and out onto the terrace which encircled the first floor of the big hotel on three sides. Gaslights glowed along the stone balustrade, and well-trimmed boxwood hedges cast deep shadows off several narrow alcoves leading down onto the grounds.

"I suppose I should offer my congratulations on your marriage," he began awkwardly. His tone of voice sounded anything but felicitous.

"Thank you," Roxanna replied, blushing uncomfortably. "I imagine you thought it precipitous. Everyone else did . . . or worse."

"I don't really have any right to criticize you, considering the circumstances," he replied gravely. "I only wish you to be happy, Alexa. You are happy . . . aren't you?"

She gave him her most brilliant smile. "Yes, Larry, of course I am." *Bad acting, Roxy,* she chided herself. Her timing had never been more off.

"Cain's always been such a loner. I never thought he would marry."

"You mean you never thought he'd marry a white woman

from a good family," she retorted, still reflexively defending Cain. Then she added bitterly, "Of course my own social standing was little better than that of a half-breed gunman, so perhaps we were always fated to be together." Utterly out of nowhere, the images from her dream about the lone bull flashed into her mind as she finished speaking.

"You're being unfair to yourself—you deserve far better than Cain—or me. Oh, Alexa, I was such a fool to let my father break us apart."

Roxanna sensed the guilt and self-loathing in his voice, familiar emotions to her. Moving away from him, she walked slowly into the shadow of an alcove as he followed her. "There never was an 'us,' Larry," she said gently.

"But there could have been . . . if I hadn't been such a weakling. I've let my father run roughshod over me ever since I was a boy."

"He's a very daunting man," Roxanna said sympathetically, remembering Andrew Powell's towering presence, the harsh slash of his mouth and most of all his piercing blue gaze.

"That's no excuse for me. I've had a lot of time to regret losing you. Seeing you here tonight, looking so breathtaking, only makes the loss seem more painful. You have such fire, Alexa, such courage. Cain should never have let you face these people alone. He—" Lawrence broke off abruptly and turned away from her, swallowing audibly. "Alexa, why did you agree to marry him? You could've gone east, left all the ugly gossip behind. You could've—"

"I didn't want to run away. No, that's not the truth." She set her glass on the balustrade and placed her hand on his arm. Perhaps it was time to start admitting the real reason she stayed out West. "I have loved Cain from the start . . . when he came to Leather Shirt's village to rescue me. I was heartbroken that he didn't ask me to marry him then."

"Are you saying that you would never have gone through with our betrothal even if my father hadn't broken it?" He reached out and took her hand, drawing closer to her.

Roxanna could see that she'd hurt him, and that had not

been her intention. She placed her hand on his chest and confessed, "I tried to tell myself it was all for the best, that you would be better for me than Cain. In light of the way things have turned out, perhaps I should have heeded my own advice. But I could not."

"You love that rotter this much after he's treated you abominably," he said with startling vehemence, taking her into his arms. "If there's anything I can do, Alexa . . . I shall always be here for you. . . . You do believe me, don't you?"

His arms felt warm and consoling and she was in such sore need of consolation. She lay her head on his shoulder and said, "Yes, Larry, I do believe you."

"Get your hands off my wife, Powell." Cain stood silhouetted in the brilliant light streaming through the glass doors to the ballroom. The swell of the music had covered their intimate conversation, but there was no mistaking the way Roxanna was draped over the fop's chest.

Roxanna froze as Cain stalked across the terrace and seized her by one wrist. The stark fury etched on his face made him look as savage as his cousin Weasel Bear. She almost backed away from him, but before she could think or speak he had jerked her against his side and held her with one steely arm, glaring at Lawrence.

"See here, Cain, you can't treat her—"

"I can treat her any damn way I please." Cain's voice was low and silky, utterly deadly. "I married her, Larry. You didn't."

Lawrence remained motionless as Cain turned away, still holding Roxanna tightly around her waist.

She did not want to create a scene or endanger poor Lawrence. In spite of his elegant evening clothes, she could feel the unmistakable shape of the Smith and Wesson Model 2 concealed inside her husband's suit coat. When they reached the glass doors she stopped, bracing one palm against the frame.

"Please, Cain, we have to talk."

"It seems as if you and Larry have already had quite a conversation. Me, I'm not in the mood for talking."

"What are you going to do?" Genuine alarm threaded her voice. She had never seen him this way, so ice-cold, so deliberate.

"Why, I'm going to do exactly what Jubal wanted. Dance with my wife."

He jerked open the door and pushed her into the ballroom. As they made their way through the crowd, people stepped aside, staring, whispering. Then Cain swept her into the waltz and they whirled across the floor with everyone watching in fascination. They did make a striking couple, a few would later admit. He was tall and bronzed, she slender and silvery. His understated black evening clothes fit his dark forbidding mien perfectly, contrasting with the pale orchid tones of her billowing silk gown. He seemed to absorb the light which reflected from her.

"Forgive me if I tread on your feet, princess, but Enoch's instruction was a little light on social amenities like waltzing."

"I can just imagine who taught you to dance." He was, in fact, quite naturally adept at it.

"You think I learned it around a campfire when I was a kid in Leather Shirt's village?" he asked bitterly.

"I was thinking more along the lines of some floozy in a bordello," she grated out between gritted teeth. Enough was enough! She had done nothing improper with Larry. He refused to come to Denver, then stormed in giving her no chance to defend herself and dragged her onto the dance floor to make a spectacle of them both!

"You know as much about floozies as I do . . . considering your previous line of work."

The barb cut wickedly, but she refused to let him see her shrink from the pain. Instead she tried to slap him, but he seized both her hands just as the music ended and raised them to his lips in a mock salute. Hard black eyes glared down into defiant turquoise.

"You don't really want a scene, do you? Jubal would be embarrassed in front of all his colleagues." He led her from the floor and they wended their way through the press of people toward the hallway to the lobby.

"Where are you taking me?" she finally asked when they were clear of the crowd.

"To our rooms. Where else? I think it's time we had that long-delayed honeymoon, don't you?" When they reached the curved staircase, he scooped her up into his arms and began to climb.

From across the lobby, Jubal MacKenzie had watched the whole scene, from the dance to their stormy exit upstairs. The pair of young fools might be fighting, but at least they were together where they belonged. That was at least a start. He smiled and lit up a cigar.

Chapter 16

Roxanna could feel the steely tension radiate from every hard muscle of his body as he carried her into their suite and kicked the door closed with his booted foot. He was furious. What would he do to her?

"Ma'am, are ye wantin'—" Eileen's words died on her lips as soon as she saw Cain. Her normally merry hazel eyes widened in fear and she froze at the sight of the dark menacing stranger carrying her mistress.

"This is my husband, Eileen," Roxanna finally managed to get out when Cain set her on her feet, still holding one arm proprietarily around her waist.

"Mrs. Cain won't require your services tonight, Eileen," he said in a silky arrogant voice that rippled with danger.

The little maid backed out of the room with a hurriedly mumbled good night while Cain turned to Roxanna. She squared her shoulders and faced him. "You have no cause to be jealous of Larry Powell."

"Don't I? He was the blueblood you set your sights on before you had to settle for me."

"That's a lie and you know it," she cried.

"Is it? I wonder, Roxy. Hell, I even wonder if we're legally married," he muttered half to himself, raking his fingers through his hair as he tugged at his silk tie.

That very thought had occurred to her, but she would not

give him the satisfaction of replying. When she made no answer, he continued, "I suppose we are. If that damn preacher pronounced us man and wife after kicking up such a ruckus about my chosen name, I don't imagine it much matters if you signed Alexandra or Roxanna on the marriage documents. *You are my wife.*"

He bit off those last words as if laying down a challenge to her. She stood still, silent, waiting to see what he would do next. He shrugged off his suit coat and started to unfasten his shirt studs, then stopped. "Undress me," he commanded. His voice was low, sexually charged, as he reached out and seized her hand, placing it against his collarbone where the shirt gaped open. "Finish it."

She tried to read what was behind his shuttered gaze and could see only lust. *He must be in pain, thinking I'd prefer a man like Larry to him.* How could she ever convince him that she loved him? Speaking the words was useless. He was less likely to believe her now than he would have in Leather Shirt's village. All she could do was show him. Slowly she began to remove the rest of the sapphire studs from his cuffs and shirtfront, then slide the silk fabric off his shoulders, letting her fingers brush softly over his skin. He felt blazing hot to her touch, like dark fire.

He sucked in his breath when her cool pale hands pressed against his chest as his shirt floated down to the floor. Remembering that night in Chicago when she had undressed him and then herself, she asked, "How am I doing so far?"

"I'll reserve judgment till you finish the job," he replied, walking over to the jack in the corner and quickly removing his expensive dress boots. Then he turned back to her and stood, waiting.

Roxanna swallowed and moistened her lips, then approached him, reaching out to touch the belt at his waist. The washboard-hard muscles of his abdomen quivered imperceptibly as she slid it through the loops and let it drop. When her hands grazed his fly, she could not still her own trembling. The first time she did this he had quickly pulled away from her and finished undressing himself, unable to control his passion for her. What would he do now? She began to open the buttons with clumsy fingers, feeling the tight bulge of his phallus pressing against the confinement of cloth. When the last button was open, she pulled at his trousers and underwear until his sex sprang free as the clothing fell around his ankles.

"Touch me." There was as much plea as command in his voice now.

Yes, my love, she thought, wanting to return to the past. She took the thick hard length of him in both her hands and his whole body shuddered.

A woman can have power over a man . . . if he was the right man, and she the right woman.

Abruptly he stilled her hands, pulling away from her. He kicked off his trousers and yanked off his hose in a few swift movements, then stood barbarously naked, staring at her with those hot hooded eyes. She had observed the Cheyenne warriors in Leather Shirt's village with scarcely more covering their bodies. None compared to Cain, although he looked as savage as any of them. Straight black hair framed a harshly chiseled face which was ferally hungry. His skin glistened bronze in the flickering gaslight, the ripple of lean sinuous muscles accented by fascinating patterns of body hair running from his chest down to the male potency of his erection which stood out rigidly, pulsing, beckoning. He was the most splendidly beautiful animal she could ever imagine. He was her husband.

"Turn around so I can unfasten your gown," he murmured.

Roxanna complied. He reached up to the deep vee where her gown was fastened and began to unhook the whispering watered silk. As he bared the soft white flesh of her back, the fabric rustled sensuously when he shoved it out of his way. "I was right about the color on you." He had not intended to say the words aloud. He felt her reaction even before she spoke.

"I never thanked you for the silk and the jewelry. They're so lovely, so perfectly chosen. When—"

"I just found them, that's all," he said quickly, not wanting to admit how he had seen the bolt of changeable purple silk and the amethyst jewelry the day after the awful betrothal ball in Denver and bought it on some insane impulse. At the time he wondered if he would dare ever give the gifts to her. Perhaps some part of him knew even then that he would ask her to marry him. He had left them hidden in a trunk for months.

Instead of answering her question, he splayed his hand on the delicate vertebrae of her back, wrapping his fingers around the deep curve of her slim waist, then gliding over the flare of her hip. She wore no corset, only silk undergarments so sheer he could almost see through them. Letting the weight of her gown and petticoats fall in a whoosh onto the floor, he quickly peeled off her chemise and pantalets. His hands cupped the curves of her small silky buttocks, so creamy pale against his darkness. He could feel her tense and smiled to himself, then turned his attention to her elaborate coiffure, pulling out pins and jeweled combs until the whole mass tumbled in a silver cascade down her back.

Cain could have drowned in all that shimmering moonlit hair as he raised fistfuls up to his lips in a silent salute, pressing kisses to the side of her neck. She turned slowly into his arms and he picked her up, striding into the bedroom. He placed her on the bed and sat down beside her, gliding his hands over her legs as he rolled down her garters and silk stockings, tossing them on the floor beside the slippers she had already kicked off.

"Do you want me, Roxanna?" he asked, kneeling over her like some dark pagan god.

His phallus arched suggestively, the dark red head glistening with a pearly drop of semen. She could not seem to pull her eyes away from it. Her hips arched back in ancient invitation and her thighs opened as he lowered himself to plunge deep inside the wetness and warmth of her body. Roxanna dug her nails into his back and wrapped her legs around his waist, crying out against the sweat-slicked skin of his throat, "Yes, Cain, oh, yes, I want you."

He took her hard and fast, pumping furiously into her until his body, unable to endure the blinding surfeit of pleasure, spun out of control. Just as his shaft swelled and began to pour out its life-giving fluid, he felt the sharp contractions of her sheath and knew she was answering his release with her own. He spent himself utterly, falling onto the softness of her body, sweat-soaked, panting like an animal. And he realized that she too was spent from their mutual burst of passion.

Roxanna held him tightly, reveling in each labored breath he took, each tremor of his body, pressed so intimately into hers. Her limbs felt leaden, replete, yet she struggled to raise her arms and caress his head as it nestled against the curve of her neck. How coarse and heavy his night-dark hair was since he had let it grow longer. Had he eschewed the barber to flaunt his savage good looks in the midst of the rich and powerful railroad barons? How much pain and insecurity lay hidden beneath the cool and arrogant facade Cain had presented to the world since his childhood?

He felt utterly at peace in her arms, cradled between her slim thighs. She held on to him fiercely, as if daring anyone or anything to come between them. *Pretty fanciful stuff,* he scolded himself. Then she began to press soft delicate kisses against her throat, along his jawline. When her tongue rimmed the thin scar across his cheek, he was undone. He could feel his body leap to renewed life, feel the velvet walls of her sheath tighten around him, wanting him. She buried her fingers in his hair and pulled his head to hers for a deep savage kiss.

With a muttered oath that spoke of endearment and fear at the same time, he took her again, this time slowly, languorously, holding back, savoring each thrust, each tiny nuance of her flesh melded to his flesh, prolonging the pleasure . . . and the intimacy, unable to stop himself from craving something he could not even name.

When Roxanna awakened the following morning, Cain was standing by the mirror in the dressing room, shaving, wearing only a pair of trousers. Roxanna sat up in bed, wincing from a slight soreness between her legs. Their passion had run out of control last night, as if all her husband's jealousy and insecurity drove him to demand from her body what he would never dare ask of her heart. She watched him slide the gleaming straight edge of the razor through the thick white suds, clearing a path of smooth bronzed skin. The soft rasping sound was both soothing and domestic yet erotic and exciting.

Sensing her eyes on him, Cain turned when he had finished, wiping bits of soap from his face with a towel, which he slung negligently across one shoulder. "Morning," he said noncommittally.

"Good morning," she replied, hating the breathless way her voice sounded. Swallowing, she said, "You never did tell me how I did as your valet last night."

He arched one eyebrow sardonically. "Well enough, I reckon. I never had a valet before, so I can't really say." A wicked grin flashed across his face. "Bet none of the nobs at the shindig last night ever had a valet do what you did after they were undressed."

She blushed scarlet and he chuckled. "I take it that means you were satisfied."

"Oh, I was satisfied, all right," he replied dryly. "So were you." He paused a beat, then added, "I ordered your breakfast."

"You're leaving." She tried not to sound disappointed.

"More infernal meetings, wrangling over grading routes, meeting points." He sighed in vexation. "I don't think Powell and Huntington ever intended to settle the issue. This is just a smokescreen to pacify Grant and those men in Congress the Central Pacific hasn't succeeded in buying yet."

"You believe the general will defeat Horatio Seymour in the election?"

"Saint Nicholas couldn't defeat Ulysses Grant. Durant and his cronies are fools to put the Union Pacific in the embarrassing position of having the brother of their consulting engineer run against the general. Jubal tried to get

Silas Seymour to resign when his brother received the Democratic nomination.''

Although it felt good to discuss the everyday matters of politics and work the way other ordinary married couples might, Roxanna ached to speak of things nearer the heart. Yet she knew it was unwise to press Cain so soon and break their fragile truce. He seemed to have let go of last night's jealousy. Perhaps she should settle for that. ''But Jubal is a friend of Grant's. Shouldn't that help our cause?''

''Thank heaven he is. I only hope he can finally pull the Union Pacific out of this mess. I've seen the overbudget costs for supplies, the mile-consuming detours designed to raise more government subsidies. The Union Pacific directors back East are lining their pockets at the railroad's expense—and that of the taxpayers. This whole thing could explode,'' he said grimly.

''But the Central Pacific does the same thing.'' Roxanna knew he had worked for Andrew Powell long ago. Jubal told her he had quit because of their policies.

''Yes, the Central Pacific certainly does. And soon we're going to nail the high and mighty Powell's hide to the wall.''

She could hear the bitter satisfaction in his voice, but before she could ask anything about his life with the Central Pacific, a bellboy knocked on the door to their suite. ''Cain, our clothes are strewn all across the parlor carpet!'' she whispered hoarsely, pressing her cool palms to her flaming cheeks.

''Don't worry, Eileen picked them all up earlier this morning while you were still asleep.'' Grinning, he slipped on a shirt and strolled into the other room to open the door.

After dealing with the bellboy, Cain finished dressing and left, telling her he would be tied up in meetings all day. She was to amuse herself in Denver with shopping, perhaps visiting with some of the ladies she had met. That prospect seemed dismal. She felt bereft at his desertion with no more than an admonition not to venture out without the guard he had placed outside her door to act as her protection against Isobel Darby.

Had Cain done anything to address the problem of the hateful woman yet? He had said nothing specific about his search. In spite of dreading the pain it would cost Jubal if he learned the truth, Roxanna was no longer fearful of being exposed as an impostor. Cain had not set her aside because of the deception. Could he one day come to love her? Soon she would have to tell him about the baby. She patted her still-flat abdomen and smiled. Suddenly she was ravenously hungry.

The problem of how best to spend the day was quickly settled when she remembered Sarah Grady's open invitation to visit the next time she was in Denver. The Gradys had not attended last evening's gala. After sending a note to Sarah, Roxanna learned that was because one of the children had suddenly taken ill. This morning young Justin was well on the way to recovery from what had turned out to be an overindulgence in fudge, sneaked into his room by a well-meaning young cook's helper.

Sarah's message included an invitation for luncheon and an afternoon of shopping. Considering that her waistline would soon be thickening, Roxanna knew she would need new clothing. In spite of Jubal's objections, she hoped to convince Cain to bring her back to the Union Pacific camp for the winter. If he agreed, she would be hundreds of miles from a dressmaker. She set out for a day ripe with promise.

Across the city Cain and Jubal spent the morning in negotiations with several high-ranking officers of the Central Pacific. The top floor of the Grand Union Bank had been converted into a spacious meeting room. A long mahogany table ran its length, with heavy armchairs for the gentlemen. Huge potted palms in Chinese urns filled the corners and an ornate sterling coffee server was attended by two waiters, who also lit the patrons' cigars and provided crystal ashtrays and polished brass cuspidors for disposing of tobacco waste. One eastern journalist had written, quite accurately, that the railroad barons surrounded themselves with elegance . . . and spittoons.

Lawrence Powell represented his father but had little to say during the often heated arguments. The younger Powell leaned back in his chair with his fingers steepled, seeming to drift in and out of awareness about the business at hand, puffing on an expensive Cuban cigar more for affectation than from a genuine enjoyment of the smoke.

Bored little rich boy, Cain thought disgustedly when Collis Huntington fired Powell a question about the Central Pacific's grading contracts with the Mormons and Lawrence stuttered an excuse, fumbling through the papers before him to find the correct information.

Jubal passed Cain a note midway through the tedious proceedings. From the self-satisfied expression on the Scot's usually dour face, he knew it was good news even before he opened and read it. Their agents had located a bank clerk in San Francisco who was privy to the transfers of almost two million dollars. The funds had gone from Central Pacific accounts to pay Magus Shipping Enterprises and the Felder-Smythe Iron Foundry, and from there into the accounts of several private individuals. The clerk was willing to produce records proving that all these accounts were owned by Andrew Powell.

A slow smile touched Cain's lips, then vanished like the smoke wreathing the conference room. A deep flush of satisfaction engulfed him like a warm ocean tide sweeping in to cover dry sand. *I've waited a long time to nail you, Powell.* Then Lawrence stood up to make his report. He could read well, Cain would give him that, although he was certain some underpaid clerk had no doubt toiled into the night gathering and preparing the facts and figures Lawrence ticked off so smoothly.

Cain studied his appearance as he spoke, admitting that young Powell was handsome in that pale waxy sort of way so many women favored. Fair hair, clear ruddy complexion, blue eyes, even the recent affectation of muttonchop whiskers. *At least he's man enough to shave now.* Did Roxanna find him attractive? Certainly he had polished manners and was a meticulous dresser.

"So you see, the Central Pacific will reach Salt Lake no later than April of next year using the route our crews have graded. Given the Union Pacific's present position in Wyoming Territory with winter coming, we see no reason to place the meeting site anywhere near the one they proposed," Lawrence concluded, looking around the room with smug assurance.

As the "Here, here's" of the Central Pacific men began to die down, Cain said, "I see a dandy reason."

"Oh, Cain, what's that?" Lawrence asked, taken aback to have a man so recently a mere hired hand dare to speak out in the august assembly.

"Our work crews and yours have been grading parallel routes across Utah for two hundred miles already and your Central Pacific track layers aren't as close to Salt Lake as ours are. We're holding all the aces, Powell," Cain replied evenly.

"Do na' think the public won't protest such a shameful waste of taxpayers' dollars subsidizing duplicate routes when only one will be used," Jubal added with a sour scowl.

"Gentlemen, gentlemen, I'm certain this will all be sorted out in the fullness of time." Leland Stanford spoke slowly in a pompous pontificating voice. With his carefully trimmed beard and deep-set eyes, the beefy-faced president of the Central Pacific was a consummate politician, always oiling the waters.

While Stanford droned on, saying absolutely nothing of substance, Cain and Powell studied each other quietly. Cain's level gaze was disdainfully amused; young Powell's was affronted and angry. When the session finally broke for the afternoon, MacKenzie observed the tension between the two younger men with an uneasy feeling of foreboding.

Lawrence Powell, born to privilege, had never been forced to confront a man he considered his social inferior across a boardroom table. The very idea of such a thing had never occurred to him before. Jubal was familiar with that attitude and the mocking relish Cain had just exhibited. As an impoverished young Scots immigrant, MacKenzie had risen far beyond his social station in the brash no-holds-barred world of American enterprise. He understood how good it felt to thumb your nose at affronted bluebloods, old-money aristocracy. But the possibility that Alexa might get caught between these two men worried Jubal. He did not want to see her hurt by their animosity, but somehow he felt in his guts that it was inevitable.

Cain decided to walk the short distance back to the hotel. He needed time to think, away from the political maneuvering going on around him. He opened the note he'd received that morning from the detective he'd hired to locate Isobel Darby. After brief stops in Cheyenne and Denver, she had surfaced in San Francisco late last spring, in Andrew Powell's lair. Too much of a coincidence to be one. His wife's vindictive and dangerous enemy allying with Powell was cause for real worry.

Damn Roxanna for her deceiving ways, for embroiling him in such a mess . . . for not being the Alexa he had married. Life would have been so much simpler if she really were Jubal's granddaughter. Reconsidering that, he shook his head. No, nothing about life with Alexa/Roxanna could ever be simple. But Lawrence's sudden pursuit of his wife was certainly complicating an already difficult situation. What possessed the Powell heir apparent to set his sights on her at this late date? Did it have something to do with Isobel's appearance in San Francisco?

Several solutions to the conundrum presented themselves: Wring the truth out of the Darby woman and frighten her away from Roxanna for good. Go to San Francisco and beard the old lion in his lair. Face down Lawrence and see what he knew right now. The latter one held the greatest appeal because he could act on it at once. His knuckles itched to wipe that air of shocked condescension off Powell's whey face, but he would resist the temptation. No sense in embarrassing Jubal and proving himself to be the savage most of those captains of industry already thought he was. Tonight before the reception he and Lawrence would have a small private talk.

Cain strode into the Imperial Hotel blinking his eyes to adjust from the brilliant autumn sunlight to the dim interior of the lobby, which was nearly deserted. Just as he started to make his way toward the stairs, he caught sight of his quarry heading out the side door onto the private terrace. A slow smile spread across his face, but it did not reach his eyes as he followed.

Lawrence Powell lit up one of his father's Cuban cigars and inhaled deeply, feeling the sweet thick smoke curl soothingly through his lungs. One of life's many fine pleasures. His presentation at the meeting this afternoon had gone well . . . except for Cain's jibe, he grudgingly admitted to himself. Not that he didn't expect some protest from the Union Pacific crowd. But it galled him that the Scot's Injun had dared to make it.

As if conjured, Cain's tall dark figure strolled casually through the open doors and approached him. "Did you come to make a deal for MacKenzie, Cain?" he asked, wishing he were taller when they stood face-to-face. Cain had a good three to four inches on him. He'd always resented that . . . and other things.

"I make my deals with the men in charge, not their wet-behind-the-ears flunkies," Cain replied.

Powell's face reddened. "You made some sweet-talking deal with Alexa, conning her to marry so far beneath her station."

Cain laughed mockingly. "It really galls you, doesn't it, that I have her? You were too spineless to stand up to the old man when you wanted her for yourself. What did he tell you—that you couldn't take the leavings of his half-breed bastard? That she might be carrying a red baby in her belly?" The guilty flush on Powell's face was easy to read. Cain pushed relentlessly, relieved, even eager to have it out in the open after letting it fester for so many years. "I finally beat you both, Larry. I made a deal with Jubal after you jilted Alexa. No Indian ever touched her, not even me. MacKenzie needed someone to marry her once the rumors started and I wanted to be operations chief.''

"You're saying he sold her to you in return for a promotion," Powell said scathingly.

"Not just a promotion, Larry. Right now I'm in a position to ruin our father—and you, if you get in my way. I'd advise you to stay out of it." The silky threat was unmistakable.

"You always did resent my being the legitimate son, the heir, didn't you, Damon?" When Cain's expression tightened imperceptibly, Lawrence smiled. "You hate your given name, don't you?"

A hard edge of sardonic humor laced Cain's voice as he said, "Too bad while the old man was giving it to me he didn't throw in his last name along with it."

"Not very likely. You know how he despises Indians."

"Funny he didn't seem to despise my mother whenever he came riding into Leather Shirt's village."

"That was a long time ago. Things have changed now."

"Yeah, he's a hell of a lot richer. But I'm going to be just as rich as he is one day, just as powerful. I'm going to beat him at his own game. Why don't you run back to San Francisco and tell him that? Better yet, I have some other business to take care of there. I'll deliver the message in person."

Lawrence Powell stood with his cigar clenched tightly in one hand, staring at Cain's back as he walked away. The ash on the tobacco burned down several inches, then fell on the tops of his highly polished shoes, but he did not seem to notice.

Cain walked through the lobby and headed to the bar, pleased with his day's work. His spineless half-brother wouldn't be sniffing around Roxanna anymore and he was pretty certain the Powells didn't know that she was not Jubal's granddaughter. If the Darby woman had told them, how could Lawrence have resisted turning the taunt around by blurting out the truth?

Cain decided he would leave the rest of the boring posturing here in Denver to Jubal. Nothing would be decided until after Grant was elected. Once in office, he could force the Central Pacific to agree to a meeting site. Meanwhile, it was long past time for Damon the bastard to face his father. The very thought of confronting Andrew with documented evidence that would end his career with the Central Pacific quickened Cain's step. Yes, he would leave at once!

Roxanna stood frozen inside the terrace door long after Cain had walked by her unaware. Pain, great red waves of pain, exploded behind her eyes and squeezed the breath from her lungs, but most of all it centered in her heart. The heart he had shattered. Damon. The Lone Bull. Cain. By any name a treacherous embittered man who used those around him without a care for their feelings.

How ironic that the icy Andrew Powell, Jubal's arch enemy, was Cain's mysterious father. *His Eyes Are Cold.* Now she could see the resemblance between them, father and son, both tall and lean, hawkish and hard. Their souls were as bleak as their pitiless cold eyes. Cain hated his father for using his mother, but he was no better. *I made a deal . . . MacKenzie needed someone to marry her.*

Roxanna pressed her fingers to her temples and stumbled woodenly to a leather sofa in the lobby. She had spent the day with Sarah, who had just let her off from her private carriage outside. On her way upstairs to dress for dinner this evening, Roxanna had seen her husband walking out onto the terrace and followed him, eager to learn how the meeting with the Central Pacific had gone. *Eager to hear his voice, to touch him.*

What a fool she was! She had lived for months in fear, riven by guilt because of her shameful past. But her husband had deceived her in a far more calculated and coldhearted way than she ever had him. She had pretended to be Alexa, but she had never pretended her love for him. No wonder he had never spoken of love. He considered their marriage to be a business arrangement. *I made a deal . . .* Tears burned behind her eyelids, but she refused to let them fall.

She had to think, alone, somewhere private, away from

Cain. Rising, she made her way inconspicuously to the front door and had the bell captain summon a hackney. Once inside, she directed the driver to head down Larimer Street. "Just drive. I'll tell you when to stop," she said woodenly.

Thank God she had not told Cain about the baby. What leverage he could make of that! Jubal's great-grandchild! She had to leave her husband. The very thought of ever facing him again made her stomach clench with fear, for she knew if he touched her she might believe his lies again and weaken. "I won't be used and neither will my child," she whispered to herself.

But where could she turn for help? Certainly not to Jubal MacKenzie. The old Scot's betrayal stung almost as badly as Cain's. She had begun to feel that he really was her grandfather, that once more she had a family. But like Cain, he had betrayed her with far greater callousness than any deception she had worked upon either of them.

Once again she was alone and penniless, cast adrift to live by her wits. Only this time she had her unborn child to consider too. In all too short a time her pregnancy would begin to show. Somehow she would protect her baby from Cain, from Jubal.

Then the old line from a play came to her: "The enemy of my enemy is my friend." The irony of it did appeal. Besides, she was desperate, with nowhere else to go. She would ask Lawrence Powell for help.

Chapter 17

When Roxanna returned to the hotel, Cain was gone. She felt profound relief as she crumpled one of his typically terse notes, announcing that he was attending another in the endless series of meetings. Then she sat down to compose her final message to him. Her first impulse was to pour out all the heart-searing pain, the bitter betrayal she felt, but her pride quickly asserted itself. Damn him! She would not give him the satisfaction. Her message was brief and pointed, as emotionless as she could make it.

Once she had finished it, she threw a few changes of clothing in a valise. Her life as Alexa Cain was over. She wanted none of the elegant finery or jewels that Cain and Jubal had bought her. The amethyst necklace and combs were so lovely they almost made her weaken—until she remembered they were a wedding gift from the man who had used her to obtain his position as operations chief. All she had ever meant to Damon Powell was a means to an end. Roxanna walked out of the hotel and hailed a hackney.

Cain left the Union Pacific bigwigs bickering endlessly, fueled by port and cigars. The bitter rivalries between the backers of the Durant and the Ames factions could not agree on the location of the sun if it was high noon. Jubal had already spoken his piece and departed for bed. Cain was inclined to do likewise . . . although thoughts of his wife stirred a desire to do much more than sleep. In spite of his anger with her and the very real fear that her deception might cost him his job, he could not get enough of her. Cain could not trust Roxanna, but he was as powerless as she against the need that drew them irresistibly together.

Her hold on him was dangerous. He had continuously reminded himself of it. Everyone in his life he had ever needed had left him. Blue Corn Woman and Enoch had died. Andrew Powell had denied him his birthright, even his name. His father's betrayal had cut him so deeply that he had vowed to trust in no one except himself. Roxanna had almost overcome those betrayals . . . when he believed she was Alexa. Which only proved that he should have stuck to his old resolve.

Thinking of his father enabled him to tamp down his desire for Roxanna. He would act immediately on the information Jubal had given him about Powell. He could be in San Francisco to face down the old man in less than a week if he rode hard. The expression on that haughty patrician face when he realized his empire was crashing down around his ears brought a grim smile to the face of his bastard son. Cain had waited twenty years for this day.

Why delay it a moment longer? Especially considering they didn't want to give Powell any chance to cover his tracks. The old man's carelessness still nagged at Cain. Not that Andrew Powell or any of the other railroad magnates was above stealing from his own company. They had not been dubbed ''robber barons'' in the press without reason. But this had almost seemed too easy. He worried the thought like a tongue returning to a sore tooth.

Before he realized it, he was opening the door to his suite. The moment he stepped inside, Cain knew something was amiss. Roxanna was not there. When had he become so attuned to her presence, her very scent, that he could feel her absence? Then he saw the note on the table. A premonition of dread touched him. He plucked the envelope from the center of the lace tablecloth and opened it. The heavy gold wedding band tumbled out into his hand. He squeezed it in his fist until the metal cut his palm as he read Roxanna's delicate feminine script. Her words left him numb with disbelief. Cursing, he read again.

Cain,
    Perhaps I should address you as Damon Powell. I overheard your boast to your brother Larry. You accused me of using you. Now I have learned you are far more guilty of using me. You have what you want, the position, the power, the means to destroy your father. I wish you joy in your vengeance. Before it is over, perhaps you will come to realize that you and Andrew Powell are just alike.
    In any case, I will no longer be a party to the deal that you and Jubal made. Tell him what you will about my disappearance.

                                        Roxanna Fallon

I made a deal with Jubal . . . His words echoed in his mind. Roxanna had been there, heard him fling his insults at Larry. God, how calculated and mercenary, how utterly cold-blooded he must have sounded. Just like his father. He had become the very thing he hated most. He unclenched his fist and stared with burning eyes at the small circlet of gold.

Cursing savagely, he crumpled the note as his heart squeezed painfully in his chest. Reading between the terse bitter lines, he could sense her desolation, the outrage and the betrayal. Where could she go? He quickly searched the bedroom. She had taken almost nothing, not even her jewelry. Without funds, how could she hope to leave the city? What if Isobel Darby found her? The madwoman had tried twice to kill Roxanna.

"I have to find her," he muttered, with a string of angry oaths. She was his wife, dammit! And he wanted her back. He would get her back!

*   *   *

The angry pounding on Jubal's door did not relent. Checking his timepiece, the old Scot grimaced, then swore. One in the morning! "Do na' break the sash in," he yelled as he belted his dressing robe and padded barefoot across the carpet. Rubbing sleep from his eyes, he opened the door, took one look at Cain and said, "This had better be good, laddie."

Cain stared past him into the sitting room, almost a duplicate of the one he shared with Roxanna, right down to the maroon and blue carpet. With a pang he remembered how they'd undressed each other on that carpet only a night ago. "My wife's left me. I mean to get her back, but first there are some things I have to tell you," Cain began without preamble.

Jubal poured two stiff tumblers of bourbon and thrust one at his young protégé before Cain could gather his thoughts. "That yer wife isna' Alexa? . . . or that yer really old Powell's bastard son?" He had the satisfaction of watching Cain's normally shuttered expression turn to poleaxed incredulity.

Cain took a long pull on the bourbon and let it burn a trail down his throat straight to his knotted guts before he replied, "How long have you known?"

"About you? From the first. When you saved my hide in North Platte I had my agent investigate yer past. If I hire a man with a gun to watch my back, I want to know he willna' put a bullet in it."

"Learning I was Powell's bastard should have convinced you not to trust me."

"Do na' be daft, lad. It was all the more reason for me to keep you on. Powell never acknowledged you. He was a fool, ashamed of yer Injun blood, and you hated him for it. You were eaten alive with ambition. The desire to beat him burned inside you even fiercer than it did in me."

"And so I became the Scot's Injun." It made sense in a perverse manipulative way that Cain could understand. "But what about Roxy?"

"Roxanna Fallon," Jubal said softly, taking another sip

of his whiskey. A faraway look haunted his wintry gray eyes for a moment, then passed. "I wasna' certain for a while . . . until the reports came back from my investigators." He chuckled softly. "Yer father tried to blackmail me with her past—and yers. He was livid that I already knew the truth and dinna' care."

"Was that why you let me have her?"

MacKenzie could hear the ice crack in Cain's voice. *Like your pride,* the old man thought. "Laddie, I grow a wee bit weary of that stiff neck of yers. No. I dinna' find out about Roxanna's identity until after yer marriage, but her being Alexa would have made no difference. She has a good heart, Cain, and courage to match yer own. There's more to her past. I'll leave the telling of it to her . . . if she chooses to share it with you."

The implication was clear to Cain. "I won't lose her, Jubal. She's my wife."

"She loves you, Cain. I asked you once if you loved her and you only replied you'd treat her kindly." He snorted in disgust. "I can see how well you've kept yer word on that, laddie."

Cain blanched. The barb struck home. How often had she wanted to tell him she loved him? And how often had he been afraid to return her love? "She overheard my conversation with Larry. I said some things . . . things I didn't mean . . . or didn't want her to hear so baldly," he amended. "She blames you too, for the deal we made." He handed Jubal the crumpled note.

Now it was the old man who blanched. "I played God with yer lives and I had no right," he said wearily, rubbing his eyes as he took a seat in a balloon-backed chair.

"Did your agents find out about Isobel Darby?" At MacKenzie's perplexed look, Cain said, "She's the one who hired those men to kill Roxanna. I don't know much, only that Roxanna was involved with the woman's husband."

Jubal blinked as the cogs shifted in his mind. "Aye, that'd be Captain Nathaniel Darby." A great deal was coming clear to him now.

"What the hell was it all about?" Cain asked. Roxanna's life as a spy must have been as dangerous as his had been hiring out his gun.

"As I said, it's for her to tell you that, not me," Jubal replied almost gently. The same was true of the child she carried. He would not tell Cain he was to be a father. Best if he found his wife before he knew. Then she could be certain he'd come after her because he loved her, not for the sake of duty.

"I learned that Isobel Darby went to San Francisco several months ago. I'd bet she beat a path straight to Powell's door."

MacKenzie stroked his beard worriedly. "Aye, that would make sense. That would explain how he found out Roxanna was an impostor. But do you think after all these years the Darby woman's trying to kill Roxanna?"

"Who else hates my wife enough to want her dead? Roxanna is convinced it's Isobel and I'm inclined to agree. It's dangerous for her to be alone without protection, Jubal. I've sent three of our men to make inquiries at the stage stations, telegraph office and livery stables. Wherever she's gone, I'll go straight after her, but I could use your help."

"You know you have it, lad," MacKenzie answered as Cain took an envelope from his coat pocket and handed it to the old man.

"Everything I've been able to find out about Isobel Darby is there. She may be here in Denver . . . or she may have sent those killers from San Francisco. Hell, I don't know."

MacKenzie watched as he raked his fingers through his hair and finished off the bourbon. *He really is in love with her, even if the young fool does na' know it yet.* "I'll deal with the Darby female. You just attend to yer wife."

With a terse nod, Cain jammed his hat back on his head and walked to the door. "I won't be back until I find her."

Roxanna had vacillated too long making her decision. Now she stood despondently in the telegraph office as the sleepy clerk waited with leering curiosity for the wife of a Union

Pacific bigwig to compose her wire to the son of a Central Pacific director. Lawrence had left Denver by the time she arrived at his hotel. Not wanting to attract attention, she had bribed a bellboy to deliver a message to his room, only to learn he had checked out earlier that afternoon. She found he had purchased several good horses at a stable and rode northwest into Mormon land, ostensibly to check the Central Pacific crews working on grading.

There was nothing to do now but wire the address on the card he had given her and pray the message would be relayed to him. Whether or not he would help her was conjectural. If he refused, Roxanna had one half-formed fall-back plan. The only thing she was certain of was that she would not go crawling back to Cain and Jubal. She handed the boy the message, then left the office.

She had no choice but to take the mare Jubal had given her. The animal waited at the livery with the rest of the mounts brought to Denver by the Union Pacific entourage. She was not dressed for riding, but there had been neither time nor a place to change. Going to Sarah Grady for help had occurred to her, but Sarah's stern husband was a life-long friend of Jubal's. She could not place the woman in the position of having to choose between them.

"How could I have been so wrong about Cain? Or about Jubal?" she asked herself as she retraced her steps to the livery. Roxanna had prided herself on the hard-earned ability to judge people. In her past life as a spy and then an actress, she had observed more than her share of the good and bad in human nature. It was ironic, cynic she had thought herself to be, that she should fall so easily for the duplicity of these two ruthless men.

Well, she could be ruthless too. If Cain pursued her, she had arranged to send him on a merry chase in the wrong direction. She had purchased a ticket on the afternoon stage to Cheyenne. He would believe she was going to make connections from the Union Pacific railhead. By the time he caught up to the coach and found she was not aboard, she would have enough of a lead to leave a cold trail. Jubal would want his great-grandchild even if Cain did not want his wife. For that reason alone she was certain her husband would pursue her.

By the time dawn streaked the horizon in the east, Roxanna was hours away from Denver. With a small bit of luck, and pressing her mare, she might catch up to Lawrence in a hard day's ride. If she could not find him, or he would not help her, then she would continue on to Salt Lake. Perhaps the Mormons, themselves persecuted for so many years, would aid her in reaching San Francisco. In a large city she hoped there would be work for an experienced actress. She would have several months before her pregnancy showed in which to save some money. After that . . . well, she'd have to deal with it when the time came.

As for Isobel Darby, Roxanna refused to worry any longer. The worst had already happened. It was highly unlikely any of the widow's minions would be able to follow her into the wilderness. She had eluded Isobel for a year living with Alexa in St. Louis. She would outsmart her enemy again. She simply had to, for the sake of her child.

Cain almost fell for Roxanna's ruse. When Pat Finny came back from the stage depot saying she had purchased a ticket to Cheyenne, Cain was ready to burn leather north. Luckily, when he reached the station, one of the off-duty drivers remembered the late afternoon coach's passengers—all males. Then Ham Benning caught up to him with a copy of the wire she had sent to Lawrence Powell in San Francisco. If her letter to him had been a blow, the terse missive to his brother was almost as devastating.

Dear Larry,
    You offered help if I needed it. I do. Am on my way.
    Gratefully,

Alexa Cain

She had turned to the man she had come west to marry in the first place. The irony of the situation did not escape him. He wondered if Larry appreciated it, doubted he did. "You had your chance, brother. Now it's too late. She's mine," he whispered savagely, crumpling the copy of the wire. She had hours of head start on him, but he could ride her down—if he could pick up her trail.

No one had seen her since she left the stable. He would have to gamble on her taking the road to Salt Lake. If she was lucky enough to pick up a coach along the way, he might not catch up to her until she was in San Francisco. Would his father take her in? He doubted it, but since it presented an opportunity to thwart his bastard son, the old man might just enjoy "protecting" Roxanna.

Larry's motives in offering to help her were considerably more puzzling. Was his brother smitten with his wife? A far darker thought nagged at him, one he refused to think about—that Roxanna and Larry were having an affair. He had been insanely jealous when he found her in his brother's arms the other night, but after the way she responded to him, Cain simply could not believe there was anything between her and Larry.

For his own reasons, Larry had defied their father to offer Alexa Cain his protection. "Hard to imagine you've finally grown a backbone at twenty-eight." But was that less difficult to believe than that Roxanna would betray her husband? The punishing ride took his mind away from such troubling thoughts. He chose the big chestnut and took remounts from the fine string of horses Jubal always brought on any trip.

By camp that night Cain was forced to admit that Roxanna had most probably picked up the express coach headed into Salt Lake. Even with his spare horses he could not hope to catch her before she arrived in the Mormon capital. Once there, she could vanish again on another coach or have met Lawrence in a prearranged rendezvous. The only thing he could be certain of was that she was bound for San Francisco.

If Roxanna remained alone, she would have to travel the northern route, sooner or later selling her horse, if she had not already done so, and riding the overland stages from Salt Lake through the mining towns of Nevada down into California. All he could do was follow her the whole damn distance.

He settled back on his bedroll and looked up at the starless night sky with a grim smile. He would solve two problems at one time in San Francisco—face down his father with the news of imminent ruin when word of his thievery reached the other Central Pacific directors, and bring Roxanna back with him. Somehow he would make her understand that he had not married her only to become Jubal's operations chief. But what if he found out that she had been unfaithful with his brother?

Once he had read her wire to Larry, the question simply would not go away. Nor would the insidious pain in his heart when he thought of losing what he had told himself all along he did not want—Roxanna's love.

Lawrence Powell stood with the wire in his hand, printed out in the telegrapher's neat cribbed script. It had been delivered to him directly by a rider as soon as his San Francisco office telegraphed back his location along with Alexa's message. A smile flashed across his face. Was Alexa finally finished with his bastard brother? He would soon find out. After all, he'd offered her his help and he intended to give it. A quick calculation of the distance she could have traveled indicated to him that he might intercept her before she reached Salt Lake. Luckily he had decided to ride north on a pressing business matter before returning to San Francisco.

"Zebulon, tell the others to mount up. We have a damsel in distress to rescue."

After selling her horse to purchase passage on the coach to Salt Lake, Roxanna finally let the numbness of shock give way to bone-weary exhaustion. Crammed between a drummer whose clothes smelled of camphor balls and an obese woman who munched greedily from the basket of fried chicken on her ample lap, Roxanna fell asleep in spite of the pitch and roll of the fast-moving stage.

The next morning, as she picked at the greasy stew at the way station, the drummer engaged in an argument with the proprietor.

"Your place is a pigpen. I've seen better food in Chicago tenement kitchens."

"Why don't you go on back to Chicagy, then?" the wiry little station owner said, sending a slug of tobacco juice pinging off the hard-packed dirt floor well shy of the overflowing cuspidor.

The drummer jabbed a none-too-clean spoon in the direction of the bowl before him. "There's a fly in the stew!"

The owner, who doubled as cook, lifted one shaggy beetled brow and squinted into the food. "Yep. If'n th' stew warn't so damblasted good, it wouldn't a flown in it neither," he answered, crossing his arms over his scrawny chest.

In spite of herself Roxanna smiled, forcing down another spoonful. At least hers had no flies in it—that she could see. As the wrangling continued, she thought about the jouncing ahead. Lord, if only she were not so tired. How many days to San Francisco? Should she have kept riding horseback in the slim hope of running into Lawrence? She pondered her decision. One way or the other she would reach Salt Lake tomorrow. After that . . . She rubbed her eyes and tried to think.

"You look as if you could use a friend."

Roxanna's head flew up at the soft, familiar voice. Seeing Lawrence's round smiling face and sympathetic blue eyes, she impulsively stood up and threw her arms around him. "I was afraid I'd missed you!"

He patted her back in a brotherly fashion. "If your wire to San Francisco hadn't been redirected to me, you would have. Let's get out of this noisome place so we can talk," he said, looking around the small squat adobe room with its high little windows and food-encrusted cookstove. The smell of stale grease and sweaty horses hung on the air until they made their way out into the station yard. A fresh team had already been hitched to the coach. The driver called out for everyone to board and the drummer, still fuming, rushed past her, followed by the fat lady, still clutching her enormous hamper of food. Perhaps she'd share with him.

The morning sky was hazy with low pale gray clouds massing on the western horizon. Already heat hung like an old horse blanket, enveloping them. "I paid my fare to Salt Lake," she said, wondering if she could retrieve part of it from the driver, doubting it.

Larry shook his head, smiling. "Forget about the coach. I'll see you get safely to San Francisco—if that's where you want to go, Alexa."

"Yes. It's as good a place as any to start over," she said dismally.

He took her elbow gently and steered her to a copse of trees where they could sit on a rock, shaded against the merciless heat. "Now tell me what happened."

"I've left your brother."

He paled at that, then shook his head. "How did you find out? My father has gone to great pains to conceal our relationship."

"I overheard your conversation with Cain the other day on the hotel terrace. My husband did most of the talking as you may recall."

He could hear the bitterness in her voice, underlaid with desolate pain. "He's used you. Just as he uses everyone, but I'm not sure I should place all the blame on Damon. Father was not always . . . kind. My brother learned to survive in spite of everything, though."

"So did you. I have a feeling growing up with Andrew Powell wasn't easy for either of his sons. But that didn't turn you into the same kind of person."

Lawrence flushed. "You're very kind, Alexa."

For an instant it was on the tip of her tongue to confess that she was not Alexa, but she was risking enough already without adding further complications. Perhaps if he knew she was not Jubal's granddaughter, he might be afraid to offer his help. Lawrence was not a man who dared fate like his brother. "You are the one who's kind for responding to my plea. I can't imagine your father would approve of it."

He sighed. "No, he won't, of course, but that doesn't matter. If I'd not been such a wretched coward in the first place, you would never have fallen into Cain's snare."

I already had, before I ever met you. "What happened between Cain and me isn't your fault, Larry."

"I can't help but feel it is. You must know that I was smitten with you from the first time we met. If only . . ."

She could not bear the earnest guilty look written across his face. "When I told you in Denver that I was in love with Cain, it was the truth."

"But you can't still love him?"

"I don't know," she replied softly, as her hand curved protectively over her belly. "But I do love the child I'm carrying. And I'll never let Cain or Jubal MacKenzie or any other man use it the way they've used me."

Lawrence stiffened. "Does Cain know about the baby?"

"I didn't tell him, but Jubal guessed. He was so pleased," she said bitterly. "I imagine by now he's told my husband. He'll most probably come after me—to secure MacKenzie's heir for his boss."

Lawrence could hear the scorn in her voice. "Then it might not be wise to go directly to San Francisco. That's the first place he'll look, you know." He stood up and began to pace, combing slender elegant fingers through his sandy hair. "If you're feeling well enough, I could take you with me while I ride up into the Snake River country to arrange a timber contract. That would give us time to figure out how to deal with Cain and MacKenzie."

That must have been where he was heading when her wire interrupted his plans. She smiled. "Of course I feel well enough. It sounds like a marvelous adventure."

San Francisco had not changed much since he left it over a year earlier, except to grow even bigger and more crowded and dirty. Early autumn rain fell, hanging chill and sullen in the foggy evening air. Cain reined in his horse and dismounted in front of Andrew Powell's immense gargoyle of a house, situated on the far southern edge of the city. Its splendid view of the bay was the only good thing he could see about it. The three-story stone monolith had a mansard roof, a twenty-foot portico on three sides and acres of topiary, which must require a dozen gardeners year-round to maintain. The guard at the scrolled wrought-iron gate had wanted to deny him admittance but was too frightened to do more than bleat a halfhearted protest when Cain drew his Smith and Wesson and ordered it opened.

He studied the large front windows hung with heavy lace curtains. The lights glowed dimly through the dusk like the eyes of a jack-o'-lantern. A cold welcome for any man. He had never before set foot on the estate and would never again after tonight. Was Roxanna inside?

He felt the keen itch of anticipation racing through his blood as he climbed the three tiers of stone steps and lifted the heavy brass door knocker. A pity Andrew's fancy city wife had died before he had the chance to introduce himself. He wondered if she had ever known about Blue Corn Woman . . . about him. Then the door swung open on well-oiled hinges and an imperious-looking man with the bearing of a major general looked him up and down with melting thoroughness. Unshaven, his hair shaggy, wearing the same ripe buckskins he'd ridden in during the past week, Cain could easily imagine what the disdainful butler was thinking.

"If you're here for employment, the stable master is 'round back. Now, see here—"

Cain placed one dark hand on the pristine starched whiteness of the servant's shirt and shoved him out of the way, stepping into the large marble foyer. A glittering crystal chandelier hung suspended from a twenty-foot ceiling, and Louis XIV tables covered with Chinese vases lined the French silk covered walls. His boots echoed on the polished surface of the floor as he strode around, whistling low. "So this is what you sold your soul for, Andrew Powell." He raised his eyebrows sardonically. "And for your soul, maybe it was worth it."

"It was." Powell's icy clipped words cut across the distance separating them like the blade of a knife. He stood at the top of a curving staircase, dressed as always in an elegantly tailored suit. He made no move to descend the steps.

"Sir, I tried to stop this ruffian," the butler said, huffing angrily at Cain, then backing off when those cold glittering black eyes swept from his employer to him.

Deliberately, Cain turned his back on the servant and faced Powell with a dare implicit in every move of his long lean body.

The older man nodded a curt dismissal to the butler, then started down the stairs to face his enemy. "What the hell are you doing here?"

Running his fingertips over the satiny surface of an ornate table, Cain replied, "Maybe I thought it was past time to see how you and my brother have lived all these years, now that I'm moving up into your rarefied circles."

Powell snorted inelegantly. "You still look like the breed gunman you always were. Marrying MacKenzie's damaged little darling will never change that . . . especially now that the truth will come out. She isn't even his kin . . . just a cheap actress posing as Alexa Hunt. But she is still your wife." His cold blue eyes glittered with triumph as he let fly the barb.

Cain nodded calmly. "Roxanna is still my wife."

"So, you already know. I wonder, did you take the news with the same equanimity as old Jubal?" The words were delivered with an almost disinterested air, but his eyes continued to skewer Cain like a hawk focusing in for the kill.

"I imagine the charming Mrs. Darby gave you the information. Pity it won't do you any good. I'm still Jubal's operations chief, Powell. And in that capacity, I have a bit of information to share with your associates . . . about the Felder-Smythe Iron Foundry back East and their rather sizable sale to the Central Pacific, the one which Magus

Shipping Enterprises contracted to bring around the Horn to San Francisco.''

''What the hell are you talking about?'' Powell's eyes narrowed but did not betray any disquiet, only annoyed perplexity.

Cain thrust a copy of the documents Jubal's agents had secured about the shady transactions into Powell's hand. He had always known the old man to be one hell of a poker player, but his admiration for his father's calm facade grew exponentially. Faced with certain ruin, the old son of a bitch didn't even break a sweat! ''The originals are in Stanford's and Huntington's hands by now. Jubal MacKenzie is no man to cross. Neither am I.''

Powell skimmed the first few pages, then began to read with more care in several places. No, it couldn't be! This said he had siphoned off millions from the Central Pacific's accounts to purchase and ship supplies which never existed, never reached the West Coast. Sheer force of will held his hand steady as he quickly flipped through the rest of the documents. It was all here. A trail so clear a Philadelphia greenhorn could follow it—leading straight back to him.

Cain watched the subtle shift in Powell's demeanor as the older man perused the evidence. ''You thought I was bluffing,'' he said lazily. ''Now I assume you realize the noose has been slipped down and tightened.'' *I have the son of a bitch at last.* He waited a beat, expecting a surge of intense satisfaction, vindication, peace . . . something. Why didn't it feel the way he had always believed it would? ''Where has Larry taken my wife? Is she here?'' The abrupt questions popped out before he could stop them.

Andrew Powell recovered himself sufficiently to pick up on the anger and vulnerability in Cain's voice. ''Why on earth Lawrence or I should know anything about your wife is beyond me,'' he responded with his usual icy contempt. ''He is on the rail line, attending to Central Pacific business. Tell me, have you mislaid your scheming little actress somewhere between here and Denver?''

''She left me,'' Cain admitted baldly, realizing that Powell's vitriolic satisfaction did not matter in the least. All he really wanted, all he'd chased hundreds of miles for, was Roxanna! "She wired Larry asking for help. It seems your heir is still smitten with her. He'd promised to help her—in spite of you."

A flush of anger finally tinged Powell's cold patrician face. "That arrogant young fool," he ground out. "He's taken his last slap at me. I'll see him in hell. I'll see you both in hell!"

Cain sensed that Powell was telling the truth about Larry. His brother had not brought Roxanna to San Francisco, which meant he had most likely taken her with him into the dangerous country where the Central Pacific was laying track. "I damn sure know you're bound for hell, Powell. I can help you arrange it for Larry boy, too," Cain said, turning away from his father.

"Cain." When his son turned, Andrew said with a grim parody of a smile, "I'll be at the finish line in Salt Lake first."

Without bothering to respond, Cain walked through the door and out into the chill blackness of nightfall. It was going to be a bitch of a ride back over the mountains. When he got his hands on Roxanna, he would lock her away in their private railcar until the transcontinental was complete! That he might not find her unharmed he refused to even think about.

Chapter 18

THE SNAKE RIVER COUNTRY

Roxanna felt the sharp sting from razor-edged fragments of stone when the rifle shot ricocheted off the rocks. As the tiny missiles flew all around her, she threw herself behind a large boulder. Heart pounding fiercely, she crouched low, prepared to make a dash for different cover. If the assassin circled around, she'd be dead in his sights in these rocks.

Surely someone in the camp would have heard the shot. Then again, perhaps not. The timber cutters were a noisy and industrious lot. Between their loud banter and the sharp cracks of their axes biting into wood, one or two rifle reports might not be discernible from the distance she had ridden. If only she'd not dismounted to drink at the stream. The rifle in the saddle scabbard of her spooked horse was out of reach now. At least the stupid beast should eventually wander back into camp.

By then I could be dead. She listened for sounds of movement in the brush. The dry autumn woods would have made stealth nearly impossible if not for the murmur of the swift-running stream nearby. A faint noise in the aspens to her right had her poised for a dash. There, she heard it again. Nothing was visible through the dense screen of kinnikinnick bushes. She decided she had to chance it.

Tossing her hat to the right, she sprinted off to the left

just as a quick shot pinged in the rocks, striking the ruined headgear. As she zigzagged toward the dense woods behind her, another shot whistled past her. When she reached the shelter of the trees, she could hear someone yelling and cried out for help. The sound of her attacker retreating left her dry-mouthed and quivering with relief. She leaned against the trunk of an aspen and waited. Soon the sound of hoof-beats drew closer and Lawrence was calling for her.

"Roxanna!"

She stepped from behind the tree, still winded more from fear than the quick run she'd made across the rock-strewn clearing. "I'm here, Larry. Be careful. He has a repeating rifle."

He dismounted beside the stream, looking around. "There's no one here now," he said, slipping his fancy British revolver back into its holster. "I must've scared him away." He walked quickly to meet her, his expression distraught. "Are you all right?"

"Yes. He must've been waiting for me to dismount by the water. I've become too much a creature of habit this past week, riding every morning at the same time, stopping here for a drink."

He picked up her hat, which had a bullet hole through the crown. His hands clenched it so tightly it crumpled before he tossed it angrily away and took her in his arms, inspecting her. "You're certain you're not hit."

"Certain," she said, gently disengaging from his grip. "See, no blood." She strove for a light tone, knowing how upset he was.

"Thank God I decided to ride out to join you. When I saw your horse down the road, I didn't know what to think. At first I feared you'd been thrown. Then I heard a shot." He shook his head. "You said that this Darby woman sent some men to kill you in the Union Pacific work camp. I'm afraid the one who escaped the first time—or some other hireling—has found you again."

Roxanna sighed. After they arrived in the rough lumber camp five days earlier, Roxanna had reached a difficult decision. Larry was risking too much for her, he was too decent and kind a man for her to deceive any further. She had told him the truth, gambling that he cared for *her*, not just that she was Jubal's granddaughter. Lawrence Powell, of all people, understood what it meant to be a powerful man's sole heir, valued only for that and nothing more.

He had not disappointed her, smiling wistfully and telling her that he was honored because she had trusted him enough to reveal her past. Then she'd revealed the potential danger from Isobel Darby and he had promised to protect her. Now she could see how upset he was that one of their worst fears had been realized. All she needed was for Cain to ride in and demand her back at gunpoint. "It must be Isobel. I can't endanger you or your work crew any longer. If you'll loan me a horse, I'll—"

"Don't be ridiculous," he interrupted, his face flushed with affront. "I'd no more let you ride away from here all alone with an assassin on the loose than I'd hand you back to Cain."

"But I can't stay, Larry. Surely you see that."

He raked his hands through his hair in frustration. "Yes, you're right. It's too dangerous. I promised to protect you and look what's happened right under my nose."

He looked at the ground and seemed to shrink before her very eyes. Roxanna placed her hand on his arm. "Don't blame yourself for the enemies I've made."

"I'm hopeless, a failure, just as my father has always said I was."

"That's not true. You are a good and kind friend, loyal, gentle." *All the things your brother is not.*

"We have to find someplace safe for you to hide while I have my agents track down this Darby woman." He paced back and forth, stroking his chin, then paused and looked down at Roxanna, who was seated on the grassy bank of the stream, using her handkerchief to bathe her face with cool, soothing water. "Those Indians who held you for ransom . . ."

"Leather Shirt's Cheyenne?" she responded, puzzled.

"You said they treated you kindly—that you actually enjoyed your time with them. I found that amazing . . . was it true?"

"Yes. Most of the women were kind, especially Willow Tree and Lark Song, Sees Much's granddaughters. The old medicine man reminded me of my father in some strange way." Thinking of Sees Much brought a smile to her face. She missed him. Had he forgotten her by now? Somehow she was certain he would never do that. He was the only person with whom she could ever discuss Cain and the confusion, anger and pain he evoked. Sees Much would understand.

"I know this sounds crazy, but what would you think of returning to spend a short while with this Leather Shirt's band?"

"Actually it doesn't sound as crazy as you might think," she replied, remembering Sees Much's words. *There are greater things . . . which will unfold . . . before we meet again.* Almost as if the old shaman knew that she would return to the Cheyenne.

"If you would be safe with those Indians, then you'd certainly be safe from any hired killer sent after you. They couldn't get near an Indian encampment. While you were there, I could deal with Isobel Darby. Would you consider such an outlandish suggestion?" he asked doubtfully.

"Yes, I think it's a marvelous idea—almost preordained, you might say." At his startled look she just chuckled. "It will be all right, Larry. But how can we find Leather Shirt's band? They move around so much. They could be hundreds of miles from where I last saw them."

"I think one of the men who scouts for the railroad can locate them. He's a breed. . . ." His face reddened in embarrassment, betraying his realization that she had deigned to marry a breed and still wanted the baby he had given her. When she only nodded, he continued, "I'll wire the Central Pacific railhead and have them locate him and the men who ride with him. If anyone can find your Cheyenne friends, he can."

DENVER

"I have names," Jubal MacKenzie said, shoving the papers across the desk, "enough hard evidence to link you to at least one attempt on Roxanna Fallon's life."

Isobel Darby pursed her lips in a frugal smile that only served to accent the coldness of her dark eyes. She glanced at the sworn affidavit of Gable Hogue affirming that he had contacted a gunman named Butch Green on her behalf, hiring him to break into the private railcar where Roxanna slept to rape and murder her. Hogue had always been a craven lickspittle, for sale to the highest bidder, she thought contemptuously. "This will never hold up in court. Who would believe that a woman of my impeccable background, a flower of the South, would even think such a thing, much less commission a criminal to do it?"

She studied MacKenzie coldly, still seething inwardly that he already knew Roxanna's identity. She had come to play her trump card, to destroy the bitch's last bid for security and respectability by revealing everything to "Alexa's" grandfather. The old Scot had a reputation for ruthlessness almost as single-minded as Andrew Powell's. MacKenzie had amazed her when he said he already knew of Roxanna's identity. He was livid that the widow had threatened the sordid·hussy, and countered her revelation with this evidence about her conspiracies which his agents had gathered. Her calm demeanor gave away nothing. Perhaps she could use his wrathful anger to her advantage. She waited for his response.

"I do na' think you'll get off quite so easy. Even if yer not convicted, think of the scandal it would cause. You'd be considered the very sort of woman you've spent the past five years saying Roxanna is. Ruined," he pronounced with sepulchral finality. His gray eyes were wintry as a Wyoming sky in January.

"Then why don't you turn me over to the law?" she replied like the excellent chess player she was.

"Much as I'd like to see yer neck snap at the end of a noose, the best you'd probably get is a few years in prison," he admitted baldly. "And I do na' want Roxanna to be dragged into the mess if I can avoid it. You've made her suffer enough already."

"So we have an impasse." She sat back, still unruffled. Although Andrew Powell would be angry because she had left San Francisco and interfered in his plans for Roxanna Fallon, she felt sure he would still come to her aid, if only to thwart his old enemy MacKenzie. Besides, the Scot did not intend to have her arrested.

"Not exactly an impasse," he replied, stroking his beard gently, as if petting a cat. Andrew Powell could have warned her this was Jubal MacKenzie at his most deadly. "I will give you two choices and no others. Neither involves the law."

A faint chill snaked down her spine. Surely, right here in the middle of the city in a public building he would not attempt to kill her. Or would he? The fool was as besotted by that Fallon harlot as any man half his age. "What choices?"

She was a cold one, didn't even blink. Captains of industry from Paris to Pittsburgh had learned to tremble when Jubal MacKenzie was ready to pounce, but this female sat in stony composure. Was she mad? It would explain her persecution of Roxanna. He could find out little about her marriage to Nathaniel Darby, other than that the man was a sadistic bastard who enjoyed playing games with other people's lives. What bizarre twist must there have been to their relationship to drive her to such hatred over his death? He stood up and walked around the desk, using his considerable bulk as a weapon of intimidation. Eyes cold and hard as steel pierced her.

"I know you blackmailed Roxanna more to humiliate and frighten her than because of the money . . . but I also know yer broke and Andrew Powell hasna' ever been accused of being a generous man with his mistresses." He scored a point at last when she sucked in her breath faintly. "He dinna' pay you the money you thought you'd get, did he? Yer out of money. You owe exactly seven thousand two hundred seventy-two dollars and twenty-seven cents in back taxes and interest before you can reclaim yer estate Edgewater. I'll pay you fifty thousand dollars so you can go back South, get back yer land and start over.''

Isobel digested that. The old fool was offering her a fortune! ''I take it that in return for your largesse I must agree never to bother the Fallon woman again?''

MacKenzie nodded. ''You take it correctly.''

With a growing sense of triumph, Isobel continued. ''As for your second choice . . . let me guess. If I do not leave your 'granddaughter' alone, you personally will throttle me. Also correct?'' She was almost taunting.

The old Scot's eyes widened. ''Mrs. Darby, do na' mistake me! Murder? No, indeed. If you take the money and stay here, out West, you will have an 'accident' . . . soon, I expect. And if you take my money and go back South and then double-cross me, well . . . perhaps one night the cook will unintentionally overload the kitchen stove and there'll be a devastating fire. . . .'' Jubal shook his head sadly, as if he had just read a distressing article in the newspaper. ''Or perhaps one afternoon, yer trusted overseer will take you on an inspection tour of yer fields—say, one where a wagon road runs along the high embankment of the river. The wheel comes off yer buggy; it overturns, throwing you into the current; his rescue attempt fails. . . . Tragic, absolutely tragic!''

All through MacKenzie's narrative Isobel felt the muscles along her spine tighten. Staring up at the old Scot, who was gazing at her with the benign smile of a kindly grandfather, she felt as though her bladder might disgrace her at any moment.

Damn you and that bitch you are besotted with! she thought furiously. But she knew he had eyes everywhere, and to protect that slut, he would be even more callously ruthless than Andrew. She fought to keep her voice steady. ''When will I receive my . . . stipend?''

"Why, my dear lady, it has already been deposited in yer account."

Without another word, Isobel Darby rose on trembling knees and walked out of the office.

Cain tracked Lawrence for nearly a week through the Nevada grading camps of the Central Pacific. Powell's former troubleshooter, now working for the competition, did not receive a warm welcome. Many of the Central Pacific crew chiefs viewed him with covert suspicion, but none had the courage to mention his runaway wife—until he asked point-blank if she was with Lawrence. Several knew that young Powell had a blond-haired woman with him. Gossip spread fast as heat lightning through the rail camps. When Cain finally located his brother all the way back in Salt Lake, he expected to find Roxanna with him. If Lawrence had touched her, he was prepared to commit fratricide for the second time.

"A man named Cain is asking for you, Mr. Powell. A mixed-blood, rather a rough-looking sort," the young bookkeeper said with the avid curiosity of a greenhorn newly arrived from back East.

"Show him in, William." Powell laid aside the papers he had been working on and straightened his tie nervously.

Before William Smithers could do more than reach for the door to the Central Pacific's small temporary office, Cain shoved it open and stepped inside. "Where is she, Larry?"

"Mr. Powell, shall I—"

"You may leave us, William. It's all right," Powell replied firmly.

Disappointed to be excluded from what looked like an exciting confrontation, the youth bowed out, closing the door behind him.

"I knew you'd come. She thought you wouldn't, but I don't think she knows you as well as I do, Damon," Lawrence said calmly. In spite of his brother's shuttered expression, Powell sensed the murderous anger in those glittering black eyes. *As lethal as Father's.*

"Knowing me isn't the question, it's how well you *know* my wife," Cain replied in a silky voice.

"In the biblical sense, I presume." He raised his hands, palms up, then sighed and shrugged. "If she'd have had me, I would have taken her away from you. I made a mistake letting her go in the first place."

"Like I said before, your mistake." The tension that had coiled so painfully tight inside his gut eased. *He's telling the truth. She didn't let him touch her.* "Alexa is my wife and I keep what's mine."

"Maybe you don't deserve a remarkable woman like Roxanna." Lawrence watched in satisfaction as Cain's bronzed face leached of color.

"She told you."

"Does that decrease her value to you? If so—"

"I said I keep what's mine, Larry. I don't give a damn if she's Jubal's granddaughter or not. She *is my wife.*"

Lawrence watched Cain's hand rest lightly on the Smith and Wesson at his hip. "If you shoot me, you'll never find her."

Cain was surprised at the near taunt in his brother's voice. "If she's tucked in some hotel room in the city, I'll find her—if I have to tear the whole of Brigham Young's New Jerusalem to the ground. I don't need you."

"She's not in the city, but before I tell you where she went, I want your word you won't hurt her."

"My word?" Cain echoed dryly. If he wasn't so worried about Roxanna, it would be amusing. "Since when would a Powell take a breed's word?"

"You'll always hate me because I'm the old man's heir, won't you?" Lawrence asked stiffly.

Cain studied the pale smooth-faced man fashionably dressed in English tweed, his light brown hair meticulously barbered, his hands soft and manicured. "Frankly, Larry, I've never given you much consideration one way or the other . . . until I thought you might have slept with my wife. It's old Andrew I hate."

"The worthy adversary. Yes, I imagine you would think

of him that way. He does you," Lawrence replied bitterly.

"We can do this easy . . . or we can do it hard. You choose. Either way, I'll have her." Cain advanced a step.

"She's with the Cheyenne, your mother's people," Lawrence replied, stepping back.

"In old Leather Shirt's camp?" Cain asked, stunned.

"There was another attempt on her life. We believed she'd be safest there while I try to locate the Darby woman."

Cain cursed. "They move around. Must be over a hundred miles east of here. They could even be down in Colorado Territory. How the hell did you locate them?"

"The Central Pacific has scouts the same as MacKenzie," Lawrence said smugly.

"Yeah, I'm acquainted with their work." Lawrence gave him a blank look, then backed away as Cain placed his hands on the desk and leaned forward. "She better be with my grandfather and she better be unharmed—by anyone— or you'll wish you were dead before I'm through with you."

NORTHEASTERN COLORADO TERRITORY

The old man sat staring into the flames. The sharp chill of late autumn put a bite in the ceaseless High Plains wind. Sees Much gathered his blanket closer around his shoulders, remembering how it had been when he was young and his blood ran thick and hot in the coldest winters . . . like the Lone Bull's did now. "He will be here soon."

Roxanna did not pretend to misunderstand even though they had not discussed Cain since the day she arrived several weeks earlier. She had not explained about Cain's betrayal or her own masquerade as Jubal's granddaughter. Among these people she was still called Her Back Is Straight.

"Tomorrow?" she asked, settling on a pile of furs with graceful ease, a bowl of fragrant antelope stew in each hand. Strange how easily she once more fit in with the routine of the camp, she thought as she passed the food to the old man.

They ate in companionable silence for several moments

before he replied. "Yes, tomorrow, I think." His rheumy dark eyes studied her. "Are you ready to see him?"

She put down her bowl. "I . . . I don't know. There is so much that has gone wrong . . . lies and deceptions. At first when I learned who he was and why he had married me I blamed him for everything. But now I realize that we were both guilty."

Sees Much did not speak, only waited in patient silence, as was his way. In her own time she would unburden her heart. From the day she rode into their camp, he had felt her anguish. She as much as his nephew needed to be healed.

"I've had these weeks away from him to think. I suppose I will always love him, but I don't think I can ever trust him again."

"Your pain is great. Sometimes it is lessened when it is shared."

Roxanna took a shaky breath and launched into the whole story, beginning with her own desperate masquerade as Alexa Hunt, her plans to wed the Powell heir and the subsequent events leading up to her marriage to Cain instead. He did not seem surprised, nor was he condemning. She realized now that she had known he would not be. It gave her the courage to tell the rest of it, the most painful part about the deal Cain and Jubal had made and the shocking way she learned of it and her husband's true identity. By the time she was finished, tears brimmed in her eyes, but she refused to let them fall.

"Does your husband know about the child?" he asked after a moment.

She bit her lip and smiled sadly. "I should not be surprised that you know." She shook her head. "I did not tell him, but I'm certain Jubal MacKenzie will. After all, providing that heir was the only reason he needed his granddaughter. Cain will come after me for the child and because I'm his guarantee that he'll keep his new position with Jubal."

"Perhaps he comes for another reason."

"Out of love?" she asked, half scornful, half hopeful in spite of herself.

"I do not think he accepts that he loves you yet, but you are his woman and he is a proud man who has already lost much in this life."

"Will you make me go back with him if I don't want to?"

Sees Much shrugged. "A Cheyenne woman may divorce her husband anytime she has just cause."

"I have just cause," Roxanna said, hotly.

"Do you?" he asked. When she sat back, stung at the gentle rebuke, he said, "Only wait until you speak with him, child. Then listen with your heart."

Cain had searched arduously for another two weeks after leaving Salt Lake, beginning with Riccard Dillon, who had been busily scouring the areas adjacent to Union Pacific land for hostiles. The colonel had not been overly happy with Cain's explanation about how Leather Shirt's band came to possess so many Yellow Boy Winchesters, but he had elaborated on the information Jubal and Cain already possessed about the renegades. When he explained that full-bloods riding with the raiders had been tracked into Leather Shirt's camp, Cain knew Weasel Bear was one of them.

Cain did not tell Dillon he was searching for his wife. He planned to ride into the Cheyenne village and drag her out himself before she was caught in a full-blown Indian war! The best thing would be for the colonel to head in the opposite direction. He described some Crow sign he had run across a week earlier, farther west. Perhaps Dillon would take the bait, perhaps not. Either way, Cain meant to have Roxanna safely out of harm's way as soon as possible.

He rode into the camp at midday. The way of life there was timeless as always. With winter coming on, the women were busy drying antelope meat taken from their last hunt. Ponies fattened on the remnants of tall summer grasses. The warriors sharpened their weapons and prepared to move the village farther south into the shelter of the Arkansas River country. Children ran naked in the warm autumn sun, laughing and playing a game of stickball.

His eyes searched for the glint of silver-gilt hair as he made his way to where Leather Shirt stood, waiting impassively. He dismounted and greeted the old man. "I have come for my woman," he said in English.

"Sees Much said you would return. I did not believe him until she came to us," Leather Shirt answered in Cheyenne, a wintry smile touching his lips. "Her Back Is Straight may not wish to return to the white eyes with you."

"She is white. She cannot remain here." It had not occurred to him that the old man might interfere between them. "The soldiers could come after her," he said, switching to Cheyenne. "I spoke with the one called Dillon. Already he does not trust this band."

"Because of Weasel Bear and the others." Leather Shirt considered this, waiting to see what else Not Cheyenne would say, pleased that he now spoke in their language.

"I sent the Blue Coats riding west after Crow, but if Weasel Bear has joined the raiders attacking the Iron Horse he will only bring grief to his people."

"He has been banished by the council. He is no longer our concern."

"Just as I am no longer your concern either."

"You both made your choice," the old man said.

Perhaps a tinge of regret flavored the words. For Weasel Bear or the Lone Bull? Cain wondered but did not ask.

"Your woman is with Willow Tree and Lark Song gathering roots." He gestured to the brushy area beyond the creek on which they were camped, not indicating what he would do if Her Back Is Straight asked for sanctuary.

Cain mounted his chestnut and rode slowly across the creek, rehearsing in his mind what he might say to her. How could he make her understand his feelings when he did not understand them himself?

She sat with Willow Tree and Lark Song at the edge of the stream where it curved around a copse of chokecherry bushes. The sound of their laughing chatter drew him. He reined in his horse and sat silently watching her for a moment. The afternoon sun gleamed off the silken waterfall of her hair, turning it to molten silver. She wore a simple buckskin tunic and leggings, probably the ones she had worn back from her captivity here. He knew she had always treasured the garments. They fit her slim body as elegantly as her most expensive gown. A shaft of desire pricked him, just thinking about how smooth and soft and supple that body would be when he removed the clothes and touched it. She tilted her chin up and laughed at something Willow Tree said. He drank in the music of it like a man dying of thirst.

Roxanna felt the heat of his eyes and turned her head slowly. He sat the chestnut with the same rangy grace every Cheyenne male seemed born with, leaning on the saddle horn with one arm, his black eyes boring into her. The other women quickly gathered up their baskets and scurried away, understanding that this was between Her Back Is Straight and Not Cheyenne.

Her mouth was dry as she returned his stare. He looked hard and dangerous and dirty, carrying an arsenal of weapons, just as he had that first time he'd ridden into Leather Shirt's camp. Dismounting, he walked toward her with the same pantherish stride, arrogantly male, predatory. And hungry. Roxanna remembered that hunger from their first encounter. It had taken her in thrall and she had never been free of it since.

"I won't go back with you," she said breathlessly.

"You're my wife."

"We're with the Cheyenne. A woman can divorce her husband with cause. You've given me cause, Cain."

He smiled grimly. "I'm Not Cheyenne, remember. I'm a 'cut hair.' I live white and in white society divorce isn't so easy. You're still my wife."

"Whom you vowed to love and cherish. You never spoke of love, though, did you, Cain? Because you didn't marry me for love—you married me to get promoted." God, it hurt, sucking the breath from her just to get the words out!

He winced inwardly, knowing she had a right to the anger. "I didn't plan it that way when I first found you . . . naked in a creek. . . . Then I only wanted you the way a man wants a beautiful woman."

"Oh, when did you plan it, then? After the gossip ruined me—or when your father broke the engagement with Larry?"

She stood, slender and defiant, her turquoise eyes blazing with wounded fury. He fought the urge to crush her in his arms. "I thought about it when the gossip got out. I knew what Powell would do," he admitted, watching those glorious turquoise eyes close against the pain, then open to stare back at him in silent agonized accusation. "I wanted the job Jubal could give me. . . . I—"

"You used me. You went to Jubal MacKenzie and cut a deal."

"That's the way I told it to Larry. Hell, Roxanna, I was tired and fed up after hours of meetings, sick and tired of Larry—all right . . ." He clenched his jaw until the tendons stood out in his neck, then swallowed painfully, looking away at the far horizon. "I was jealous of him. He always had it all—the Powell name, the money, the power . . . our father's only son and heir. But I had finally beaten him—I took something away from him that was worth more than all the money on the transcontinental."

"You thought I was Jubal's heir when you married me. That made it a better than even trade—the money, the power—and revenge against your father all at the same time."

He could not deny what she said and felt an irrational swell of anger . . . or fear building up inside him. "I knew damn well who you were when I said those hurtful things to my brother. I was rubbing his nose in it because I had *you*—not just the job. The problem is that I didn't realize how much more important you were to me than the railroad until I lost you, Roxanna. When I read your note and realized what I'd done—"

"I bet it was almost as bad as when I confessed that I wasn't Alexa." She knew that remark stung. In spite of his shuttered expression, he winced visibly. "No wonder you were so furious with me. I could've cost you your job if the truth came out." She wanted him to hear the bitterness in her voice, needed him to hurt as she hurt. Why didn't he honestly admit that he wanted to return Jubal's great-grandchild to the old man? She found it difficult to believe that Jubal had not told him about the baby when she vanished.

"Was Jubal angry with you for driving me away? Is that the reason for your sudden solicitude?"

She had a right to her anger, he reminded himself. But fear of losing her, combined with his nagging jealousy over Larry, goaded him to the cold fury that made tough men quake the length of the transcontinental. "What about Larry's sudden solicitude? He walked away from your engagement without a backward glance. The next thing I see is you in his arms the night of the party. Then you fly off to meet him instead of facing me so we could work this out. I married you, Roxanna—he didn't."

"You don't own me! Neither does Larry, but he's been kind. He offered to help me escape from you."

"He used you to get to me."

"Well, it's not as if I haven't been used already." She turned away from him, hugging herself. "I'm weary unto death of being caught in the middle of your vendetta against the Powells. Go away. Leave me in peace, Cain. Tell Jubal what you will."

"I don't have to tell Jubal anything. He knows all about us—that I'm Powell's bastard, that you're Roxanna Fallon."

Chapter 19

Roxanna turned back to him, her expression numb with shock. "That . . . that's impossible. How could he?"

"He's a devious old son of a bitch," Cain said with obvious affection. "Always was. He's known who I was since he hired me, known you weren't Alexa for months."

"And yet he didn't denounce me?" Her mind whirled with the possibilities. What was Jubal's game? *What was Cain's?* Was he telling her the truth? "How can I trust you?" she asked defensively, plaintively.

"I suppose it's a leap of faith we both have to make. I could accuse you of running off to Larry."

"I didn't stay with Larry," she said indignantly.

"That's the only reason I didn't kill him."

She looked into his eyes . . . cold, black, pitiless . . . and she shuddered. "Who are you, Cain? Damon Powell?"

"I have no right to the Powell name," he replied bitterly.

"Lone Bull, then." She thought of Sees Much's dreams, and her own, and wondered.

"No. I'm Not Cheyenne. I killed my brother. The only name I have is the one I gave you. Cain. I'd take back those words I said to Larry if I could. I never meant to hurt you, Roxanna. I want you back."

Me or the baby? She almost asked it, yet something held her back. He did not know. Jubal, for whatever mysterious reason of his own, had not told her husband that he was to be a father. "Give me time, Cain. Let me talk to Sees Much. He's on your side, you know." She could see the disbelieving expression on his face. "He has some idea—or dream or vision—that my capture was ordained by his Powers. That I was the means to bring you back to your people."

He scoffed. "I have no people. You above everybody should know that."

"You choose not to belong. You're so scarred by Andrew Powell's rejection that you can't see anything else."

"You sound like Leather Shirt now." He gave a shaky laugh. "He accused me of choosing to be white, rejecting my Cheyenne blood, but I'm really neither red nor white. Hell, if I had a choice, I sure wouldn't choose to be a breed."

"You'll never be free to love anyone until you can learn to stop hating yourself," she said with sudden insight. "I fell in love with a man of mixed blood, Cain." And in loving him, she had learned to forgive herself—or thought she had until he had betrayed her.

"And now, Roxy? Are you telling me that love died? That I killed it?" He studied her intently, praying that she would do as she always had—come to him. Irresistibly he was drawn to step closer, to reach out for her, for that old physical intimacy that blotted out the rest of the world. But she drew back.

"No. Don't touch me . . . please. I need time to think." She stumbled as she turned away, then broke into a headlong run when his warm, firm hands touched her.

Cain let her go. A feeling of bleak desolation swept over him. He felt suddenly more alone than he ever had in his life.

Why hadn't she told him about the baby? Roxanna still was not certain. But she was certain that Jubal had not done so for a reason. Was he trying to be some sort of matchmaker, however misguided? Whatever his motives, Jubal was the least of her concerns. Cain had come after her without knowledge of his child. She had to make a decision that would affect that child as much as it did her. No matter how much she still loved her husband—and there was no killing that love in spite of his fears—she had to think of their child first.

Without realizing it, her wandering reverie had taken her directly to the lodge of Sees Much. The old man sat outside the door, puffing on a pipe. He set it carefully aside, and motioned for her to sit across from him as if he had been expecting her.

"Her Back Is Straight is troubled. Your talk with the Lone Bull did not go well."

She sat wearily, feeling for all the world like a child at her father's feet once more, seeking wisdom and council. "No, it did not. He expects me to return with him because I am his wife. He still has not said that he loves me."

"It is difficult for a man to love another person when he has never learned to love himself," he said gently, feeling the hurt in her confession.

Roxanna smiled sadly. "Strange, that is the very thing I said to him. There is such self-hate, such a feeling of rejection and unworthiness burned into his soul."

"And into yours as well," the old man replied. "But I think you are learning the truth of your own worth now . . . perhaps because of the child you have created together."

"He doesn't know about the baby."

"And you did not tell him." The old man made no further comment, only waited patiently for her to continue.

"Something held me back. I don't know what . . . or why . . . unless . . ."

"A mother always wishes to protect her child."

She looked at him in amazement, then nodded. "Yes, that is why I couldn't tell him. He hates his own Cheyenne blood. I will give him a child who shares that blood. What if he comes to see a mirror of himself in his son or daughter? Another mixed-blood whom he cannot love, just as Andrew Powell could not love him, just as he cannot love himself?"

Sees Much nodded, considering this. "He must first come

to accept himself. To see that what is deep inside here"—
he pounded his fist against his chest with surprising
strength—"is good. Then he will be able to see good in his
child."

"But how can that ever happen?"

The old man smiled serenely now. "There is a sacred
ceremony among our people for wholeness and rebirth, to
strengthen the spirit of each man who pledges himself to it.
This we call the Making of the Medicine Lodge, or Sun
Dance. When the Lone Bull swings to the lodgepole all
things will be made new before his eyes. He will see himself . . . he will again be one with the People . . . and he will
be at peace."

Roxanna knew Cain had always rejected Indian mysti-
cism. He would scoff at the old man's idea. "How will you
get him to agree?"

"I will not. You will."

"But . . . but how?"

"If he heals his soul, comes to peace with himself and
who he is, will you take him back as your husband?"

"Yes, of course."

"Then you will convince him that he must pledge to
make a Medicine Lodge."

"You believe this will heal him?"

"I know it is so. When you first came among us, I was
given to see that you would draw the Lone Bull after you.
But I did not know for what purpose. Now I do. His long
exile from the People and from himself will be ended."

Cain might doubt the old man's mystic powers, but after
spending time with Sees Much, Roxanna was not so quick
to dismiss them. "Then I will try to convince him."

"Oh, you will convince him," Sees Much replied dryly.

Cain sat in front of the low-burning fire in the lodge, staring
at Roxanna in stupefaction. "You want me to do *what*?" It
was a good thing they were already sitting down, else he'd
have fallen over. "Me participate in that barbaric ritual!"

Roxanna sighed. "I knew you would react this way. You

don't want to belong here . . . but don't you see? If you don't come to terms with this part of who you are, we can have no happiness. No matter how hard you've tried to prove yourself as white, all your life you've been thwarted . . . inadvertently even I've played a part in that. Perhaps there was a reason for the way we met.''

"That sounds like my uncle talking. Fate's grand design—visions from the Powers." He could not believe she had fallen for the old man's bizarre schemes.

"Don't scoff! You have to know and accept who you really are—not just Cain the outsider, the man who needs no one, who lives for his hate, but Damon the lost son, too. The Lone Bull is the key." Should she tell him about her dream? Roxanna was not certain. Perhaps that was best left unspoken. He must find his own way . . . if only he would agree to search for it. "Sees Much believes this ceremony will help you see who the Lone Bull is. It would reunite you with your people. Then you wouldn't be Not Cheyenne—you wouldn't need Cain any longer. You wouldn't have to hide behind the stigma of outcast.''

He stiffened angrily. The words bit deep. "Hide? The last thing I've ever been able to do in either world is hide my mixed blood.''

"No, you've thrown it down like a gauntlet in front of your grandfather, in front of your uncle . . . in front of me. You dare anyone to love you, just because your father refused. You keep us all at arm's length. You're a coward, an emotional cripple who's never come out from behind the wall he built when he was deserted as a ten-year-old boy!'' Roxanna scrambled to her feet and fled from the lodge, tear-blinded.

Cain sprang after her, but she was nearer the door flap and slipped out of his grasp. With an angry oath he pursued her, his long-legged strides quickly catching up to her as she reached the stream flowing along the west side of the camp. She stood with her back to him, slightly out of breath, fighting back the tears.

Whatever made Sees Much believe she could convince

him? For once the old shaman had been wrong. Or had he?
There was one trump card she had not played. Would it
matter enough to him that he would agree? She would be
taking a grave risk to tell him. How much did she believe
in Sees Much's vision? How much did she love her husband? "I am with child, Cain," she said quietly, turning to
face him. They stood alone in the twilight. She tried to read
his expression but could not.

For the second time that night he felt poleaxed as confused thoughts—joy and fear—tumbled around in his mind.
"How long have you known?" he asked at length, certain
that she had withheld the information deliberately.

"Six weeks, a bit more, perhaps. The time never seemed
right. I learned it the day of the first attempt on my life. By
the time you returned from the grading camp, Isobel Darby
sent the second assassin and I was forced to tell you who I
was. Then . . ."

"You were so unsure of me you didn't want to tell me,"
he finished for her, remembering how he had lashed out at
her for using him. A painful wry smile played about his
lips, then vanished sadly. He ached to take her in his arms,
but some instinct held him back. "Hell, Roxy, we are a fine
pair."

"I won't let this baby grow up with a father who will see
his child's mixed blood the same way he sees his own."

"So that's what this is all about," he said angrily.

"Did you ever in all your plans and schemes to become
a railroad baron, to destroy Andrew Powell—did you ever
think about a wife and children—children who would share
one quarter of their blood with Leather Shirt and Sees
Much?"

"No," he admitted, "I never thought to marry at all until
you. I knew it would be hard on you . . . and on any children."

"Leave me, Cain," she said coldly, numb with hopeless-
ness. "It's better if I go away. Anywhere—back East, to
San Francisco—"

"Back to Larry." He placed his hands on her shoulders

and spun her around to face him. "I don't think so."

"You can't force me to stay with you," she said stubbornly.

"You called me a coward. What if I make a Medicine Lodge? Would it prove to you that I cared about you . . . about our baby?"

Was this the way Sees Much intended for him to make the pledge? There was a note of quiet despair in his voice that she had never heard before, beyond jealousy, beyond anger. Was it love? That would be a start. Perhaps it was all that was needed . . . for now. "Yes, Cain. It would prove that you care," she replied.

Cain approached Sees Much to make the arrangements. The old man seemed completely unsurprised that his cut hair nephew was willing to undergo the Medicine Lodge ritual. "You were certain that I'd agree to this?" he asked.

Sees Much smiled. "I was certain. Her Back Is Straight did not quite believe . . . but you are here."

"She has no idea what it means to swing to the pole, does she?"

"I did not speak of that part, no. Do you fear it?"

"I'm not afraid of pain," Cain answered quickly, but he knew what his uncle meant. Was he afraid of what the ancient ceremony would reveal? He had spent his whole life trying to escape this world. Now he was being trapped inside its circle once more . . . *for her, for the child.* Dread of the unknown seized his guts, twisting them until he sweated in the cool night air.

The old shaman squinted at his nephew through rheumy dark eyes. "You are not afraid of the physical pain, I know," he replied.

"You've convinced her I'll have some sort of mystical vision," he said dismissively, then leaned forward, adding, "or is this an atonement for my past sins?"

"You have much to atone for . . . both with the People and with your woman, I think. It will be good. I will speak with your grandfather and we will plan the ceremony."

"Do you believe Leather Shirt will permit me to be the pledger? He has never forgiven me for the death of High-Backed Wolf."

"It is time that too ended. This will be the means for a new beginning. My brother will agree."

Later that night, as Sees Much made his way to Leather Shirt's lodge, he was not at all as certain as he had led Cain to believe. His brother's heart was bad toward the one he called Not Cheyenne. But Sees Much had faith in the dreams he had experienced, dreams which had become increasingly vivid in the months after the Lone Bull and Her Back Is Straight had left them. He entered Leather Shirt's lodge and made his request as soon as they had shared a pipe.

Leather Shirt sat in the gathering darkness, staring into the flames in the fire pit. "Many of the people will remember how he killed High-Backed Wolf. He is still Not Cheyenne."

"After four years a banishment may be lifted. The autumn hunt will be blessed by the blood sacrifice of the Medicine Lodge. There will be many buffalo. Our people will have full bellies once more."

"Will the Powers be pleased when the Medicine Lodge is pledged by one who is half white? Who has shed Cheyenne blood?" Leather Shirt played devil's advocate, worrying the idea in his mind.

Sees Much smiled. "I have seen his dance in many dreams now. Come, I will tell you of them. Then you may speak with the warrior societies about breaking camp."

Cain awakened suddenly, hearing the old familiar sounds of the crier riding through the village announcing the day's activities. He remembered listening eagerly as a small boy, each morning awash with fresh hope that His Eyes Are Cold would return that day. Brushing the old pain away, he sat up, looking at the empty pallets around the fire pit.

Roxanna had slept on the opposite side of the fire from him with Sees Much's granddaughters, while he had been forced to share this side with his aged uncle. The night had been still and close and he had slept poorly, angry to have her so near yet so far from him after searching so long to find her. Then the nightmare had come. When he woke from it, he had lain awake for hours, refusing to sink again into the morass of blood and pain. He felt a deep dread of the unknown. Or perhaps simply of what he wished not to know. Eventually, he had drifted off again into a deep dreamless sleep.

What insane impulse had made him agree to this barbaric ordeal? Roxanna was his wife. She carried his child. He had every right to pack her on a horse and ride out of here, the Medicine Lodge, his uncle, the whole Cheyenne nation be damned! But he had made a pledge for her sake. Now he must carry it through. Would it do what she hoped? What Sees Much believed would happen? Cain doubted . . . but he would have to try anyway.

As Cain was listening to the morning crier, another watched the Elk Soldier making his rounds. Johnny Lame Pony was too far away to make out his words, but it did not matter. Cain had come to Leather Shirt's camp after his white woman and that was as it should be. The old chief apparently was not letting her go back with her husband so quickly. Johnny smiled. "There will be plenty of time to bring the Blue Coats to the camp in search of MacKenzie's granddaughter," he said.

"Then we make certain both the half-blood and his woman die when soldiers ride in," Weasel Bear replied in serviceable Lakota.

Johnny motioned to the two other Cheyenne renegades with them and they slipped away from their hiding place. It would take them a day's hard ride to reach Dillon, another to return here. Then they would collect their pay from the Iron Horse man. Weasel Bear would receive a fine new string of horses and have revenge on the band who had disowned him. Johnny Lame Pony would receive enough whiskey to stay drunk for at least a month.

Down in the camp, Roxanna and Willow Tree brought pails of fresh water from the stream and set about making the morning meal. "Is true Lone Bull pledge to make Medicine Lodge?" the Cheyenne asked Roxanna, while chopping wild onions for the bubbling pot.

"A Sun Dance? Yes. He has agreed."

Willow Tree smiled knowingly. "He does for you." At her friend's nod, she added, "Will be good for whole village. Bring many buffalo."

"Just so it brings him peace," Roxanna replied.

Willow Tree studied the white woman shrewdly. "Why you no sleep with your man?"

Roxanna flushed, thinking of Cain lying across the lodge from her. She had ached with the need to feel his arms around her, to have the solid comfort of his big hard body spooned against hers. "The time is not right. This is a testing period for him." She could not jeopardize it by giving in to her own weakness. "If I lie with him, he might decide to take me away, back to the Iron Horse camp. Then nothing would be settled between us."

Willow Tree grunted in approval, understanding abstinence before a pivotal event in a warrior's life. "Lone Bull sweat, pray, then make big sacrifice to Powers."

Sees Much had described the ceremony to Roxanna, so she possessed a vague idea of how it would go. Cain must perform a vision quest through an elaborate four-day ritual of fasting and dancing. If the shaman was wrong and Cain had no dream, at least he would have come to terms with the customs of his mother's people. Surely there would be some benefit in his participation, even if he did it only to prove his love for his wife.

He still has never spoken of love. Before she could worry that thought any further, Cain stepped outside the lodge. Several days' growth of beard made him look piratical. His expression when he looked at her was unreadable.

Nodding to Willow Tree, Cain paused by Roxanna and said, "When that water boils, bring me a bowl of it for shaving," then continued on his way down to the stream.

Roxanna gritted her teeth at the arrogant male presumption, but Willow Tree seemed to see nothing amiss in the command. Cheyenne women performed many such menial tasks. She supposed white women did too, but it helped when their men were at least polite enough to say please!

Bowl of hot water in hand, she made her way to the curve of the stream, searching for Cain. She found him drying off after a brisk swim in the cold water.

He smiled at her when she averted her eyes as he pulled on his breeches. "Remembering the last time we met at the water?" he taunted. "I believed I'd cured you of maidenly modesty."

"Marriage to you has cured me of a good deal more than my modesty," she snapped, fighting the urge to fling the scalding water in his smirking face.

When she stood and turned to walk away, he reached out and clamped his hand around her wrist. "Stay and keep me company."

His voice was cajoling now, that low seductive rumble that made her mouth go paper dry. Small wonder. All the moisture in her body had fled in the opposite direction! "Why are you doing this? You know Sees Much said you must remain celibate until after the ceremony."

"He said it was best, not that I *had* to." He touched a loose curl at her cheek, brushing it softly back. "Hold the mirror for me while I shave."

He knew what that would do to her, damn him! His hold on her wrist did not lessen as he waited. "All right," she replied, taking the small polished steel mirror he held out.

He let her go then with a crooked smile and knelt beside a flat rock where he had tossed his saddlebags. Extracting a razor and soap from inside, he used the hot water to work up a stiff lather and spread it across his whiskers, then set to work shaving them away, directing her to position the mirror close to his face.

She perched on the edge of the rock close beside him, her eyes downcast, listening to the soft raspy flick of the sharp blade. Snick, snick, snick. After several strokes, she was unable to stop herself from looking up. With each pass of the blade, he cleared another piece of smooth bronze skin. Her fingers tingled with the urge to touch it. How well she remembered the warm firm feel of his jawline. How often she had lain beside him and traced the high planes of his cheekbones, the thick ridge of black eyebrows, the wide sensuous curve of his lips. . . .

The mirror wavered just as he made one final stroke with the razor. He set aside the blade. She lowered the mirror, clutching it in her lap with trembling fingers. Their faces remained inches apart, their eyes staring deeply, hungrily at each other. Cain reached up and laid his palm against the side of her cheek. ''I've missed you these past weeks, more than I could ever have imagined possible. Roxanna, I—''

A loud series of shouts erupted suddenly from the camp. Roxanna would have given much to know what he was about to say, but he understood the cries in Cheyenne and broke away from her with a troubled look on his face. ''What is it? What are they saying?''

''His Eyes Are Cold has been brought into camp.''

''Your father? What on earth would Andrew Powell be doing in Colorado hundreds of miles from the Central Pacific's farthest eastern grade?''

''I'm not certain,'' Cain replied as an idea niggled in the back of his mind.

She followed him reluctantly back to camp. He walked like a restless mountain cat warily scenting the wind, moving in for the kill. What would Leather Shirt do to the man who had disgraced his daughter and deserted his grandson? What might Cain do? A chill premonition washed over her.

Two members of the Dog Soldier Society had bound Powell's hands behind him. They shoved him roughly, but he refused to give in, holding his footing as he came face-to-face with the old chief who waited at his lodge in the center of the circle, arms crossed, face unreadable. Roxanna remembered how she had felt when she was dragged before Leather Shirt, a daunting experience indeed.

Andrew Powell's expensive twill riding pants were

smeared with grime and dust and his shirt was torn open, hanging more off than on his tall frame. A thin trickle of blood ran from the corner of his patrician mouth. His thick mane of steel-gray hair was plastered to his sweat-soaked head with several locks falling over one eye. He coolly blew them away in lieu of his being able to shove them off his brow, standing as arrogantly as if he were presiding over a San Francisco boardroom.

Leather Shirt and Powell were the same height, both tall men, in the prime of vigor in spite of their ages. They faced each other in silence, cold dark blue eyes daring fathomless black ones. A palpable current of hate seethed between them. The excited crowd gathered around them, their gazes moving from the chief to his prisoner and back.

Finally Leather Shirt broke the silence, speaking in Cheyenne. "You have returned at last. Too late to sing a death song for your wife."

"I did not come for that. I knew she was dead," Powell replied in cold clipped English.

"Then you are a fool for coming onto our land again. Blue Corn Woman would plead for your life. No one else will."

"I am a powerful man among the whites now. If you kill me, the Blue Coats will come to avenge me. Women and children will die along with warriors. The soldiers will burn your lodges and drive what is left of the band onto reservations in the hot country to the south."

"The men who rode with you are all dead. If I kill you, who will ever find your body in the vastness of the land?" Leather Shirt gestured eloquently with his arm, adding chillingly, "The buzzards will pick your bones clean. Then who will recognize the great Powell?" He allowed a brief flicker of satisfaction to cross his face. "Dead bones, red or white, all look alike."

If those words daunted Powell, it was not apparent from the way he stared haughtily back at Leather Shirt. *The old son of a bitch is one hell of a poker player.* Cain observed the exchange, curious about what his grandfather would do, more curious by far about what had brought his father into this wilderness.

"Get used to red bones. There will be many bleaching across the mountains if you don't release me," Powell replied calmly as if he were negotiating a right of way through some pumpkin roller's back forty. "I am still a trader, a rich man now. I can bring presents—whiskey, guns, sugar, coffee. Whatever you wish."

"You can't buy your way out of this one, Powell," Cain said, walking into the open space between his grandfather and father.

For an instant, Andrew Powell's composure broke, then the facade slipped quickly back into place as he turned to face his half-breed son. "What the hell are you doing here?"

In an unconsciously identical manner, Cain's eyebrow raised sardonically as he surveyed his father. "I might ask you the same thing. This is quite a ride from the Central Pacific's eastern terminus."

The two men studied each other in a subtly different fashion than had Powell and Leather Shirt, yet the hatred was every bit as pervasive. Cain offered less challenge, more mockery. Roxanna stood fixed as he circled Powell with insolent slowness. She held her breath, wondering how the older man would respond.

"I have my reasons for being here."

"Reason enough to risk your life? My grandfather will kill you, you know," Cain replied conversationally.

Powell's eyebrow rose. "Grandfather, is it? The last I heard, you'd been banished. I would imagine you're no more welcome than I after you killed the old man's favorite grandson."

"His banishment has been lifted," Leather Shirt replied in what could only be described as a smug voice. "Now he seeks a vision to find out who he truly is. The Lone Bull pledges to make a Medicine Lodge."

A look of utter incredulity swept over Powell's face. "The Sun Dance?" he asked, turning to Cain. "So, all your attempts at being white end in this. I always knew mongrel blood will out,'' he said contemptuously.

Beneath the mockery in his voice, Roxanna detected anger. So did Leather Shirt, who smiled broadly now. Cain stood rigidly still, his face expressionless as the eyes of both older men returned to him.

Damn them both! Leather Shirt was using his apparent reversion to primitive superstition to goad Powell. Powell was furious that any son of his—even if scorned and rejected—would dare to sink into savagery. Perhaps he had overlooked the best way of all to defy Andrew Powell; if only he did not have to sell his soul to do it. A feral grimace of a smile twisted his lips as he replied to his father, ''Like you said, I have my reasons.'' His eyes flashed to Roxanna for an instant, then he turned and stalked away.

Leather Shirt made no attempt to stop him. Turning his attention to Powell, who scowled at Roxanna now, the chief said, ''Together we will watch your son make the sacrifice for his people. Then we shall see if he has the heart of a Cheyenne or the heart of a vulture like you.'' He nodded to the Dog Soldiers, who seized Powell, dragged him into a lodge and bound his feet, leaving him to lie on the hard earth.

That afternoon the People broke camp. The women dismantled the buffalo-hide teepees, lashing together the lodgepoles for travois to transport all their possessions, which were packed into large rawhide parfleches. Youths herded their families' extra horses while small children rode squeezed between the furs and bundles piled on the travois. Most of the women and old people trudged in a long file toward the north, where the buffalo herds had fled from the noise and stench of the white man. They would have to cross the hated Iron Horse tracks to reach their destination deep in the wide-open basin of the Medicine Bows.

The leaders of the warrior societies, mounted and heavily armed, led the way while others rode point, all keeping a wary eye out for signs of enemies. When Lawrence's escorts for Roxanna had left her here, they had taken the horse and saddle she used back with them. She rode one of the skittish Cheyenne ponies, rigged with a cumbersome wooden saddle which made her posterior ache interminably. Cain was mounted on his big chestnut, as graceful and skilled a horseman as any of his Cheyenne cousins. Andrew Powell, the prisoner, walked behind Leather Shirt's horse, his bound hands secured by a long rawhide tether held by the chief.

As much as she disliked the man, Roxanna did not want to see Powell harmed. And his claim to Leather Shirt was no idle boast. Once it was discovered that he was missing, the army would sweep down viciously on the Cheyenne. She kneed her pony into a swifter pace to catch up with Sees Much.

"What will Leather Shirt do with my husband's father?" she asked.

"They are old enemies. I know only that my brother is pleased that His Eyes Are Cold is here to observe his son make a Medicine Lodge."

"You mean because he's taken Cain away from Powell."

Sees Much nodded. "You are wise beyond your years, daughter."

Roxanna felt warmed by the praise, yet she could not quit worrying about the fate of her father-in-law. "If Leather Shirt kills Powell, it will bring destruction down on the People."

"What you say is true," was all the old man would answer.

They made camp the second night by the banks of a shallow stream that trickled with autumn sluggishness across water-worn pebbles. The wide-open basin was ringed on three sides by the stark peaks of the Medicine Bows and domed by the vastness of a brilliant azure sky, which blazed with the incredible incandescence of a million stars that night. The rich loamy smells of thick high prairie grasses blended with the savory aroma of freshly killed antelope roasting over the campfires.

Sleeping arrangements on the trail were the same as in

:campment, Roxanna with the women, Cain across the ..site side of the fire with his uncle. At dawn everyone ..ose and began to break camp, each individual in the band performing his or her tasks with brisk efficiency as if the whole had been organized by an army general. After a simple meal of cornmeal porridge they again moved out.

Just before noon, Sees Much raised his hand and Leather Shirt gave a command for everyone to stop. The leaders of the warrior societies sat poised on their horses as an air of expectancy swept through the long column of people.

"What is it?" Roxanna asked Lark Song.

"Cannot feel? Come, down off horse. Touch earth," she replied, moving her moccasin-clad foot through the thick soft dust.

Roxanna felt the vibrations before the low rumbling sound rolled across the valley floor. Then, beginning as tiny specks on the flat horizon to the northwest, a thin broken line of brown began to grow larger.

Willow Tree and Lark Song chattered excitedly in their language, then shared the conversation with Her Back Is Straight in broken English. "Big herd of buffalo. Plenty blessings. The Powers pleased with Lone Bull's pledge."

The buffalo must have counted in the tens of thousands, an awesome spectacle rarely seen on the High Plains in the last decade. A vast undulating sea of brown moved slowly to the west and north of them, circling around, breaking up and reforming into different patterns as the Indians moved across the immense bowl of the basin floor.

At first Roxanna was frightened that they would be caught in the awesome waves of horn and hoof and trampled. But whenever the great shaggy beasts came downwind of the scent of humans, they retreated, giving the band a wide berth. The People traveled all that day through the bison and made camp at the edge of the first rolling foothills to the northeast. A clear stream, larger than any they had yet encountered, ran down from the snowy peaks of the mountains. Along its banks thick stands of cottonwoods and willows grew in verdant abundance.

Sees Much announced that their journey was over.

Chapter 20

"What are they doing in there?" Roxanna asked Willow Tree. Sees Much and Cain had been closeted together in what her Cheyenne companion referred to as the "lonely lodge" since dawn that morning. The sun now blazed high in the sky as the women finished the myriad tasks associated with setting up a new camp.

"They prepare, sweat, pray to Everywhere Spirit," Willow Tree replied. "Must be alone. No others go in, out."

Roxanna could see the smoke from the lodge's fire pit rising. In spite of the warm autumn day, the sides and door flap of the lodge were securely closed, isolating the two men. Wryly she thought Cain might indeed be sweating, but she much doubted that he was doing any of the praying. As his instructor in making a Medicine Lodge, Sees Much would prepare him to enter the vision world.

Earlier the leaders of the band's various warrior societies, Elk, Fox, Dog and Bowstring, had ridden from the camp. As they passed by, the people had cheered them on, the women making high trills while small children clapped their hands gleefully. Some of the men beat their fists against their breasts in a sign of respect. Roxanna had been told that they were going to cut down the poles for the Medicine Lodge, a large edifice which would be constructed that morning.

Sees Much had selected White Owl Woman to be the bearer of a sacred buffalo skull which would be used in the ceremony. She was the mother of Weasel Bear, a fact which had struck Roxanna as strange. Surely White Owl Woman must resent Cain, since it was enmity toward him which had caused her son's banishment. Yet last night when Sees Much had conferred the honor on her, she had seemed highly pleased, calling Cain "cousin" in the formal manner of address used to denote one who is being honored among the People. Apparently she had been shamed by her son's dishonorable behavior as had many others. The defection of the young hotheads following Weasel Bear had brought bad medicine to the band. This ceremony would renew and unify their whole society, so they were grateful to the one who pledged to it.

The felling of a tall straight cottonwood for the center pole of the Medicine Lodge took only a short while. Several other lesser trees were also cut for the supporting beams of the large edifice, then all were dragged on ropes back to the village to the sounds of great revelry among the assembled people, who now ceased their chores for the day in favor of celebrating the erection of the lodge. The leaders of the societies, under Leather Shirt's direction, set the tall center pole in the central clearing, around which the other teepees had been situated in their usual orderly manner, all facing east.

Roxanna and Willow Tree sat in the shade of their lodge, watching as the skeleton of the Medicine Lodge took shape. "It's much larger than any of the others."

"So warriors can sing, dance," Willow Tree said, gesturing to the inside of the lodge.

Apparently some favored few would be witnesses, even participate with Cain and Sees Much. She had already been told that, as pledger, Cain would fast for the four-day duration of the ceremony, taking no food or water. Considering how warm the autumn weather had turned, this concerned her, but her friends assured her that many warriors had undergone this discipline before her husband with no lasting ill effects. Still, they spoke of the "great pain" which the Lone Bull would offer for the People and she felt uneasy. Her eyes continuously returned to the "lonely lodge" where Cain had spent what surely must have already been a long and arduous day.

When the skins had been stretched over the sides of the large oblong lodge, various of the participants brought into it sacred artifacts entrusted to their possession. Leather Shirt and Sees Much, who had left Cain alone in the "lonely lodge," directed the placement of the trophies. All of this was done to the beat of drums and low solemn chanting. At length, White Owl Woman, decked out in an elaborately quilled doeskin tunic and leggings, walked to the site of the "lonely lodge," followed by Sees Much, who opened the flap of the lodge. She stepped inside.

A moment later she emerged, holding aloft the most honored trophy of the ceremony, the skull of a large buffalo bull. It gleamed whitely in the blazing sun as she carried it across the clearing to the Medicine Lodge. Because she was not a member of the tribe, Roxanna could not enter the lodge, but Sees Much's granddaughters explained to her that White Owl Woman was placing the skull in the rear of the Medicine Lodge, facing out the open doorway to the east.

When she emerged, everything was in readiness for the pledger. All eyes in the crowd turned expectantly to the lonely lodge. Old Leather Shirt and the other leaders waited outside the Medicine Lodge in utmost respect. While the chants continued, the flap of the "lonely lodge" was once more opened by Sees Much. He stood aside and held the buffalo hide up in honor of the pledger.

Roxanna worked her way through the crowd of tall men, eager for her first sight of Cain since the ceremony had begun. When he stepped out into the light, she gasped in shock. She would never have dreamed her husband, who had aspired all of his life to be white, could look so utterly Indian. His long bronzed body was practically naked, with only a loincloth around his narrow hips. He was painted with vermilion slashes and geometric designs across his face, chest, arms and legs. His hair, although much shorter than that of the other men, had been without the attention of a barber for enough time that it hung nearly to his shoulders. Long beaded earrings and feathered leather leg and arm bracelets completed his savage adornments.

Watching him as he walked through the crowd toward the lodge, she bit her lip, frightened suddenly by what she had asked him to do. *How he must hate this.* Cain looked neither to the left nor right, staring stonily ahead as he passed by the others. But when he approached her, he slowed his stride imperceptibly and his eyes met hers in a burning exchange.

See what you have made me.

Then he was gone, vanished inside the big lodge with the other celebrants. Roxanna stood, numb with remorse, as the people rushed by her, closing in around the lodge to hear what was going on inside. ''What have I done?'' she whispered to herself.

She stood for a moment, staring at the lodge, then became aware of someone's eyes on her. She turned to meet the piercing blue glare of Andrew Powell. His hands were bound and two young Dog Soldiers held his arms. His cold eyes narrowed on her as the guards brought him closer to the lodge. Leather Shirt obviously planned to have him watch his son perform the Sun Dance.

''You've married a savage. Now is a bit late to regret it.'' His voice held a note of pity mixed with condescension.

''You're the only one here with regrets, Mr. Powell. Your son is renouncing your hold over him by participating in this sacred ceremony.''

His patrician nostrils flared as his face went rigid with shock, then anger. ''Sacred ceremony,'' he spat. ''Nothing but gory barbaric superstition. I would say I found it difficult to comprehend how a gently raised young woman could stomach the Sun Dance, but it would seem you've become one of them as well.'' He eyed her buckskin tunic and moccasins scornfully. ''Hardly surprising, if half of what Mrs. Darby says about your checkered career is true. You're a fraud well suited for a man like Cain.''

"I take that as a compliment, although I know you didn't intend it that way," she replied, covering her shock about Isobel. Revealing her true identity was no longer of significance, considering what was transpiring here in the Medicine Lodge. "You have two fine sons, yet you appreciate neither one."

A flash of anger blazed on his face, then dissipated into a strange weariness. "I had only one son. I never acknowledged Cain."

"And now he no longer acknowledges you. You resent that, don't you?" Roxanna could see that her barb struck by the reddening of his face, but before he could reply, one' of the Dog Soldiers said something in Cheyenne and they dragged Powell away, forcing him to sit near the door of the lodge. He would be able to hear everything. Leather Shirt's revenge would be sweet. Deeply troubled, Roxanna rejoined the other women.

The dancing, drumming and chanting continued through the rest of the day, along with the shrill cries from whistles made of eagle bone which many of the dancers blew repeatedly. At full dark the dancers and singers began to file out, leaving Cain and his instructor Sees Much inside. After a bit, Sees Much too emerged. Roxanna had spent her lonely vigil sitting in front of their lodge. As the old shaman approached, Willow Tree offered him a bowl of stew. All day various of the women in the band had been cooking special feast foods for the celebrants—all but the fasting pledger.

Sees Much accepted the stew gratefully and sat down beside Roxanna. "Have you eaten, daughter?" he asked.

She shook her head. "I could not."

He gently touched her pale hand with his gnarled dark one. "It will be well. You must not fear for him. Already he shows good heart. Hear the drum?"

"Yes. Is someone still dancing inside the lodge?"

His smile beamed proudly. "That is the Lone Bull."

"I—I don't understand. I thought . . ."

"You feared he was angry with you. Perhaps he is . . . but it will not last once he sees the truth in his vision. I

have made him understand what it means for the People—
that the sacrifice of the Medicine Lodge must be made with
a strong heart. That is why he will dance through the night,
alone. It is most pleasing to the Powers.''

''And for the people who see his heart,'' she supplied.

''Just so.''

Roxanna lay on her pallet that night feeling weary, yet a
bit hopeful. Perhaps Cain might be drawn to reconciliation
with his family and the other members of the band through
this ritual. *I am with you in my heart, my love. Be strong.
Be well.*

''They crossed here, Colonel. Three, maybe four days ahead
of us,'' the scout said, kneeling on the muddy bank of the
Little Laramie.

There was something about the Pawnee that made Riccard
Dillon distinctly uneasy. He had brought a paper signed by
Major Frank North reassigning him and three of his men.
North's Pawnee Battalion was famous for helping the cavalry to pacify the Cheyenne and Sioux. The men certainly
seemed to be good trackers, but they just didn't have the
look of Pawnee about them. Too tall, not dish-faced enough.

*Hell, maybe I'm just getting 'spooked because we lost old
Leather Shirt and MacKenzie's granddaughter.* He had been
incredulous when the wire arrived from MacKenzie saying
Alexa Cain had been taken prisoner by Leather Shirt. Cain
had not indicated that his wife was in any danger when he'd
run across the half-breed the week before. Very peculiar,
that. He wondered what Cain was up to.

Having the Pawnee scouts was a lucky break. They'd
found Leather Shirt's camp in just two days. Worse luck
that the hostiles had moved on, but given the way they lived,
not surprising. Dillon figured they'd catch up easily in a few
days.

That was before they ran into the massive herds of buffalo
which obliterated all traces of the Indians. They had wasted
days searching through the churned-up earth for some sign
of Leather Shirt's band. At last they had struck paydirt. Dil-

lon wondered what Cain was doing now. Was the breed too on his wife's trail? The colonel only prayed that she could survive with the savages until he could rescue her. Of course sometimes it was better for a white woman not to make it out alive. . . .

"All right, Flint Arrow, tell your scouts to move ahead," Dillon commanded.

"Flint Arrow," the "Pawnee," smiled slyly as he signaled to Weasel Bear to mount up. Johnny Lame Pony could almost smell that whiskey.

At dawn Roxanna awakened when the other women arose, chattering as they dressed for the second day of the ceremony. The three hurried outside just as the first purple and orange streaks of sunrise were climbing over the western mountains. The men who had been designated to participate inside the lodge sang their morning songs to the sun. Then they filed into the Medicine Lodge and the full-scale dancing and drumming resumed, along with the piercing cry of the eagle whistles. The women continued to prepare feast foods—rich stews, roasted meats, luscious fall fruits gathered fresh that morning.

"May I help with the cooking?" Roxanna was too nervous to continue watching from the outside with nothing to do but fret and wonder how her husband fared.

White Owl Woman, in charge of the food, nodded. "The Lone Bull does well. Our cousin has a good heart for the People. You do too, I think. You may grind that corn for porridge," she replied in Cheyenne, pointing to a mortar and pestle and a pile of dried red ears.

Willow Tree translated for Roxanna, who was relieved to have some useful task to perform. She felt gladdened by the praise from White Owl Woman and haltingly thanked the woman in her own language.

The third day went on much as the preceding one had. Roxanna worked diligently at the cookfires and later in the afternoon was asked by White Owl Woman to carry food to the Medicine Lodge for the dancers. The edifice was surrounded by people, some chanting, some simply sitting in reverence. The food was received by Sees Much at the door. He took it gravely from her. Several other women bearing similar offerings also handed their bowls to warriors who carried them inside. Roxanna waited with the women, not certain what would happen next. She dearly wished to see what was going on inside, but the opening was blocked by several men who stood in front of it.

In a few moments the food, mostly untouched, was carried back out. Sees Much then began to distribute it among the men and women who sat around the lodge. At length he approached her, offering a bowl of dark red plums. "Will you eat now? It has been blessed in the sacredness of the lodge."

Like a Eucharist, Roxanna thought, struck at once by numerous similarities between Christian and Cheyenne beliefs. Cain had told her Enoch Sterling admired the Cheyenne religion. She was beginning to understand how that was possible. "Thank you," she replied, accepting a plum from the bowl and biting into the sweet juicy fruit.

Her eyes strayed over to where Powell was sitting. He stared stonily, not sharing in the food. "What will happen to him when this is over? Will Leather Shirt be satisfied after he has forced Powell to watch his son here?"

"You understand much," the old man replied. "Yet it is not important what either old man feels. They feed the bitterness of their hearts. What matters is that the Lone Bull is alone no more. He has rejected the one who rejected him and found that his true family is here. As to the fate of His Eyes Are Cold, I do not think Leather Shirt will kill him. Yet my brother wishes to know what has brought him here after so many years. There may be mischief in that."

Roxanna thought of the raiders the Central Pacific had sent to attack Union Pacific crews and sabotage their supplies. "It may have to do with the great race between the Iron Horse men." She explained about the competition and the skulduggery, and Powell's involvement.

Sees Much listened intently. "After the Medicine Lodge

is completed, I will discuss this with my brother and
the Lone Bull. Then we will decide what is to be done.''
He arose with that agility that still surprised her because he
looked so frail. ''Tomorrow is the most sacred day. Rest
well this night and prepare yourself.''

Roxanna wanted to ask why she needed to prepare. What
would tomorrow bring? But Sees Much quickly disappeared
into the Medicine Lodge. She did grow weary that evening
and returned to her pallet as the moon rose splendid and
golden over the tall cottonwoods along the river. At first she
drifted in and out of a restless slumber, hearing the relentless
pounding of the drum, thinking of Cain still dancing alone
in the lodge. For some reason Sees Much had not returned
tonight to the lodge he shared with the women. A feeling
of unease swept over her, but then she fell into a deep
dreamless sleep.

Just before dawn she awakened with a suffocating sense
of dread laying so heavy on her that it felt as if a great
invisible hand pressed her whole body into the furs on her
pallet. She sat up slowly, orienting her muzzy senses in the
darkness. The lone drum had ceased its pounding. Across
the lodge Willow Tree and Lark Song slept soundly. The
panic clawed at her with such fierceness that she scrambled
up and began to dress awkwardly, her fingers clumsy with
fear. She had to get out of the confines of the lodge, yet she
had no idea where she would go.

When Roxanna emerged from the lodge, she could see
the first pearl-gray light of dawn stealing over the eastern
sky. No one stirred in the silent camp as she walked toward
the big Medicine Lodge, drawn to share in her husband's
suffering. How weak he must be with hunger and thirst by
now. Could he endure another day of such suffering?

Just as she approached the big lodge, Sees Much emerged
as if he had been expecting her. Odd, she thought, how often
he seemed to anticipate events. ''I feel foolish disturbing
you,'' she said softly. ''Is my husband resting? I—I was
worried about him. The drumming stopped and I thought—''

"There is no time for him to rest now That will come at sundown tonight."

"I have had this feeling of terror. It awakened me. At first I thought it must be because I'm with child, yet it seems so real, so oppressive." She waited for the old shaman to reassure her, but instead he changed the subject.

"The Lone Bull prepares for his vision. It will come by the end of the day. There were some in the warrior societies who did not believe one who is half white should be allowed to make a Medicine Lodge. They said his white blood would displease the Powers, that he would be denied a vision, that he lacked the heart to fast and dance, to make the final sacrifice. Already they know they were wrong and say they have never seen one make a stronger sacrifice for the People. For the three days he has not rested as he might have at night. He has danced with good heart. He shows great courage. Now he will swing to the pole in the center of the sacred lodge."

"You have explained about the dancing, the fasting, the vision, but not what swinging to the pole means." The feeling of dread seemed even more oppressive now. She could not shake it.

"You will see. The lodge skins will be rolled up this afternoon so that all may watch the final time when his vision comes."

A low keening chant began on the other side of the lodge near its open door, a woman's voice, growing louder and stranger with each note. "Who is that?"

"White Owl Woman sings a strong-heart song for the Lone Bull, to cheer him on through his ordeal so that his sacrifice will bring many blessings to the People."

Sacrifice. Ordeal. Roxanna felt a prickling along the hairs at the nape of her neck. What exactly was going to happen today? She felt oddly constrained from asking Sees Much any further questions. He vanished back inside the Medicine Lodge.

The sun rose cloaked in orange and gold now and people began to emerge from their lodges. The ritual of the morning song echoed across the camp. Then the sound of the drums resumed inside the big lodge, the beat loud, steady, relentless. A wave of renewed excitement swept over the camp as people converged around the sacred edifice.

Roxanna was joined by Willow Tree and Lark Song, who urged her to break her fast in preparation for the day. She demurred, finding that the hearty appetite of pregnancy had suddenly deserted her. The hours seemed to drag through the morning as Roxanna helped with the cooking and carried offerings of food to the Medicine Lodge.

When the sun reached its zenith, an excited murmur ran across the assembly as the dancers from the ceremony began to roll up the lodge coverings. Roxanna worked her way carefully to the front of the assembly, staying far from where Andrew Powell was seated. She was dimly aware that the crowd parted deferentially for her, giving her honor as wife of the pledger.

Some sixth sense centered her concentration on the tall center pole of the lodge, rising above the walls. She could see a rope attached at the top of it being pulled from below slowly, back and forth in a semicircle. This was swinging to the pole. Cain must be pulling on it as he danced. The lodge covering was rolled high enough now for her to see his feet moving in the circle. She knelt down to see the rest of his body, then fell to her knees, suppressing a cry of shocked horror. Both hands flew to her mouth, covering it lest she scream.

Blood. There seemed to be blood everywhere, rolling down his chest, mixing with the red ocher paints and perspiration, running in smaller rivulets over his thighs, streaking his legs, soaking his moccasins with crimson. His chest had been cut by some sharp instrument. The skin over the pectoral muscles on both sides was skewered with leather thongs which were fastened to the braided rope suspended from the top of the center pole.

He moved slowly in the circle, dancing to the steady beat of the drums, oblivious to his surroundings. His eyes were closed, his hair matted to his head, soaked with sweat. Each step he took was deliberate, each jarring bounce when his foot came down on the hard-packed earth must have been agony. His lips were pulled into a wide thin slash, his expression a feral grimace of pain and determination.

She sank onto the ground, unable to tear her eyes away from his face. He was utterly silent as he circled the pole. Roxanna bit down on her lips, drawing blood, to keep from crying out when he lunged backward in a deliberate attempt to yank the cruel thongs from his flesh. His eyes opened then, blank and fathomless, as he stared up past the lodgepole towering above him into the blazing noontime sun.

It was as if he were in some sort of trance which carried him beyond the pain. She knew he had abstained from all food and drink for the past three days. Did the heat and his natural lightheadedness produce such a state? Perhaps that was how the pledger received his vision, the desperate hallucination caused by starvation and exhaustion compounded by unspeakable pain. There was a burning behind her eyelids, but tears would not form. She was beyond tears.

Did he do this for her? To prove to her that he had not married her only for his job with Jubal, that he had come to love her, that he could love their child? *I wanted you to love me, Cain, but I never wanted this!*

Roxanna forced herself to watch as he made his way back and forth in front of the pole. Each time he threw himself back, pulling against the thongs, she felt his pain as tangibly as if she too were pierced and bleeding with him. All the murmuring of the crowd, the beating of the drums, the shrill sounds from the eagle-bone whistles, the songs of the other warriors who danced with him—everything faded. She saw only her husband.

Sees Much observed the Lone Bull's head lift skyward again, turning his face toward the fiery heat of the sun. Soon the vision would come. He could feel its power and knew it would be good for the young man who endured so bravely. And for his woman. The old man turned his attention to Her Back Is Straight. Luminous eyes, the color of polished turquoise, stared in rapt horror at the pain her man

was undergoing. *She does not realize why this must be done.*
He made his way outside and sat down next to her. In tacit
understanding, Willow Tree and the others around her arose
and cleared a space, allowing the shaman and his young
charge to speak privately.

"He shows great courage. So do you, my child."

Roxanna sucked in a breath. "He knew what would happen this day. What did you say to him before the ceremony
to make him throw himself into this as he has?"

Sees Much was silent a moment. "When a man pledges
the Medicine Lodge it cannot be done in half measures. This
the Lone Bull knew." He smiled faintly. "I know he did
not believe in the medicine as I did. But he believed in
you."

Roxanna squeezed her eyes closed and the earth beneath
her seemed to spin. "Then this is all my fault."

"There is no fault. He could have taken you away. None
would have stopped him."

"But I made him—"

"No," he said forcefully. "You did not force him to do
this. There was something—some small spark deep inside
of him, long buried, that flamed to life because of his love
for you and his child. That is what took hold of him when
he began to dance on the second day. I watched it grow as
he fasted and danced through the nights and the days until
this morning . . . the final day."

"How can we do this to him? How can he endure it?"

His eyes were sympathetic. She had not been raised in
their way. That was why he had withheld from her this
information about the fourth day of the ceremony. "He en-
dures because it is the only means to receive his vision. Pain
does more than purge past sins and prove great courage to
the people who watch. It also teaches him that he has great
heart, strength." He pounded his chest, which also bore the
scars of the Sun Dance. "In the Medicine Lodge a man
faces himself and sees who he is."

"And what if he does not like what he sees?" The question seemed to ask itself. This was her greatest fear for Cain.

"He did not like himself because he refused to look until now," Sees Much replied.

"If he must finish this, then I must watch him," she said, turning her eyes back to her husband once again. Steely determination was etched in every plane of her face as she sat rigidly still. Only her tightly clenched fists buried in her lap betrayed her anguish.

Each time he threw himself backward, working the cruel thongs through his flesh, a low hum of approval was elicited from the observers. Roxanna's nails dug deeper into her palms until she too bled with Cain.

Time stood still. Or it seemed to. Heat rose in shimmering waves from the plains grasses undulating to the far horizon. The drum's rhythm seemed to be one unified heartbeat which was shared by every man, woman and child present. The high wailing songs of the other dancers grew gradually louder, the shrill piercing sound of eagle-bone whistles more frequent as the drums' tempo slowly accelerated.

Sweat poured off the Lone Bull, diluting the rivulets of blood and paint, bathing his whole body in crimson. Had he danced forever? There had seemed no end at first. Now there seemed no beginning either, only the eternal now of heat and drums and blood, the pounding of his feet on the earth below, the blazing gold of the sun above, the fierce insistent agony of thirst and pain . . . and the vision. He blinked, opened his eyes wide and stared into the sun, not seeing its bright rays.

A hush fell over the assembly when the Lone Bull stood still, transfixed by the sun. Everyone seemed to lean forward in anticipation. The chanting of the other dancers, the beat of the drums grew swifter, fiercer. Then he made one final lunge and tore free of both thongs at once. The "Aaah" of the People broke the silence as all rose to their feet.

Roxanna saw two pinpoints of light dancing in the blackness swimming before her eyes. Willow Tree helped her to her feet, where she stood swaying for an instant. Then she fixed her gaze on the Lone Bull, who at last sank to his knees, then crumpled to the earth. No one rushed to aid him until Sees Much, walking slowly, reached his side.

Willow Tree held Roxanna's arm in a firm grip. "You do not touch now. Shaman will tend him. Learn his dream. Come, I take you to our lodge. You wait for him."

Numbly, Roxanna let her friend guide her back to their lodge as Sees Much and Leather Shirt knelt beside her husband. Was he conscious or had he at last passed out from exhaustion, dehydration, pain? She could not tell as the crowd converged, blocking him from her sight.

The Lone Bull lay on the ground, staring up into the face of Leather Shirt. "Grandfather?" he said in Cheyenne. His voice was a hissing rasp, so faint he was not certain the old man heard him until Leather Shirt smiled and leaned over, offering him a small sip of cool water.

"Do not speak yet, my son, child of my child."

Gently Leather Shirt let a few more drops trickle onto his tongue. The Lone Bull closed his eyes in gratitude, letting the blessed balm of moisture ease the parched agony of lips, tongue, throat. *All will be set right.* Had Sees Much said it—or his grandfather? Or had it been some voice inside of him? Then Leather Shirt spoke.

"You are no longer Not Cheyenne. You will claim a new name among the People. Never has any warrior made a finer Medicine Lodge. Never have I seen one so pleasing before the Powers. The buffalo have come. The fall hunt will be good. Our women and children will not go hungry. The Everywhere Spirit blesses us all for what you have done. My heart overflows with gladness that you are my grandson."

"Grandfather," he said, raising his arm and clasping it around the old man's. "I am proud to be the grandson of Leather Shirt." They held on tightly for a moment.

"Now go with Sees Much back to your lodge. Tell your uncle of your vision. Your woman worries for you. She has a strong heart."

The old chief helped his grandson to his feet, then released him and stepped back as Sees Much guided him toward their lodge. Reverently people stepped aside, murmuring praise for the pledger who was truly one of the People now.

With a wintry smile the old chief turned to meet the hate-filled glare of His Eyes Are Cold. "The darkness inside you no longer holds your son. He takes his place in the light now."

"Savage superstition," Powell spat. "I don't believe in such things." There was a hollowness in his voice that even Andrew Powell himself could hear . . . and suddenly he heard something else as well. For the first time in almost twenty years, His Eyes Are Cold had spoken the Cheyenne tongue.

Chapter 21

Roxanna waited inside as Sees Much assisted her husband into the lodge. Cain walked under his own power, although Roxanna could not understand how he had managed to make it from the Medicine Lodge. Sees Much held one of his arms to guide him. His head hung limply and his steps dragged in the dust. Once inside, he faltered, then sank to his knees without seeing her. When Roxanna started to scramble up to assist him, Sees Much waved her back to the outer perimeter of the teepee where she had been instructed to sit.

The old man helped him onto the pallet specially prepared for the pledger, piled high with freshly cut willow boughs and covered with rich furs. Roxanna bit down on her lip to keep from crying out for his hurts. The torn flesh of his chest seeped blood more slowly now. There would be scarring from the wounds, a badge of honor he would share with Sees Much, Leather Shirt and other leaders of the Cheyenne.

She ached to touch him, to reassure herself that he was alive, that within his cruelly lacerated chest his heart still beat. But the old shaman positioned himself between them, then opened his medicine bags and began to arrange the items he needed. Roxanna's gaze remained fixed on her husband's face. His eyelids fluttered open. There was an unfocused opacity to the usually sharp black glitter in his eyes as he watched Sees Much feeding sweet grass into the flames in the fire pit. Then his eyes closed once more and he seemed to drift in and out of consciousness.

"We will need living water," the old man said quietly to her, indicating a bucket beside the fire pit. She took it and quickly left the lodge to draw fresh water from the river.

When she returned a few moments later, the silvery smoke of the sweet grass rose in a thin curl, drawn up through the hole at the apex of the lodge. Its pungent aroma hung in the warm evening air. Sees Much placed his hands over the smoke and rubbed them, then stretched them out across Cain's chest over the twin wounds, chanting in a low voice for a moment. Then he extracted some sacred white sage plant from one of his bags. Accepting the water bucket from Roxanna, he motioned for her to take her seat in the darkness across from him.

Cain continued to drift in and out of consciousness, restlessly moving his arms and legs as he lay on the pallet. She knew he must be in terrible pain. The old shaman was a skilled healer. She had watched him work wonders with his herbal remedies and the soothing touch of his gnarled hands. *Please, help him.*

As if responding to her silent plea, Sees Much poured some water from the bucket into a drinking gourd and let a few drops at a time trickle past Cain's parched lips. At length he set aside the gourd and used a pair of metal pincers to remove two red-hot rocks from the fire pit, placing them one at a time in the bucket to heat the water. The sizzling hiss roused Cain for a moment, but then consciousness faded again. Once Sees Much was satisfied with the temperature of the water, he added fistfuls of the white sage to the liquid, immersing it until it was pliant and soft.

After testing it with his hands, he squeezed the excess moisture from a handful of the sacred herb and began to sponge the wounds, one, then the other, leaving a clot of sage on each. When the poultice began to penetrate, its cooling balm seemed to partially revive Cain. The old man leaned over him and gazed into his eyes.

"Now, nephew, it is time for us to study the vision you received in the Medicine Lodge."

His voice raspy, Cain replied so low he could barely hear himself over the crackle of the flames. "How do you know I was given one?"

Still half conscious, he replied in English just as his uncle had spoken to him in that language. Roxanna too leaned forward to hear what he said. She could see both their faces etched in the flickering light of the flame. Daylight was fast dying outside and the lodge was cast in shadows. The old man's eyes looked up for a moment and met hers. They glowed like the embers in the fire pit. *Like a cat's eyes.*

"You received a vision," the shaman replied with certainty. "Even full-blood whites are given them . . . if their hearts are good. Tell me your vision." He picked up the gourd and this time raised Cain's head, allowing him to take a few sips of water for himself.

Cain struggled to remain conscious as bits and snatches of his vision flashed once more through his mind. He was incredibly weary, more exhausted from dehydration and lack of sleep than from his injuries, which now had settled down into a dull ache as the poultice did its work. When he finally gathered his scattered thoughts enough to speak, his voice was low and hoarse. Halting and weak, he relived the vision bit by bit.

"I saw a great bull buffalo. Seemed to come straight at me in the lodge . . . as I danced . . . then the lodge vanished and we . . . no—not me . . . the buffalo and the woman . . . woman with hair glowing gold and silver like sun and moon melded together . . . she was . . . she was dressed all in white . . . coming toward the bull . . ."

Cain tossed fitfully and Sees Much placed a restraining hand on one shoulder, saying nothing, only waiting. When the shaman raised his head once more and looked across at Roxanna, she was struck again by the glowing incandescence of his eyes. A strange prickly tingle traveled down her spine as her husband resumed his narration.

"She shouldn't approach the buffalo bull . . . blood . . .

there's blood on his horns. He shakes his head . . . warning her . . . but she does not stop . . ."

For the first time Sees Much interrupted at a pause in Cain's story. "Is the buffalo bull angry with the woman?"

Cain shook his head. "No . . . not angry . . . afraid. He is afraid . . . of her . . . she can hurt him . . . she'll leave him . . . but she does not leave . . . does not stop. She keeps walking, her hands outstretched . . . to caress his shaggy mane . . ."

His voice faded as he drew in a deep breath and let it out slowly. The restless tension in his body seemed to drain away then. All at once he resumed speaking. "Sun and Moon Woman reaches up to touch his horns . . . the bloody horns. And the blood vanishes at that touch. The hurt and fear go away."

His breathing was even now, although he did not sleep, only lay staring up at the night sky overhead, visible through the lodge opening. Sees Much looked over at Roxanna. The tears which had burned behind her eyelids ever since that awful day in Denver when she had overheard his cruel words to Lawrence, those tears now flowed freely for the first time. Her cheeks were wet with shiny silver rivulets. Through their blurry sheen, she looked back at the old shaman, whose eyes now glowed so intensely she seemed to feel their warmth from across the lodge. Then he once more offered the water gourd to his nephew for a few more sparing sips.

Still unaware of his wife's presence, Cain spoke to Sees Much once more. "The sacred buffalo skull White Owl Woman brought into the Medicine Lodge seemed to speak to me then. I was myself again, back in the lodge, dancing around the pole, when it said, 'Behold.' I looked outside the door. High-Backed Wolf stood there with his arms folded across his chest. He wore no war paint. There was no anger, no hate. We exchanged a look for a moment and he was gone. In his place stood Blue Corn Woman. I could feel her pride in me and it made me glad. Then Enoch appeared beside my mother, smiling his gentle Good Heart smile.

They waved, then vanished as my brother had.

"The sacred buffalo skull spoke again, telling me that I was no longer the Lone Bull. From this time forth I would be Brother of the Spirit Bull. He will always be with me and I with him. Wherever I go, the People will be with me."

Sees Much's wizened face suddenly seemed smooth and clear, all the lines of age and care erased as Roxanna watched him smile. "Sleep well, Brother of the Spirit Bull. You have earned your rest. The Spirit Bull has cleansed you of your rage and your guilt. Sun and Moon Woman has healed you and made you whole," he said.

Cain's head turned to the side and his eyes closed as an exhausted sleep finally claimed him. All the restless energy, the tension had been purged from him in the telling of his vision.

The old shaman arose and motioned for Roxanna to follow him outdoors. "You must never speak of what he has said until he is ready to share it with you. Before he does, you must tell him of the vision you had the first time you came to us. The Powers clearly mean for you to join your lives. There is no other reason for the way you have shared in his sacred Medicine Lodge vision." He paused, studying her with shrewd dark eyes. "You will once more be his wife?"

"I will always be his wife."

Sees Much grunted in pleased assent. "It is good. Let him rest awhile, then bring him broth with these herbs in it to strengthen him." He handed her a small pouch. "He will need to be bathed. You have already had practice at this, I think," he added teasingly as she flushed.

"I will care for him."

Smiling, Sees Much went in search of his brother. Leather Shirt would be greatly pleased when he explained the medicine dream of Brother of the Spirit Bull. Then they would have to decide the fate of His Eyes Are Cold. After all that had passed, the shaman was certain Leather Shirt would be inclined to show mercy and release the Iron Horse man.

Roxanna spent the day hovering over Cain, watching him

sleep, trickling water over his lips and sponging his injured chest with the healing white sage poultices. Several times he awakened during her ministrations. She was able to get two bowls of Sees Much's herbal broth down him in those brief intervals, but his eyes were clouded by the medicines Sees Much had given him to promote rest and healing. He smiled at her and called out her name but did not try to speak more before drifting back into slumber each time.

By the following morning he was awake and sitting up when she returned from the river with fresh water. He leaned against one of the heavy parfleches, using it as a backrest. When he sat forward and reached out his hand to her, the wound on his chest ached sharply, causing him to wince and sit back.

"You're too weak to be up," she scolded, kneeling by his side. "Here, let me help you lie back down."

Cain let her reach out to him, her soft hands touching his arms. He could smell the faint essence of lilacs and woman that belonged uniquely to his wife. "I'm more weak than sick, Roxy. All I need is some solid food and water—to drink and wash in," he added, wrinkling his nose at the blend of blood and red paint smeared over much of his body. "I smell like a cross between a livery stable and a slaughterhouse."

"You've been through a terrible ordeal. You need to rest," she said, trying to ease him back onto the pallet, but he took hold of her arms with surprising strength.

"I know you were shocked by what I did—that you didn't know it would be so bloody, so savage—"

"Yes, I was shocked," she admitted. "I never dreamed I was asking you to suffer such agony when I accepted your uncle's suggestion about the Sun Dance." She forced herself to meet his eyes, clear glittering onyx now. "When you walked out of the 'lonely lodge' that first day and looked at me, I . . . I was afraid that you hated me."

A faint tinge of sadness touched his smile. "I suppose I did for a little while, but it was my decision to make the pledge. I knew what I was getting into. Did it repel you?

Did I?'' He studied her, the Sun and Moon Woman of his vision, and wondered how he could ever explain it to her. Would she think it was superstitious nonsense . . . or would she believe as he had come to believe?

Roxanna shook her head and the fat silvery plait of her hair slid from her shoulder down her back. ''No, you could never repel me. I felt guilty for causing you to suffer but . . . how can I explain it? . . . you seemed to find yourself in the ceremony those first two days. Sees Much told me you barely rested but danced all through the night, that it was a sign the Everywhere Spirit was working in you.''

''And when you witnessed the fourth day?'' Cain held his breath, meeting her eyes steadily. He had to know how she felt now that she had finally seen the red half of him which he had kept so deeply buried—even from himself—until now.

She could see the uncertainty in his face. *He still fears I'll leave him.* Tears filled her eyes as she reached up and touched the scar on his cheek. His breath caught and his hand shot up, wrapping around her wrist, pulling her hand to his lips and pressing his mouth on her palm. ''The fourth day you made a sacrifice for me and for your people that I will honor all the days of my life.''

A blaze of joy lit his eyes, but before he could reply, the raspy sound of Leather Shirt clearing his throat outside the lodge interrupted them. ''Come, Grandfather.''

The old chief entered, smiling shrewdly at the way Her Back Is Straight sat beside Brother of the Spirit Bull. ''Our warriors go out on the hunt. Buffalo are plenty and there will be a feast tonight when they return with fine meat. Now there are many in the village who would offer you presents in gratitude for the good medicine you have brought us.''

Cain nodded. ''I would be honored.'' In truth he felt uncomfortable accepting gifts from these people who had so little, yet he knew if he refused it would be considered an insult.

A steady stream of men, women and children came through the lodge during the day. One of the first visitors was White Owl Woman, who brought him a magnificent leather vest worked with one of the most treasured of Cheyenne talismans, elk teeth, perfectly matched in gleaming amber gold rows all across the front of the exquisite garment.

"Now you too shall be a leather shirt," she said with a smile.

Cain thanked her warmly, as Sees Much translated her words for Roxanna. There were many other presents, some humble, such as a small boy's treasured favorite arrowhead, others grand, such as a pair of beaded moccasins and a finely carved medicine pipe. In between visitors Roxanna saw to it that her husband rested and ate more nourishing broth and even some small pieces of solid food to regain his strength.

That evening old Leather Shirt himself offered his grandson his most prized possession, the heavy leather war shield which he had carried into battle against the Crow and Pawnee as a young man. "I know you do not fight with lance and arrow, but it is good medicine to protect you against danger."

Cain let his fingers trace the shiny surface of the shield, which had been stretched and cured over a low fire until it was hard as metal. "I will keep it with me always and my children's children will tell the stories of Leather Shirt's bravery around their campfires."

The two men sat sharing a pipe while Roxanna was out with the other women preparing for the feast. They sat in companionable silence for a bit. Then Cain asked, "What will you do with His Eyes Are Cold?"

Leather Shirt looked at his grandson. "What would you have me do?"

"I honestly do not know." Cain thought about the renegades hired to raid the Union Pacific and throw the blame on the Cheyenne. They had to be stopped. But not this way. "His death will only bring the Blue Coats."

Leather Shirt grunted sourly. "They will come anyway. Your Iron Horse has seen to that. It carries the soldiers to us even as it drives away the buffalo."

Cain could not dispute that fact, which troubled him

greatly. "The whites are as grains of sand on a riverbank. We cannot stop them from bringing the Iron Horse trails into Cheyenne land. But I will do what I can to keep peace between the People and the invaders."

"Perhaps I will let you have His Eyes Are Cold," Leather Shirt said with faint amusement.

Once he had wanted evidence to prove that his father was responsible for Johnny Lame Pony and his renegade's actions so that he could turn Powell over to Dillon. Now the idea held little appeal. Soon Powell would be publicly humiliated by the other Central Pacific directors, his financial empire in ruins. After all the years Cain had lived for vengeance, their confrontation in San Francisco had shown him that his vendetta was no longer the most important thing in his life—his wife was, and now that he had a second chance with Roxanna, he found Andrew Powell's fate was of little matter to him.

"I will think on what to do with him," Cain replied, passing the pipe back to his grandfather.

Although still faintly lightheaded, Cain felt surprisingly well after his ordeal. His wounds throbbed dully, the sharpness of the pain reduced by Sees Much's herbal poultice. There was no sign of infection, always the worst thing to fear from the scarring ceremony. With help from several of the other warriors he made his way to the river and waded in to cleanse himself fully. They left him there. Roxanna had sponged away the worst of the paint and blood. He carried the last remnants of a bar of soap taken from his saddlebags. As he stood waist deep in the cool running water sudsing his lacerated chest, the dichotomy of his life struck him.

"White man's soap, red man's ritual," he murmured to himself. For the first time in his life Cain realized that he did not feel the clash of his two natures, nor feel any desire to deny that he was Cheyenne. Deep in thought, he did not hear Roxanna approach.

She stood on the riverbank partially concealed by the dense growth of kinnikinnick, watching him bathe. A sudden surge of desire caught her by surprise, but she suppressed it. Here he was, only two days after such an ordeal, standing in swift running water! She started to call out an admonition, then realized how foolish it would be. He had managed to get down to the river and wade in without being swept away and he did not look in any immediate danger as he soaped carefully around the angry wounds on his chest.

Watching the glide of his hands over the hard muscles of his shoulders, chest and belly left her mouth cottony dry, her heart beating fast as the current. The ache of desire grew inside her, warm and insistent. *He is truly beautiful.* She had always thought that, even when he looked like a dangerous brigand, more so when he was elegantly dressed in a black wool suit and white silk shirt. But now she realized that he was equally magnificent wearing only a loincloth and pagan jewelry with his body painted . . . and yes, even scarred by the Sun Dance. This too was Cain, Brother of the Spirit Bull.

"Now we're even. Once I spied on you bathing in a stream. Now you've looked your fill."

His laughing words jarred her from the reverie which had let her mind wander while her gaze remained riveted to the wet, naked man walking toward her. White teeth gleamed in his bronzed face. The pallor of his ordeal was gone, but he made his way out of the water with the measured step of someone whose footing was not the steadiest. "You shouldn't be down here alone. You could have drowned if you'd passed out in the water," she scolded, knowing her voice was scratchy and breathless. He stood ankle deep in the current now, arms crossed, unabashedly naked, grinning at her. Wide turquoise eyes locked with dancing black and held for a moment. She could not help but see the visible proof of his desire thrusting proudly forward as he let his gaze rake her body from her blushing face down to her moccasined feet. "I . . . I brought medicines to tend your wounds."

"Then by all means, tend to me." The smile left his face. God, just looking at her made him ache, this Sun and Moon

Woman with her luminous aquamarine eyes and pale glowing hair. He had come so close to losing her. Even being
president of the Union Pacific was not worth that cost. Nothing was. He extended one hand, palm up.

Roxanna stepped from the kinnikinick and reached out to
take his proffered hand. "The feast will begin in a little
while. You have to dress for it."

He pulled her closer, murmuring, "I'd rather you undressed for me right now. . . . We have time." His voice was
a low silky purr, yet beneath the teasing burned a hunger
for her, a need to reaffirm his claim that she was yet and
would always be his wife.

Roxanna still clutched the medicine pouch in one hand
like a talisman. "You're too weak. Your wounds—"

"Are healing just fine. Put some more of that herbal poultice on . . . and then . . ." He took hold of the fat shiny plait
of hair hanging over her shoulder and drew her closer until
his lips brushed her cheek, then trailed down the side of her
neck to the racing pulse at the base of her throat.

Her eyes closed and every nerve in her body thrummed
with the remembered pleasure of his touch. How lonely and
cold she had been without that touch. She leaned into his
embrace, raising her hand with the pouch in it unconsciously, reaching up to hold him. Accidentally she brushed
his injured chest. The instant the buckskin came into contact
with the newly healing flesh he winced, but did not release
his hold on her.

Roxanna's eyes flew open and she tried to step back.
"You're not ready—"

"Oh, I'm ready, believe me," he replied, letting the rigid
pressure of his erection press into the soft buckskin of her
tunic. He took the pouch from her and released the drawstring, holding it open to her. "Tend my wounds, Roxy."

He stepped away from her then, walking through the shallows to where a thick copse of willows hid the path from
the camp. He took a seat on the cool, mossy earth and
waited, patient except for the burning hunger revealed in his
eyes.

She knelt beside him and extracted a handful of the poultice. "It will work best if you lie down."

"Whatever you wish," he replied, stretching out on his back, one hand resting proprietarily on her thigh.

She worked the poultice around the ragged edges of skin, already beginning to scab over, then let the moisture soak in to numb the ache. "Does that hurt?" she asked, feeling his muscles quiver with pain when she placed the medicine directly into the punctures.

"Only for a moment . . . then it cools the burning." There was another burning deep inside of him that was of far greater urgency than these mere superficial wounds.

She finished her work with trembling hands, then rose and walked over to the edge of the water to wash the poultice from them, feeling his eyes follow her.

"Take off your clothes, Roxy. I need you . . . now."

His eyes compelled her and his voice was raw, hoarse with desire—or was it something more, something he had yet to say? *You have never spoken of love, Cain.* She pulled off her moccasins, then stood up and began to unlace the ties on her tunic until she could pull it over her head.

When she reached down to unfasten her leggings, he said, "Come, let me do it."

She walked across the soft earth to him and he reached out to unlace the thin leather ties first on her right leg, then her left. As he did so, he pressed his mouth along the curve of her calves and ran his fingertips around to the sensitive skin behind her knees. Her legs buckled as she knelt beside him, afraid to touch his injured chest. "I'll hurt you. . . ."

Cain smiled. "You'll just have to be gentle with me, Roxy." He took her hand and placed it around his phallus, gasping when her small fingers, still damp from the river, slid up and down the hot length of it.

She leaned down, careful not to touch his upper body as her lips neared his. His hand tugged insistently on her braid, guiding her mouth to his for a long slow kiss of homecoming. Releasing his hold on her hair, he reached over to cup one breast, kneading gently as their kiss deepened.

She tasted of the wild mint the Cheyenne used to clean their teeth and the sweet subtle essence that he always associated with his wife. As he plunged his tongue inside her mouth, hers darted out, teasing him until he groaned and began to suck on it. His hands on her breasts squeezed and tugged in rhythm with the thrust of their deep hungry kisses and he was rewarded with the pebbling of her nipples.

Breaking away from the kiss, he pulled her breasts closer to his mouth. His palms cupped around the sweetly suspended globes until he could suckle one, then the other, loving the sighing moans she emitted with each ragged breath. Her fingers teased his staff, which throbbed urgently with the desperate need to plunge inside her. When he arched up, thrusting into her hand, she tightened her hold on it, sliding her hand down to the base. One more stroke like that and he would be undone.

He removed his mouth from one pearly lush breast and commanded hoarsely, ''Put a knee on each side of my hips.'' He placed his hands on her hips, guiding her to straddle his lower body.

Roxanna looked down into his passion-glazed face, knowing her expression was equally desperate. Then his fingers caressed between her legs, rubbing the swollen pink petals until he was rewarded with the creamy wetness of her arousal. The touch of his hand in that place so hungry for him sent tremors of ecstasy radiating up to her breasts and down her legs right to the soles of her feet. Her back arched, thrusting her breasts high. She looked glorious, with the dappled sunlight giving her ivory skin an incandescent glow.

''Take me inside of you.'' His hand reached for hers and guided it to his shaft, which pressed intimately against the inside of her thigh.

''Oh,'' she gasped, having never done this before. The scalding heat from the head of his staff brushed the wetness of her as she gingerly positioned it at the opening to her body. A new sense of power combined with the slow magnetic pull of pleasure as she lowered herself onto him, letting the thickness of him stretch her tightness, the length plumb her depths. His heat fused with hers as she seated herself all the way down and felt his hips tilt, moving to drive himself even deeper inside her.

A shiver of raw sensual pleasure blended with the sense of completeness, enveloping him as surely as her velvety sheath enveloped his staff. He wanted to remain this way forever, not moving, joined so completely to her, looking up at the proud curve and thrust of her breasts, already growing heavier with pregnancy, the perceptible swell of her silky belly, the wonder in her eyes as she gazed down at him. Was his own need reflected in those fathomless aquamarine depths?

Roxanna had never been so in control yet so uncertain of what to do. When she felt his hardness move high inside her, her body responded of its own volition, muscles tightening around him. She felt his fingers dig into her hips, raising her up from him then, almost high enough to lose contact . . . but not quite. Staring into each other's eyes, they teetered on the brink for a moment. Then, with a guttural groan, he pulled her down once more.

She quickly caught the rhythm as his big hands cupped her buttocks lovingly, fingers digging into the soft flesh as he raised and lowered her, canting her hips to meet his deep upward thrusts. Her body seemed to have an instinct of its own, bucking and twisting as she moved with him, eliciting oaths of endearment and ragged gasps of pleasure from him. The sweet, sweet madness of it robbed her of all thought. Everything centered here in this joining, in the slick gliding glory of moving with him, taking him deep inside herself, raising up on him before each hot downward stroke, driving herself as desperately near the brink as she drove him, wanting that ultimate culmination, striving for it, focused on it, yet wanting the sheer wonder of it never to end.

Cain held on to her fiercely, letting her ride him as he thrust up into her. What a splendidly wild, savage little goddess she was, his Sun and Moon Woman. Her hair had worked its way loose from its plait and showered her shoulders in silvery splendor, gliding like silk each time she raised up and plunged down. The slick heat of her sheath squeezed him, driving him to madness. He dug his heels into the ground, his whole body rigid as he arched up, totally oblivious of the dull insistent ache of chest muscles flexing and unflexing with each thrust.

He watched the growing intensity of her expression, the way she bit her lip and sobbed his name over and over, throwing her head back until her long mane of hair brushed his thighs and fell between his legs. The thrill of that caress elicited a ragged cry, "Roxanna, darling, Roxy!" Her skin glowed with the faint sheen of perspiration. Then a rosy pink suffused it, spreading from her face down her throat to her breasts and belly.

Cain could feel the first delicious contractions of her sheath, squeezing him, pulsing wave after wave, growing stronger until he could hold back no longer.

Her climax began gradually, spiraling, making her legs grow weak, her body catch fire. As the tight rhythmic contractions built, she could feel him high against her womb, swelling, pulsing his life deeply inside her once more, like an offering.

Roxanna braced her hands on either side of his head and fell forward, careful not to press against his injured chest. She could feel his swift breath against her face, his whole body panting with the same limp satiation that swamped her senses. His hands slid up her hips and he embraced her, pulling her down to lie on top of him.

"I'll hurt you," she murmured against his cheek.

"I'll risk it," he growled, burying his fingers in the curtain of pale hair tumbling around her shoulders, inhaling the exotic combination of lilacs and musk. "Don't ever leave me again," he whispered against her throat.

It was not a declaration of love, but for now it would suffice, she thought lazily as she lay enfolded in his arms and closed her eyes.

Chapter 22

Johnny Lame Pony reined in his horse and considered what he should do. He had ridden ahead of the column with the other scouts, then dispersed the three Cheyenne to search for sign of Leather Shirt's camp. The colonel was afraid that the Cheyenne might have harmed the white woman. Johnny was afraid that she and Cain might have already left the band. Now that he had finally located the camp on the banks of Deer Creek, he knew that his fears were groundless. The breed and his woman were still here.

So was Andrew Powell! That had greatly surprised Lame Pony. What was the big boss of the Iron Horse doing with the Cheyenne? Then he had risked crawling in closer and learned that Powell was a prisoner. Somehow the old man had been captured. If he followed orders and led the army down on the camp, Powell could be accidentally killed in the melee. After all, that was what he and his "scouts" would claim happened to Cain and the woman.

What would be the wisest course? Andrew Powell was the most powerful man on the railroad and Lame Pony had been in his employ for years. Yet it was not a sense of loyalty which prompted his consideration now. Rather, he thought of how he might turn the situation to his greatest advantage. It was a prickly problem.

The three Cheyenne renegades wanted to destroy Leather

Shirt's band in revenge for their banishment. Weasel Bear
had an even more personal grudge against Cain and relished
this opportunity to kill his half-breed cousin. If Johnny freed
Powell, they would probably be robbed of their prey. Then
too, he took no small risk riding into the camp to bargain
for Powell's life. Cain had trailed him relentlessly after the
raid at the grading camp and knew his identity.

Leather Shirt would be pleased that he warred against the
Iron Horse crossing their hunting grounds, unless Cain convinced the chief that he had tried to shift the blame for those
raids onto the Cheyenne. If so, the old man's wrath would
be terrible indeed. Perhaps Johnny could avoid that rage by
saving all of their lives. Would not Leather Shirt's band be
grateful for a warning that the Blue Coats were fast approaching, searching for the white woman?

Whatever he decided, he must act quickly before Weasel
Bear and the others caught up with him here at the Cheyenne camp. All of his life he had lived on the periphery of
the white man's civilization, working for little money, despised by those who used his services, existing from one
drunken debauch to the next. This was his one big chance.
If he saved Powell's life, he could demand a far larger reward than that originally promised.

After discarding the makeshift uniform worn by North's
Pawnee scouts, Johnny donned his Lakota beaded moccasins
and headband and a plain buckskin shirt and britches. Then
he rode straight toward the Cheyenne camp. The sentries
saw the Lakota half-blood approaching and brought him to
Leather Shirt immediately. Luck was with him, for there was
no sign of Cain when he was admitted to the chief's lodge.

"The Lakota are our brothers. You are welcome to our
camp," Leather Shirt said, gesturing for his guest to have a
seat. "How are you called?"

Figuring it best to stick with as much of the truth as possible, Lame Pony replied, "I am called Johnny Lame Pony.
My mother was Brulé, from Buffalo Hump's band," he replied in serviceable Cheyenne.

"Your father was white." Other than the tribal identification afforded by his headband and moccasins, he was dressed in white frontiersmen's clothing.

"I live with the whites," Johnny confessed, keeping his eyes fixed firmly on Leather Shirt. This was no time for shifty evasions. "Sometimes I scout for the soldiers."

Leather Shirt's expression hardened. "My sentry said you have some urgent message for me."

"The Iron Horse soldiers approach. They have been tracking you for many days."

"You mean you have tracked us for them. What do these Blue Coats want with us?"

"They have come to rescue the white woman who is with you. They mean to punish you for taking her prisoner."

Leather Shirt drew himself up. "Her Back Is Straight is no captive. She is now my granddaughter. She has come to us of her own free will. Who speaks such lies?"

Johnny shrugged. "I do not know. I only work for the soldiers. Colonel Dillon said you captured this woman and he must get her back."

"If you work for the Blue Coat chief, why do you come to warn us that he will attack?" Leather Shirt asked suspiciously.

"Do not believe anything he says. He is the renegade who attacks the railroad and places the blame on the Cheyenne," Cain said as he entered the lodge.

"I speak the truth. Dillon will come here to get the white woman back for her grandfather. He is only half an hour behind me. If you think I lie, send out your own scouts and you will find him a few arrow flights down the river."

"I will do this," Leather Shirt replied, calling for the Dog Soldiers who stood outside the lodge. He dispatched several warriors to search for the Blue Coats.

Cain studied the renegade for a moment, trying to sift out his motives. "What's in this for you, Johnny?" he asked softly in English. An idea was beginning to take shape in his mind.

"I have come for the Iron Horse man, Powell. You and the woman can show the soldiers she is no prisoner, but he has been held against his will. Give him to me and let us ride away.'' Johnny addressed the old chief, cursing his ill luck that Cain had intervened.

"Bring His Eyes Are Cold here and let us speak with him," Leather Shirt said to Brother of the Spirit Bull.

Nodding, Cain stepped through the door, then said, "Do not turn your back on this one while I am gone, Grandfather."

He walked quickly across the camp and entered the lodge where his father was confined. Powell looked up at Cain, dressed in breechclout and leggings. "You look like a full-blooded savage. I wonder how MacKenzie would feel if he could see you this way."

Ignoring the jibe, Cain said, "I know why you came so near Leather Shirt's band."

Powell's graceful eyebrows rose as he got to his feet, meeting his son's level gaze. "Do you, now?"

"Yes. You were—"

The pounding of horses' hooves and a loud cry of alarm interrupted the tense confrontation. "Blue Coats! Soldiers are coming," the Dog Soldiers yelled. "Many times more than our warriors! They are only a little ride off. Soon they will be here!" Everyone in the camp began scrambling frantically to find children and gather horses for an escape.

Cursing, Cain stepped outside the lodge and called to one of the Dog Soldiers. "Take the prisoner to Leather Shirt. Do not let him escape," he commanded, reaching back inside to seize hold of the braided leather rope binding his father's hands. Once he had delivered Powell to the warrior, he went in search of Roxanna. If the army swooped down on the camp before they could get away, she could be cut down in the crossfire—just as he would be.

Women called frantically for children, and warriors grabbed their weapons and mounted the best horses in preparation for defending the camp. Everywhere people rushed about, preparing to flee, leaving behind all their worldly goods to escape the fury of the soldiers. Cain called out for

Roxanna, then saw her emerge from Sees Much's lodge followed by the old shaman.

She ran over to him. "What's happening? Why is everyone fleeing?"

"The army. Dillon's coming with a large column of cavalry—they were told you're being held prisoner by the Cheyenne."

"That's absurd! Who—"

"There's no time—you have to get out of here before you're caught in the crossfire."

"I can tell the soldiers I'm no prisoner. Let me talk to this Dillon," she said as he took her arm, walking swiftly to the roped-off corral and whistling for his chestnut.

"It isn't that easy. I want you safe first. Then I'll stop Dillon."

She could see by his expression that he was not going to listen and gave up arguing as he bridled and saddled the big stallion. Then he roped the gelding she had been riding, quickly saddled it and helped her mount. "Ride for those alders down by the river," he instructed her, pointing in the far distance at the cluster of trees. "Wait there for me. Don't come out or let anyone see you until this is over. I mean hide, Roxanna."

She blanched. "There's more going on here than a misunderstanding, isn't there?"

"Get going," he instructed as she reined in the gelding and faced him.

"Cain, listen to me. If you ride up to the soldiers dressed like that they'll think you're Cheyenne. They'll shoot you. If they see me, they'll know—"

"No," he said with a curse, but she spurred her horse past him, headed downriver toward Dillon's cavalry, her bright silver hair streaming like a banner behind her.

Sees Much stood in the midst of the pandemonium, watching as Cain roared a fierce oath and galloped after his headstrong wife. Then the shaman walked calmly toward Leather Shirt's lodge, where his brother and His Eyes Are Cold were standing with the Lakota renegade. Gesturing to one of the Dog Soldiers, the chief said, "Bind the Lakota and then conceal them both. We will wait for the Blue Coats here."

"Brother of the Spirit Bull and Her Back Is Straight have gone to meet the soldiers," Sees Much said. "They will listen to him—he is an Iron Horse chief among them."

"If the one called Dillon recognizes him," Leather Shirt said worriedly.

"Let us go. I have warned you. In return you are honorbound to give me Powell," Johnny Lame Pony protested as his hands were being tied at gunpoint.

"You have no honor, therefore I am not bound," Leather Shirt replied impassively, dismissing the prisoners with a chop of his hand.

As they were dragged into the lodge by the Dog Soldiers, Powell looked at the renegade with contempt. "You fool. He isn't going to let either of us go."

On the rise, hidden behind an outcropping of shale, Weasel Bear looked down on the camp, cursing the Lakota traitor who had to have given the warning. Perhaps he could still stop the half-blood and his woman from reaching Dillon before the army attacked. His companions had already given a false report to the colonel that the woman was being dragged out to be put to death. That should incite the soldiers into a headlong rush to attack. But he had to kill Not Cheyenne and his woman. He wheeled his horse around and streaked after the two riders in a course which would intersect them before they reached the soldiers.

As soon as Roxanna was free of the camp and headed toward the route the army was taking, she slowed her horse. She realized that if she raced into their sights with her husband in pursuit they would surely shoot him, mistaking him for a buck intent on harming her. As he reined in beside her, the look on his face was thunderous.

"We have to ride together. Take me on your horse, Cain, please. There's no time. You can't stop them dressed like a Cheyenne. Don't you see—"

"Don't you see, you little fool, we'll make a perfect target when—"

The high-pitched whine of a bullet echoed from a copse of willows across the narrow fork of the river, missing Cain by scant inches. At once he flattened himself on the chestnut and seized her reins, yelling, "Lie flat and hold on!"

Cursing, Weasel Bear fired again, but the riders were moving swiftly and the low leafy willow branches waved in the breeze, obscuring his aim. He missed two more shots as they vanished behind some boulders. He cursed his marksmanship, then crossed the river, splashing through the shallows, his eyes fastened on the rocks. There was not much time before the blue bellies would ride up the river valley. Not Cheyenne and his woman must be dead! Then he could watch the destruction of Leather Shirt's village and his vengeance would be complete. The Iron Horse man would reward him instead of that traitor Lame Pony.

Cain helped Roxanna from her horse, shielding her with his body as he shoved her into the rocks. "Stay down. It looks as if Lame Pony's friends have arrived and I don't know how many of them there are." Over the barrel of his Spencer carbine he scanned the edge of the trees by the river, watching for a movement.

"While we're pinned down here, the army will ride into the village," Roxanna said desperately. "I can't let all those innocent people die because of me! I'm going to slip out—"

He turned and seized her wrist in a bone-crushing grip, pulling her against his chest as he sank down behind a large boulder. "You'll be killed if you try to ride past those trees."

"Not if you cover me. I'm a good rider, Cain, I'll stay low. Let me use your chestnut. He's faster."

She was right about the village. There would be a bloodbath. "Stay here and stay down," he said, releasing her arm. "You can fire across to the trees without raising your head any farther than this." He fired off a round crouching behind the shadow of the boulder. "You *can* fire a carbine, can't you?"

"Yes, but the soldiers will shoot you—"

"Dillon knows me. If I can reach him, he'll listen," he said, moving carefully back to where the horses stood. He rummaged in his saddlebags and pulled out a soiled buckskin shirt. Slipping it over his head, he pulled off his Cheyenne jewelry. "I look as white as I ever have and they haven't shot me yet."

"Cain, be careful." *I love you.*

"Just start shooting when I mount up, but don't raise your head!" he admonished, tossing her a box of shells.

She nodded when he swung up on the chestnut and kicked him into a gallop. Then she turned and fired off several shots as the big stallion streaked away through the trees. An answering series of shots rang out from the willows, but none hit Cain or his horse. Roxanna tried to pinpoint where the shooter was located but could not be certain. So she settled for firing into the dense willows, where she thought she had seen movement.

Cain heard the exchange as he rode out of range, praying that Roxanna was safe. *I'll kill him for this! Him and all his renegades!*

He spotted the cavalry column about the same time they saw him from across the river. He had ridden out of his way in a wide circle to avoid the open river flats, which afforded no cover from the shooter in the willows. A near thing. Just a few moments more and they would have ridden straight to the village. He raised his hand and waved, calling out Dillon's name.

Riccard Dillon squinted at the lone rider on the big chestnut. "Looks like one of them bucks, Colonel. If them Pawnee is right we ain't got time to palaver or they'll kill the woman," his corporal said, raising his Springfield carbine.

"Wait. I recognize the horse. It's Cain's."

"The breed who runs the Union Pacific work crews?" the corporal asked dubiously, looking at the swarthy longhaired rider. "He's probably stole the horse'n saddle from Cain."

"He's alone," Dillon replied, trying to make out what

the rider was yelling as he rode headlong toward them over the desultory firing in the distance. Some gut instinct made him distrust the report from the two scouts. Flint Arrow and the big buck who rode with him had not returned. This whole situation smelled like a buffalo skinner on a hot summer day.

Then he heard his name and recognized Cain's face. "Column halt," he commanded, signaling to the troopers, then riding ahead to meet Cain. "What the hell's going on?" he yelled as soon as they were within earshot of each other.

"Not what you think. My wife was with Leather Shirt's band, but she wasn't a prisoner."

"Then she's in no danger? My scouts told me—" Dillon broke off with an oath as he realized the two "Pawnee" had broken away from the column at Cain's approach and were riding hell-bent for the river. "Damnation, I knew I shouldn't have trusted those bastards."

"No time to explain, Dillon. My wife is in danger—pinned down by a bushwhacker who tried to kill us both." With that Cain wheeled his chestnut about and took off toward the sound of the firing.

Dillon signaled the troopers to follow. By the time they arrived, the shooting had ceased. Cain leaped from his horse and ran toward a pile of boulders calling a woman's name—Roxanna, not Alexa.

Roxanna threw down the rifle when she heard Cain approaching and scrambled down the rocks to meet him. "Cain! Thank God you're safe! I was so frightened," she said, leaping into his arms as she peered over her shoulder at the soldiers who drew near.

A square-faced officer dismounted and approached them. The colonel was a fortyish man with eyes that looked as if they'd seen more than enough of military life and the world at large. He tipped his hat respectfully at her, revealing a head of thinning gray-brown hair with a distinctive widow's peak.

"Mrs. Cain," Riccard said uncertainly. The silver blonde

was a real looker, even decked out in Indian buckskins. What had Cain called her—Roxanna?

"Roxanna, this is Colonel Riccard Dillon, late of Fort Russell. Colonel, my wife, Roxanna Cain."

Ignoring the question about her name, Dillon gave her proffered hand a gentlemanly salute. "I can see you haven't been harmed. My Pawnee scouts reported old Leather Shirt was preparing you for a public execution."

Roxanna gasped in outrage. "Why, that's absurd. These people are my friends, my relatives."

"Where did you acquire Pawnee scouts?" Cain asked.

"They rode into my camp a little over a week ago with papers signed by Frank North . . . or at least it resembled Frank's scrawl. Funny, but I never thought they looked like Pawnee."

"Was their leader a big flat-faced bastard, kind of barrel-chested and banty-legged with a scar here?" Cain asked, running his fingers across the left side of his neck.

"Yeah."

"Rope burn from a brush with a hangman. He's Sioux, not Pawnee. Name's Johnny Lame Pony."

"Cain, that's the Lakota who rode into camp earlier," Roxanna said, thoroughly confused by what was going on.

After saying to her, "There's no time to explain now," Cain turned to Dillon, who cursed under his breath. "He and the men with him are involved in the sabotage on our grading and surveying crews. I have a hunch I know who the other scouts were too. I plan to track them down, but first I need to see that my wife is safe. Can you spare an escort to take her back to the railhead at Medicine Bow?"

"No, I'm safe with the Cheyenne. I don't want to leave you."

"You can't go with me, Roxy, and Jubal will be frantic until you're back home," he said, giving her a swift kiss, then turning to Riccard. "Can I count on you?"

Dillon nodded. "I can spare six troopers. Should have her down to the railhead by nightfall if they ride steady. My job is to get these renegades, Cain. I want the whole story out of you.''

''See to my wife and I'll explain everything when I get back from Leather Shirt's camp. I'll bring you Lame Pony.''

Roxanna was torn between fear for Cain and seething fury at his high-handed dismissal of her as she watched him swing onto his horse and ride toward the village. She turned to the officer with a worried frown. ''Do you have any more idea than me what's going on?''

Riccard shrugged. ''Only that those phony 'scouts' intended to lure me into attacking Leather Shirt's camp in hopes of rescuing you.''

''But why did you come after me in the first place?''

By the time he had explained about the telegraph supposedly signed by Jubal, both of them were perplexed. Roxanna judiciously did not mention in the exchange that Andrew Powell was being held by Leather Shirt. The Cheyenne had escaped disaster once already. Let the old rascal see to his own salvation.

True to his word, the colonel picked six men to escort her back to civilization. ''You can wire your grandfather as soon as you reach Medicine Bow. I'm certain he'll send a car at once to bring you back to him,'' he said to her.

Although Roxanna was far from certain she wanted to confront Jubal just yet, she decided it might be best to have the matter of his ''arrangement'' with Cain out in the open. If only she were not worried sick about the danger her husband was in, riding after those renegades. ''Before I go back to the rail line, I intend to say good-bye to Leather Shirt and Sees Much and my other friends with the Cheyenne. They took me in when I came to them as a supplicant and in return I almost got them killed.''

''Now, Mrs. Cain, you heard your husband.''

''Yes, I did.'' She gave him her most beguiling smile, then scrambled up into the rocks where her gelding was hidden. ''Have the detail wait for me down by the river. I won't be long,'' she called out cheerfully, kicking her mount into a trot as the colonel swore to himself.

*   *   *

By the time Cain reached the village, everyone knew the danger was past. Order was returning among the People, who calmly began unpacking the items they had seized when they fled. He rode straight to Leather Shirt's lodge, where the chief and Sees Much waited with grave faces.

"My warriors say the Blue Coats will not attack us," Leather Shirt said.

"No. I took Her Back Is Straight to them. They are returning her to the Iron Horse trail."

"In good time," Sees Much replied enigmatically, but Cain was too preoccupied to attend him.

"Take me to Powell and Lame Pony. I must get some information from them."

Leather Shirt nodded and led Cain across the camp to the lodge where they had confined the prisoners. Sees Much remained in the center of the village, looking expectantly toward the south.

Leather Shirt opened the lodge flaps and Cain slipped inside, then snarled a furious oath in English as he knelt by the body of one of the Dog Soldiers. "His throat has been cut," he said furiously as his grandfather entered the dark interior. "Lame Pony and Powell are gone."

"It must have happened during the confusion when we thought the soldiers would attack," Leather Shirt said angrily.

"I must send a message to the Blue Coat leader explaining that the renegades have escaped. He too will wish to join in the hunt for them." Cain quickly returned to his chestnut and extracted a pencil and a scrap of paper. After scrawling a terse message, he handed it to his grandfather. "Have one of your warriors take this to Dillon under a white flag. One of the men with Lame Pony is Weasel Bear. I am certain of it. I am going after them."

The old man placed a restraining hand on his arm as he accepted the note. "I will send warriors with you. They have shed the blood of the People. This is our concern now."

*   *   *

Cain rode north toward the mountains with several of Leather Shirt's finest young warriors. In the village the family of the slain Dog Soldier slashed their arms and legs in mourning as they prepared the body for burial.

Roxanna hid in the trees at the riverbank until Cain was gone, then rode up to where Sees Much stood with his arms crossed, as if expecting her.

"I could not leave without telling you good-bye," she said as she dismounted. "I'm so sorry to have brought this danger to the People and grateful that you took me in when I needed a place to stay."

"The danger is past now, child, thanks in large measure to you as well as my nephew. You risked your life to stop the Blue Coats from riding down on us. We too are grateful. Have you told Brother of the Spirit Bull about your dream?"

Roxanna sighed. So much had happened since the Medicine Lodge ceremony that she had almost forgotten about the dream. "No, there has been no time."

"There will be time."

"Then you are certain my husband will be safe?" she asked worriedly.

"I have not been given to see all that will happen, no. But it does not seem to me that the Powers would grant you both the same vision only to deny your sharing of it. It was a portend of the future."

Roxanna felt his serenity and her own troubled emotions calmed magically. She smiled and said, "I shall look forward to sharing my dream and my life with Brother of the Spirit Bull."

He returned her smile. "And sharing in the life of the child you carry . . . and many more children as well, I think. We will talk more when we meet again."

Cain and the warriors with him followed the trail left by Powell and Lame Pony for nearly an hour before losing it in the rocky bottom of a shallow stream. "We'll have to split up and search the banks to find where they came out of the water," he said to the others, damning Lame Pony for the cunning bastard that he was. Perhaps Dillon would have better luck, but he doubted it, since the soldiers no longer had scouts to track for them.

The warriors split into four groups and began to comb both sides of the river upstream and down. Cain, on a hunch, led his two companions downstream, heading in a westerly direction, unaware of the hate-filled eyes narrowed on him from a stand of cottonwoods a hundred yards away.

Weasel Bear had left the others, who went in search of the Iron Horse man. He knew after they had failed to kill the half-blood and his woman that their employer would be furious. They would not be paid. All he cared about was vengeance now. Leather Shirt's band was unscathed and the blue bellies would pursue Weasel Bear and the raiders until they were all either killed or captured. The only satisfaction left for him was the man in his rifle sights.

He would kill Not Cheyenne. He grunted in disgust at the name, for now because of the hated half-blood, he too had been sent away in disgrace, a man who belonged nowhere. "I will not kill you quickly with bullets. I will wait my chance and kill you slow," he muttered to himself, lowering the rifle.

In fact, he was not a good marksman, or his enemy and the woman would have fallen before his rifle earlier. His long-range vision was too poor, a deficiency he had attempted to conceal since boyhood, which only became worse as he grew older. But he was very good with a knife. Patting the wicked looking blade at his side, he began to stalk his prey.

Roxanna and her escort rode until they left the open country around Deer Creek far behind, heading toward the desolate looking foothills to the southwest. The corporal in charge of escorting her to the railhead was a dour Prussian immigrant who replied to her attempts at conversation in monosyllables. Gustave Fenshlage was furious at being left behind to baby-sit a redskin-loving hussy dressed like a squaw while the colonel chased after the renegades without him. What respectable white female would voluntarily live with savages, much less marry one of them? It did not matter that Dillon said he was some high-ranking official on the Union Pacific. He was still a dirty breed to Corporal Fenshlage.

The sun was blistering hot and Roxanna found she tired far more easily because she was pregnant. "Do you suppose we could rest a bit when we reach the next water?" she asked as she wiped the trickling perspiration from her forehead with the back of her hand.

"*Nein.* The railroad we will not reach by nightfall if we do not *mach schnell.*"

Roxanna debated telling the hateful man that she was in a family way, then decided he would not care. She had seen the way he looked at her beaded buckskin tunic. *He thinks I'm some sort of traitor for marrying a breed.* Damn his ignorance, she would simply dismount when they reached the next water and refuse to ride until she had rested and cooled off. He had been given a direct order by Colonel Dillon to escort her to Medicine Bow. He could scarcely ride away and leave her.

She doubted he would have nerve enough to try to forcibly place her back on her horse. *Let him try,* she thought with a grim smile, *and he'll be eating those corporals stripes by reveille.*

When they reached the creek, Roxanna followed her plan. Just as Fenshlage reluctantly ordered his men to dismount and water their horses, they were alerted by the sounds of another small party of riders approaching. He signaled for them to draw their weapons, but as soon as the men came into view it was apparent they were white—and that Mrs. Cain knew their leader.

"Larry! What on earth are you doing out in the wilderness?" she said, amazed and pleased to see him.

Lawrence Powell dismounted and walked over to her, nervously crushing his hat brim in his hands. "Thank God you're all right," he said in an impassioned croak. His face was beet red, part sunburn, part the natural flush which he could not subdue when agitated.

He shuffled awkwardly from one foot to the other as she smiled and gave him a hug. ''Yes, I'm all right.''

Before she could launch into an explanation of the dangerous turn of recent events, he blurted out, ''I'm afraid I sent Cain to Leather Shirt's camp. He came to my office in Salt Lake, Roxanna. I . . . I guess I'm still afraid of him,'' he said, shamefaced, looking off at the pale lavender mountains rising in the distance. He swallowed audibly, then continued, ''I told him where you were and he stormed out after making some pretty ugly threats. The more I thought about it, the more worried I became. I didn't know if he'd harm you—if the Cheyenne would let him just drag you away because he was your husband. So I hired these men—expert trackers—to take me to Leather Shirt.''

She patted his arm reassuringly. ''I can imagine you had a long dusty ride tracking us down. The army certainly did.''

His shoulders slumped dejectedly. ''We lost the Indians' trail days ago. I could scarcely believe my eyes when I caught sight of this cavalry patrol and you were with them. No missing all that silver hair,'' he added with an embarrassed smile.

''I have so much to tell you, Larry.'' She thought about his father, who remained a prisoner of Leather Shirt. Should she tell him? Best to leave Andrew Powell's fate to Cain. She would only describe her reconciliation with her husband and the brush with death they'd had. Then an inspiration struck her as the corporal cleared his throat behind her.

Turning to him, she said, ''Corporal Fenshlage, this is Lawrence Powell, an officer on the Central Pacific railroad and an old friend. I'm certain he would be happy to escort me to the railhead so you could rejoin your command.''

''Yes, of course,'' Larry chorused at once. ''The only reason I'm even in this ghastly wilderness is to see that Mrs. Cain is safe.''

Fenshlage scratched his graying yellow hair in uncertainty. ''I have my orders. . . .'' He was torn between his desire to chase renegades and his duty to follow orders. Yet he had heard of the Powell name. And the fellow had as much firepower as he did. Obviously his men were seasoned veterans who knew the country. The woman knew Powell and the younger man was willing to take her off his hands.

"Ya, I suppose it will be all right."

Chapter 23

Cain felt a prickling along the back of his neck, a subtle tingle traveling down his spine that had often alerted him that someone was watching him—usually someone unfriendly. He had separated from the other warriors when they picked up the trail of two ponies headed west away from the river. The third man was unaccounted for. Cain sent his companions after the pair while he remained behind, searching for signs of that last man.

He had a hunch who it was. Veering off toward a small stream that ran into the river, he dismounted and knelt to drink, watching the surface of the placid water while he feigned fatigue. *Not much of an act,* he thought with grim humor. He was still weak from his Sun Dance ordeal. One mistake could be fatal.

Although he heard nothing, not so much as a leaf rustle, he could sense his stalker drawing nearer. Cain leaned forward just slightly and slowly dipped his left hand into the water, careful to disturb the placid surface as little as possible. Just as he raised the handful of water, he saw the reflection of a man directly above him.

Weasel Bear brought the club down in a swift deadly arc. An instant before the blow landed, Cain lunged to his left, thrusting out one leg to knock Weasel Bear off balance. With a grunt of angry surprise, the Cheyenne stumbled but righted himself before he fell.

Cain drew his Smith and Wesson, but before he could level the .44, Weasel Bear's club connected with the barrel, sending the weapon flying. The half-breed jumped to his feet and took a step backward, drawing his knife.

"Have no fear, *Cousin*." Weasel Bear made the word sound like an obscenity. He tossed away his club. "I have no wish to brain you, only to take away your short gun." Without taking his eyes off his half-blood cousin, he gestured in the direction of the handgun laying several feet away. "I knew you would choose the white man's way rather than the Cheyenne's." He drew his own blade and began circling.

In a crouch, Cain shifted position only slightly to keep his opponent directly in front of him, better to save his strength and let Weasel Bear do the moving. He goaded the other man. "Ah, *Cousin*, you are the one who should fear. The Everywhere Spirit frowns on cowards. This is the second time you have attacked me from behind. You are the one who does not choose the Cheyenne way."

With a howl of rage the renegade launched himself at Cain. Weasel Bear's knife came in high, aimed straight for the half-blood's throat. Cain blocked the wicked thrust with his own blade, but the force of the Indian's body slammed him backward. Both men fell to the ground, Cain on the bottom. They rolled over and over, each with a death grip around the other's knife arm.

Cain tried knocking Weasel Bear's blade from his grasp by slamming his hand against a rock but could not dislodge the weapon from his grip. When they rolled again, Weasel Bear positioned his knife over Cain's throat and slowly, inexorably forced it closer and closer to his target. Beads of sweat popped out on the half-blood's face as he struggled to hold death at bay. The muscles in his arm suddenly felt weak as a newborn foal's. He could not match Weasel Bear's strength in his present condition. He would have to outsmart him instead.

Abruptly he released his hold on Weasel Bear's knife arm while at the same instant scissoring his legs to throw off his foe's weight. The blade plunged into the earth, grazing his neck as he rolled free. Blood seeped in a thin trickle down his chest as he gulped in several deep breaths, trying to clear his head. He could see the feral smile of satisfaction on Weasel Bear's face as he recognized his foe's failing strength.

"We will soon see which of us the Everywhere Spirit favors, cut hair," Weasel Bear sneered as Cain backed away, circling to the right.

The two men slashed, thrust, parried and backed off, Cain keeping out of the stronger man's reach, Weasel Bear trying relentlessly to wear out his enemy. Although Cain's arms felt leaden and his body was now soaked with perspiration in the afternoon heat, he forced his mind to focus, while he moved in fits and starts gradually toward the edge of the water. As he had knelt earlier he had seen a series of smooth moss-covered rocks hidden inches beneath the surface.

"When I defeat you I will open your belly so you will die slowly," Weasel Bear said with relish.

Cain could see the bloodlust gleaming in his eyes. "You are the one who will die," he said with quiet certainty, stepping carefully into the water where the bottom was soft and sandy opposite the rocks.

Weasel Bear followed him in, making another thrust. At that instant, Cain lunged forward, parrying the blade, knocking Weasel Bear off balance. The big man stepped back to regain his footing and his moccasins came down on the slimy hard surface of the rocks. He started to pitch backward. Desperate to regain his equilibrium, he instinctively threw both arms wide.

Cain thrust his blade with every dram of strength behind it he could muster. The knife sank into Weasel Bear's solar plexus up to the haft. He crumpled backward into the water, wrenching free of his cousin's grasp. His own weapon dropped from his nerveless fingers as he went down, all the while staring incredulously at the heavy leatherbound handle of Cain's knife protruding from his body. Heaving a breathless sigh, he went limp in the shallow water, which soon ran pink, fouled with his blood.

For a moment Cain stood weaving beneath the blazing heat of the sun, watching his fallen enemy. Then he walked over to Weasel Bear's body and pulled his knife free. As the waters ran red, he said, "I still don't know what the Everywhere Spirit feels about me, Cousin. But I'm pretty sure he doesn't care much for you."

By the time he rejoined the other warriors from Leather Shirt's band, they had caught up with Weasel Bear's two companions but had found no trace of Johnny Lame Pony and Powell. Three of Johnny's renegades were dead, the traitors who had misled Dillon into believing Leather Shirt's band was responsible for the sabotage on the Union Pacific. Cain knew the colonel would be eagerly tracking Lame Pony and Andrew Powell by this time. Perhaps the soldiers had already caught them, but he doubted it. Bidding farewell to Leather Shirt's men, whose business was concluded, he set out after the renegade Lakota and his employer. By dusk he picked up Dillon's trail. Within an hour the smell of coffee boiling led him to the cavalry bivouac.

As soon as he calmed the sentry, a green recruit frightened enough to shoot first and ask questions later, Cain rode up to where Riccard sat studying a map by the flickering light from the fire. The officer watched him dismount, then poured another cup of the bitter black brew he was drinking and offered it to the half-breed.

"Here, looks as if you could use it," he said, taking in the exhausted slowness with which Cain moved as well as the dried blood caked on the knife wound on his neck.

Gratefully Cain accepted the steaming tin cup and took several gulps of fortifying liquid. "I take it you haven't cut Lame Pony's trail."

Dillon gave a disgusted grunt. "No. But I take it you caught up with some of the bastards."

"Three Cheyenne from Leather Shirt's band who'd already been banished for betraying the People. By now I figure Lame Pony's met up with the rest of his bunch of cutthroats. I'm glad Roxanna is well out of harm's way. By this time she should be on her way back to Jubal.''

''I'm certain she is. Corporal Fenshlage left her in good hands.''

Cain looked up suddenly, his eyes narrowing. ''What do you mean? I thought your men were personally going to see her to the railhead.''

Roxanna lay down on the hard ground, so bone-weary that the discomfort no longer mattered. They were lost. Larry's men were from California, new to Wyoming Territory, he had sheepishly explained after they had ridden for hours without reaching the Union Pacific tracks. Apparently they had taken a wrong turn in the unfamiliar surroundings and ridden parallel with the rails for dozens of miles, overshooting Medicine Bow, heading south toward Rock River.

It would be easier to locate the railroad line in daylight, so they made camp for the night on the banks of a small stream. Poor Larry, he had been so embarrassed and distraught about the debacle, she thought as she drifted into slumber. She knew he sat awake near the campfire, too upset to sleep. If being pregnant had not tired her so much, she would have kept him company, trying to reassure him that everything would turn out all right.

When Roxanna awakened in the morning, the men were breaking camp. Weary to the bone, she sat up, rubbing sleep from her eyes, then smiled at Larry. He must have gotten some rest after all, for he returned her smile brightly.

''Good morning. After you eat a bite of breakfast, we'll be on our way,'' he said.

She shook her head as she rose, rubbing her back, which always seemed to ache lately. ''No, I don't think food first thing in the morning is such a good idea for me.''

''Very well then, I'll—'' He broke off, turning at the sound of a rider approaching.

Roxanna gasped in surprise when Johnny Lame Pony rode boldly into the camp as if he were expected. What was the renegade doing loose? Last she had seen of him, he was being held along with Andrew Powell in Leather Shirt's camp. Had the old chief released him—and if so, why had he come here?

Johnny threw his leg over the saddle and jumped smoothly to the ground in front of Larry as the hard looking men gathered around him. "We no longer work for this one," he announced peremptorily, pointing to young Powell. "Ride to our hideout and wait for me there. I will explain everything then."

"What the hell is going on, Lame Pony?" Lawrence asked in a cold voice.

Johnny turned back to him with a contemptuous smirk on his face. "You are the cub. I work for the old bear now."

"Wait. I'll pay you double whatever he offered you," Lawrence said to the renegade's men. One of the whites named Gibbs and a Mexican pistolero called Coyote appeared to consider, but all the rest shook their heads and started to mount up. Lawrence turned back to Lame Pony and hissed furiously, "This whole mess was your doing, wasn't it? You double-crossed me, you son of a bitch, after I paid you top dollar!"

A slow smile spread across the half-breed's face, revealing crooked blackened teeth with gaps between several of them. "I made a better deal." He turned to Gibbs and Coyote. "Are you in with me or out?" The smile was gone.

"*Sí, jefe,* I am in," Coyote said. The Anglo nodded agreement and both turned toward their horses.

All of the men were starting to ride away. Roxanna was terrified. What would happen to her and Lawrence now that the renegade had them in his clutches? Then, to her utter amazement, Lawrence started to draw his fancy Adams revolver. Johnny Lame Pony turned with a faintly amused look on his seamed face.

"What the hell you think—" The Lakota suddenly read death in the greenhorn's calm demeanor. He clawed for the old Army Colt at his side, but it was already far too late.

The heavy .450-caliber slug slammed into his guts like a

mule kick. As the renegade started to fall, Lawrence fired again.

"I should've known better than to ever trust a breed," he said as he watched the Lakota's lifeless body crumple to the ground.

"That was a grave tactical error, one of many you've made out here. Your machinations are far better suited to the boardroom than to dealing with dangerous men like these," Andrew Powell taunted as he rode out from behind a cluster of boulders and dismounted in front of his son. His eyes were as blue as the sky and as dead as agates. The confused gunmen, who had reined in when Johnny went down, now hightailed it away from the two deadly Iron Horse men.

Roxanna stood on the other side of the campfire, numb with shock. "What are you going to do—kill your own son?" she asked the old man, drawing closer to Lawrence.

Andrew quirked one gray eyebrow at her and replied, "It would be fitting, considering he's single-handedly engineered my ruin as well as attempted to destroy the competition from the Union Pacific. Tell me, Larry, did you intend to go after Stanford and Huntington when you'd dispensed with me?" he asked, looking back to his son.

Lawrence Powell's face turned the color of old brick, but his voice was eerily calm as he stared at his father with hatred gleaming in his pale eyes. "I already have dispensed with you," he said scornfully. "You're finished on the Central Pacific. But you're right, I am exceptionally gifted at corporate intrigue. A pity you've always held my abilities in such low esteem. It was child's play for me to purchase those supply shipments in your name, then divert the skimmed money to holding companies I'd set up so they'd be traced back to you."

"It might have worked if Cain hadn't come to San Francisco to accuse me," Andrew replied darkly.

At the mention of his brother's name, Lawrence Powell's face lost its smug scornfulness. The cold blue light in his eyes matched that in Andrew's. "Cain!" He said the word like an epithet. "Your paragon bastard. I've lived my entire life in his shadow."

"I gave you everything, him nothing," the old man said, his voice thick with anger.

"Oh, yes, I was the heir, waiting in the background, invisible, powerless. You wouldn't trust me to fill a freight order. My opinions you laughed at, but you listened to him—you respected him—a filthy half-breed gunman. 'Why can't you be a man like Cain, Larry?'" He mimicked Andrew's voice perfectly. "'He's a breed, but he has more brains in his left hand than you do in your head, Larry.' God, how sick I got of having him thrown up to me. And then the final insult." He turned to Roxanna, seizing her arm roughly.

"Larry, no!" She tried to pull away, but his fingers bit into her flesh like talons as he jerked her closer. She had always thought him mild-mannered, sweet, boyishly awkward and endearing. His round face seemed to take on harsh angles she had never perceived before. There was a ruthlessness in his stance, and the blazing hatred of insanity glowing in his eyes as they raked her, lingering on her belly. Fear such as she had never known ripped through her like a lightning bolt.

"You stupid little bitch. I wanted you, would even have married you if you hadn't gone and gotten yourself captured by savages."

"I certainly didn't do it on purpose, Larry," she replied as calmly as she could. *He's mad. Utterly mad.*

"But you did fall for Cain, didn't you? I would've ignored the ugly gossip about your captivity and made you my mistress once my plans for ruining the Union Pacific and taking over the Central Pacific were in place. But you had to turn to that breed. Do you have any idea how it revolted me to have you tearfully confessing your love for him that night in Denver? I could've killed you then with my bare hands."

"Why have you let me live this long?" The instant she

asked the question, Roxanna could have bitten her tongue. Was she fueling his rage?

His expression abruptly shifted from fury to chilling calm. "You became part of my master plan, the means to get to that breed. First I tried sabotage on that little pleasure jaunt from Chicago. That should've wiped out Cain and half the key people on the Union Pacific."

"*You* sent that man to unhitch the freight cars!"

"But, alas, it failed. Your mongrel lover has more lives than a damned cat."

"Yeah, I do, Larry," Cain's voice cut in. "Your fake train wreck was as sloppy as that gunhand with the faulty aim in the work camp," he added, walking calmly up to the campfire. He paused when he drew nearer, standing across from Andrew. Lawrence stood between them, with Roxanna tightly in his grasp.

"That wasn't Isobel trying to kill me—it was your assassin sent to kill my husband," Roxanna said to Lawrence, her horror growing.

"My baby-faced little brother here had a whole bag full of tricks. The theft of those shiploads of supplies always did strike me as a bit too clumsy to be your style," he said to his father. "Then when you showed up at Leather Shirt's camp, I knew you had to be after Larry. The whole thing reeked of a trap."

"A trap into which you fell neatly," Lawrence replied with a death's-head grin, pressing his revolver against Roxanna's breast. "But you had to go and spoil my plans. I could've devastated old Jubal by wiping out his granddaughter and heir apparent—and done it in a way that would never have made him come looking for the murderer. I had to move fast before that stupid Darby slut told him you weren't Alexa Hunt."

"You're a fool if you think the old Scot didn't already know the truth," Andrew said with a flicker of amusement overlaying the chill in his expression. "I approached him with the information months ago. Men like us are beyond your ability to comprehend, you with your puling boyish jealousies and hurt feelings.'' There was terrible anger in his voice but perhaps more . . . pain, loss, resignation? "Jubal told me he already knew and didn't give a damn—the same way I'd have bluffed him if our positions were reversed.''

" 'Boyish jealousies? Hurt feelings,' is it?'' Lawrence parroted with cunning malice. "It was pure bloody genius. I had you fooled the same as her. You saw me as weak and ineffectual because that's how I wanted you to see me.''

"You did have us all fooled, Larry,'' Roxanna replied, as her eyes met Cain's. *What can we do?* He looked utterly calm, but she could sense the fear for her deeply buried inside of him. She could also feel the hate radiating from Lawrence and tried to step back but he rammed the gun barrel harder into the tender flesh of her breast. Cain moved a step closer while Lawrence's attention was diverted, then stopped when his brother looked at him again.

"I think I'd still have kept her to warm my bed after you were dead if not for your brat in her belly,'' he said with sneering contempt, looking from Cain to their father. "At least I have principle enough not to claim a breed bastard.''

"I never acknowledged Cain,'' Andrew replied quietly. "Perhaps that was a mistake. He has my brains and nerve, something you'll never possess. You take after your dear unlamented mother and her sly, grasping little clan. Greedy but gutless.''

The scathing words dropped like shattered icicles. Cain tensed, prepared to make a desperate lunge if his brother turned his rage on Roxanna, but Lawrence's attention now riveted on their father.

"Greedy? Gutless?'' he echoed tonelessly. The gun jabbing Roxanna's side moved slightly as Lawrence's eyes narrowed on the man who had dominated him all of his life. "You've belittled me, ridiculed me, preached, goaded, threatened . . .'' His voice began to rise, growing thinner as his grip on the earlier calm slipped. "You *played* with me as if I were an insect in a glass jar!''

"I tried to make a man of you,'' Andrew replied calmly.

Like Cain, he had moved closer. Now each of them stood within six feet of Lawrence on opposite sides of him. "But all you'll ever be is a spoiled little sneak thief. Collis Huntington will eat you alive."

"You fucking son of a bitch!" Lawrence shrieked, turning the gun on his father.

As soon as the sharp pressure of the barrel moved, Roxanna lunged free of his grip, flinging herself toward Cain. Two shots rang out almost simultaneously. Lawrence took his father's bullet directly in the heart, falling back like a rag doll onto the hard dusty earth, his face expressionless in death. Andrew looked down at Lawrence's blue eyes, the only physical resemblance between them. "I may be a son of a bitch . . . but I know you were one, boy," he whispered as his knees slowly buckled.

Dropping his gun, he crumpled while a red stain began to widen across his chest. Quickly sliding his own unfired .44 back into his holster, Cain caught him and lowered him gently to the ground, then began to unbutton his shirt to examine the wound.

Andrew shook his head with a thin smile. Faint flecks of blood foamed on his lips as he said, "No use. Funny . . . I guess he did have nerve after all . . . just not enough . . . brains. . . . You always had . . . the . . . brains. You beat me . . . Cain . . , satisfied now?"

"No . . . not satisfied at all," Cain replied quietly as his father's narrow aristocratic features grew slack in death. Sightless blue eyes stared up at the sky until Cain closed them.

Roxanna placed her hand gently on his shoulder, knowing that in spite of everything her husband grieved for the father he never had.

"I wonder if he intended to kill Larry all along," he said to himself.

"Regardless, he saved our lives. I'm certain Larry would have killed us once he finished venting his spleen."

"I never imagined how much he hated Andrew. I guess

I was too wrapped up in my own hurt and anger to really see him.''

"He never let anyone see who he was, Cain. I honestly believed he was my friend." Her voice choked. The harrowing experience of standing with death all around made her suddenly light-headed.

Cain stood up and took her in his arms. "When I heard those first shots I was terrified that I was too late. I came scrambling through the brush just after Andrew showed himself. Larry was holding you so close I couldn't risk a shot. I—"

A volley of shots echoed from over the rise. Roxanna flinched, but Cain rubbed her back to calm her. "That's probably Riccard Dillon taking care of Johnny Lame Pony's men. I wrung a promise out of him to hold back while I came in after you."

She looked up into his eyes. "You always come after me, don't you?" *Say you love me, Cain.*

He brushed a stray curl from her cheek as he smiled at her. ''Yeah, I'll always come after you, Roxanna. The minute I found out from Dillon that his men had turned you over to Larry, I rode hell-bent to reach you."

She waited expectantly, but just then the sound of approaching hoofbeats made him turn from her. "That's probably Dillon's men, but let's not take chances," he said, taking her arm and hurrying into the cover of the rocks a few yards away.

When the blue uniforms of several cavalrymen became visible, Cain stepped out into the open, followed by Roxanna. Dillon and several of his men reined in their horses. Riccard looked around the campfire at Johnny Lame Pony and the Powells. "Christ, looks as if you had your own small war here."

"You get all of those 'Indian raiders'?" Cain asked.

The colonel threw up one hand in admission of his mistake. "You were right. They were working for Powell," he replied, looking down at Andrew.

"Not the old man—Larry," Cain corrected.

Dillon's world-weary countenance gave way to an expression of frank incredulity. "That greenhorn kid?"

Even in death Lawrence Powell would receive no respect. "Yeah, that greenhorn kid."

A detail of Dillon's troops saw to the burial of the renegades. The Powells were wrapped carefully in blankets and strapped to their horses for the long journey back to civilization.

"Will you take them to San Francisco?" Roxanna asked as they rode with the column later in the day. In a few hours they would reach the railhead at Rock River.

Cain shrugged. "I guess there's no one else." He smiled at the sad irony of it all. "He was always so damn careful to keep anyone from finding out that I was his son, Larry's half-brother. Now I'm the only blood kin left to see to their burial."

"I'll go with you."

He looked at the dark smudges beneath her eyes. She had been through so much in the past weeks and most of it was his fault. What would he do if something happened to her and their child? He refused to think about it. "You need to rest, not spend the next five days on overland coaches and trains."

"I'm perfectly fine," she remonstrated.

Cain shook his head firmly. "You're carrying our baby and you're exhausted. I want you to spend at least a week sleeping in a real bed while I'm away. That big place Jubal had built in Cheyenne ought to be finished by now."

An expression of dismay crossed her face, followed by uncertainty. "I don't know . . ." she said softly, still feeling the sting of hurt the old man's scheming with Cain had caused.

"You have to make your peace with him, Roxanna. He was a lot less guilty than me. I came to him and offered to marry you."

"And he made a deal to get rid of the embarrassment of the sullied woman he believed was his granddaughter."

"If that was the way he felt about you, he could have disavowed you when he found out you weren't Alexa," he countered. "I think he cares for you more than he ever did any of his family."

She sighed. "Perhaps, but whatever he feels for me, I do owe him enough to face him and sort this mess out." Right at that moment she was too weary to even feel, much less think.

They left Dillon and his command at the Union Pacific railhead and boarded a night train eastbound for Cheyenne after sending a wire to Jubal. In the absence of his chief of operations, the Union Pacific director was overseeing the work crews on the Utah line. Cain's message explained what had transpired since Roxanna had left him. Jubal wired back at the following stop saying he was returning on the next train east to see that Roxanna was comfortably ensconced in his new house while Cain took care of family obligations. Jubal included a cryptic postscript indicating that Isobel Darby should no longer trouble them.

Late the following day Cain stopped the small rig he'd driven from the railway station in front of the impressive new white frame structure on the outskirts of Cheyenne. The house was three stories high with a large tower on one side and beautifully wrought gingerbread trim on the porch railings. The shutters and latticework were painted charcoal-gray, giving a clean pristine accent to the house. A pair of large bay windows with leaded glass panes in rich hues of ruby and deep blue gleamed in the evening light.

"Almost as big as a Scottish castle," Cain said as he helped Roxanna down from the buggy.

"All it lacks is a moat," she replied, eyeing the immense tower with foreboding. It was made of granite blocks hewn in the Medicine Bow Mountains and loomed over the house.

They walked up to the wide wooden porch and climbed the steps. A smiling Li Chen opened the front door and bowed in welcome as they entered. Chattering excitedly in Cantonese, he explained to Cain that Jubal had sent Roxanna's trunks here as soon as the house was finished, along with a skeleton crew of servants to wait on them when Cain returned with his "missy."

After thanking Chen, he turned back to his wife. "He'll have a bath drawn for you and supper waiting as soon as you're ready. They're holding the westbound cars at the depot until I return, so I'd better go. Get some rest while I'm gone. Jubal will be here in a couple of days." He drew her into his arms for a kiss.

She held him tightly as he brushed her lips tenderly. "We've had no time alone to talk since that awful renegade Sioux came riding into Leather Shirt's camp—"

"We'll have all the time in the world when I return from San Francisco—to talk . . . and do other things," he replied with a smoldering smile.

She felt a tremor of urgency but dismissed it. This was not the time to explain her dream or for him to describe his Medicine Lodge vision. That must be a very special moment of sharing between them. . . . first he must begin it.

Cain could feel her disquiet—or was it something in the house? That was absurd. It was brand new. No spirits haunted it. He looked at her quizzically, a frown creasing his forehead. "Roxy, is something wrong?"

She felt a queer malaise stealing over her, almost as if someone had brushed her with a silk scarf, then vanished into the gathering darkness outside. "No, it's nothing, just a flight of fancy common to pregnant women. Hurry home, Cain." *I love you.*

He raised both her hands in his and kissed the palms, then drew her back into his arms for another kiss. "Rest well while I'm gone."

She stood silhouetted in the front doorway until he had driven the rig back down the street. The peace and quiet would do her good and Jubal would watch over her, protective as a bulldog. Cain was certain of that. Still the premonition of danger would not leave him as he boarded the westbound train.

Chapter 24

Jubal climbed out of his rig and motioned for the driver to take it around back to the stables, then stood looking up at his new home. He was making a fresh start here in the West. Railroading was in his blood. Steel manufacturing, textiles, shipping, all the other business ventures he had established back East no longer held his interest. Chuckling, he wondered if Cain would consider taking the helm of his highly diversified holdings.

Jubal doubted it. Building railroads to crisscross the West from California to Canada, Missouri to Mexico, that was what his young protégé wanted. They would do it together, for in Cain he had at last found the business associate he had hoped for when his daughter wed that shiftless aristocrat Terrence Hunt. They would sell out his eastern interests for a tidy profit and pour it all into railroad expansion and subsidiary industries out here.

Cheyenne, as the Wyoming territorial capital, was a convenient stopover on the Union Pacific line, an excellent base of operations. Although their brief exchange of telegrams had not allowed much elaboration, Jubal intuited that Cain might want to keep in touch with his mother's people now. Yes, Cheyenne would suit just fine. But first he had to clear the air with Roxanna.

The lass was no doubt spitting mad, feeling that he and

Cain had bargained over her as if she were a racehorse or a piece of real estate. Sighing, he set his steps toward the house. For the first time in longer than he could remember—and Jubal MacKenzie had a very keen memory—he was nervous.

Roxanna had slept, eaten and read from the extensive collection of books in Jubal's library for the past three days. She was rested—and restless. "I'm just bored," she scolded herself impatiently. It was past time for her to drive into town. Perhaps she could find something worthwhile to do. Although the raw young capital had no hospital, several physicians had hung out their shingles. Perhaps her nursing skills might be useful to one of them.

That resolution made, she set down her fork and shoved away the remains of the lavish luncheon the cook insisted on preparing for her. Everyone thought she needed to be fattened up, it seemed. *As if I won't soon be fat enough!* Just as she stood up and stepped around the small table in the rear sitting room, the door opened and Jubal MacKenzie's imposing body filled the sash.

"Oh, Jubal . . . I didn't know when to expect you." In truth, their reunion had been preying on her mind ever since her arrival. "Have you had luncheon? I can have the cook serve some cold roast beef and vichyssoise." Her voice sounded stilted, awkward.

He watched her standing with one hand braced on the table, her expression guarded, no more the smiling young woman who had hugged him and teased him and drank bourbon whiskey with him. "I ate on the train, thanks just the same. Yer lookin' in the bloom of health. Motherhood agrees with you." He too was stiff and formal. With a mumbled oath, he stepped into the room and blurted out, "Is everything all right between you and yer husband?"

"Yes. I believe he cares for me . . . that he didn't marry me just to become your operations chief. . . ." She smiled wryly and added, "Or at least if he did, that's changed now. While we were with the Cheyenne, he underwent a terrible ordeal for me and our child. Everything is fine between Cain and me.''

''But not between you and me, eh?'' He smiled mirthlessly.

''How did you find out I wasn't Alexa?'' The question had gnawed at her ever since Cain told her that the old Scot knew the secret of both their identities.

''I suspected a wee bit from the first,'' he replied, pacing across the room to the window, then turning back to her. ''Oh, you looked like the child I remembered close enough—physically. It was yer grit that surprised me. Alexa was like her parents, I think. Staid, timid, afraid of a challenge. How would a lass who refused to leave her home in St. Louis survive an Indian captivity?''

''She could've grown, changed,'' Roxanna said. Remembering Jubal's repeated entreaties to join him and how terrified Alexa had always been, Roxanna knew her friend would never have voluntarily left the shelter of the house in Lafayette Square. If Alexa had been on that stage when Leather Shirt's warriors surrounded it, she would have died of sheer terror on the spot. ''No, I suppose you're right. Alexa wouldn't have been able to do what I did,'' she admitted.

''At first I was so delighted with yer courage, yer wit, yer sense of humor, that I puffed myself up thinking it was me you inherited them from.''

''Did you have me investigated?''

He shook his head. ''Maybe I dinna' want to know the truth. But one day, a month er so after yer marriage to Cain, I received some documents from a law firm in St. Louis. They were assigned by the courts to sell the house and handle the probate after Alexa's death.''

A wave of remorse washed over Roxanna as she looked into his eyes and read the regret, the pain of loss. ''I am so sorry that your granddaughter died. When I began the masquerade, I never thought I'd hurt anyone—''

''You've brought me only joy, lass. Have no fear on that,'' he replied fiercely. ''Once I read the documents, I knew Alexa had died of consumption and her companion had closed down the house and arranged her funeral. It dinna' take much to figure that she'd also come west in Alexa's place.''

He hesitated a moment, then asked, ''Do the names Tam O' Shanter and Elizabeth R mean anything to you?''

Roxanna paled, then sat down on the chair beside her as memories flooded back. ''Elizabeth R was my code name during the war. A fine conceit,'' she added bitterly, ''likening myself to the virgin queen of England. Tam O' Shanter was the code name for the man in Washington who . . . I sent my reports to,'' she said with dawning recognition. ''You—you were Tam O' Shanter?''

''As President Lincoln's Undersecretary of War I was assigned to organize and run a network of spies in rebel territory. I suppose the reasoning was if I could outmaneuver the likes of Commodore Vanderbilt and Daniel Drew, I would be good running a spy ring. You were the best agent I had in the field.''

''Until Vicksburg in '63.'' Her voice was quiet and she sat tracing the pattern on the linen tablecloth with one finger, unable to meet his eyes.

''Aye, until then. I received word you'd died in prison, lass,'' he said with genuine concern in his voice as he took a seat across from her. ''You seemed to drop off the edge of the earth.''

''I intended it that way, Jubal.'' She pressed her fingertips to her temples as the memories returned, vividly clear, ugly. ''I've told no one what really happened in that prison.''

''Not even yer husband,'' he said gently, knowing she had not.

''Perhaps someday I'll be able to talk about it, but not yet . . . not now.''

He reached over tentatively and patted her hand with awkward solicitude. ''Do na' think of it now. When I decided to learn yer real identity, I never intended to tell you that I knew you weren't Alexa. I was dumbstruck when the reports came back saying you were Roxanna Fallon.''

"Roxanna Fallon, spy, actress, fallen woman—hardly the sort you'd choose as the heiress for your empire," she said bitterly.

"There's where yer wrong, lassie. Dead wrong. Yer exactly the woman I'd choose to be my granddaughter, just as Cain's the man I'd choose to run all my business ventures for you."

She looked up, startled, then read the earnest expression on his face. *This is the Jubal MacKenzie who's played poker with the Commodore,* she reminded herself, but she wanted to believe him. "Tell me about the arrangement you made with Cain to marry me off."

He winced at her choice of words. "Och, lassie, you make me sound cold as Loch Ness in January," he said in a thickened brogue. "I repented my bargain with old Andrew Powell an hour after I saw that whey-faced boy following him around like a lapdog, but I dinna' want the engagement broken because of ugly gossip. Then Cain came to me. He said that none of the Indians nor himself had touched you."

"And you believed him?"

"Aye. I always thought I was a good judge of human nature, Roxanna." His eyes were shrewdly assessing as they met hers. "Cain dinna' touch you, but it wasna' because he dinna' wish to. The lad wanted much more than the job—much more than even he knew."

"But you knew. . . ." It was not quite a question.

"I thought I did. For a while when he worked so much, leaving you alone . . . I worried that I'd been mistaken, especially when I could see how much you loved him."

"He's never spoken of love . . ." she admitted.

"For a man like Cain it's not an easy thing to do. Nor for me." His face, always ruddy and sun-darkened, turned red as he cleared his throat. "I've missed you, lassie. Yer the granddaughter I never knew, the one I've come to love. Yer all the family I have, Roxanna, and far better than an old curmudgeon like me deserves." He studied her guardedly with tears glistening in his eyes.

She felt her throat tighten as she rose and reached out to hug him. He returned her embrace, enveloping her awkwardly in his arms. The scratch of his untrimmed beard and the faint aroma of Cuban cigars were as dearly familiar as if he had been her own father. "I've missed you too, Jubal, but you're right—you are an old curmudgeon!"

Jubal remained in Cheyenne attending to railroad business for the next several days. He and Roxanna resumed their old comfortable relationship, sharing meals, discussing problems with his work and now planning for the new baby. She described the ordeal Cain had undergone in the Medicine Lodge ceremony and their brush with death because of Lawrence Powell's treachery. At the end of the week, Jubal received a wire from rail's end indicating that a strike was imminent if the workers were not paid.

"It's criminal, the greedy stupidity of Durant and the other directors, lining their own pockets with dividends from the Crédit Mobilier while cash for payrolls is always short," Jubal groused as he prepared to take the westbound cars for the Bear River camp.

"You can't keep paying the men out of your own cash reserves," Roxanna remonstrated. "You've said yourself, the Union Pacific isn't going to show a profit for years after the transcontinental linkup—not until all the lands between California and the Missouri River are settled and developed."

His gray eyes twinkled. "Aye, but in time that will happen. Meanwhile I intend to keep my reputation intact as a boss who pays his employees so they'll keep working for me when we expand rail links into the Rockies, to the Northwest, even south to Mexico."

"You dream big," she replied, kissing him on the cheek before he headed out the door.

"Aye'n so does that husband of yers. Take care of the bairn until he returns."

"We'll both be fine," she assured him, patting the slightly rounded swell of her belly with a smile.

Roxanna watched his rig pull away in a swirl of light snow. The weather, unseasonably warm all fall, had suddenly turned cold as winter pounced with freezing temperatures and icy blasts of wind howling down from Canada. The abrupt shift in seasons was one of the most difficult things she had to adjust to living on the High Plains.

As she closed the massive oak door and turned, her eyes were drawn to the foyer stairs which wound up to a high balcony extending across the second floor to the tower. A shiver of foreboding skittered down her spine. "It's just the sudden change in the weather," she said over the echo of her own footsteps crossing the polished slate tiles.

Several days later Roxanna rose with brilliant late autumn sunshine pouring into the windows of her bedroom. How large and lonely the big bed seemed without Cain. But soon he would return from San Francisco, she thought with eager excitement. Then she would have to convince him to allow her to go with him to the winter camp on the Utah border.

The Union Pacific track crews would work through the winter this year. With the Central Pacific already well into Nevada, the race was growing fiercer with each passing day. The men would somehow withstand gale-force winds, bone-freezing temperatures and torrents of snow just as their counterparts had crossing the Sierras in California. They would be hundreds of miles from Salt Lake, the nearest settlement. Would Cain and Jubal believe it safe for her, considering her pregnancy? Well, if they didn't . . . too bad for them!

Pulling off her nightrail, she stood in front of the mirror and eyed her naked body critically. No doubt about it, her waist had begun to thicken noticeably. Already her breasts were considerably enlarged and tender to the touch. All of her clothes were getting tight. Corsets would not have been an option even if she had been still wearing them.

"I suppose it's time I went into town and visited the dressmaker," she said to herself with a sigh.

If Cain noticed her clothes pulling unbecomingly across

her breasts and waistline, he would be more inclined to worry about her "delicate condition." Perhaps some new looser-fitting gowns would disguise the changes until she could wheedle him into agreeing to her plan. Also, she would require quite a few confinement dresses cut without waists for the latter stages of her pregnancy. Ugh, not exactly the sort of shopping trip to elicit eagerness, even if she enjoyed dress fittings—which she did not.

Within an hour Roxanna had polished off a hearty breakfast of scrambled eggs, waffles and bacon. She and Li Chen were both overjoyed at the return of her appetite, but if she continued to be this hungry, she'd require the services of a tentmaker rather than a seamstress! After giving the household servants a well-deserved afternoon off, she set out to spend the day poring over pattern books and having her new, more ample measurements taken.

Over their liveryman's protests, she insisted on driving the small phaeton herself. "I'm not certain how long I'll be in town and you have work to do here at the stables. Really, Juan, I'll enjoy the exercise. It's only a short trip."

"You be careful, señora," the grizzled little Mexican replied dubiously as he helped her into the rig.

Why was it men always assumed women were helpless, especially when the women were increasing? Thinking of the self-sufficiency of the women in Leather Shirt's band, she had to smile. The Cheyenne viewed carrying a child as a natural occasion, not a confinement. If only "civilized" society were half so sensible.

She spent the duration of the morning in Cheyenne at Mrs. Whittaker's shop. Mercifully, the selections and fittings did not take as long as she had anticipated. Although an estabished station on the Union Pacific line, the town was still small, with only a few respectable ladies to patronize a dressmaker. The selection left something to be desired, but she had chosen several fabrics that were practical and sturdy, sensible for the months ahead in the wilderness.

As she slapped the reins and the frisky white mare trotted off, Roxanna studied the sky. Thick gray clouds billowed over the northwestern horizon. The air was chilly and a light dusting of snow covered the ground. Were they in for the first big storm of the season? She urged the horse to a swifter pace, looking forward to a few hours of blissful solitude without servants hovering. The morning of being pinned, poked and pulled on had been quite enough.

She drove the rig down to the stables and left it with Juan, then walked back up the long winding footpath to the servants' entrance at the rear of the house. She entered the kitchen and set about making a pot of tea, then poured a large cup and carried it with her down the hall. This would be a perfect afternoon to curl up with one of the books from Jubal's library. She could watch the snowfall from her sitting room window and be safe and cozy inside. First she had to select a book from the collection which lined the circular walls of the second-floor tower room.

She entered the foyer and that eerie prickling sensation returned as she looked up the steep winding staircase to the tower room. There was something about the tower room and these stairs that made her uncomfortable. Grinning at herself, she murmured, "It's probably that I'm on my way to becoming a fat and lazy pregnant lady." Picking up her skirt in one hand, holding the teacup and saucer in the other, she began the ascent.

When she reached the top, she made a mental note to suggest to Jubal that he have the hard oak risers carpeted. She entered the big room with its floor-to-ceiling bookshelves and began to browse. At one point she thought she heard footsteps on the stairs, but when she called out, no one answered.

It was scarcely half past one. None of the servants would return for hours yet. Shrugging, she turned back to the shelves and plucked a volume of Aristophanes' plays from the shelf. With a smile bowing her lips, she decided to re-read *Lysistrata*, even if not in the original Greek. Perhaps there was more than one way to convince Cain to take her with him.

Book tucked beneath her arm, she picked up her empty

cup and headed out the door. Halfway to the stairs, she froze. The cup and saucer slipped from her fingers and shattered as they hit the floor, jagged pieces bouncing through the railing to the tiles far below like brittle raindrops.

"What are you doing here?" Roxanna asked as steadily as she could.

Isobel Darby's face contorted with the venom that had eaten away at her soul and her sanity for five long years. "I am going to exact justice," she replied in a high-pitched voice, producing an ancient percussion cap pepperbox pistol from the folds of her heavy plum velvet dress.

"You'll be arrested. My servants—"

"I listened as you dismissed them for the day. No one but that dirty greaser is around and he's down at the stables, too far away to hear."

Keep her talking, Roxanna thought desperately as she placed her hand on the railing and took a tiny step forward. "How did you hear what I said?"

An almost childish smile came over Isobel's pinched aristocratic features. "Why, I've been here ever since the house was completed, in the attic over the tower room." She glanced up for a second, but leveled the gun the instant Roxanna moved another step closer.

"I had everything planned, you see. When the house sat empty I sneaked in with enough food and water to last until you arrived. I knew you'd be here alone sooner or later. All I had to do was wait. I've waited so many years already. But I'm through being patient."

Cain stood rigidly in the foyer below the two women. Dear God, was he too late? When he reached the railhead at Bear River, Jubal's agent in Mississippi had just wired him that the Widow Darby had vanished from Vicksburg, had not even gone to her plantation. His fifty thousand had been withdrawn from the bank the same day.

Cain had immediately hopped a train heading east and instructed the engineer to open the throttle wide. Now he stood in the deserted house, powerless as the two women faced each other. Roxanna was directly in his line of fire. If he tried to move out farther in the room where he could get a shot at Isobel, she would see him and shoot his wife.

What could he do? He had to get behind Isobel. The back servants' stairs to the second floor! Edging along the wall underneath the balcony, he dashed down the carpeted hallway and raced for the back steps as Isobel continued her demented ranting.

"That old fool MacKenzie thought he'd bought me off, but I've outsmarted him. I have my ticket for the four-thirty train eastbound. By this time next month I'll be living high in London . . . and you will be dead . . . you and that filthy half-breed's brat you're carrying, lying at the bottom of those stairs with a broken neck . . . probably everything else broken too," she added with relish. "My noble Nathaniel will at last be able to rest in the peace he deserves."

"Your noble Nathaniel was a thief and a traitor," Roxanna said, deliberately goading Isobel, hoping she would slip over the brink of madness and fire wildly. She still held the book beneath her arm. Please, God, let her aim be true when she threw it! "He deserved to hang—not only for stealing—"

"You lying slut! You enticed him into your bed!" Isobel shrieked, moving closer to Roxanna, her teeth bared in a snarl as her thin lips pulled up, twisting grotesquely.

Swallowing the bile her memories evoked, Roxanna said, "I traded my virginity to Colonel Nathaniel Darby in return for his word that he'd release me from that hellhole of a prison in Vicksburg. Do you know how much his word was worth—your fine Confederate cavalier?" *Come closer, Isobel, closer.*

"I won't listen to—"

"Do you?" Roxanna's voice too rose sharply as the horrors of that hellish night came bubbling up, still festering in the back of her mind, like sewage, black, filthy, noisome beyond endurance. "He took me until he'd slaked his lust. He even told me what a splendid fuck I was."

Isobel drew back in shock. ''Nathaniel never used such language!''

''Those were precisely his words. After commending me, he smiled and called in the guard. Instead of the horse and free passage north he promised me, he sent me back to that stinking cell in the bowels of the prison—where three guards waited.''

Roxanna shivered uncontrollably, then regained control of herself. Isobel's eyes were round, almost popping from their sockets as she relished the idea of her hated enemy's degradation. But Roxanna had to finish it. The telling of it was her only hope of escape from certain death.

''He turned me over to those animals. The lowest dregs of humanity, rotted teeth, sour breath, unwashed bodies. They tore off the clothes your noble Nathaniel had allowed me to put back on. Then they took turns . . . all night long . . . until they didn't even have to hold me down anymore.''

She could feel the tears thickening her voice, feel the sting of them gathering behind her eyes. *Don't let them blur my vision.* She slid the book from beneath her arm and clutched it in both hands. ''They left me for dead near dawn and went to get drunk. They were passed out in the guard room when I crawled out of that cell. I stole one of their horses. To this day, I don't know how I managed to stay on it until I reached Union lines.''

''You deserved what you got,'' Isobel said viciously. ''My Nathaniel is dead. You ruined him.''

''Do you know the real irony in this, Isobel? I wouldn't have turned him in to General Johnston if he'd kept his word to me. He could still be alive today.''

''No! You're lying—lying about it all! You've made up this whole tale!''

Just after Roxanna hurled the book, Isobel fired her gun. The slim volume struck the barrel and the shot went wild. Cain raced the last dozen yards down the hall, but before he could reach them, Isobel leaped at Roxanna and the two women stumbled backward as they clawed and gouged at each other. The force of their combined weight slammed against the wooden railing, which gave a sickening crack. Isobel seized a fistful of Roxanna's hair and yanked it free of its pins as Roxanna landed a fist in her foe's lower abdomen below the protective whalebone stays of her corset.

With a bleat of rage and pain, Isobel renewed her attack, intent on forcing her victim over the banister. Once more she careened into the railing, with a talonlike grip on Roxanna's arm. Her strength was incredible, as Cain found out when he reached them and attempted to extricate his wife.

His appearance only seemed to add to Isobel's blind rage. Flecks of spittle flew from her thin white lips as she held on with a grip of steel, using the weight of both their bodies as she slammed against the banister yet a third time. She was rewarded by the sharp crack of wood giving way behind her.

Cain braced his legs and pulled backward, with his arms wrapped around Roxanna's body. As he fell to the carpet, Isobel lost her grip on Roxanna. They could hear her anguished cry, ''Nooo . . .'' Then there was only the dull solid whump as her body hit the slate tiles below.

Cain rolled onto his side with Roxanna cradled in his arms, holding her gently, drinking in the feel of her body, so warm and alive against his, the ragged rise and fall of her ribs as she gasped for air. He sat up, then carefully helped her rise. ''Are you injured?''

Roxanna shivered. ''Not nearly as bad as Isobel.''

Together they climbed to their feet and peered over the smashed railing. Isobel Darby lay splayed out in the center of the foyer floor, her body bent at grotesquely malformed angles. Her heavy plum velvet gown billowed out around her legs, and from beneath it, spilled all across the tiles, lay small bundles of banknotes, hundreds of them.

''She must've hidden all the money Jubal gave her in her clothes,'' Cain muttered to himself as he turned Roxanna's head away from the bloody flesh that had once been Isobel Darby.

Chapter 25

Cain and Roxanna left the broken remains of Isobel lying on the foyer floor and walked down the hall to her sitting room. "We'll have to send for the authorities . . . do something . . . about her body . . ." She shivered, remembering Isobel's hate-filled cry as she fell to her death.

"Don't think about it. I'll handle it later," he replied, urging her to take a seat on the sofa. He knelt beside her and examined the scratches on her face and arms. "When I think how close I came to losing you all over again . . ." His voice trailed away. "Are you injured anywhere else?"

"I think she pulled half the hair from my head. Other than that, just these scratches and scrapes," she responded.

"I felt so helpless when I saw the two of you up there. I couldn't get a shot at her. You were directly in my line of fire. I raced to the back stairs, but by the time I reached that hall, you'd both moved and I still didn't dare shoot. I tried to sneak up on her and then you threw that book."

"You saved me once again." She paused, staring down at her hands, clenched tightly in her lap. "You heard, didn't you?" Her voice was choked.

"Yes, Roxanna, I heard," he said, placing his hand over hers.

"I—I had to keep her off balance, angry, to move closer . . . or at least that's what I was telling myself. Maybe I just wanted to spew it all out at her. She's tormented me for so long . . . all over a man who existed only in her imagination.''

''Jubal said you'd have to be the one to tell me about it . . . if you wanted to.''

She choked on a sob and bit down on one tightly clenched little fist. ''Reliving it brought back what I thought I'd escaped . . . feeling so defiled . . . so dirty. . . . It's as if it happened only yesterday. I'll never be rid of the memories.''

He sat beside her and placed his arms around her, holding her tightly. ''Roxanna, you weren't to blame for any of it— not Darby, not those guards—you were their victim, may the bastards rot in hell.''

She felt his hands, those gentle hands, stroking her hair, holding her so securely. He didn't understand. She looked up and met his eyes, struggling for control of her runaway emotions. ''I sold myself, my honor, to escape a hangman's noose. I should've died for my country the way a man in my place would have.'' Her face crumpled. ''But as you said, a woman has weapons that a man doesn't. I gave that swine Darby my virginity—what I should've been able to give you—''

''If you hadn't, I never would have met you—you're worth more than your damn maidenhead, Roxanna!'' His hands cupped her shoulders, fingers digging into her soft flesh as he willed her to believe him.

Her eyes glistened with tears as they met his. ''Don't tell me it didn't matter to you on our wedding night—that's why you believed I'd been unfaithful with Larry.''

''I was a fool, Roxanna.'' He tried to gather his chaotic thoughts, taking her clenched fists in his hands and forcing them open, interlacing his fingers with hers and bringing them up to his lips. ''I didn't know on our wedding night. After all, I'd never had a virgin before, but I imagine it's highly overrated.

''What made me jealous of Larry was a hell of a lot more complicated. You know how I felt about my Cheyenne blood, my bastardy. For once I'd been given the prize instead of my brother. You were my wife and I wasn't about to share you with any man. It had nothing to do with what happened to you before we met.''

"But I lied to you and deceived you into thinking I was a sheltered St. Louis belle.''

"I deceived you in a far worse way. I hid my past and I made that deal with Jubal. All along, I tried to convince myself I was doing it for the promotion, the power—my revenge against my father. But the harder I fought against you, the more I fell under your spell. And I resented it, Roxanna. I was afraid of your hold over me. I couldn't admit the truth—not even back in Leather Shirt's village after the Sun Dance. I know now that even if they made me president of the Union Pacific, it wouldn't matter worth a damn without you. I love you, Roxanna, love you more than life, wealth, anything.''

Roxanna looked into his eyes, which were glowing with unshed tears—and love. She reached up and touched her fingertips to the scar on his cheek, caressing it softly, letting the wonder of the moment wash over her like spring rain, clear and sparkling with new promise, so utterly wonderful that it robbed her of breath. His heart was revealed in his eyes, open and vulnerable. *He is still afraid that I'll reject him.*

"I have wanted to hear those words from the time we met on the banks of the Niobrara.''

He could hear the tremor in her voice, see the smile on her lips reflected in her eyes. "Then it isn't too late?''

"If you can leave the past behind, so can I—we can do it together. Oh, Cain, I love you, I love you, I love you,'' she cried, throwing her arms around his neck with a sob of joy. "I've spoken the words a thousand times in my heart, but I've waited so long to say them out loud.''

"I love you, Roxanna—and I'll say those words every day for the rest of our lives.'' He could feel the tears on his cheeks and did not care, for her soft lips kissed them away as he did the same for the salty drops on hers.

They held on to each other for several moments, communicating in silent joy. Then he reached into his pocket, pulled out a tiny box and handed it to her. Eagerly she opened it and gasped. The heavy gold wedding band she had returned to him when she left Denver lay nestled beside a magnificent brilliant cut diamond ring mounted in delicate filigreed gold.

"I always intended to give you an engagement ring. I had Jubal send the gold band to me in San Francisco so the jeweler could match it for the set." He waited expectantly as she slid the rings on her finger.

"It's the most beautiful thing I've ever seen in my life—but Cain, the size of the diamond—it must've cost the whole earth!"

He smiled, bemused at the past week's revelation. "I can afford it. I can afford to shower you with diamonds, Roxy. When I reached San Francisco and made arrangements for my father and brother to be buried, Andrew's attorneys contacted me. It seems after I confronted him, accusing him of stealing from the Central Pacific, and told him I was going to ruin him, he changed his will. Then he came after Larry." A haunted expression shadowed his face. "What must have gone through the old man's mind? He left me everything, darling—his shares in the Central Pacific, his shipping business, the land."

"He finally realized that you were more deserving than Larry—he planned to acknowledge you as his son."

He raked his fingers through his hair and shook his head. "Hell, I don't know. I know he still hated my Indian blood. Maybe that's why he was so appalled when he learned I'd pledged to make a Medicine Lodge. I'll always wonder if he came back here deliberately to kill Larry for his treachery—or, if things had come out differently, to give him a second chance."

"Then why would he have cut Larry out of the will and given everything to you?"

Cain sighed. "I suppose I was the lesser of two evils at that point."

She could hear the lingering pain in his voice. "Remem-

ber, he told Larry that he made a mistake by not acknowl-
edging you.''

"No, he said *perhaps* it had been a mistake. His last
words were, 'You always had the brains. You beat me'—
damn, it was always a game to him. He pitted Larry and
me against each other all of our lives. I was the tough one
who'd learned to survive on my own. He sicced me on my
brother like a damned dog.''

"Larry had his own way of fighting back, Cain. You can't
put that entirely on Andrew Powell—if he were completely
at fault, you would've turned out worse than your brother
did.''

"I almost did," he said with regret. "And you paid for
my sins.''

"I think you paid for them yourself in the Medicine
Lodge.''

An ironic smile touched his lips. "Sees Much told me I
had a lot to atone for when I was preparing for the ritual.''

"A very wise man, as is your grandfather. What will become of them with the army and the railroad invading their
hunting lands?''

"Dillon knows Leather Shirt's people are peaceful. He'll
let them alone. As for the rest . . .'' He sighed. "Sooner or
later those that survive will end up on a reservation somewhere.''

"Can we visit them after the transcontinental is complete?
I think Leather Shirt will be as pleased with his great-
grandson as Jubal.''

Cain smiled. "So you think it'll be a boy, do you? I rather
had in mind a little silver-haired vixen like her mother, but
in either case, we can locate them after the baby's born.''

"You will let me come with you this winter? Dr. Milborne will be there to deliver the baby, and the railcar Jubal
gave us is a veritable palace. Say yes, Cain, please!'' She
lowered her lashes and added slyly, "Unless you can't bear
to watch me get so fat I don't have a sideways anymore.''

His hands moved to her waist, then up to her breasts. "So

far I don't see that you're getting all that fat. . . . Tonight
I'll—''

A loud oath in a thick Scot's burr exploded from downstairs, then the sound of Jubal's footsteps clambering up the
stairs followed as he called out their names.

"We're in here, Jubal. Roxanna is all right," Cain replied.

Winded and white-faced, the old man leaned against the
doorjamb. "When I saw that devil woman laying there, it
peeled a decade off my life." He looked at Roxanna's
scratched face and half-unfastened chignon. "Yer sure yer
all right, lassie?"

She went over to him and gave him a fond hug. "Yes,
I'm fine, thanks to my husband."

"And Jubal. He kept an agent in the small town near the
Darby plantation to watch her. If I hadn't intercepted a wire
from the man, I'd never have reached here in time," Cain
said, placing his arm around her shoulders.

Seeing that the young couple needed time alone, a relieved Jubal MacKenzie went to handle the disposition of
Isobel Darby's mortal remains. Within an hour the Cheyenne constabulary had accepted his glib tale about the
widow's "tragic accident." But first the frugal Scot had
retrieved the remainder of his fifty thousand dollars from
her person saying, "She dinna' keep her part of our bargain.
The money is still mine." The undertaker carried off her
body for burial in the local potter's field.

The cook, maid and Li Chen all returned later in the day,
unaware of the harrowing events. Dinner was served on
time. After enjoying the meal with Cain and Roxanna, Jubal
asked them to share some fine ten-year-old bourbon with
him. The big man poured three glasses, then paused, a bit
unnerved, and said, "First there's something I want to ask
the both of you."

He looks nervous, Cain thought with surprise as he replied, "Go on, Jubal. Spit it out."

Roxanna too leaned forward expectantly, watching as Jubal harrumphed, clearing his throat, loosening his tie with one hand. *What is he going to do?*

"Have you given any thought to what the newest director of the Central Pacific should call himself? Will you be Damon Powell again?" he finally asked Cain.

"Well, first off, I'm not a director, just the owner of a sizable share of stock. Next, I never had any legal claim to the Powell name. Still don't, even if the old man left me his estate. I honestly don't think I'd want to be called Powell anyway."

"How do you feel about the MacKenzie name?" Jubal's big hands trembled slightly as he placed them flat on the table, leaning forward. No more the calculating bargainer here. He wore his emotions as plainly as he ever had in his life. "If you agree, I'd like to legally adopt you as my son, make you and Roxanna and yer children my heirs. And you do na' even have to call me 'father.'"

Roxanna's eyes filled with tears. So did her husband's as he replied, "I'd be honored to be a MacKenzie . . . to be your son."

The two men clasped hands, then stood up and embraced, sandwiching Roxanna between them. When everyone had regained their composure, Jubal handed them their glasses and raised his. "Here's to America, the land of opportunity—"

"And damn good whiskey," the two newest MacKenzies chorused.

When the celebration had finished, Jubal returned to his new office to apply himself to Union Pacific accounts. The young lovers went upstairs to their bedroom suite . . . to apply themselves to other matters. . . .

Cain stood in the door between the sitting room and the bedroom, watching Roxanna take the pins from her hair.

Seeing his reflection in the mirror, she turned as he approached and smiled. "Remember that . . . er, lesson you gave me while we were in Chicago?"

His mouth went suddenly dry. "I'll never forget it. Do

you plan to give me another demonstration?'' he asked hoarsely.

"No, I don't think so," she replied consideringly as she stood up very close to him, letting her fingers glide up his shirtfront and skitter over his shoulders. "I think you should undress me . . . take off everything but my rings." She flashed the diamond in front of his face and chuckled at his growl of pleasure, then added, "After that, I'd like to watch you."

"Watch me?"

"Sometimes a woman likes her *man* to strip for *her*."

One black eyebrow raised as he looked down at her with a wicked, wicked grin spreading across his face. "She does, does she? . . . Well, never let it be said that I'd disappoint my woman." He took her hands and led her to the big canopied bed in the center of the room. She perched on the edge. Then he knelt with one knee on the stool and slid off her shoes, letting his hands caress the arches of her silk-clad feet until she all but purred.

"Now come here," he commanded as he stood and took her in his arms, lifting her once more to the floor with her back to him. With deft fingers he worked the dozen satin-covered buttons from their loops and slid the smooth butter-soft fabric from her shoulders. His mouth, hot, moist and insistent, followed, pressing kisses on the pale creamy skin above her chemise.

When the dress was bunched at her hips, he reached around to cup and lift her breasts inside the sheer silk of the chemise, murmuring against her neck, "Mmm, they are growing heavier." He flicked his thumbnails across the nipples, which instantly puckered as she gasped, arching forward into his hands. "More sensitive too."

His hands glided lower, around her waist. "Not much thicker yet," he commented, then quickly unfastened the tapes of her petticoats and shoved the whole satiny mass to a glistening puddle around her feet. "Now let me examine that little belly," he said, running his palm over the rounded swell of it as he turned her in his arms.

She held on to his shoulders as he pulled the drawstring holding closed the neckline of her chemise, then let him pull it up over her head and send it floating down to the floor, while he bent his head and nuzzled one breast, then the other. Before she realized it, he had her pantalets sliding past her hips and pooling at her ankles. She stepped out of them in a haze of sensual pleasure, her fingers buried in his long night-dark hair.

He stood back and looked at her, naked but for her garters and silk stockings. She felt his eyes sweeping over every inch of her and had to ask, "Am I shapeless already?"

A low wicked chuckle rumbled deep in his chest as he scooped her into his arms, saying, "You—ten months pregnant—could never be shapeless, Roxy, my love." He laid her on the bed, then sat down beside her and began to peel off her garters and hose slowly, kissing his way from thigh to toes, then back up on both legs, until she was writhing with excitement.

Roxanna gloried in his hands gliding all over her tingling flesh, his lips caressing with licks, nips, soft brushing kisses. Then he withdrew abruptly and stood back. Her eyes flew open wide in surprise and dismay as she raised her head and propped herself up, resting on one elbow, looking at him hungrily.

"You wanted me to strip for you," he said, watching the little pink points of her nipples tighten even harder.

She blinked and gave a breathless nod, letting her eyes feast on his tall, lithe body. His eyes met hers hotly, dancing with deviltry as he shrugged the black wool jacket from his broad shoulders and tossed it carelessly onto a chair. His hands, those marvelous long-fingered hands, reached up and began to loosen the knot of his tie, slipping the steel-gray silk free with a long slow swish, then letting it dangle from his fingers and slide to the floor. He held up one cuff and pulled out one diamond link, then the other.

"Catch," he said, tossing them one at a time to her. She sat up and reached for the sparkling jewelry, grabbing the first one, missing the second as she licked her lips and watched him pull the studs from his shirt, slowly peeling away the starched white linen to reveal that fascinating pattern of curly black hair on his chest. He let one hand rub over a bulging pectoral muscle, touching the freshly healed scar from the Sun Dance, and she moaned softly.

"Don't stop now," she whispered raggedly when he stood with the shirt half on, half off his body.

"Your slightest wish . . ." He shoved the fistful of jewelry into his pants pocket and walked with pantherish grace to the bootjack, shrugging the shirt off and tossing it away. Then he pressed his palms against the wall, back turned to her as he worked off his boots.

Roxanna watched the muscles move in sinuous ripples beneath the bronzed skin of his back. His long arms were extended, emphasizing the breadth of his shoulders and narrowness of his waist. Straight black hair, still without the attention of a barber, covered his neck, barely brushing his shoulders. She shuddered, thinking of the feel of his hair when she buried her hands in it, pulling his head to her for hot wet kisses.

Cain turned halfway around, with one palm still braced against the wall, and pulled off one sock, then the other. Then he strode slowly back to the bed. "How am I doing so far?"

"Keep going," she whispered hoarsely. God, he was beautiful! Her eyes traveled hungrily from his face with its smoldering heavy-lidded eyes to the scars on his chest—a badge of honor, a pledge of love. Soon she would tell him about her dream . . . but not right now. The bulge in his fitted black wool trousers was visual proof of the urgency they both felt. Her breath hitched when his hands began to unfasten his belt and pull it through the loops, then toss it to the floor and move back to the buttons at his fly.

"If you tear them off I'll be happy to sew them back on later," she urged raggedly.

He grinned, working the placket open quickly, then took a deep breath to steady himself as his sex sprang free of the tight confinement. Kicking the britches and underdrawers away, he stepped directly in front of her and stood looking down. "Was that something like you had in mind?" he said with a grin, repeating her words to him.

"Something like," she echoed breathlessly, returning the grin as his rigidly erect phallus jutted out at eye level. A single pearly drop of semen glistened on the dark head of his staff. She reached out and wrapped one hand around the length of it, sliding back and forth until he cried out. "Come to me, Cain . . . come deep inside of me," she invited, still holding on to him as he climbed onto the bed and knelt between her spread thighs.

He covered her body as she guided the pearly tip to her wet swollen petals. He plunged deep inside of her then, unable to stop himself after holding out for so long, especially when she arched up to meet him, tightening her thighs around his hips and pulling his head down to her breasts.

Alternately suckling the delectable feast of one pink nipple, then the other, Cain set a deep, slow rhythm, thrusting as she rolled her hips. "I've ached . . . wanting to do this each . . . day . . . I was gone," he said as he kissed his way up her neck to her face, then centered his mouth over hers.

Roxanna moaned as his tongue met hers, digging her nails into the hard satiny muscles of his shoulders, pulling him closer as the spiraling waves of ecstasy built higher and higher until she thought she would go mad with the pleasure and the craving, wanting that shimmering culmination, yet wanting the searing sweet friction to continue forever . . . forever . . . forever.

Feeling her begin to slip over the abyss, he murmured into her ear, "Now," then let go, plunging harder, faster, swelling and pumping his seed deep inside her as her silky sheath squeezed him dry.

He collapsed on top of her, feeling her arms hold him tightly while she feathered small swift kisses across his face and down his neck. He hummed in contentment when her tongue licked a trickle of perspiration off his skin.

Carefully, he rolled over onto his back, carrying her with him, not breaking their joining. "I think Sees Much will have to find a new name for you," he said, smiling.

She propped her chin on her hands, which were crossed over his chest, and replied, "Oh?"

"Her Back Is Straight doesn't fit a woman who can wriggle and arch and buck and—"

She pummeled him playfully, then began to kiss his chest, letting her fingers rifle through the springy black hair, pausing to touch and caress the Sun Dance scars. "Do they hurt, Brother of the Spirit Bull?" she asked.

"Not any longer. I never told you about my dream. I think—"

"There is something I must tell you first, my love. Sees Much instructed me very specifically."

His brow crinkled in perplexity. "What is it?"

She described her dream about the lone bull, watching the look of incredulous wonder spread across his face.

"If I ever had any doubt about the meaning of the vision I had in the Medicine Lodge, you've just put it to rest forever. In my vision you healed me. You—"

"A Sun and Moon Woman healed you." She nodded. "I was there in Sees Much's lodge, helping him treat your wounds when you described it all. He already knew about my dream. Do you think he knew you'd have the final fulfillment of it in yours?"

He smiled tenderly at her. "We'll ask him next summer."

PROMONTORY POINT, UTAH, MAY 10, 1869

There was a hushed air of expectancy hanging over the crowd. The heat was stultifying, with scarcely a hint of a breeze to dispel the golden scorch of the sun high overhead. The two locomotives, one pointing east, the other west, stood only a few yards apart. The dignitaries clustered around the small space between them, preparing to complete the final act of the drama which had begun a dozen years and fifteen hundred miles ago. A small man with a green eyeshade hunched expectantly over his telegraph key.

"Damn Leland Stanford's long-windedness," Jubal

groused as he wiped at the sweat trickling down into the starched collar of his shirt. ''If he'd rambled on with that speech any longer, the rails would have melted in this heat.''

Cain MacKenzie chuckled as he leaned over to shade his wife and their daughter Jubalee beneath the protection of the large sun umbrella he was holding. His little silver-haired vixen of a daughter looked up at him with adoring wide dark eyes and cooed. Roxanna smiled, rocking the child, when a sudden cheer erupted across the assembly.

The golden spike had been driven into the last rail, linking a continent from sea to sea. Hats flew up into the air as men yelled and women waved their kerchiefs in excitement. The message tapped out by the telegrapher sang across the wires to all points east and west. The transcontinental railroad was complete. Slowly the two engines puffed and chugged, inching across the last few feet until the cowcatchers touched. People swarmed all over the two trains, everyone laughing and talking at once.

Jubal exchanged a smile with the newest director of the Central Pacific, who happened to be his son and business partner, and said, ''Damn me if I'm not almost as good at building railroads as I am at building families.''

Author's Note

The Great Race across the American continent was much more than the last act of Manifest Destiny. It was an epic exercise in piracy against the American taxpayers, who ultimately financed the rails. The building of the transcontinental symbolized the American dream in all its grandeur and its rapacity: noble aspirations went hand in hand with the basest greed. The coming of the railroad sounded the death knell for the hunters of the High Plains, dozens of Native American tribes whose way of life was destroyed by the Iron Horse. The era was as violent as it was opulent, thrilling as it was tragic, all in all the perfect backdrop for the tale of a ruthless man and a reckless woman.

I wanted Cain to be an outsider burning with ambition, desperate to prove himself to a world—and a family—who had rejected him. Being a half-breed placed him beyond the pale of white society. In this instance I decided to reverse the characterization of the mixed-blood protagonist: Cain is a hero who rejects his Native American heritage. He longs to be a white man and is ashamed of the ''savagery'' he perceives in the Cheyenne. His is a long and painful road to reconciliation with the people who love him, both red and white.

Roxanna's character too is complex and difficult. She is a chameleon, an actress playing the role of her lifetime.

While Cain conceals his identity as Andrew Powell's bastard from her, Roxy escapes her tragic past by becoming Alexa. Like the husband she grows to love, she is filled with guilt because of the deception.

Although our angst-riven lovers are fictional, a great many of the other characters in the story are actual historical persons or fictionalized versions of such figures. The irascible and devious Jubal MacKenzie is a composite of Charlie Crocker and John Casement, while the cold and calculating Andrew Powell is loosely based on James Strobridge with a dash of George Francis Train thrown in. In Charlie Crocker's place, I "promoted" Cain's father to become one of the infamous Big Four who ran the Central Pacific. Leland Stanford, Mark Hopkins, and Collis Huntington are portrayed as accurately as I could draw them. Dr. Thomas C. Durant and his smarmy sidekick Silas Seymour and the brothers Oakes and Oliver Ames are also described as history reveals them, although I took the liberty of fictionalizing Mrs. Durant and Mrs. Seymour for purposes of the plot.

A few other literary licenses taken are as follows: The meeting between the Union Pacific and Central Pacific leaders described in Denver in the fall of 1868 was wholly my fiction; several attempts were made by the Union Pacific leaders, most especially Grenville Dodge, to force an agreement on a Utah meeting site for the transcontinental, but it was not until Ulysses Grant took office as president that Promontory Point was settled upon. Fort Russell outside Cheyenne was an infantry post, not cavalry. There was no through transit from Chicago to Cheyenne until 1870, when the bridge between Omaha and Council Bluffs was completed. Although Dr. Durant and Silas Seymour made frequent junkets west, the journey described in the story is a fictionalized version. All the members of Congress in the book are fictional, but their venial interests in the transcontinental are true to life. (Readers may recognize Senator Burke Remington and his wife Sabrina from *The Endless Sky*.)

The research necessary to depict this complex and colorful era was extensive. Once more I relied heavily on the dean of Cheyenne historians, George Bird Grinnell, whose two-volume work *The Cheyenne Indians* is still the standard reference for these remarkable Horse Indians. In the Time-Life Old West Series, two books were especially useful: *The Townsmen* and *The Railroaders*. Keith Wheeler edited both.

One of the most authoritative popularizers of American history, Dee Brown brought the era to life for me in two diverse books—*Wondrous Times on the Frontier*, a superb collection of western humor and hyperbole, and *Hear That Lonesome Whistle Blow*, which chronicles the building of the transcontinental and describes each ''Hell on Wheels'' and its inhabitants in lusty detail.

A Great and Shining Road by John Hoyt Williams and *The Great Iron Trail* by Robert West Howard are two solid accounts of the ''Great Race.'' My inspiration for the runaway freight cars sequence was inspired by Nellie Snyder Yost's article ''The Union Pacific'' in the Western Writers of America anthology *Trails of the Iron Horse*.

Carol and I hope that you have enjoyed our tale of villainy and victory on the High Plains. Please write to us and let us know how you felt about Cain and Roxanna's turbulent relationship. A stamped, self-addressed envelope is appreciated for replies.

Shirl Henke
P. O. Box 72
Adrian, MI 49221

or e-mail us at:
shenke@c4systm.com